PRAISE FOR *The Trapped Girl*

"In Dugoni's outstanding fourth Tracy Crosswhite mystery, the Seattle homicide detective investigates the death of Andrea Strickland, a young woman whose body a fisherman finds in a crab pot raised from the sea . . . In less deft hands this tale wouldn't hold water, but Dugoni presents his victim's life in discrete pieces, each revealing a bit more about Andrea and her struggle to find happiness. Tracy's quest to uncover the truth leads her into life-altering peril in this exceptional installment."

—*Publishers Weekly*, starred review

"Dugoni drills so deep into the troubled relationships among his characters that each new revelation shows them in a disturbing new light . . . An unholy tangle of crimes makes this his best book to date."

—*Kirkus Reviews*

"Dugoni has a gift for creating compelling characters and mysteries that seem straightforward, but his stories, like an onion, have many hidden layers. He also is able to capture the spirit and atmosphere of the Pacific Northwest, making the environment come alive . . . Another winner from Dugoni."

—Associated Press

"All of Robert Dugoni's talents are once again firmly on display in *The Trapped Girl*, a blisteringly effective crime thriller . . . structured along classical lines drawn years ago by the likes of Raymond Chandler and Dashiell Hammett. A fiendishly clever tale that colors its pages with crisp shades of postmodern noir."

—*Providence Journal*

"Robert Dugoni, yet again, delivers an excellent read . . . With many twists, turns, and jumps in the road traveled by the detective and her cohorts, this absolutely superb plot becomes more than just a little entertaining. The problem remains the same: Readers must now once again wait impatiently for the next book by Robert Dugoni to arrive."

—*Suspense Magazine*

Praise for *In the Clearing*

"Tracy displays ingenuity and bravery as she strives to figure out who killed Kimi."

—*Publishers Weekly*

"Dugoni's third 'Tracy Crosswhite' novel (after *Her Final Breath*) continues his series's standard of excellence with superb plotting and skillful balancing of the two story lines."

—*Library Journal*, starred review

"Dugoni has become one of the best crime novelists in the business, and his latest featuring Seattle homicide detective Tracy Crosswhite will only draw more accolades."

—*Romantic Times*, Top Pick

"Robert Dugoni tops himself in the darkly brilliant and mesmerizing *In the Clearing*, an ironically apt title for a tale in which nothing at all is clear."

—*Providence Journal*

Praise for *Her Final Breath*

"A stunningly suspenseful exercise in terror that hits every note at the perfect pitch."

—*Providence Journal*

"Absorbing . . . Dugoni expertly ratchets up the suspense as Crosswhite becomes a target herself."

—*Seattle Times*

"Dugoni does a masterful job with this entertaining novel, as he has done in all his prior works. If you are not already reading his books, you should be!"

—*Bookreporter*

"Takes the stock items and reinvents them with crafty plotting and high energy . . . The revelations come in a wild finale."

—*Booklist*

"Another stellar story featuring homicide detective Tracy Crosswhite . . . Crosswhite is a sympathetic, well-drawn protagonist, and her next adventure can't come fast enough."

—*Library Journal*, starred review

PRAISE FOR *My Sister's Grave*

"One of the best books I'll read this year."

—Lisa Gardner, bestselling author of *Touch & Go*

"Dugoni does a superior job of positioning [the plot elements] for maximum impact, especially in a climactic scene set in an abandoned mine during a blizzard."

—*Publishers Weekly*

"Yes, a conspiracy is revealed, but it's an unexpected one, as moving as it is startling . . . The ending is violent, suspenseful, even touching. A nice surprise for thriller fans."

—*Booklist*

"Combines the best of a police procedural with a legal thriller, and the end result is outstanding . . . Dugoni continues to deliver emotional and gut-wrenching, character-driven suspense stories that will resonate with any fan of the thriller genre."

—*Library Journal*, starred review

"Well written, and its classic premise is sure to absorb legal-thriller fans . . . The characters are richly detailed and true to life, and the ending is sure to please fans."

—*Kirkus Reviews*

"*My Sister's Grave* is a chilling portrait shaded in neo-noir, as if someone had taken a knife to a Norman Rockwell painting by casting small-town America as the place where bad guys blend into the landscape, establishing Dugoni as a force to be reckoned with outside the courtroom as well as in."

—*Providence Journal*

"What starts out as a sturdy police procedural morphs into a gripping legal thriller . . . Dugoni is a superb storyteller, and his courtroom drama shines . . . This 'Grave' is one to get lost in."

—*Boston Globe*

CLOSE
TO
HOME

CLOSE TO
HOME

ROBERT DUGONI

THOMAS & MERCER

Published by Thomas & Mercer, Seattle

www.apub.com

Amazon, the Amazon logo, and Thomas & Mercer are trademarks of Amazon.com, Inc., or its affiliates.

ISBN-13: 9781542045018
ISBN-10: 1542045010

Cover design by David Drummond

Cover photography by Chrissy Wiley

Printed in the United States of America

To Meg Ruley, Rebecca Scherer, and the team at Jane Rotrosen Agency—the best literary agents in the business. Words cannot express how much I appreciate your guidance and support over these years. I was blessed to walk in the front door of your brownstone and you have made me a part of the JRA extended family. Can I get an "oorah"!

PART 1

CHAPTER 1

D'Andre Miller pushed open the glass doors of the Rainier Beach Community Center and stepped out into the frigid night. The temperature had dropped considerably, a sharp contrast to the humid, sweat-soaked air inside the basketball gym. His breath burned in his throat, and goose bumps tickled his arms beneath his hooded sweatshirt as he shuffled his rubber sandals down the concrete steps. His basketball shoes, laces tied together, dangled over his right shoulder, his leather basketball tucked securely into the crook of his arm. His prized possessions would never touch anything but the hard court.

"Hey, Baby D!"

D'Andre turned, though still shuffling backward on the concrete patio, no time to lose. Terry O'Neil had pushed open the glass doors of the community center. "Sweet J, Baby. Sweet J," he yelled.

D'Andre smiled at the praise and thought again of his crossover and three-point jump shot to win the final pickup game.

"You were balling tonight, Baby D," Terry said. Terry opened the rec center's gym three nights a week and supervised the basketball games.

"Thanks, Terry," D'Andre said. He had been balling. Threes and floaters like Steph, drives to the bucket like KD. He'd drained them all, and he'd been playing against guys at least three years older. Just twelve, D'Andre had been the youngest player that the older boys at the center let play, though tonight it had been because they were short players. In the future, they wouldn't even question his age. Not if they wanted to win.

"You coming back tomorrow night?" Terry shouted, now standing on the top step, his breath like cigarette smoke in the tinted yellow light.

"Can't," D'Andre yelled, still shuffling backward. "I got a math test Thursday and I have to study."

"All right then. You get right with school. But then you come back. Anytime, Baby D. You proved yourself tonight."

D'Andre liked the sound of that. The best played at the center, and D'Andre had plans to be better than all of them. He'd hung around the gym since he was nine, mimicking their moves—crossovers, Euro-Steps, hesitations—the best each had to offer. And he had showed game tonight . . . though maybe for one game too many. He'd have to bust his butt to get home by his curfew. He should have begged out of the last game, but how could he? He'd finally gotten his chance; he didn't want to tell them his mama would whip his butt if he was late getting home.

Though she would.

Mama had said to be home by nine. She'd also said D'Andre best have his homework done when he walked in the door. No home-work . . . No basketball. A *C* on his report card . . . No basketball. Forget to do his chores, talk back, get home late . . . No basketball. Mama wasn't playing either. That's what she told him. "I ain't playing and neither will you." Mama didn't have time for nonsense, not while trying to raise three sons on her own. D'Andre did things Mama's way.

End of story.

The oldest child, he understood Mama had it tough. She worked all day and didn't get home until after six. Grandma made dinner while

Mama checked homework. By the time Mama got to bed, D'Andre knew she was beat. "I don't want this for you," she told him one night as they sat at the kitchen table going over his math. "You do right in school, get your degree. Become a doctor or a lawyer."

School came first. She'd already grounded D'Andre once for getting home late, and she wouldn't hesitate to do it again. "I'm not raising a fool. You got a one-in-a-million chance to play professional basketball, but you can do anything if you study and work hard in school."

He wasn't like some of the fools at his school, bringing home Cs and Ds. D'Andre had straight As, except for math. He needed to ace his test this Thursday. Not that he'd get anything for it. Mama didn't promise anything for straight As. "Why would I reward you for doing what you're supposed to be doing?" she'd said.

D'Andre cradled the basketball and checked his cell phone. He had ten minutes to get home. He could make it, but only if he moved his butt. He slid on his Beats headphones, listening to Lil Wayne—whose music Mama forbade in the house. She called Lil Wayne a "tatted up felon fool"—which D'Andre actually found funny. He pulled the hood of his sweatshirt over his headphones and started jogging, each breath marking the air in a white burst. It felt cold enough to snow, though he'd never seen snow in Seattle. People said it snowed a lot in 2008, but he'd been too young to remember. He glanced up at the sky, not really sure what he was expecting to see. The clouds looked like cotton balls against an ink-black sky, the edges tinted silver from the light of a full moon.

D'Andre hurried down Rainier Avenue with the lyrics of "Tha Block Is Hot" busting in his ears. In his mind, he juked a would-be defender and changed direction, heading west on Henderson. That was D'Andre's best skill, changing direction without losing speed. He learned that from Terrell, and Terrell was going to the UW, at least for a year, before he turned pro. D'Andre wouldn't be going pro after just one year in college. He'd get his degree. "Don't give me that nonsense about going pro," Mama would say. "You tear up your knee, then what are you going to do?"

D'Andre booked it on Henderson, picking up his pace to Lil Wayne's lyrics. He'd cross Renton Avenue, cut over the Chief Sealth Trail, hop the back fence, and push through the kitchen door with minutes to spare. Mama would give him that look, just to let him know she had him on the clock. Then she'd heat up a plate of spaghetti and sit down, and they'd talk while he ate. He liked those moments, when his brothers were in bed, and it was just him and Mama at the table.

"Someday I'm going to buy you a big house," he'd tell her. "Big enough that you'll need one of those scooters to get around."

"Why would I need a house like that? It's hard enough to keep this one clean."

"I'm going to get you a maid too."

She'd smile. "You buy yourself a big house."

"Then you and Grandma can come live with me."

"Your wife might have something to say about that."

"Who's she?" he'd say, and break out in a smile.

Mama would pour him another glass of milk and kiss him atop his head. "Eat your spaghetti and get to bed. The best growing hours are before midnight."

D'Andre thought again about that final crossover and jump shot. Marvin had been talking smack all night, trying to get under D'Andre's skin, trying to make him lose his cool. It was just smack and it didn't bother D'Andre none. Mama once told him, "You lose your cool on a basketball court and I'll walk down from the stands and pull you from the game right then and there."

D'Andre hurried to the corner and crossed 46th Avenue South, getting close to home. It had been so sweet, his crossover. D'Andre busted the ball up court, dribbling low with his left hand, then gave a burst of speed to get Marvin on his right hip. Nearing the three-point line, he dipped his shoulder, like he intended to drive to the basket. Marvin bit and also dropped low. When he did, D'Andre planted his left foot hard. Marvin couldn't stop. He kept going, right on by, already stumbling when D'Andre crossed the ball from his left to his right hand.

D'Andre leapt from the curb at Renton Avenue South, his orange basketball floating from his fingertips and arcing upward toward the imagined basket. In his mind he watched the ball slip through the rim, compressing that white net in a sweet ripple.

A dark blur in D'Andre's peripheral vision caught his attention. He turned his head. Too late. The basketball exploded from his hands, seeming to momentarily hang in the air, suspended above the car's hood. It hit the windshield hard and shot forward. Striking pavement, it bounced high at first, then a little less with each bounce, over and over, until it rolled into the gutter, ricocheted gently against the curb, and came to its final rest.

Not moving.

CHAPTER 2

Tracy Crosswhite had read in some magazine somewhere that the Smith Tower in Seattle's Pioneer Square had once been the tallest building west of the Mississippi. Now, the building wasn't even in Seattle's top thirty, and its significance was largely historic. The city was rapidly changing, and not necessarily for the better.

Seattle was headed for a record year for homicides.

On average, Tracy and the fifteen other detectives in the Seattle Police Department's Violent Crimes Section investigated thirty homicides a year, but like the height of the downtown buildings, that number had been steadily increasing—another downside to being one of the fastest growing cities in America. It meant more work for them all, work they'd all just as soon do without.

Tracy removed her corduroy jacket and hung it with Kinsington Rowe's leather coat on a hook at Shawn O'Donnell's American Grill and Irish Pub. Kins started to sit, but grimaced and abruptly stopped.

"Your hip hurting again?" Tracy asked.

"It's been catching," Kins said. "It's worse in the cold weather." He rotated the hip and it freed with a small pop. Tracy cringed. A football injury had become degenerative.

"When's the surgery?"

"Don't remind me." He sat across from her.

"You're worried about it?"

"Hell yeah, I'm worried about it. I told you the story about the woman who stroked out in the middle of the same surgery, didn't I?"

"You said she was eighty."

"Eighty-three, but still. They say that's how that actor died, Bill Paxton. Stroked out after a surgery."

"He had a bad heart. What, are you reading obituaries for people that died of a stroke?"

Just forty, Kins had put off the surgery for years by chewing ibuprofen. He said he only wanted to go through the procedure once, and the warranty on hip replacements was about thirty years. But lately the pain had become more frequent and more intense. "The doctor said I'd let him know . . . when the pain got too bad."

"Sounds like you have."

"Two weeks," he said. "And I'll be glad to get it behind me. Feels like a hot knife stabbing my joint and radiating to my knee." He picked up the menu, studied it for a bit, then tossed it aside. "What number did you get in the pool?"

The detectives and SPD officers paid twenty bucks to enter a pool predicting the number of homicides each year. The number this year had become a hot topic. The skull of death hung from Tracy's cubicle wall, a macabre reminder that she and Kins were the detective team "next up" for one of those homicides, though they still had two open investigations. She was hoping to get through the week without another killing, but given the way things had been the first months of the year, the odds of doing so were poor. The Violent Crimes Section was still digging out from the previous week, when a jealous young man killed three high school students at a party with an AK-47 assault rifle he'd purchased online. The deaths brought the total number of homicides in Seattle—for just the first two and a half months of the year—to twenty-two. "Thirty-eight," Tracy said, perusing the menu. "I thought it was going to be too high. Now I'm thinking it's going to be too low."

Many attributed the increase in crime, including homicides, to being a byproduct of both the spike in population and the use of heavy drugs like meth and heroin, which was epidemic in Seattle and becoming epidemic in just about every other US city.

"Well, if you're too low, I'm screwed." Kins tossed a slip of paper on the table. He'd pulled number thirty-six. "I think we might pass that by June."

It was warm inside the pub, which had become one of their regular haunts when working the night shift, or maybe Tracy just noticed the change in temperature from the chill outside. March usually brought wind and rain. Not this year. This year it had brought temperatures in the low twenties and, maybe, snow. It had felt cold enough walking down the hill from Police Headquarters at Fifth and Cherry Street. Tracy liked the pub's ambiance. Across the room, a green digital clock counted down the days, hours, and minutes until Saint Patrick's Day. It had just dropped below two weeks at thirteen days, two hours, and thirty-six minutes, which explained the heavy mix of the Irish band U2 on the playlist, and the decidedly green décor—even more than normal. Pennants hung overhead with sayings like: "Kiss Me. I'm Irish." And three-leaf clovers on the wall advertised Guinness. Over Kins's head, a sign in a wooden frame said:

If I ever go missing I want my picture on a beer bottle instead of a milk carton. That way, my friends will know I'm missing.

Tracy checked her cell phone, though it hadn't rung; she'd provided dispatch with her number when they left the office.

"Everything all right with you?" Kins asked. "You've been acting like you're the one going under the knife."

After years as partners, they knew each other's moods, knew when they were fighting with their spouses, when Kins had kid problems, when they'd gotten laid. "I'm fine," she said. But she wasn't fine. She'd been considering her appointment to see a fertility specialist the following afternoon. In the six months since her wedding, she'd never had so much sex and been so frustrated. At forty-three, Tracy was learning that deciding to have children and getting pregnant no longer went hand in hand.

Far from it.

Kins picked up the menu again. "I should lose weight before the surgery. That minimizes the chance of a stroke."

"Would you stop worrying about a stroke? That was a fluke. She was twice your age."

"I should order a salad. I say that every time, don't I?" He did say it every time. "And then I get a burger. I have the willpower of a sausage."

Tracy ignored him. Kins used "sausage" to describe just about everything and everyone that bothered him. Lousy driver on the freeway—sausage. A slow cashier at the grocery store—sausage. A lying witness—sausage. He'd told Tracy he'd gotten in the habit as a kid when he'd slipped and said the F-bomb in front of his mother. After a good whacking, she told him to come up with something else. He'd come up with "sausage."

She looked over the menu again. Kins's mention of a burger was tempting, but she'd order a salad. At five foot ten, she wasn't petite. Working out was good for the cardio, but it was getting tougher and tougher each year to keep the weight off. What went in the mouth migrated to the hips and thighs.

Kins slapped his menu down on the tabletop. "Salad. I'm getting a salad." His cell vibrated. He checked it and set it aside. "Faz and Del are coming down."

Vic Fazzio and Delmo Castigliano constituted the other half of the Violent Crimes Section's A Team. The letter was just a designation, but that didn't keep the four of them from professing to the other three teams that it was a designation of quality.

"Del's back at work?" Tracy asked.

"Started back tonight. He and Faz were out running down that witness in White Center. Faz wants me to be sure to ask whether they still have the corned beef on rye." Kins shook his head. "It's an Irish pub. He's just being Faz."

"Did he say how Del is doing?"

Kins played with a pack of sugar, folding the corners. "I talked to him yesterday about it. He said he's still pretty down. Can't blame him."

The previous Saturday, Tracy and Kins had joined Faz at the funeral for Del's niece. Just seventeen, she'd overdosed on heroin. She'd started on marijuana at fifteen, progressed to prescription drugs, and eventually became hooked on heroin. Del got her into a detox program in Yakima, and when she'd returned home, he'd said she'd turned a corner. Then she'd overdosed and died.

"Faz said she'd overdosed four times. Did you know that?"

"Del told me," Tracy said.

Kins shook his head. He had three teenage boys. "Four times? It would kill me if one of my kids was taking that shit."

Liam, the owner, approached their table. He worked tables and behind the bar when it got busy. "You guys must be working the night shift again."

"It's just us and prostitutes, Liam," Kins said. "Only they make a whole lot more money than we do, and they don't have to report it on their income taxes."

"You're preaching to the choir," Liam said. "The city is telling me I have to pay my employees fifteen dollars an hour. One of the busboys asked me to cut his time so he wouldn't lose government aid. Sometimes I wonder if the city council actually thinks this crap through." He groaned. "You want something to drink?"

"I'd take the soup special if I wasn't on duty," Kins said. A billboard at the entrance advertised the soup special to be whiskey on the rocks.

"I hear you." Liam looked to the window. "Full moon tonight. The crazies will be coming out. Ordinarily we're dead on a Monday night."

Violent Crimes got the crazies *every* night, like the woman who called claiming she knew who'd killed the singer Kurt Cobain, or the man who said his dead wife was threatening to cut him up and deposit his body around town in suitcases. When Tracy had been single, she'd liked working the night shift, which was from 3:00 p.m. to midnight. At least the crazies were entertaining, and the solitude allowed her to get caught up on paperwork. Since her marriage to Dan, however, Tracy wanted to be home nights.

"Iced tea," Kins said.

"Put some lemon in mine," Tracy said.

"I assume you're waiting for the two gumbas?"

"They're on their way," Kins said. "Faz asked me to find out if you had the corned beef."

"What self-respecting Irish pub wouldn't have corned beef this close to Saint Patrick's Day?" Liam crossed himself, kissed his thumb, and departed the table.

Kins glanced past Tracy's shoulder in the direction of the front door. "Here they come now."

Tracy turned. Del and Faz entering a restaurant were like two moons eclipsing the sun. Each stood at least six foot four and weighed better than 250 pounds. Each wore a suit, though without the tie. Seattle might be changing, but Faz and Del were not. No tie was dress casual for them.

Del removed his raincoat and hung it on the hook. Tracy thought he looked tired. Bags under his eyes indicated a lack of sleep, and he moved as if doing so was a chore. Faz said Del had been spending nights on his sister's couch while caring for his twin nine-year-old nephews.

Del slid into the booth beside Kins. Faz slid next to Tracy. He was on Kins like a Labrador on a shot duck. "Did you ask about the corned beef?"

Kins grimaced. "Damn, I forgot, Faz."

"How could you forget? I just texted you." He pulled up the text and held up the phone.

Kins shrugged. "I got distracted."

As Faz swiveled in his seat, searching for Liam, Tracy turned to Del. "How are you doing, Del?"

"Hanging in there," he said, voice soft.

"Where the hell is Liam?" Faz said, head on a swivel.

Del motioned to Liam, who'd been behind the bar and came over quickly. "Coffee," Del said. "Black."

"You got the corn beef?" Faz asked.

Liam grimaced. "Kins ordered the last one, Faz, but we got a Polish sausage with sauerkraut."

Faz looked wounded. "Polish . . . You're shitting me." He looked to Kins. "Is he shitting me?"

Kins and Liam laughed. "What do you take me for, an Italian?" Liam said. "An Irish pub without corned beef this close to Saint Patrick's Day—that's a felony."

"What, are you trying to give me a heart attack?" Faz said to Kins. "Don't do that to me."

"Anything to drink?" Liam said.

"Coffee," Faz said. "I'm trying to warm up—cold as my Nets the last ten games." A New Jersey native, Faz still rooted for his hometown teams.

Tracy ordered a salmon Caesar salad.

"Irish whiskey mac and cheese," Kins said. He looked at Tracy as he handed back the menu. "Told you I have the willpower of a sausage."

Liam waited for Del. "Just the coffee," Del said, which was unlike him. Del loved food as much as Faz.

After Liam departed, Tracy said to Del, "How's your sister?"

"Not too good. It's gonna take some time."

"Just so you know," Faz said to Tracy, "we're going after the dealer."

"We who?" Tracy asked.

"We 'us,'" Faz said, catching Tracy's look of concern. "But Del's not officially involved."

There was no way Del should be working a homicide involving his niece. "You ran this by Nolasco?" she asked, referring to the Violent Crimes Section captain.

Faz gave her a look intended to convey that he'd talk to her more about it later. "He gave his blessing so long as I'm the lead."

She wondered if Nolasco's capitulation, rather than assigning a different team, had to do with the extraordinary rash of recent murders. *Every* homicide detective on *every* team was struggling just trying to keep up.

"Does your sister have any leads?" Kins asked Del.

"She's not ready to go there yet," Del said. "We're going to give her a few more days. I'm guessing my niece used her cell phone to make the buys and there's a boyfriend involved. If he is . . . he'll give up his dealer."

Tracy glanced again to Faz, who gave her a gentle nod that things were under control. "She just needs some time," he said.

Del considered Tracy. "I keep thinking about that saying, you know? I keep thinking about you."

"Me?" Tracy said.

"You know that saying, 'No parent should ever have to bury their child'? I don't think I fully appreciated what that meant. I'm sorry about your sister. I'm really sorry for your parents. I can see now what it did to them, what it did to your father."

Two years after Sarah disappeared, Tracy's father, overcome with grief, depression, and likely prescription drugs, took his own life.

The thought of a child made her think again of her attempts to get pregnant. As much as she wanted a son or a daughter, she couldn't imagine the grief and the agony of losing a child. Her sister's kidnapping and disappearance had devastated her, but it was nothing compared to the havoc it had wreaked on her parents.

A cell phone rattled on the table. Both Tracy and Kins picked up their phones. Tracy's phone lit up. "Dispatch," she said, shaking her head.

Kins groaned. "That homicide number just keeps inching higher, doesn't it?"

CHAPTER 3

A basketball rested motionless in the gutter near a white sheet draped over a body. Tracy and Kins had speculated on the drive about the reason for the A Team's presence at a traffic fatality, which was ordinarily handled by the Traffic Collision Investigation Unit. For homicide to be called out was unusual.

Kins parked along the curb on South Henderson Street. Del and Faz pulled their car in behind Kins and Tracy. The call to Tracy's cell had been from Billy Williams, the A Team's sergeant. Williams had received a call from the TCI sergeant, Joe Jensen.

"Billy say what we're doing here?" Kins asked.

Tracy shook her head. "TCI thinks it's a hit and run. That's all I know."

They stepped out into the cold, waiting on the sidewalk for Del and Faz. Blue and red lights painted the stucco walls and barred windows and doors of the local businesses. Multiple patrol units had been parked at angles, blocking off Renton Avenue South. Uniformed officers dressed in gloves and thick jackets redirected approaching traffic.

A fire truck and ambulance were also part of the ensemble though the firefighters and paramedics stood still, looking frozen.

Tracy said, "What do you think about Nolasco allowing Del to work his niece's death?"

Kins glanced at her, then continued to survey the scene. "Faz will keep Del in check."

"He shouldn't be working it."

Kins gave her a look. "You going to tell him that?"

"That's not my job. That's Nolasco's job."

"You think you might be letting your personal feelings influence you?" Tracy and Nolasco had a long and rocky relationship that went back to the police academy.

"Nothing to do with my personal feelings. It's section policy."

"Faz said he's got it under control. I'd say you and I should let it be." Kins turned and looked up the street toward the white sheet. "How far do you think the body is from the intersection?"

Tracy knew he was changing the subject, but she let it go and gave his question some thought. "Maybe twenty-five feet."

"This is not going to be pretty," he said.

Del and Faz joined them, and they started toward Williams.

A heavy cloud layer that gave every indication of snow had dampened all sound. Williams stood speaking to two men wearing fluorescent yellow jackets with gray reflective tape, the words "Seattle Police" across their backs. Williams, a dead ringer for Samuel L. Jackson, looked fashionable in a red-and-black-checked driving cap and matching scarf, which he'd wrapped around his neck and tucked beneath his coat.

"Wouldn't have guessed you were Scottish," Faz said to Williams. "Sean Connery give you that hat and scarf?"

Williams responded with a sardonic smile. "According to Ancestry. com, I'm a lot of things you never would have guessed. I have your people to thank for that."

Faz said, "I'm a hundred percent Italian; you can thank me for good food and *The Godfather*."

Tracy spoke to Joe Jensen, the bigger of the two men, who wore a black ski cap pulled low on his head. "You call us in on this one, Joe?"

Jensen had served in the TCI unit for nearly three decades. When Tracy had worked patrol, and a promotion to homicide seemed a pipe dream, she'd looked into TCI as a way to expand her base of knowledge and experience. The unit's requirements included a boatload of math and physics, and theories such as linear momentum. She'd always been good in chemistry, which she'd taught for three years at the high school level. However, after her sister's disappearance and Tracy's decision to become a cop, she'd left math behind for good.

"When are you coming over to Violent Crimes?" Kins asked Jensen.

"After I retire," Jensen said, his standard refrain. He'd been asked to move to homicide often. He told Tracy the cases were too generic, that "This week's suspect is next week's victim." Besides, he was a proud math geek. Jensen adjusted the ski cap. "This one's tragic." He looked down Renton Avenue to the white sheet. "It's a twelve-year-old boy."

"No," Tracy and Kins said in unison.

Del stepped away.

"African American kid on his way home from playing basketball," Jensen said.

"Some of the brass are concerned, given the current climate, that this be handled with some sensitivity," Williams said.

"'Black Lives Matter'?" Faz asked. Like the rest of the United States, the movement had hit Seattle hard, and no one had to tell them they were standing in a predominantly African American community.

Williams nodded. "The brass wanted a homicide team." He looked to Jensen. "No offense."

"None taken."

"It's politics," Williams said. "We'll work with TCI."

"That okay with you?" Tracy asked Jensen.

"Not my call, but as far as I'm concerned, the more the merrier, though nothing merry about this one."

"What happened?" Tracy asked.

"Car knocked him out of his flip-flops. His basketball shoes are another ten feet down the road."

"I'm assuming no ID?" Tracy asked.

Jensen gestured with his chin to a group of men and women standing on the street corner. "No, but one of the witnesses said the victim's name is D'Andre Miller."

"Did he witness the actual accident?" Tracy asked.

Jensen shook his head. "No. He was walking up South Henderson and heard a thud. You know how that is."

Tracy did. The vast majority of witnesses to a car accident were not helpful. They often wanted to be, but it was more the norm that they didn't see the actual crash. They'd only heard it and saw the aftermath. The mind filled in the blanks, which were often inconsistent with the physical evidence, making the witness more damaging than helpful, if the matter went to trial.

Jensen pointed to another man on the street corner. "That man was driving home and stopped when he saw the patrol cars. He said the kid played basketball at the community center tonight and was hurrying to get home." Jensen pointed down the street. "He said the victim cuts over the Chief Sealth Trail."

"That's the opposite direction," Kins said, meaning opposite to where the body lay.

"I know," Jensen said. "If he came up the sidewalk to the intersection, he had to have been hit at a high rate of speed."

"Parents know yet?" Tracy asked.

"Not from us. Someone here, though, probably."

Tracy looked up at the array of dangling traffic lights and black wires strung between the telephone poles. The lights on Renton Avenue changed from green to red. "Any problem with the lights?"

"None that I've detected," Jensen said. "But we'll get it confirmed." He noticed Tracy looking south, at the significant hill coming down Renton Avenue before the street flattened at the intersection. "And no, we didn't find any skid marks," he said.

"So the driver didn't try to stop?" Tracy said.

"No evidence of it," Jensen said. "My guess, this was either a wrap or a forward projection."

Tracy knew a wrap was when the victim hit the car and wrapped around the hood. A forward projection was exactly what it sounded like.

"Given the distance of the body from the intersection, I'd say it's likely there was some damage to the front of the car," Jensen said. "We'll work to get the word out."

"What about cameras?" Faz considered the businesses on the four corners. An auto body shop had black gates over the windows and the door, as did the ground-floor windows of a three-story apartment building on the southeast corner. On one of the other two corners stood a mustard-colored commercial building with a dry cleaner. Across from it was a restaurant with a faded red awning. Weeds growing in the street-front windows indicated the restaurant had been out of business for some time.

"Don't know yet," Jensen said.

Williams removed his hands from his pockets. "Let's get going. Del, Faz, find out if the tenants in the apartments saw anything or if the auto body business uses any cameras that picked up anything."

As Del and Faz departed, a female officer approached the group. "Detectives? Sorry to interrupt, but I think we found something."

The group followed her up the street to about ten feet from the intersection. "We didn't initially see it because it's clear," the officer explained. She directed the beam of her flashlight to the ground, to a triangular piece of glass. To Tracy, it looked like the kind that covered a headlight.

"Good find," Jensen said. "Now all we need is the car to match it."

Tires screeched on the pavement, drawing everyone's attention. A white, older-model Honda had come to an abrupt stop in the intersection. The driver's door pushed open, and an African American woman jumped out from behind the wheel. Frantic, she left the engine running, the lights on, and the door open. "My son," she said to no one and everyone. "Where's my son?"

Patrol officers moved quickly to restrain her, but she slapped at their hands. "I want to see my son. Where's D'Andre?"

The people on the street corners started to voice their agitation. The man Jensen had noted earlier stepped into the street. The mother turned to him. "Terry, where is he? Where's D'Andre?"

Crying, Terry pointed down the street to the white sheet.

The mother put a hand to her mouth, but otherwise stopped moving. She melted, knees buckling and body collapsing onto the pavement, where she moaned and wailed. Tracy made her way to the woman. The man stood over her, seemingly uncertain about what to do. Tracy knelt and the woman raised her eyes. Tracy saw the same overwhelming grief she'd seen in her father's and mother's faces the night Sarah went missing.

"I'm sorry," Tracy whispered, thinking again of what Del had said in the restaurant.

No parent should have to bury their child.

—

The two dogs had not burst from the bedroom barking when Tracy entered the front door. Apparently they'd become accustomed to her working the night shift. She put her shoes on the bench seat, hung her jacket on one of the hooks, and made her way into the kitchen.

Dan had remodeled the inside of the single-story stone-and-mortar cottage, opening the floor plan and refinishing dark oak floors that contained all the nicks and scars one expected in a farmhouse. The ceiling was pitched, with large wooden crossbeams, and a stone fireplace dominated the living area. Dan had found a company to build an insert with a blower so that a fire could heat the entire house for hours. A red leather couch, love seat, and area rugs delineated a living room, while an antique oak table and chairs defined the dining area. In the far corner, a comfortable chair and lamp provided a place to read. At the back of the building, a single bedroom barely fit their queen-size bed. The kitchen, adjacent to it, didn't have room for a dishwasher, or more than two people at the same time.

Tracy pulled a glass from a kitchen cabinet and filled it at the sink while staring out the back window, thinking again of the mother in the street, and of her own mother. A full moon shimmered over the horse pasture, painting the grass a sorrowful, pale blue. The world was weeping tonight.

Dan had bought the five-acre farm and cottage because he liked how isolated it felt, much like his home in Cedar Grove, but Tracy had lived for years in downtown Seattle, and then in a West Seattle neighborhood. It was taking her longer to get used to how remote and quiet the farm could be, especially on nights like this, when she wanted a distraction, anything to divert her mind from the image of the white sheet and the grief-stricken mother who would never completely heal.

Sherlock padded out from the bedroom, followed by Tracy's cat, Roger. Tracy shut off the water, which had overflowed the rim of her glass. Roger popped up onto the kitchen counter, pacing and emitting a low mew. It had taken months, but Dan's two dogs, Rex and Sherlock, 140-pound Rhodesian mastiffs, seemed finally uninterested in the cat.

"You didn't have to get up," Tracy whispered to Sherlock, the more chivalrous of the two dogs. Sherlock gave her an inquisitive look. "Yeah, I know what you want." She opened a cabinet and fetched him a dog biscuit. He didn't immediately take it, looking up at her with mournful eyes, as if he could sense her pain. "It's okay," she said. "Go ahead."

Gently, he mouthed the biscuit. She kissed his head. "Don't tell your brother."

She stepped lightly into the bedroom and undressed in the dark, slipping on a nightshirt and sliding beneath the comforter. She nuzzled into the pocket of warmth created by Dan's smoldering body.

"Hey," Dan said, his voice groggy with sleep. He wrapped his arms around her. "You're late. I tried to wait up."

She could still smell mint toothpaste on his breath. In the dark, Rex gave a high-pitched yawn, as if to tell them both to keep quiet. Roger jumped onto the bed, purring.

"Sorry to wake you," she said. He'd been busy at his law office in downtown Redmond, his reputation and caseload having followed him from Cedar Grove. With Tracy working the night shift, they didn't see each other much in daylight. "We got another homicide."

"I figured as much. Bad?"

She thought again of the body beneath the white sheet. Just a boy. A child. "Hit and run," she said. "Twelve-year-old boy."

He kissed the top of her head and gently caressed her hair. "You okay?"

In all the years that she'd gone home to an empty apartment, she'd always told herself she was okay, even when she hadn't been. She didn't have much choice. There wasn't anyone to comfort her, and so she'd never learned how to be comforted. She was trying.

"Not great," she said.

"I'm sorry." He squeezed her tight. She felt his breath on her hair and the gentle rise and fall of his chest. "You want to talk about it?"

She smiled. She'd be talking about it for many days. She'd be thinking about it for years. But tonight, Dan was tired. She was too. "Go to sleep."

"What time is your doctor's appointment tomorrow?"

She'd forgotten about Dr. Kramer at the fertility clinic. "Two."

"I can rearrange things and meet you there."

"It's just to get the test results," she said. "We can make a decision about what to do after we know."

Dan adopted a staccato, military cadence. "Well, for my part, I continue to remain fully available for the task at hand. And let me assure you that neither snow nor rain nor gloom of night shall keep me from my appointed task."

"We're making a baby," she whispered. "Not delivering the mail."

Dan had no worries. He'd already been tested, after having his vasectomy from his first marriage reversed. He'd walked into their Redmond home loudly proclaiming that he was "locked and loaded and shooting live ammo!"

In other words, whatever their problem, it wasn't him. So while a part of Tracy would have liked having Dan go to the doctor with her, another part didn't want him present, didn't want him to hear what she already suspected to be the test results. The problem, whatever it might be, was her.

Dan released her and rolled onto his side. Within less than a minute, she could hear his peaceful breathing. She thought again of Shaniqua Miller, about the way she had crumbled in the street, her son's death consuming her. She thought too of Del's sister, Maggie, and how she must have felt when she'd walked into her daughter's bedroom and found her child dead. She thought of her own mother's complete and inconsolable agony, like a deep cut that would never heal.

It made her think again of her desire to have a child, and she wondered if, maybe, not getting pregnant was a blessing, instead of a curse.

CHAPTER 4

Early Tuesday morning, before the wheels of justice had started
to spit out civil decisions and criminal punishments, Delmo
Castigliano walked the hallways of the King County Courthouse. The
well-lit marble floors still emitted the faint odor of lemon from the janitor's mop, but they did not yet teem with lawyers, courthouse personnel, or the citizens who had business within the courtrooms.

Del found courthouses fascinating representations of a city and
its population. Within its rooms people recited wedding vows, wills
were probated after lives lived, and titles changed hands on land and
on buildings. Fortunes were made and lost in civil suits. Lives were
condemned in capital murder cases. Families were irrevocably altered.
The building held so much joy and so much sorrow.

And now Del had business in it.

He'd lost his niece. His sister had lost her child. No arguments
could be made or appeals filed to alter that fact. Man could not change
what had occurred. Allie was not coming back.

But he could bring those responsible to justice. Yes, he would.

He'd called in a favor, unbeknownst to his captain, Johnny Nolasco, who had reluctantly given Faz the green light to find the dealer who'd sold Del's niece the drugs. Del had agreed to take a backseat in that investigation, but he would not take a backseat when it came to finding closure for his sister. That was family business. That was Del's business.

He stepped from the hallway into the King County prosecutor's office and advised the receptionist he had an appointment to see Rick Cerrabone.

"He's in trial," the receptionist said.

"He's expecting me."

Moments after a phone call, Cerrabone appeared in an interior doorway and motioned for Del to follow him. Faz had once pointed out that the senior King County prosecutor, with dark bags beneath his eyes and a hound dog's jowls, was a dead ringer for Joe Torre, the former Yankees manager. The description had become fixed in Del's head.

Del followed Cerrabone down a narrow hall into his cramped office. Every inch of space on his desk and floor was occupied by binders and stacks of paper. Cerrabone was Prosecuting Attorney Kevin Dunleavy's right-hand man and handled most of the first-degree murder cases, including the death penalty cases, and he was in the grips of another one.

"Sorry about the mess. We're in the middle of the Westerberg trial." Cerrabone closed the door, making the office feel even smaller. Del detected coffee and saw a mug on Cerrabone's desk.

"I heard. I hope this isn't an inconvenience," Del said.

Cerrabone waved away the comment. "The judge gave us the morning off; one of the jurors called in to say her nanny was running late." He sat in an ergonomic chair behind his desk—his back gimpy. Del sat in one of two cushioned chairs. The only indication Cerrabone had a personal life was a five-by-eight framed picture of his wife, also a prosecutor, though she used her maiden name. When you sent murderers to prison, you guarded your privacy. The prints on the wall were standard black-and-gray photographs of Seattle throughout the decades.

"I'm sorry about your niece, Del."

"Thanks," Del said, for what seemed the thousandth time. "Thanks for coming to the service."

"You look tired. You getting any sleep?"

"We had a hit-and-run fatality last night. A twelve-year-old boy."

"I heard," Cerrabone said. "It may end up on my desk."

The comment caught Del by surprise. Cerrabone usually only handled the MDOP cases, an acronym for the Most Dangerous Offender Program. "Why?"

"Same reason you're involved. The brass is worried about the public's perception."

Del sighed. "Well, I appreciate your help on this matter," he said, feeling guilty for having called Cerrabone for a favor, given how busy the prosecutor was.

Again, Cerrabone dismissed it. "It's not a problem, but I did ask an associate to run down the research and handle this while I'm in trial." Cerrabone sifted through the stacks of papers on his desk, found the memorandum he was looking for, and handed it to Del. "Are you all right with that?"

"Yeah, fine," Del said.

Cerrabone picked up his desk phone, hit a button, and said, "Can you come in?"

A minute later, an attractive black woman opened the door as she knocked. "Come on in." Cerrabone introduced them. "Celia McDaniel. Del Castigliano. Del's the person I asked you to do that overdose research for."

McDaniel closed the door and crossed to Del, who'd stood to greet her. "The detective," she said, her arm extended.

Del shook her hand, a firm grip. He'd never met Celia McDaniel and estimated her to be between thirty-five and forty. She adjusted a navy-blue jacket over a cream blouse. A clip held long light-brown braids in place. He detected little, if any, makeup.

"You're new," Del said.

She sat in the chair beside him. "Hardly." She smiled. "I'm new *here*."

"Celia worked drug cases in Georgia," Cerrabone said. "She moved here just about six months ago and has been with us for two months."

"Long way to come," Del said.

"I was looking for a change of scenery."

"I think you got it. Wet and wetter."

"I like the rain," she said.

Cerrabone said, "I thought it might be faster to have you tell Del your findings, in case he has questions."

"Sure." McDaniel angled to face Del, crossing her legs. "First, I'm sorry about your niece."

"Thanks," Del said. One thousand and one.

"As I understand the facts, she . . . or a boyfriend, purchased heroin in the evening and she was dead the following morning."

"That's what we believe. My sister hasn't been in any shape to be of much help, but from what I do know, Allie suffocated on her vomit." The final words caught in Del's throat. He cleared it.

"So we can most likely prove that the heroin she used that night is the heroin that killed her?" McDaniel asked gently.

"Absolutely. She'd been clean for more than two months," Del said, recovering. "We sent her to a rehab facility in Yakima."

"That's not unusual," McDaniel said, almost to herself. "If we can identify the person and prove he supplied the heroin that led to your niece's death, we can charge him . . . or whoever the dealer is, with a controlled substance homicide under RCW 69.50.401."

"Homicide?" Del glanced at Cerrabone.

"That's correct," McDaniel said.

"What if he only delivered the heroin? What if he didn't manufacture it?" Del asked.

"The statute is relatively new and broad in its reach. It makes it unlawful for any person to manufacture, deliver, or possess with intent to manufacture or deliver a controlled substance."

Del wasn't familiar with the statute, but liked what he was hearing. "What's the punishment?"

"It's a Class B felony. If convicted, a person can get up to ten years, a maximum fine of twenty-five thousand dollars, or some combination of the two, if the crime involved less than two kilograms, which I'm assuming to be the case."

Ten years. Del was skeptical. "When's the last time somebody was convicted under that statute?"

"The penalty is being used more often with the recent proliferation of heroin and meth," Cerrabone said, viewing Del over the top of bifocals, a legal pleading in his hands.

"But I've only found a few instances in which the person was charged," McDaniel added. "None went to trial. They all pled."

"What kind of sentences did they get?"

"Two to four years and three to five thousand dollars."

"That's not very much for taking a life."

"I agree, but it's better than what it was, and there are other factors at play here."

"Such as?" Del asked.

Cerrabone's desk phone rang and he reached to answer it. After listening for a bit he said, "What kind of motion? That's ridiculous. Yeah, tell the judge I'm on my way down." He hung up, stood, and unrolled his shirtsleeves to button his cuffs. "I have to go argue a disqualification motion of one of the jurors. Feel free to stay here and use my office."

"Do you drink coffee?" McDaniel said to Del as Cerrabone grabbed his jacket.

"Too much," Del said.

Tracy stepped into the conference room on the seventh floor of the Police Headquarters building after just a few hours of sleep. Kins and Faz already sat at the table, talking about NBA games.

"Where's Del?" she asked Faz.

Faz sipped from a large mug of coffee embossed on one side with "Italians Make the Best Lovers" . . . and on the other side with . . . "Of Food!" The bittersweet aroma made Tracy's mouth water, though she knew she'd be in for a day of heartburn if she drank a cup on an empty stomach. "He had a meeting this morning and said to start without him."

"How's he doing, really?" Tracy pulled out a chair on the opposite side of the table and sat. Outside the tall, thin windows, rain fell on the concrete patio.

"He's all right." Faz shrugged. "He's pissed, you know? He wants somebody's ass."

"Enough to do something stupid?" Tracy asked.

"I'll keep an eye on him," Faz said, the New Jersey accent thickening. "He'll be all right."

"He shouldn't be working his niece's case," Tracy said.

Faz shrugged. "Everyone in the department is up to their eyeballs, and Del's trying to do right by his sister, you know? The husband hasn't been around in years. Don't worry, I'll watch him."

Kins turned to Tracy. "Is Joe coming in?"

"He called and said he was up late and early and is working to get something for us by this morning."

"Weren't we all." Faz flexed his shoulders and popped his neck. The long night and early morning showed in his bloodshot eyes.

Tracy felt like somebody had punched her in the back of the head. She hadn't slept much. "Anything turn up when you and Del canvassed the buildings?"

Faz shook his head. "Nobody saw or heard nothing. I'll get something written up for the file."

"It confirms what Jensen said," Kins offered, "that the driver of the car didn't brake."

Their captain, Johnny Nolasco, stepped into the room. Tracy had not been expecting him. They coexisted as well as a stick building and a tornado. "Heard you had a hit and run last night?"

"Twelve-year-old kid," Faz said.

"Fatality?"

"Unfortunately," Tracy said.

Nolasco said, "I'm going to push to have TCI handle it."

"It's a homicide," she said. "Billy says the brass is pushing for us to handle it, or to at least work with TCI."

"I'm well aware of that, but that multiple homicide last week is heating up and they need help with the interviews. This is a hit and run with a fatality," Nolasco said, "which is what TCI does."

"What if it was a homicide?"

"Then we'll cross that bridge if we come to it."

Jensen stepped to the doorway. Nolasco gave him a glance, turned, and departed down the hall. Jensen peeled off the strap of a computer bag slung over his shoulder and set the bag on a chair. "Sorry I'm late, but I was running down something I think you'll find useful."

Jensen looked decidedly different without the knit ski cap and bulky jacket. He had a full head of red hair and a stocky build. This morning he wore jeans, low-cut hiking shoes, polo shirt, and down jacket, which he quickly discarded over an empty chair.

"You get any sleep?" Kins asked.

Jensen removed the laptop from his bag and flipped it open, waiting for it to power up. "Yeah, I'm good. Adrenaline is pumping."

"Put some of that in my coffee," Faz said.

Jensen pulled out several sheets of paper and handed them to Tracy, then looked at his watch. "We might make morning roll call."

"Should we call the sergeant?" Tracy asked.

"Take a peek."

She read the paper. "Subaru Outback?" She looked to Jensen. "You got the make and model of the car? Already? Was there a video?"

"There's a video, but too far away to be definitive."

"So how do we know it's a Subaru?" Kins asked.

"I took that car part found in the street to the Washington State Patrol Crime Lab first thing this morning. They provided me with a serial number and determined it had come off a Subaru. My buddy owns Walker's Renton Subaru," Jensen said. "So I drove the part over to him and, based on the number, he says it came off a headlamp on the passenger side of a 2003 Subaru Outback. Black."

Tracy quickly looked at her wristwatch, then looked across the table. "Faz—"

"I'm on it." Faz pushed back his chair, the sheet of paper in one hand and his coffee mug in the other. If they could get the information to the sergeant on the morning roll call, they could get the word out to the patrol officers on First Watch to keep their eyes open for the car. Faz would then get the information distributed through all the other law enforcement agencies throughout the state, including the highway patrol, as well as distributing it to car repair companies.

"You said something about video?" Tracy asked Jensen as Faz departed.

"There's a traffic camera down the street. It isn't great, but knowing the type of car and approximate time of the accident, we were able to fast-forward through the tape looking for it." He tapped the laptop keyboard and spoke to Kins. "You might want to come around to this side of the table."

Kins joined them, peering over Jensen's shoulder.

"There's a traffic camera for the bus line on top of the light pole on South Henderson, about a hundred yards west of the intersection. It's a good camera, but the distance and the lighting . . . The video isn't the best. And the car was traveling south to north so there's no chance to get a license plate." Jensen tapped the keys. In seconds they were watching a grainy, slightly yellowed, black-and-white video. "The lights distort the coloring," he said. He tapped a few more keys, speeding up the film while checking notes on a sheet of paper. He pointed with his finger. "Right here, if you look closely, you'll see someone coming up the sidewalk on the left-hand side of the street."

Tracy could barely make out a slightly lighter image. "Hard to tell."

"It's consistent with the time the witness said D'Andre Miller left the community center. And he appears to be running. Now watch, right here." Jensen tapped keys to slow the video. "The car enters the frame here, at the top of the slope in the street. The image gets a little better as it approaches the intersection."

Tracy watched a dark-colored car drive down the hill and blow through the intersection without slowing. "The stucco building on the corner blocks the view of the kid stepping from the curb."

"Like I said, it's not great, but the timing, the car, and the image of the kid coming up the street all confirm what the car part tells us—that the kid was hit by a dark-colored Subaru."

"Can you enhance the image any more?" Tracy asked.

"Not without making it grainier. You're not going to get a license plate unless we can find other cameras down the line that picked the car up."

Tracy straightened. "You have someone working on that? Maybe we get lucky and get a plate, or at least a partial."

"We're on it," Jensen said. He smiled at Tracy. "I told you this was more interesting than your run-of-the-mill homicides."

CHAPTER 5

Leaving the King County Courthouse, Celia McDaniel had been a woman on a mission. Del just tried to keep up. She'd walked past a Starbucks and a Seattle's Best Coffee, continuing without hesitation until she came to Top Pot Doughnuts on Fifth Avenue, a couple blocks north of the courthouse. As she opened the door, she told Del, "I don't do coffee unless donuts are along for the ride."

Inside, the smell of fresh-brewed coffee and fresh-baked donuts was both intoxicating and torturous. The last thing Del needed was a donut; he'd had his annual physical the day before and his blood pressure was up—no surprise, given the last few weeks, but his doctor had also been riding him about his weight.

Del purchased a coffee, black, and refrained from a donut. McDaniel ordered a latte and two donuts, an old-fashioned and a glazed. They sat at a table away from others, McDaniel on the bench seat, Del in a chair across the table. She cradled the coffee cup between her hands like it was a fire in a snowstorm. "I hate the cold," she said. "Thankfully, at least, you all don't get snow here."

"We might this year," Del said. "Usually it's December and January. I don't remember a March this cold."

"I was trying to be optimistic." McDaniel smiled, which seemed to come easily to her. She had a positive energy about her that he surmised was good with juries. Del envied her. He hadn't really smiled since the morning his sister called to tell him Allie was dead. "You sure you don't want a donut?" she asked.

"My doctor already thinks I'm a few donuts over my playing weight." Del had removed his raincoat and draped it across the back of an adjacent chair.

"No cream or sugar either," McDaniel said, nodding at Del's coffee. "You're a man without vices."

"My bathroom scale would tend to disagree with you."

"Well, you're looking at one of mine. I can't survive without my donuts. It's the only way I can drink coffee."

"Why don't you give up coffee?"

"And forego my donuts?"

"Sounds like circular reasoning."

"It's called rationalizing."

"You eat like this every morning?"

"God, no." She gave him a sheepish smile. "A couple times a week."

"How do you maintain your . . . ?" Del stopped and sipped his coffee.

"My figure?"

"I didn't say it," Del said, raising a hand. "OPA is in my cubicle enough as it is."

"You say inappropriate things often?" McDaniel asked.

"I'm closing in on fifty; I am an inappropriate thing."

"To answer your question—and thank you very much—I'm as obsessive about exercise as I am about donuts."

"I wish exercise went with my love of lasagna."

"I do Pilates every weekday morning at five a.m. just so I can eat like this." She dipped her donut and brought the end to her mouth.

"I'm up at five every morning too," Del said. "I go to the bathroom and go back to bed."

She laughed and quickly put her hand to her mouth, just below her nose. She looked for a moment like she might spit out her coffee. Then she waved at him and turned her head, using a napkin to wipe her mouth. After a moment she said, "Give me some warning next time."

Del liked her. She seemed real, without pretenses. He'd also noticed that her left hand was not sporting a ring. He sat back. His legs felt heavy and his body weary from the lack of sleep, but the anxiety he'd felt the past week had evaporated.

"Can I ask you something?" he said.

"Sure," McDaniel said.

"In the office, you said what happened to my niece wasn't an unusual situation. What did you mean by that?"

McDaniel set down her coffee and wiped the tips of her fingers on a napkin. "You said she'd been in recovery just before her overdose?"

"She'd come home one day and told my sister she was done, that she wanted to quit. She said she was tired of the drugs and what they were doing to her. My sister called me, and I pulled some strings and got her into a rehab facility over in Eastern Washington. She'd been clean nearly three months. She attended NA meetings and was seeing a counselor; I got her a job at a Starbucks and she seemed to be really turning a corner—we all thought so. This hit us out of the blue." Feeling emotional, Del stopped.

McDaniel set down her coffee. "When a heroin addict falls out of recovery, they'll often go back to using the same amount of heroin . . . or the same strength of heroin they were using before they quit. Their bodies aren't prepared for the dosage and, unfortunately, they'll unintentionally overdose."

"Cerrabone said you worked narcotics in Georgia."

"I was prosecuting drug offenders. More recently, I was working on legislation to secure judicial alternatives for addicts."

"What brought you out here?"

McDaniel shifted her eyes to the glass walls that looked out on to the sidewalk. "I needed a change of scenery after my divorce."

"I needed a different planet after mine."

"That bad?"

"Not good."

"Do you have kids?" Celia asked.

"Thankfully, no. You?"

"A son." She paused, then said, "I was looking to do some advocacy and I'd read that King County has a heroin task force exploring ways to combat the rise in usage. I'm on that task force."

"I read about that," Del said. He refrained from saying that he didn't agree with it, not wanting to offend her.

"The rise in heroin use has become epidemic pretty much all over the country," she said. "And the number of accidental deaths from opioid overdoses now exceeds fatal car crashes."

Del shook his head. "Back in my day, only the real junkies did heroin."

"Things changed with the legalization of marijuana. The Mexican drug cartels saw their revenue stream fading, plowed their pot fields, and planted poppies. People didn't think about that when they were lobbying to legalize marijuana. It never made the media."

"Increase the product and decrease the cost," Del said. "Good old capitalism."

"Big-time," she said. "You can get heroin now for less than a pack of cigarettes. It wasn't just the legalization of marijuana. Researchers also trace the dramatic increase in addiction to a shift in health-care philosophy that started to emphasize treating a patient's pain rather than treating the underlying ailments. That led to an increase in opioid use."

"I read about that too."

"Opioid use previously restricted to the treatment of things like cancer or physical trauma suddenly became widely available for more broadly defined problems, like chronic pain. Not surprisingly, the drug companies introduced and aggressively marketed certain opioids, like oxycodone."

"They had me on it when they operated on my shoulder," Del said.

"Addicts quickly figured out how to circumvent the time-release pain medication by crushing or dissolving the pill, then snorting or shooting it."

"So how did they get from that to heroin?"

"Availability and cost. When the addiction problem came to light, state legislatures passed laws making it more difficult to get opioids prescribed, and the manufacturer reformulated oxycodone so it couldn't be crushed or dissolved. It seemed like two good responses, but both ignored the fact that you had a lot of addicted people who could either no longer get the drug or no longer afford it. That just paved the way for the Mexican drug cartels."

"They moved to heroin and had a ready market."

"They flooded the market with cheap, affordable heroin, making it the most commonly used drug by eighteen- to twenty-nine-year-olds. Not surprisingly, that demographic has had the largest increase in overdose deaths."

"So we put the dealers in jail and give them significant sentences like ten years," Del said, thinking of the new law.

"You put one in jail and you open a slot ten others will be waiting to fill."

"Not if we ramp up the punishment. Not if we start ensuring they get the full ten years. A lot of dealers would think twice."

She shook her head. "Dealers, maybe, but we can't legislate habits that have formed over the last decade. If there are users, there will be suppliers, Del. An addict is an addict. Your niece was an addict.

Criminalization only drives the addicts farther away from the people who love and can help them, to the people who will abuse them."

Del felt his anxiety returning. "Yeah, well, I'm not going after the users. I'm going after the dealers. I say increase the penalty for dealing from ten years to twenty-five years to life and we'll get rid of the dealers."

"And put them where? Our jails are already overburdened. And what do you do with the addicts?"

Del didn't have an immediate answer.

"You're unfortunately seeing the problem from a side unfamiliar to you. And you're upset and angry. You want someone to pay for the death of your niece."

"I can't say you're wrong."

"And that's a common response. But the key now isn't charging the criminals. It's freeing the addicts of their addictions. We need more people like you, Del, who've seen the problem at its worst."

Del stifled a grin. "I hope you didn't bring me here to pitch me."

"That's not fair. I did the research and I provided you with the law. That's what I was asked to do."

Del wasn't in the mood to argue. He was too damn tired. He slid back his chair and stood. "You're right. Thanks. I appreciate it."

"Look, I know what you're going through."

Del raised a hand. "You know, I really wish people would stop saying that because, with all due respect, you don't know what I'm going through. And you don't know what my sister is going through. People say 'I know.' I used to say 'I know.' I used to tell people how sorry I was for their loss, but until you've been there . . . until you've been through it, you don't know."

He grabbed his coat, throwing it over his arm. "Thanks for the memo."

"What would you have given to have saved your niece's life?" McDaniel asked. "What would your sister have given?"

"Anything," Del said without hesitation. "I would have given any-thing, and my sister would have too. But that isn't going to happen. Allie isn't coming back and that isn't going to change."

"No, she's not. You paid for her rehab, and yet she died anyway." Del bristled. "So what are you saying—that it was a mistake?"

"Of course not. I applaud you for it. I applaud her for going. What I'm saying is that to be addicted is to be continually in search of the next fix. It becomes an all-consuming focus."

"If we start getting rid of the dealers, start putting them away for significant sentences, and make it more and more difficult and expen-sive to buy the heroin, maybe those addicts at least have a chance."

"I don't disagree. But what do you do with the addicts in the interim?" When Del didn't answer, McDaniel said, "There's a proposal to create two safe injection sites here in Seattle—the first ever in this nation—to give addicts that chance."

Del scoffed. "Yeah, I read about that. And you know what? I think it's crap. Have somebody fill the needle for them? Shoot them up? Let them get high? How is that giving them a chance to get clean? It's just feeding their addiction."

"Vancouver has done it since 2003 and it has reduced public inject-ing and increased participation in addiction treatment."

"So how does that solve the *problem*? You still have addicts."

"Because no one died, Del, which is what you and your sister wanted most of all."

Del felt like he'd taken a blow to the chest.

"They've had more than fifteen hundred overdoses, but not a single loss of life. Allie might still be alive. My son might still be alive. And if he was, at least I'd have the chance to get him into treatment."

McDaniel looked off and exhaled. Then she crumpled her napkin and threw it on the table beside her unfinished donuts.

Del froze, uncertain what to say. "I'm sorry. I didn't—"

"No, you didn't." She grabbed her coat. "I know what you're going through, Del. I did everything I could to convict those who supplied my son, and I succeeded. But I would have given so much more if someone had just saved him; if someone had given me just one more chance to get him clean."

CHAPTER 6

Tracy sat in an uncomfortable plastic chair in a Spartan office at the Seattle Fertility Clinic, waiting to learn if science could do what nature apparently could not. The overhead fluorescent tubes emitted an annoying buzz and illuminated the room so brightly the white walls and linoleum floor nearly glowed. She wanted to get up and walk, to relieve her stress, but the office wasn't much larger than one of SPD's interrogation rooms.

She vacillated between feeling depressed, angry, frustrated, and embarrassed. She'd done everything her OB-GYN had told her to do—timed her menstrual cycle, religiously peed on plastic sticks each morning to pinpoint her ovulation, and stalked Dan like a sailor on shore leave after a year at sea. Nothing had worked.

The door to the consult room pushed open, and with it, Tracy felt her anxiety rise. She spent her days and, this month at least, her nights hunting murderers and other violent criminals, but she'd never felt as anxious as she felt at that moment. She was not in control here, and she hated feeling powerless to alter the result.

Dr. Scott Kramer entered the room in a white lab coat with his name stitched in blue over his breast pocket. He offered his customary warm smile, then paused just inside the door and pointed to the gun near Tracy's SPD badge, both clipped to her belt. "I hope you're going to work after this."

She smiled. "Night shift."

Kramer pulled over a rolling stool and sat beside a computer and keyboard on a movable workstation. Tracy smelled the faint aroma of his cologne as he angled the metal stand to allow her to see the computer screen. About to begin, he removed his hands from the keys and asked, almost as if he'd forgotten, "How are you doing?"

"I guess you're going to tell me," Tracy said.

Kramer nodded, his smile now just a bit less pronounced. Midfifties and bald, Kramer had soft eyes that seemed to be perpetually squinting, and a tennis player's trim physique and tan. His physical appearance matched his mellow demeanor. "Well, the first thing to keep in mind is these tests are relative. They're not black-and-white."

"I understand," she said. So the news was not good.

Kramer tapped the keyboard, talking in a soft voice. "What is relative is the decline in fertility as women age." A graph popped up on the monitor and Kramer traced it with his index finger. "There is a gradual fertility decline in women up until about thirty-five years of age, and then a much steeper decline." The graph looked like someone falling off a cliff. "At forty-three, you have about a thirty percent chance of getting pregnant."

"And a higher percentage of having a miscarriage if I do," Tracy said. She'd been reading the articles she could find online, though she knew that a little bit of Internet knowledge was almost always dangerous.

"Perhaps, about thirty-five percent," Kramer said.

"So what do the tests show?"

Kramer had ordered several tests on the third day of Tracy's menstrual cycle to determine her ORT, or ovarian reserve testing. He had explained that the blood tests determined how many eggs she had, and how responsive those eggs would be at ovulation.

"Frankly, your ovarian reserve is poor," Kramer said, cutting to the chase. He folded his hands. "Now, as I previously advised, that is negative information but it is not absolute."

"It suggests that the odds are stacked against me getting pregnant with my own eggs." So she would not be walking in the door of their home after her shift tonight shouting to Dan that she was "locked and loaded and ready to bear."

"The window of opportunity is definitely shorter. How long have you and your husband been trying to get pregnant?"

"After his vasectomy was reversed, about six months," she said. Was she supposed to discuss frequency? She didn't know.

Dr. Kramer crossed his legs and leaned forward. He had a deliberate manner that, at times like this, could be maddening. Tracy already knew from articles that six months was about the prescribed period for a couple to try to get pregnant without intervention. She and Dan had crossed that milestone.

"That's the period of time we usually recommend," Kramer said.

"My alternatives now?" Tracy asked.

"Well, we could try fertility drugs," Kramer said.

She smiled softly. "You don't sound optimistic."

Kramer shrugged. "Given your age, your ORT score, and the length of time you've been trying to get pregnant, I'd say the percentages of a pregnancy are limited."

"Limited, meaning . . . ?"

"Low."

She considered the information. "What kind of fertility drug?"

Kramer looked as though the question had diverted his train of thought. He had probably been about to discuss the use of a donor egg, but Tracy did not want a child who was half Dan's and half from someone she'd never met. She didn't want a child conceived in a petri dish. She wanted their child.

"*If* we pursued fertility drugs, we'd start with a protocol of Clomid and monitor you with ultrasound to see if and when you were ovulating. You and Dan take care of business. After that, we wait ten to fourteen days to perform a pregnancy test. But under the circumstances—"

"What would be my chances?"

Kramer looked to be running numbers in his mind. "It's difficult to quantify, but under the circumstances . . ." He paused. "Let's be realistic. Yes, we could flog your ovaries with fertility drugs to get you to ovulate, but will your eggs even be able to be fertilized? And if so, keep in mind the high rate of miscarriages, as well as birth defects such as Down syndrome. Are you sure you can handle all that?"

"But you said that the ORT is not absolute."

"It's not a certainty," Kramer said. "But it is informative. In your case, the chances are very slim, at best, of your getting pregnant. There are other options."

"A donor egg."

"Yes."

Tracy sighed. If she were going to use a donor egg, she might as well adopt, give a good home to a child in need. She and Dan had agreed to make these decisions together. They agreed to discuss whether she should go on fertility drugs, which had some potentially negative side effects. They agreed that the decision to adopt would be one they evaluated together and in detail. But that was before Tracy knew for certain that she, and not Dan, was the problem.

"I'd like to try the Clomid," she said. "I'd like to at least try."

CHAPTER 7

Joe Jensen called Tracy as she drove downtown from Dr. Kramer's office. "You want the good news or the bad news?"

She thought of her conversation with Dr. Kramer and decided she'd had enough bad news. "How about some good news."

"The video team was unsuccessful tracking the Subaru after it departed the intersection, probably because it's mostly residential areas without cameras."

"If that's the good news, don't tell me the bad news."

"The good news is patrol received a call from a woman who lives in that neighborhood."

"They found the car?" Tracy asked.

"A black Subaru with damage to the hood and front headlight."

"Where?"

"A vacant lot behind the woman's home not far from the intersection," Jensen said.

Half an hour later, Tracy and Kins were driving to the address on Renton Avenue South. The street, under some sort of repair, was lined with orange cones and city workers in yellow jackets and white hats. Kins pulled to the curb and parked behind a patrol car in a sloped driveway. As he exited the car, he flashed his badge at an overly zealous city worker trying to tell him he couldn't park there.

"You're driving a Prius?" the worker asked, disbelieving.

They'd pulled the car from the pool. Kins called it the Toyota sewing machine.

"We're doing our part to save the environment."

Tracy slipped on gloves and wrapped her jacket tight to ward off the chill as she climbed concrete steps. A cracked walkway led to the front door of a small, single-story, clapboard home, which was typical for that area. At the top step, Tracy sensed Kins was not beside her. He stood at the bottom step. "You all right?" she asked.

"Just give me a second," he said. "I've been sitting and it's cold. That's a bad combo." He grimaced and started up the steps. Tracy waited for him. Together they approached a uniformed police officer standing near the front door. He looked frozen, hands thrust deep into the pockets of his blue SPD jacket, his chin tucked low into the collar, an SPD baseball cap pulled low on his head. As they approached, Kins sidestepped a child's bicycle lying in the crabgrass.

"My partner is in the back talking to the property owner," the officer said, his mouth emitting white wisps as if exhaling cigarette smoke. He led them along concrete pavers to a wooden gate at the rear of the property. "When we got out here I remembered the call from the morning roll call. Black Subaru, right? It looks like it was in some kind of accident."

The officer pulled a string, and the bottom of the gate scraped against a stone paver as it swung in. The lawn had been cut around the clutter—two older-model cars that didn't look like they'd been run in years, a motor home, and several rusted boat trailers. At the back of the lot, partially obscured by bushes and trees, was a black Subaru.

Joe Jensen stood speaking to a woman dressed in black jeans tucked into her boots. A down jacket extended to her knees. Jensen again had his head covered by the black knit ski cap.

Tracy and Kins introduced themselves.

"I saw it this morning and figured it was one of the neighbors'," the woman said, sounding both upset and excited by the attention. "My husband charges fifty dollars a month to park a car or trailer, and a hundred dollars for the motor home. This morning, after I took my daughter to school, I knocked on doors and asked the neighbors who owned the car. It doesn't belong to any of them. So I called it in to get it towed, and I was told I'd have to pay in advance." She sounded like someone had just asked for her kidney. "It isn't my car. Luckily someone reported it as stolen."

Luckily, Tracy thought.

Jensen gave Tracy and Kins a subtle eye roll. He'd apparently heard the woman's spiel already, possibly more than once. The three of them excused themselves and crossed to the car.

"Do we know when it was reported as stolen?" Tracy asked Jensen. She felt the cold stinging her cheeks.

"Seven o'clock this morning. Owner said he went out to get in his car, and it wasn't there." Jensen held the broken car part, in a plastic evidence bag, up to the damage to the left front headlamp. "It fits," he said. "This is the car." The windshield on the passenger's side had cracked like a spider's web. The hood was also dented. "Initial impression, the driver hit the kid and he wrapped around the hood, hit the windshield, then got propelled forward. That's why he was so far from the intersection."

Tracy looked inside the car's windows, without touching them. "The air bag is deployed."

"That's a good thing," Jensen said. "If it picked up the driver's DNA we might know the driver at the time of impact—if he or she is in the system. I've called to have the car impounded at VPR and we're working on a search warrant to get inside." VPR was the vehicle processing room of the Seattle Police Department located at a satellite facility next to the Washington State Patrol Crime Lab. "You want me to involve CSI?"

CSI would process the car if homicide was going to get involved. Remembering Nolasco's reluctance that morning, Tracy opted not to involve them. "No. You guys handle it, but let us know when you get the warrant to get inside."

"Will do."

"Does the owner live around here?" Tracy figured the driver of the car had to know the lot existed.

Jensen shook his head. "According to the DMV, he lives in an apartment in Bremerton."

"Bremerton?" Kins said. "What the hell is the car doing over here?"

"I assume it has something to do with the car being stolen," Jensen said.

Bremerton was a city located west of Seattle and accessed either by ferry across the Puget Sound, which took about an hour, or by driving south and cutting across the Tacoma Narrows Bridge, which took an hour and a half.

"What's the driver do in Bremerton?" Tracy asked.

"He's enlisted," Jensen said.

"Great," she said, shaking her head.

Bremerton was also home to one of the largest naval shipyards in the United States.

—

Tracy and Kins nearly missed the ferry departure because the Department of Transportation had blocked several streets leading to the terminal, which set Kins off on one of his biggest pet peeves. Seattle had been in the process of installing an underground tunnel and tearing down the elevated viaduct. At least that had been the plan. The traffic project, like so many in Seattle, had been fraught with delays, lawsuits, and mounting expenses almost from its inception.

Hey, if you can't have it on time, the public might as well pay double for it, Kins would say.

They parked on the ferry and went upstairs for the hour-long crossing. "I'm going to get a cup of coffee. You want anything?" Kins asked.

Tracy declined and found an empty table. Out the window she watched the Seattle skyline fade behind them as the boat powered across Puget Sound's slate-gray waters, the engines emitting a low chugging sound. On her laptop, she pulled up the information she'd found running the car's owner, Laszlo Gutierrez Trejo, through DMV, military, and criminal records. Trejo had two prior speeding tickets, but no criminal record. He'd been enlisted in the Navy for five years and had achieved the rating of logistics specialist, or LS. Uncertain what that designation meant, she'd Googled the position. As far as she could tell, a logistics specialist worked in ship storerooms and/or military base warehouses.

She'd then called Trejo and told him they were gathering information in the search for his stolen car. Since he couldn't come to them—he professed to owning just the one car—she and Kins were headed to Bremerton, to an address in an area referred to as Jackson Park, Navy-owned apartment units about four miles north of Naval Base Kitsap.

Kins returned to the table with coffee and a hot dog loaded with relish and onions.

"I thought you were dieting?"

"This is dinner."

"Uh-huh," she said. "You had to get the onions, didn't you?"

"Love onions on a hot dog."

"They don't love you," she said. "I hope you brought breath mints."

"Humor a condemned man."

"For the love of God, you're getting hip surgery. Seriously, are you nervous about it or just screwing with me?"

"Of course I'm nervous about it; they have to knock me out."

"They've done it thousands of times, Kins."

"That's what the doctor told me. You know what? I don't give a damn about the thousands of times everything went hunky-dory. I care about the one or two times it didn't."

"You're young and healthy. Don't overthink it."

Kins set down his hot dog. "I got three kids, Tracy, who I still need to put through college. I'll be fifty-three when the last one graduates, and that assumes none of them go on to graduate school. Do you know what college tuition costs nowadays? I'm looking at a couple hundred grand."

Tracy did the math in her head. If she and Dan were to have a child, she'd be in her early to midsixties before their child graduated from college. God only knew what tuition would cost by then.

Kins took a bite of the hot dog and wiped mustard from the corner of his mouth with a napkin. "What do you think of our man Lazarus?"

"Laszlo?" she said, thinking she'd misheard him through a mouth full of hot dog.

"What do you think of him?"

"I think it's a long way for him to travel that late at night."

"So you think he's telling the truth, that his car was stolen?"

"I'm open to hearing what he has to say."

"Wouldn't the base keep records of people coming and going?"

"He doesn't live on base. He lives in an apartment complex."

"You said he lived in Navy housing."

"It is, but not on base, which is why we can talk to him without jumping through hoops. Haven't you ever worked with the Navy?"

"No," Kins said, taking another bite of hot dog. "You?"

"Once. A home burglary. An enlisted man robbed his ex-girlfriend and NCIS got involved." Navy Criminal Investigative Services were civilians, the Navy equivalent of detectives. "They made it a nightmare just to talk to the guy, but ultimately decided not to push jurisdiction and backed off."

"Yeah, I heard they can be difficult."

"I was told that after 9/11, the best investigators got pulled from the criminal division and transferred to counterterrorism. Those who remained aren't as good or as cooperative. Laszlo's apartments are zoned for federal and civilian jurisdiction, which means we can talk to him without going through NCIS."

An hour and fifteen minutes after departing, the boat docked at the Bremerton Ferry Terminal with a slight jolt. The sun had faded, and dusk and the low cloud layer made everything nearly as gray as the water. The temperature had also dropped to the upper thirties. Kins and Tracy had returned to their car on the car deck and were waiting to disembark.

"So how do you like living at the edge of the world?" Kins asked.

"Don't be a snob," Tracy said. Kins lived in Madison Park near the university. "Redmond is far from the edge of the world."

"You miss West Seattle?"

"I miss the commute. And the views." The house in West Seattle had been a fifteen- to twenty-minute commute to the office, and the deck provided a billion-dollar view looking back across Elliott Bay to the Seattle skyline. "Some mornings it can take me an hour to get in, but the house is homey, and when we're there, work seems far away."

A ferry worker directed cars off the ship. "Have you and Dan talked about kids?" Kins asked.

The question came out of the blue. Tracy played dumb. "Here and there. Why?"

He shrugged. "You said you wanted kids."

"Eventually."

"Are you trying?"

She laughed. "That's a little personal."

"So is busting in a new partner, which I'm not looking forward to with one good hip."

"I'm not going anywhere, Kins—you are."

"And my wife wasn't quitting her job when we got married either. Things change when you have kids."

She shook her head. She knew it was just the stress of the upcoming surgery and the downtime that would follow. "Well, you'll have nine months' lead time."

"You're not pregnant now, are you?" he asked.

"No," she said. "I'm not." The car in front of them moved forward. "Drive. If we want to get off this ferry, I'd suggest we get going."

"Feed the squirrels," Kins said, making fun of the Prius's lack of horsepower.

At first blush, Jackson Park did not appear to be a bad place to live, abutting Ostrich Bay to the east and the Kitsap Golf and Country Club to the west. Like most military bases, it seemingly included everything Navy personnel and their families could need—a day-care center, an elementary school, a hospital, a minimart attached to a gas station, and outdoor tennis and basketball courts. As they drove the labyrinth of streets, Tracy didn't see a scrap of errant paper. The lawns were manicured, and the wood-sided buildings looked freshly painted, even in the fading light. One- and two-story structures, they had all been cast from the same mold. Signs designated parking in outdoor carports, or in stalls at the bottom of long sloped lawns, which, Tracy deduced, could make it more plausible for someone to steal a car and not be seen.

"It's like that movie with Jim Carrey," Kins said, looking around at the pristine world. "The one where they're all living on a movie set."

"*The Truman Show*?" Tracy asked.

"That's the one. Creepy the way everything is so perfect."

Creepy and deserted. Tracy figured that was likely in part due to the freezing temperature. Still, it was odd to drive through a community and not see a single living soul outside walking, driving, or taking Fido out to do his business. Maybe the Subaru could have been stolen. If it had been on a night like this, there wouldn't have been anyone to witness it.

Laszlo Trejo lived on the ground floor of a building adjacent to a fenced-in basketball court. Kins parked in an area designated for visitors. Lights on poles illuminated a tree-lined walkway. At the building, they descended steps to the apartment's front door. Kins knocked, and a moment later, the door opened and a Hispanic woman, perhaps late twenties, greeted them with a smile.

"You must be the police officers from Seattle," she said with just a hint of a Mexican accent. She invited them into the hall and shut the door behind them. "Laz just got home." She led them into a neat but sparsely furnished living room of bleached white chairs and a sofa that likely came with the apartment. "I'll get him for you."

Adjoining the room was a six-by-six linoleum floor with a kitchen table. Tracy stepped to the mantel over a fireplace and considered framed photographs depicting the Trejos getting married, she in a white dress, he in his spanking-white naval uniform. It was warm in the apartment and it smelled the way Tracy's apartment used to smell when she didn't get around to cleaning Roger's kitty litter for a few days.

"Are you the officers from Seattle?"

Laszlo Trejo entered the room from the hallway. He was dressed in Navy blue-and-gray camouflage shirt and pants, which he'd tucked into black boots. Perhaps five foot six, he wasn't much taller than his wife. He had a wedge of black hair and held an energy drink, which Tracy initially mistook for a beer.

"Have you found my car?" Trejo asked. His accent was thicker than his wife's. He didn't look or sound the least bit intimidated, or as if he had anything to hide.

"We were hoping to ask you a few questions, Mr. Trejo," Kins said.

"I already told that police woman everything I know," he said, not exactly hostile, but not friendly either.

"Was that a police officer from Bremerton?" Kins asked.

"Yeah."

"Your car was found in Seattle," Kins said.

"That's what she said." Trejo gestured to Tracy.

"When was the last time you saw your car?" Tracy asked, getting to the point quickly to keep Trejo from directing the conversation.

Trejo, perhaps realizing they weren't there to hand him his car keys, sat in one of the recliners. "Monday night. I came home from work and parked in the carport." He alternately sipped the drink and flexed the aluminum can.

Tracy and Kins sat on the couch across a coffee table. The more Trejo spoke, the more Tracy sensed he'd scripted the conversation, which accounted for his initial assertive demeanor. As the interview progressed, no longer scripted, he started to look and sound uncomfortable. He had a habit of glancing down when he spoke rather than making eye contact, and he continued to crinkle the aluminum can.

"What time did you get home from work?"

"I think it was around six."

"Which carport did you park in?" she asked.

"It's just up the hill," he said, making a vague gesture.

"Can you see it from here?"

Trejo shook his head. "No."

"And you didn't go out again?" she asked.

"Not that night."

"Your wife didn't take the car out again?"

He shook his head. "No."

"And when did you notice the car was missing?"

"The next morning when I went out to go to work and the car wasn't there." He shrugged. "I told this to the woman who took the report." He was like an actor reciting his lines.

"Yeah, we haven't read that report yet," Kins said.

"So how was it stolen?" Tracy asked. "You had the keys, right?"

"Yeah, but I got a hide-a-key I keep along the bottom of the back bumper. They could have gotten that."

"Who knows about that key?" Tracy asked, skeptical but trying not to show it.

"I don't know," Trejo said. "Maybe somebody saw it."

"What did you do when you found out your car was missing?" Tracy asked.

"I came back here and asked my wife where it was," he said, back on script. "She said she had no idea. So I called the police and told them it was stolen."

"And what did they do?"

Trejo frowned. He was starting to look frustrated, which is what Tracy intended. "They sent out an officer. She asked me the same questions and said she was making out a report and said they'd be in touch. Then I had no way to get to work."

"You just have the one car?" Tracy said.

"I told you that on the phone," he said, setting down his drink and leaning forward, toward Kins. "Can I ask a question? Did you find my car?"

"Do you know anyone in Seattle, Mr. Trejo?" Tracy asked.

He glanced at her. "Know anyone? What does that mean?"

"Do you have any friends or family who live in Seattle?"

"No." He sipped his drink. Again, Tracy thought that act was deliberate, to disengage from her and the question.

"Where's home for you?" she asked.

"Here."

"I mean where did you grow up?"

"I grew up in the San Diego area. What does that—"

"You've been enlisted for five years?"

"Almost six."

"Never lived in Seattle?"

"I just told you I didn't."

"What do you do at Bremerton?"

"I'm a logistics specialist for FLC."

"What's FLC?"

"Fleet Logistics Center."

"What do you do? What's your job?"

"When I'm on ship, I work in the storeroom. When we're in dock, I work in the warehouse. What does that have to do with my car?"

"You order parts, maintain inventory, that sort of thing," she persisted.

"That's right."

"Have you been overseas?"

He nodded. "I worked in Kuwait and Iraq."

"In supply stores?"

"Correct. Oh, and Afghanistan. I've been over there too."

"What ship?"

"The USS *Stennis*."

"Which is what kind of ship?"

"An aircraft carrier. A nuclear-powered aircraft carrier."

"When were you in Afghanistan?"

"Last time? In 2013. How does this have anything to do with my car?"

Tracy persisted, hoping to continue to rock Trejo from script. "And the Middle East, when was the last time you were there?"

"Last time was 2012."

"How long have you been on base here in Bremerton?"

"Four months."

"And before that where was the ship?"

"Thailand." He looked to Kins. "Did you find my car? Can I pick it up?"

"We found your car in Seattle, Mr. Trejo," Kins said.

"I figured that much," he said, sarcasm seeping in. "Can I go get it?"

"You have no idea how it got to Seattle?" Tracy pushed.

"I told you, somebody had to steal it."

"Have there been any reports of cars being stolen from this complex?"

He shrugged. "I don't know. Maybe you should ask the police. When can I get my car back?"

"It's going to be a while."

"Why?" he said, now clearly aggravated. "I need that car to go to work."

"Your car was involved in a hit-and-run accident, Mr. Trejo." She watched for any signs Trejo already knew this information, but his face remained impassive.

"It hit another car? Oh man. How bad is the damage?"

"It hit a pedestrian. A twelve-year-old boy. It killed him."

Trejo's line of sight focused on the carpet. For a moment he didn't speak. Tracy thought it was a legitimate reaction. "That's terrible, man." He sipped his drink.

"One more question, Mr. Trejo," Tracy said.

Trejo lowered the can. Tracy waited until he looked at her.

"How did you cut your forehead?"

CHAPTER 8

From the outside, the modest, single-story brick home in Seattle's Loyal Heights looked very much like the other houses in the neighborhood. The sloped lawn, dormant during winter, showed no signs that spring was around the corner, nor did the flower beds. To Del, it was bleak, as if the house too were mourning Allie's death.

A car gave a polite horn tap. Del looked in his rearview mirror and waved an apology. With vehicles parked along both curbs—many of the homes did not have driveways or garages—the road was barely wide enough for one car. He squeezed his hunter-green 1965 Impala into a spot at the curb. He'd managed to keep it in the divorce, though his ex-wife, Norma, had made him pay a steep price. The car had belonged to Del's father. He'd handed Del the keys after the DMV refused him a license following a third stroke. Del had driven the Impala to work every day since, amassing some 289,000 miles. The original engine still purred, and the paint gleamed beneath the streetlamps. He changed the oil and filter regularly, did the spark plugs and brakes when needed, and flushed the fluids once a year. He told people he took better care of his car than his body. He wasn't joking. When his nephews were in

Little League and pleaded with him, he'd driven the car in parades. The boys loved it.

He looked again at his sister's house, framed between the branches of two mature plum trees sprouting from dirt squares in the sidewalk. The light above the front door cast a sickened glow, as if to mark the house with some biblical plague. Night came early and stayed late during Seattle winters, but the darkness enveloping this home had nothing to do with the time of year or time of night.

He'd helped his sister, Maggie, purchase the home with what savings he'd had, which hadn't been much. Neither was the home, just 1,600 square feet with two bedrooms on the main floor. Del had converted the daylight basement for the two boys, identical twins. He doubted either would be moving upstairs to Allie's bedroom; Maggie hadn't touched it since the morning she'd found Allie.

He grabbed the brown paper bag from the seat and trudged up the concrete walk. Frost covered the lawn and the leaves of the rhododendrons. A shade shrouded the front window, but it leaked blue-gray light from the gaps along its edges. The television would shut off quickly if Del knocked, but that was never necessary. The only time his sister locked the front door was when she went to bed, and lately, she hadn't been locking it at all, despite Del's admonitions.

Del pushed open the door. His two nephews, slumped on the couch, scurried like frightened squirrels. One fumbled for the remote. Too late. He'd caught them in the middle of a *Seinfeld* rerun. Del's fault. He'd hooked them on Jerry, George, Elaine, and Kramer the week he'd stayed with them when his sister traveled to a friend's wedding.

"You get all your homework done?" Del asked, stepping in.

"We were just taking a break," Stevie said, looking and sounding flustered.

The mail lay scattered on the floor where the mailman had inserted it through the door slot near an assortment of socks and shoes. Unopened newspapers cluttered the coffee table amid bowls and cups.

Del had been swinging by before working the night shift, but given the number of murders they'd already had this year, it was becoming more difficult to do so.

"Uh-huh." Del eyed an empty bag of chips and a jar of salsa amid the newspapers and magazines on the coffee table. "Did you eat dinner?"

"No," Mark said. "Mom's sleeping. I think."

Del looked toward the darkened hallway. "Did you talk to your dad today?"

"No," they each said.

It wasn't surprising. Their father worked in a Los Angeles insurance firm, which was where he'd met his new, young wife. He'd come up for Allie's funeral, blamed Maggie for Allie's death, and left the next day. If he hadn't, Del would have escorted him back to Los Angeles with a size-fourteen loafer shoved in a very uncomfortable place.

Del bent and grabbed the letters and magazines. "You boys can't pick up the mail?"

"We didn't see it," Mark said. They frequently spoke for each other.

"Maybe you need glasses," Del said. He considered the two backpacks dropped near the front door beside their discarded tennis shoes and jackets. "Doesn't look like you can see your backpack or clothes either."

They didn't respond, which, for nine-year-old boys, was always an admission of guilt. They could ordinarily think up excuses on the fly. Del flipped through the mail and saw the name Allie Marcello in one of the windows. It looked like a check, likely Allie's final payment from her job at the coffee shop. He didn't need to see that at the moment, nor did his sister.

Feeling tears, he said, "Okay. Come on into the kitchen. I got burritos."

The boys scrambled off the couch, following him like two dogs about to be fed. Del turned on the kitchen light. Pots, plates, and glasses filled with utensils littered the counter and the sink. Cabinet doors had been left open. A dish towel lay on the floor. He set the mail on the stack he'd placed on the tile counter the prior day, still unopened. His list of groceries had also not been touched.

"Get out some clean plates, Stevie."

Del opened the refrigerator and found the shelves bare but for a few condiments and leftovers from the spaghetti he'd made two nights earlier. He'd need to go shopping again if he couldn't get his sister out of her room.

"We don't have any," Stevie said, looking at the empty cabinet.

Del opened the dishwasher. "Didn't I ask you to put the dishes away last night?"

"We forgot," Mark said.

"Probably all that homework you were doing has taxed your brain."

"They can tax your brain?" Mark said, wide-eyed.

"They tax everything else," Del said. He pulled clean plates from the dishwasher and handed them to the boys. "You need utensils?"

"For what?" Stevie asked.

"Never mind."

The boys carried the plates to the kitchen table. The legs of their chairs shuddered as they slid them across the linoleum. Mark started to twist the top off a half-empty bottle of Diet Coke.

"Not for dinner," Del said.

Mark looked and sounded like he'd been deprived of a constitutional right. "What are we supposed to drink?"

"Milk," Del said.

"We're out."

Del set the bag on the counter and pulled out a carton of milk. He should have purchased two, maybe a whole cow, given how quickly the boys went through a carton.

"My man!" Stevie lifted his hand in the air. "Don't leave me hanging, Uncle Del."

Del gave him a high-five. Not to be outdone, Mark held out his fist for a bump. "Bring it home, Uncle D."

Del returned the fist bump and filled the two glasses. The boys nearly drained them. Mark burped and Stevie tried to best him.

"How about an 'excuse me'?" Del said.

"Why? Did you fart?" Mark said. That set them both off laughing.

"You guys are a couple comedians." Del handed them chicken burritos. They peeled off the tinfoil and went at them like they hadn't eaten all day. "Did you use the money I gave you to buy lunch today?"

"Yeah," Stevie said, through a mouth full of rice and beans.

"What did they have?"

"Pizza."

"When's the last time either of you ate a vegetable?"

"I don't know," Mark said.

"I had an apple slice at school," Stevie said.

"Close enough. After you eat, I want to see your day planners. I want to see what you have for homework."

"We don't have any," Stevie said.

"Thought you said you were taking a break?" Del arched his eyebrows.

Stevie looked over the top of his burrito at Mark, whose eyes widened in the universal sign for *Shut up, you idiot!*

"Never lie to a detective," Del said. He rubbed the tops of their heads and departed the kitchen, turning on the hall light. He passed the door to Allie's room, still closed, and knocked twice on the door at the end of the hall. Colored light from the television flickered out the gap between the door and the hardwood. Del pushed the door open.

Maggie sat on top of the bedcovers in pajama bottoms and a bathrobe. The lights were off. The blue-gray of the television flickered about the room. "I didn't hear you come in." She tucked her bare feet beneath her and tried in vain to straighten her hair. She looked like someone who'd had the flu for a week and hadn't showered.

"Have you gotten out of bed today, Maggie?"

"Yeah," she said, a little too quickly. "I was . . . I was out. I just climbed in an hour ago."

"Where'd you go?"

"I ran some errands."

"Did you go grocery shopping like I asked you?"

"Yeah, I got a few things."

Del walked to the window and cracked it open. The room smelled stale, like an old person's closet. He turned on a wall lamp on the other side of the bed.

"The grocery list is still on the counter."

"I forgot to bring it."

"Your car is parked in the exact same spot as yesterday."

"I parked it there when I got back. The space was still open."

Del had chalked her front tire the previous night. She hadn't moved the car. Never lie to a detective.

"Did you call the name of that therapist I left for you?" He pointed to the scrap of paper on her cluttered nightstand.

She turned as if seeing it for the first time. "Oh, uh, no. I got busy and forgot."

"If you don't call tomorrow, I'm going to make an appointment for you."

"I don't need you to make an appointment for me."

"Tomorrow. Or I call."

Maggie sighed and looked away.

He picked up clothes from the floor and tossed them on a chair in the corner. "You still got two boys out there who need their mother, Maggie. There's no food in the house. They're wearing the same clothes they had on yesterday, and they're not doing their homework."

She wiped tears with the bedsheet, then clutched it tightly to her chest. "It just hurts so bad, Del. It hurts all the time."

He bit back tears. "I know," he said. "But the boys need their mother, Maggie, more now than ever."

"So did Allie, Del. And I wasn't here for her." Her crying intensified.

"You did everything you could for Allie. You're not responsible."

"I was her mother," she whispered, the tears now racking her body, coming in great sobs of pain.

Del moved to her, wrapping an arm around her shoulders. "Heroin killed Allie—heroin and the people who supplied it. Not you." He sat on the edge of her bed, silent for a long minute. Feeling himself getting angry, he stood. "I bought you a burrito. Come out and eat with the boys."

"I'm not hungry."

"When's the last time you ate?"

"This morning. I had coffee."

"Coffee isn't food. You need to eat."

"I can't. I feel nauseous when I eat."

"Then just come and sit with them."

"I will. Tomorrow I will."

Del didn't push it. "What about work?"

"I'm on bereavement leave. I have another two weeks."

"Okay, then what?"

"Then I go back to work."

"You think you can, like this?"

She sighed. "I don't know."

"None of us wants to move on, Maggie, but we have no choice. I have to work. Faz can't keep covering for me."

More sobs. In between, Maggie said, "What more could I have done, Del? What more should I have done?"

She'd asked that question of him for more than a week, and he answered the same each time. "You did everything you could, Maggie."

"Then why isn't she alive?"

Del thought of his conversation with Celia McDaniel. What would Maggie have given just to keep her daughter alive? Everything, and then just a little bit more.

The family had tried counseling when they learned Allie was using, but Allie had left the facility. They tried to have her involuntarily committed to a hospital psych ward, but she'd bolted. When they pushed the issue, they'd learned that they couldn't have Allie committed without her permission, that teenagers could refuse treatment in Washington State—unless a mental health specialist deemed her a threat to herself or to others. Apparently, overdosing on heroin was not considered enough of a threat. Allie overdosed a second time and then a third. The paramedics brought her back, stabilized her, and left her in her room. They had no place to take her. The treatment facilities were overrun with a long waiting list. Maggie called Del and pleaded with him to have Allie arrested, but Washington law prohibited it. Besides, even if arrested, Allie would have been released within hours.

We can't police our way out of this problem, Celia McDaniel had said.

Then, out of the blue, Allie walked in the front door of the house one morning after disappearing for three days. Maggie described her as looking like hell. She said she looked like death—so rail thin her clothes hung as if on a wire hanger. Dark circles ringed her eyes. Her arms were so bruised they looked like pincushions. Allie told Maggie she was done using. She said she didn't want to die. She begged for help. Del and Maggie scraped together every penny they had to get her into a facility in Eastern Washington. It wasn't cheap. Del took out a loan using his pension as collateral and he'd have done it again and again. The thought made him recall what Celia McDaniel had said.

They got Allie away from her user friends, user contacts, and the familiar places to buy. By all accounts, Allie went through hell, physically and psychologically, even with the drugs to ease the pain of withdrawal. On the day they released her, Allie's counselors told Del and Maggie, *The loss of hope is nearly as dangerous as the drug itself. Addicts have a lot of self-hatred. They believe they're worthless. Allie has a lot of fear she's going to slip back to using again. It can be debilitating.*

When they brought Allie home, she looked better, though timid. She'd put on weight. The black circles beneath her eyes had faded. She looked like the old Allie—the happy, funny kid with the quick wit. Her eyes sparkled when she talked about finishing high school and attending Gonzaga in the fall. Del got her a job at a coffee shop. She went to NA meetings. Maggie accompanied her and Del watched the twins. Once he went with Allie and learned what he already knew. She was a good kid from a good family, but she was in a fight for her life, a life-and-death struggle to be here each day. A life-and-death struggle she'd ultimately lost. My God, how could it get that bad for someone so young?

She just couldn't beat it. Using always lingered on the edge of darkness, a devil looking for any tiny crack to squeeze through and tempt her. It came in all forms, from her addict friends to the suppliers who wanted to make a buck and didn't care whom they killed to get one.

Del cared.

They'd killed the wrong girl.

"If I'm going to find out what happened to Allie, I need to get into her room," Del said.

The tears trickled down Maggie's cheeks. She wiped them with the sheet. She'd left the room the way it had been, with the needle on the floor amid the pile of clothes, a half-finished can of Coke on the dresser, posters on the walls, unfinished homework open on Allie's desk.

"I need to get on her cell phone and her computer. I need to find out who she was talking to so I can find out what happened. So I can get the people responsible. It's time, Maggie."

"I can't go back there, Del."

"You don't have to. I'll do it for you. Moving forward doesn't mean forgetting the past. Moving forward means doing something *about* the past. Let me move forward, Maggie. Let me do my job."

CHAPTER 9

Tracy and Kins missed the 7:55 p.m. ferry back to Seattle and now waited in a short line to board the 9:05 crossing. Rather, the car waited in line. It was too cold to sit in a parked car, though that wasn't what had initially motivated Tracy to go inside the sports bar across the street from the terminal. She had an upset stomach, and she'd been having hot flashes since they got back into the car after interviewing Trejo. Dr. Kramer had indicated both were potential side effects of the Clomid. She went into the bathroom and splashed water on her face, taking short, quick breaths, briefly feeling like she might throw up.

When the nausea passed, Tracy returned to the restaurant. The walls and ceiling were adorned in Seahawk blue and green, and Mariner and Seattle Sounders paraphernalia. On a Tuesday night, the crowd was sparse and the atmosphere subdued. Kins sat at a table staring up at one of the flat-screen televisions, oblivious to the fact that Tracy had been in the bathroom long enough to write *War and Peace*, or maybe just not wanting to bring up the subject for fear her prolonged absence had been related to a "women's issue." The TV was tuned to ESPN—a tape-delayed broadcast of a Mariner preseason baseball game—not that what was on the television mattered. Dan did the same thing; he'd watch any sport, even when he already knew the outcome.

When she sat, Kins said, "You want to split an order of french fries?"

Tracy had to stifle a burp. "I thought you were trying to lose weight before your surgery?"

"I've decided that if I'm going out, I'm going out in a blaze of glory."

"You're an idiot," she said. "I hope you don't say these things around Shannah."

Kins ordered coffee. Tracy asked for ginger ale but had to settle for Sprite. They got around to talking about Trejo. "He's lying," Kins said for at least the third time since they'd left Trejo's apartment. He sipped his coffee. "And he knows that we know he's lying."

"And we know that he knows that we know he's lying," Tracy said over the sound of two men at the bar.

"Sounds like an Abbott and Costello routine," Kins said.

"About what, exactly, I'm not sure," Tracy said.

"How do we prove it?"

"The ferries have video cameras at the terminals. They film the cars getting on and off the boat. If he took a ferry yesterday, the Subaru should be on the footage." She sipped her drink and folded her arms across her stomach.

"He might not have taken the ferry," Kins said. "He might have driven around to the Tacoma Narrows Bridge and come up through Tacoma."

"Well, if he did, that could also be telling us something," she said.

"He wanted to stay off the ferry camera?"

"Maybe."

"That bridge also has cameras," Kins said. "I got a ticket once for not paying the toll. I didn't realize I was in a carpool lane. A couple days later, they mailed me a snapshot of my license plate and the ticket."

Tracy wiped down the table with her napkin. "Those are traffic cameras," she said.

Kins set down his coffee. "Washington State Patrol has access to that video system."

"What would it show—a license plate? Maybe the car?" Tracy asked, thinking out loud. "Would it even show the driver? Trejo says the car was stolen; he'd just say the video proves it."

"Maybe, but we should have the video guys contact Washington State Patrol and see if they can come up with anything, maybe find the car on tape. Trejo said he worked that day and got off at five o'clock," Kins said. "So we can narrow the time he would have either been parked here at the terminal or driving across the bridge."

She removed her coat. "Go for it, but keep in mind, even if you find the car, all that is going to give you is his car. We need to put him behind the wheel."

"We can do that with the DNA."

"His DNA will be all over that car. He owned it. The crucial evidence is if his DNA is on the air bag," she said.

"Or if there's blood inside his car," Kins said. "He has a much harder time explaining how it got there if he really did cut his head on a kitchen cabinet like he said." After a beat, Kins asked, "Don't you have to give your DNA when you enter the military?"

"Only for purposes of identification—and it can only be used to identify you if you're killed in action," she said. "It can't be used in a criminal case."

"You know this, or think you know it?" Kins asked.

"I went through it with NCIS in that other case I told you about. It can't be used to prove liability for a crime. If you want to confirm DNA, you have to get another DNA test."

"Which Trejo won't agree to do."

"He might not get that choice," she said. "As I remember it, the Navy has a permissive procedure and a nonpermissive procedure. If we have enough evidence, I think the Navy can force him to provide a sample." Tracy checked the clock on her phone. They still had another half hour before the ferry sailed. She could feel another hot flash coming on. "We should also have Jensen check the back bumper and see if he can find a hide-a-key."

"It might never have been there," Kins said.

She sipped her drink. "I doubt it was. But if he was driving, how did he get back to Bremerton without his car?"

"Or hide the car by himself," Kins said. "It's not exactly a public place, and he said he's from San Diego. We should find out where the wife is from. Maybe she knows the area and helped him hide it."

"So how'd they get home?" Tracy asked. "They only have one car."

"She could have borrowed someone's car."

"Maybe, but that puts another witness and another car in play." She checked the time on her phone again.

"We should at least ask."

"I agree." Tracy's cell rang and she checked caller ID. "It's Jensen," she said, then spoke into the phone. "You're calling with good news, right?" She listened for a beat. "Okay. We'll be there." She disconnected. "We'll know soon enough about the DNA. They got a warrant to get into the car first thing tomorrow morning."

CHAPTER 10

Del grabbed a cup of coffee from the dispenser and brought it back to his chair inside the King County Medical Examiner's waiting room on Jefferson Street.

"How late were you up?" Faz asked.

This Wednesday morning, Del felt the effects of another night of too little sleep. After leaving work, he'd returned to his sister's, arriving there at a little after 12:30 a.m. and not getting to sleep until after 1:45 a.m., which is when he last saw the digital clock on his phone. He got up at 6:00 a.m., got the boys ready for school, and drove them in. Then he rushed downtown. The Medical Examiner's Office had called the night before; they had the toxicology report on Allie.

His thoughts were foggy from too little sleep. He felt like he had when, as a younger man, he'd climbed Mount Rainier and suffered altitude sickness—light-headed and slightly off balance. Now the fatigue had settled into his joints and seemed determined to stay there.

"Too late and too early," he said.

He shook his wrist to free the gold chain his ex had given him during happier days in their marriage. With the rise in gold prices, he often had more money on his wrist than in his bank account. "I fed the boys and got them off to school, but the place looks like a bomb went off, and there isn't any food in the house. My sister's in bad shape." He sighed. "I'm not sure what to do about it."

"You gave her the name of that counselor?" "I called and set up an appointment for her, but getting her to go is another thing altogether. We both know I can't force her."

"How are the boys handling it?"

Del shrugged. "They're coming home from school and sitting on the couch eating chips and salsa and watching TV. Their homework isn't getting done."

"Are they even going to school?"

"I'm getting their butts there, but after three in the afternoon, I don't know who's keeping an eye on them. Little League will be starting soon. I have to get them signed up and take them to tryouts next weekend."

"You should coach them."

Del scoffed at the suggestion. "Yeah, right, that would be a sight, me in baseball pants."

"You were a good ballplayer. God knows you'd be better than the twenty-something-year-old dads who think their nine-year-old is destined for the major leagues."

Del had been a good ballplayer, a catcher with a rifle for an arm, and he'd never have his own son to coach. "I've got enough on my plate as it is." He sipped his coffee, which was tart. "I'm thinking of moving in. I can continue to sleep on the couch."

"You on a couch? That's more ridiculous than you in baseball pants."

"Just for a couple weeks. Until my sister gets back on her feet."

"Why don't you take some time off, Del? You're burning the candle at both ends. Get your sister into counseling and get everything square. I'll handle this."

Del stood. "I'm at my best when I'm working, you know that. I got to be doing something or I'll go stir-crazy."

"You're not even supposed to be working this case. I am. You're just along for the ride, remember? That was the deal."

"I'm fine, okay? I understand the rules." Del sipped his coffee. "I convinced her to let me into Allie's bedroom last night."

Faz arched his eyebrows. "Did you get Allie's cell phone?"

Del nodded. "And her computer. But no one knew her passwords. I dropped them off with TESU this morning," he said, referring to the Technical and Electronic Support Unit. "I signed in everything under your name, so we're good. They're breaking them down and will send everything over to Mike when they're finished," he said, meaning Mike Melton of the Washington State Patrol Crime Lab.

"Why?"

"I trust him."

"You want to go through the records yourself, don't you?"

"My niece."

Faz grimaced. "Which is why you shouldn't. Let me go through the records."

Del checked his watch but didn't answer.

Faz sighed. "You get a subpoena for her cell phone records?"

"Working on it."

"Anything else in the room?"

Del thought again of that moment when his sister had unlocked Allie's bedroom door. His sister wouldn't go in, wouldn't even open the door. She just unlocked it and walked back to her room. Del went in feeling like he was walking into a time capsule, like he did each time he walked into a room with a dead body. Everything was as Allie had left it—the syringe and spoon she'd used to melt the heroin that killed her, the BIC lighter, the plastic bag. He'd gathered it all and sent them off to the toxicology lab at the Washington State Patrol Crime Lab to be processed. The Latent Print Unit at SPD would examine the bag for fingerprints. But there were other things too, personal things in the room—Allie's underwear and shirts scattered on the floor, stuffed animals, and posters. He sat on the end of her bed and wept.

Del shook his head. "Broke my heart going into that room, knowing she was gone and never coming back. I held that kid in the palm of my hand when she was born. All the birthdays and holidays." He shook his head to shake back his emotions. "She had so much going for her. She could have done anything."

Faz spoke softly. "She was addicted, Del. It don't discriminate."

"No, it doesn't. That shit was right there on her dresser beneath her posters of Shania Twain and Justin Bieber." He bit his lower lip. Then he got angry. "I don't get it, Faz. How does a little girl go from being so innocent to shooting that crap into her veins? It's hell on earth. That's what her counselor said. Literally, hell on earth."

"I don't know, Del. I just don't know."

Stuart Funk entered the waiting room like a man searching for his lost child, frazzled and in a hurry. That was typical for Funk. So was his attire. The King County Medical Examiner always wore a long-sleeve, button-down shirt, khaki pants, and thick-soled rocker shoes that Faz had dubbed Frankenstein boots.

"Sorry for the delay," Funk said. "We had two overdoses last night."

"Together?" Del asked. "Same crime scene?"

Funk nodded. "Same scene."

Finding two overdoses at the same crime scene was indicative of a highly potent drug or a drug cut with something toxic, making it lethal.

"Heroin?" Del asked, his tired brain kicking into gear.

"Yes," Funk said, shaking his head. "That's ten overdoses already this week. Only one made it out of the ER alive."

"Where? Where were the two bodies you found last night?"

"North Seattle."

Del glanced at Faz, then asked Funk, "How old were the victims?"

"Midtwenties," Funk said. He checked his watch. "Come on back."

Funk led them down the hall into his cluttered office. Papers lay scattered across the desk along with a half-full cup of coffee and a brown bag lunch. The office was a lot like Funk; his appearance always seemed a little scattered—his hair not completely combed, the lenses of his oversized glasses smudged, shirttail not completely tucked into the waistband of his pants, but there was no mistaking that Funk was very good at what he did. He picked up a piece of paper from his desk without hesitation, despite the clutter, and handed a copy to Del.

"These are the results of the toxicology tests."

"Thanks for pushing it," Del said. Toxicology tests came from the Washington State Toxicology Lab inside the Washington State Patrol Crime Lab. They performed the tests for the entire state, which explained why it ordinarily took six to eight weeks. Given the rash of recent deaths, the time would likely have been even longer, but Funk had pulled some strings to get it done out of respect for Del.

Funk started to speak. Then, perhaps realizing this was not just another body, he stopped. "Do you want to hear this?"

"Yeah," Del said, noticing Faz watching him. "I'm good. I'm all right."

Funk took a deep breath. "The tests are of the blood, liver, and urine," he said. "Tell me if I'm repeating something you already know."

"We're good," Del said, but his stomach burned as if housing a fire.

Funk adjusted his glasses. "Okay. Injected heroin is quickly converted to 06-monoacetylmorphine, also known as 6-MAM, and its original compound, morphine. The 6-MAM is significantly more potent than morphine and, because it's injected, the brain is immediately impacted. The problem is, 6-MAM is not easy to detect. In blood, it's only detectable for about two minutes after injection. After ten to fifteen minutes, only trace amounts remain, below ten nanograms per milliliter."

"This says twenty-two nanograms," Faz said, reading from Funk's report.

"Which means one of two things." Funk looked to Del. "Either the dose your niece took was extremely potent and, as such, the 6-MAM was also potent and increased the latent levels, or your niece died very quickly after injection, which would slow and ultimately halt the metabolic processes that decompose 6-MAM."

"I don't know how quickly she died," Del said. "My sister found her in the morning. That's all I know. I talked to a prosecutor the other day who said she could have died because she injected a dose equivalent to what she'd been taking before she went into detox."

"She very likely could have," Funk said.

"But you're saying it's also possible she could have taken heroin that was extremely potent?"

"Given the very recent number of overdoses we've had, including the two last night, I'd say that likelihood is very high."

"Where in North Seattle were the latest victims?" Del asked.

"Green Lake," Funk said.

Del looked to Faz. "Close to Loyal Heights."

"Within minutes," Faz said.

"And the others?" Del asked Funk.

"I'd have to look. I know one was on Capitol Hill and one was in the Central District. Both victims were older. Late twenties."

"Did you autopsy them?"

"We did," Funk said. "But it will be a while before the toxicology reports are back."

"What about the two last night?" Del asked.

"Same. I'd say ninety percent chance it was heroin, given the foam cones detected."

Del knew that heroin was a respiratory depressant that impacted the breathing function of the brain. The foam cone formed around a person's nose and mouth from pulmonary edema fluid mixing with air in the lungs as the person's respiration and heartbeat slowed.

Funk let out a held breath. "But with the bodies from the shooting the other night . . . We're up to our eyeballs at the moment. It could be a while."

Del reached into his jacket pocket and pulled out a tiny pack containing what looked like sugar. "I understand you're busy and I appreciate everything you're doing. I'm hesitant, but I have another favor to ask. Can you get someone to take a look at this, tell me anything about it?"

"Where'd you get that?" Faz asked.

"Allie's bedroom."

"I thought you sent everything to the crime lab," Faz said.

"I did," Del said. "This was just crap I scooped up."

"Shit, Del."

"Take it easy. It was just stuff on the table, not in the bag. Remnants."

Funk took the bag and considered the contents. "Definitely not black tar."

Del knew that Mexican drug cartels had a market on the West Coast and supplied black tar heroin—so called because it looked like roofing tar and was often packaged in plastic paper. Southeast Asia supplied a heroin called China white, which resembled cocaine and had a market on the East Coast and in Vancouver, British Columbia.

"It looks like China white," Funk said, examining the contents through the clear bag. "But I've never seen it out here. If this was in your niece's room, it would be highly unusual, and potentially problematic."

"Why?" Faz asked.

Funk set down the bag. He looked like the wheels were spinning. "New York had a problem sometime last year with China white. They had a number of overdose deaths all within a short time of each other and all from roughly the same area. The ER rooms detected it and got the word out on the street. Eventually they determined the deaths were from a very pure heroin cut with fentanyl."

"What's fentanyl?" Faz asked.

"It's a powerful synthetic painkiller sometimes used to cut heroin. The two in combination can be a potent high. They can also be lethal. Black tar, because of its consistency, is very difficult to cut with anything." Funk held up the bag. "This stuff? We don't see this out here."

Del was trying to process the information, how Allie could have gotten her hands on something like China white. "Can you tell from an autopsy if the person used one or the other?"

"No," Funk said. "Both show up on toxicology reports as morphine. The best way to know is by the product. If you found that in your niece's bedroom, I'd say that's what killed her."

"Has the media called yet about the overdoses last night?" Faz asked.

"Not that I'm aware of."

"We need to get the word out on the street," Faz said to Del.

"That might be the last thing we need right now," Funk said.

"Why?" Faz asked. "People are dying."

"We get word out of a highly potent heroin going around and it's like moths to the light. Addicts will go looking for it. Overdoses are the best advertisement out there for the quality of the product. We might have a lot more bodies."

"But it's got to be bad for business—for the suppliers, to have their customers dying," Faz said.

"One might think that, but their customers are statistically going to die anyway," Funk said. "And, unfortunately, there's no shortage of new ones."

CHAPTER 11

Tracy arrived at the vehicle processing room at the Washington State Crime Lab on Airport Way early Wednesday morning. It had been another short night for sleep. After working the night shift until midnight, and arriving home after 1:00 a.m., she'd slept a few hours, then got up early to meet Joe Jensen. She'd beaten Kins, who was also burning the candle at both ends. He'd called her cell to say he was dropping off his kids at school. They were both receiving overtime for working double shifts, which had been nice when Tracy was young and single, but now she'd trade the extra money for extra sleep and she knew Kins would too.

TCI was going over the car as Tracy entered the room. Joe Jensen greeted her, but not with a smile. He frowned and shook his head. "Somebody wiped down the car, inside and out," he said.

"What do you mean? Are you telling me they're not finding *any* prints?"

"They're finding prints, just not where they would expect to find them." He walked her over to the car. "For instance, the outside door handle on the driver's side is clean."

"What about the air bag?" Tracy asked.

Jensen slowly shook his head. "None."

"None meaning somebody wiped it down, or none meaning it didn't pick up any of the driver's DNA?"

"Someone wiped it down. We're detecting the presence of isopropyl alcohol, which is common in just about every alcohol wipe out there."

Tracy blew out a burst of air. "Did they find any wipes in the car?"

"No," Jensen said.

"So we know it was deliberate."

"And sophisticated," Jensen said, "which is why I'm having the air bag processed anyway, along with the blood on the front seat, though that will take a couple weeks—"

"You found blood in the car?" Tracy asked.

"Driver's side. It's a cloth seat. Whoever tried to clean it up couldn't get it all," Jensen said.

Tracy walked to the driver's door, which was open, and peered inside at the seat. "Kins and I spoke to the owner of the car last night. He had a cut on his forehead, just at the hairline."

"Did he say how he cut it?"

"He said he hit a corner of a cabinet door in the kitchen." She thought out loud. "The problem is, it's his car. He could come up with any number of excuses for his blood being inside it."

"Maybe," Jensen said. He grinned. "But this might be more difficult for him to explain." He held up a store receipt in a sealed evidence bag. It looked to have been pressed flat after being crumpled. "We found it in the back, between the seat and one of the rear doors. It's from a convenience store in Renton." Jensen handed it to Tracy. "The person bought two Red Bull energy drinks on Monday night, at eight thirty-eight p.m."

"Most of those convenience stores now have video," Tracy said.

"If this one does, we may very well have a visual of the owner . . ."

Tracy finished Jensen's thought. "And if it's Trejo on the convenience store videotape, that blood in the car becomes a lot more relevant."

———

Tracy picked up Kins at Police Headquarters, and they drove to the convenience store, which was just off an Interstate 5 exit in Renton. Graffiti covered the concrete masonry wall facing the parking area, along with faded and torn concert posters. Along the front of the building, the stucco and the aluminum framing around the doors and windows had become soiled with soot from the thousands of cars passing on the freeway.

Hovering above the building, a green billboard with a white arrow directed drivers to a marijuana dispensary on the opposite street corner.

"One-stop shopping," Kins said, eyeing the sign. "You can buy pot, cross the street, and buy Cheetos, frozen burritos, and a gallon of Coke."

"Or energy drinks," Tracy said.

"Definitely energy drinks."

Kins pulled open the glass door. They each turned at the sound of a buzzer, and Tracy noted a chipped and scarred ruler impressed on the inside of the door frame to measure customers' heights. She looked at the corners of the building and saw a lone camera mounted to the ceiling and directed at the cashier's counter and front door.

The inside of the store smelled like a vanilla air freshener that people hung in their cars. Products cluttered the shelves, with unopened boxes at the ends of the aisles. Frozen food, soft drinks, and alcohol filled stand-up freezers along the back wall. Tracy and Kins stepped around the boxes to the counter, and Kins flashed his ID and shield to a dark-skinned young man in a light-blue smock and turban. A variety of cigarette packs and magazines surrounded him in the booth.

"Are you Archie?" Kins asked.

They didn't need a warrant to get video from the security camera unless the store owner refused, which had never happened in Tracy's years working Violent Crimes. A bigger concern was the store inadvertently taping over the video, which was usually on a twenty-four-hour loop. Tracy had called the convenience store after leaving Jensen to ask about a videotape. The owner said he had a system, though it was dated. He would search the tape to determine if it had been copied over. Tracy had given him the time on the store receipt to expedite the process.

"He's in the back." The young man pointed to a swinging door at the rear of the store. A posted sign read "Employees Only." "He said you were coming. He's in his office. Go through that door. It's the room on your left. You can't miss it."

Tracy followed Kins into a storeroom more cluttered than the store. It held the faint odor of rotting food. In the room to their left, a man in a matching light-blue smock, also wearing a turban, sat facing a small television. Kins knocked on the door and the man turned and looked at them over half-lens cheaters. He had a cell phone pressed to his ear, but waved them in. "They're here," he said. "Yeah. Okay, I'll call." He disconnected and shook their hands.

"Are you Archie?" Kins asked.

Archie swiped at a thick beard streaked with gray. "I was just talking with my attorney."

"Is there a problem?" Tracy asked.

"No. No. I wanted to be sure you didn't need a search warrant. I don't want any trouble." He spoke with a thick accent. "He said no warrant is needed."

"You have the video?" Kins asked.

Archie nodded to a television. "I was just searching the tape. Having the time imprinted on the receipt saved me a lot of work."

"Do you have it on a computer?" Tracy asked.

"No," he said moving toward the portable television on the table with the VCR player, an all-in-one machine. "Nothing that fancy."

"It's not digitized?" Kins asked.

"Digit what?"

"Is that the tape?" Tracy said, pointing to a VCR cartridge partially sticking out of the television on the desk.

"Yes."

"Can you play it for us?"

"Sure."

Archie sat and swiveled his chair to face his TV. He pushed the tape into the VCR player, then lifted his chin and looked down his glasses to press a couple of buttons on a remote control. Satisfied, he slid back his chair, stood, and stepped to the side to allow Tracy and Kins to view the television. The feed was black-and-white and definitely not the best quality. Without sound, they heard just the whir and hum of the tape, as if the outdated machine was struggling and the tape could break at any moment. On the TV screen, a man in a white shirt with a baseball cap entered the store and quickly proceeded to the glass case at the back. Tracy didn't bother to freeze the frame to measure his height using the ruler on the inside of the door. They could obtain that later. She couldn't tell if the man was Trejo.

The man opened a freezer door, paused, closed the door, and opened the door beside it. He extracted two cans and started up the aisle. As he neared the counter, getting closer to the camera, his image improved—not perfect, but certainly good enough for Tracy and Kins to know.

CHAPTER 12

Tracy called Laszlo Trejo with word that the lab had finished processing his car, and told Trejo he could pick it up at Police Headquarters. Trejo didn't hesitate at the invitation. Anxious to get his car back, he said he would make the ferry crossing after work that evening. Tracy provided him directions walking from the ferry terminal to Police Headquarters, which was just up the hill on Fifth Avenue.

The officer at the duty desk in the building lobby called Tracy at just after 7:00 p.m. to advise that Trejo had arrived. Tracy instructed him to escort Trejo to the seventh floor. She met them both in the lobby as the elevator doors opened. Trejo wore civilian clothes—jeans and tennis shoes—and kept his hands stuffed in the pockets of what looked like a letterman's jacket without all the patches. Out of uniform, he looked even younger, just a kid, really, and smaller, perhaps five foot six, four inches shorter than Tracy.

She extended her hand, and Trejo gave it a halfhearted handshake, his hand small and warm.

"Come on back." Tracy led Trejo down the hall. "Can I get you a cup of bad coffee?"

"No, thanks," Trejo said. "I just came for my car."

Tracy stepped into the conference room and pulled out a chair, motioning that Trejo do the same. A portable television with a VCR sat on the table, facing her. She and Kins had scrambled that afternoon to find one. "Take a seat," she said.

Trejo continued to look wary. He kept his hands inside the pockets of his jacket, like a sullen teenager sent to the principal's office for a scolding. His eyes flicked about the room, and he avoided any prolonged eye contact.

Kins walked into the room carrying papers, a ruse to look busy. "You made it."

"Are they done with my car?" Trejo asked, standing and sounding eager to get going.

"They're just bringing it up from the police impound," Kins said.

Trejo pulled out his cell phone from his jacket pocket and considered the time.

"You in a rush?" Kins asked.

"I'm trying to catch the 7:55 ferry back home," Trejo said.

Kins pulled out a chair and sat. "What happens if you miss the ferry?"

"They have others," Trejo said, still standing.

"Or I guess you could also just drive around," Tracy said. The Department of Transportation video from the Bremerton and Seattle ferry terminals did not reveal the black Subaru. She looked to Kins. "What bridge do you cross down there, just past Tacoma?"

Kins paused as if uncertain.

"The Tacoma Narrows," Trejo said, filling the silence and lowering himself into his chair.

Tracy looked to Trejo. "That's it. You ever go that way?"

Trejo shook his head. "I told you I don't get over here very much."

They sat in an awkward silence. Kins said, "Do the Bremerton police have any more information on what might have happened to your car, who could have stolen it?"

"I don't know," Trejo said.

"They haven't said?" Kins asked.

Trejo shook his head and continued fidgeting in his chair, perhaps beginning to realize that coming over had been a mistake.

Tracy asked, "Are you curious about what the police impound found?"

"Oh. Uh, yeah," Trejo said. "I mean, did they find any fingerprints?"

"They did," Tracy said. "We're running them down now. The DNA will take longer to get back."

"DNA?"

"The air bag deployed. They can get DNA off of the bag. So we should know who was driving at the time of impact."

Trejo did not respond.

"They also found blood on the driver's seat." She let her eyes drift to the cut on Trejo's forehead.

"I told you I got some in the car when I cut my head."

"Did you? I don't recall you saying that." She looked to Kins. "Did he say that?"

Kins shrugged. Trejo hadn't. It didn't fit with the timeline he'd provided them.

"How'd you cut your head again?" Tracy asked. She wanted to pin him to his story.

"I told you I was in the kitchen and I stood up too quick. I hit one of the cabinet doors."

"When was that?" she asked.

"I don't remember," he said quickly. "Is my car ready?"

Kins said, "That hurts like hell. I did the same thing in the garage once, nearly knocked myself out. The head bleeds like a son of a bitch, too, doesn't it?"

Trejo shrugged.

"Looks like you tried to clean it up," Tracy said. "The car seat I mean. What did you use?"

"I don't know, just a napkin or something."

Tracy nodded as if understanding. Then she said, "Lab says someone used an antiseptic wipe."

Trejo did not respond.

"When's the last time you've been over on this side?" Kins asked.

Trejo again looked at his phone. "Do you know how much longer it's going to be?"

"I'm sure they're close," Kins said. "What time is it?" He turned his body and swiveled his chair to consider the clock on the wall. "You have plans, you and your wife?"

Trejo looked confused by the question. "What?"

"I thought maybe you were trying to get home because you and your wife have plans."

"No. Just, you know, I want to catch the ferry."

"No kids, right?" Kins said.

"No."

"I have three boys," Kins said. "Two in high school. I'll be taking my oldest off to college soon. He's at that age, you know, where he does stupid things—I shouldn't say stupid." Kins pinched his lower lip. Tracy had heard and seen this act before. She'd even used it. "He'll make a mistake, you know? Then he tries to hide it. I keep telling him to just be honest. I tell him that he might get in trouble for what he did, but it won't be as bad as if he tries to hide it and gets caught."

Kins never took his gaze from Trejo. He lowered his voice. "Nobody wants to believe they were lied to."

Trejo pushed back his chair and stood. He spoke to Tracy. "Could you call about my car? I'd like to get going."

Kins said, "Why don't you tell us what happened that night, Mr. Trejo?"

Trejo's eyes darted between the two of them. He gave a nervous laugh. "What is this? Where's my car?"

"We know about the convenience store in Renton, Mr. Trejo," Tracy said.

Trejo looked like a busted teenager. He licked his lips. Unprepared, all he could say was, "What?"

"You left a store receipt in your car that night," she said. "The receipt is dated and timed."

"That's bullshit. I told you I was working. Then I went home." Getting a burst of inspiration, Trejo said, "It was probably whoever stole my car."

"You bought two cans of Red Bull," Tracy said. "The same energy drink you were drinking the night we drove out to speak with you."

"I told you I was at home," he said, now more adamant. "My wife will tell you I was at home. It was the person who stole my car."

"The store has video cameras," Tracy said.

Trejo paused and glanced at the television, perhaps realizing now why it was there. Beads of sweat had formed above his upper lip.

Tracy pressed a button and the video showed Trejo entering the store and moving to the refrigerator. When he reached the counter, it was pretty clear it was him, even wearing the hat.

"The video is dated and timed, Mr. Trejo," Tracy said. "This is roughly half an hour before D'Andre Miller was hit by your car. So why don't you tell us what you were doing in Seattle."

Trejo chewed his bottom lip. The bandage on his head had become a darker shade of red. "That isn't me. I don't know who that is."

"How tall are you, Mr. Trejo?" Tracy asked. He didn't respond. "This goes to a prosecutor and he's going to charge you with a felony. The penalties are governed by sentencing guidelines—if it gets that far. That means the judge has no choice in the matter. A hit and run involving a death, you're looking at a Class B felony punishable by ten years in prison."

"D'Andre Miller's family will demand accountability, Mr. Trejo," Kins said, which was part of his spiel. "The public will demand accountability. They'll demand that we hold someone responsible for D'Andre's death. Lying isn't going to help you."

Trejo's eyes no longer focused on anything in particular, as if he were seeing into the future, seeing a jail cell that would be his home for many years.

CHAPTER 13

Leah Battles dropped her head beneath the barrel of the handgun, reached up and grasped the weapon with both hands, and drove her knee into her attacker's groin. She stepped back quickly while violently rolling the man's wrists into his body, yanked free the gun, and aimed the barrel at his forehead.

"Nice," her instructor said, his British accent distinct. "But you hesitated."

Battles bit her tongue. Seemed there was always a "but" with this guy.

"One thing you can be sure of," he said, talking now to the entire class, "when you move to attack, your attacker will fire his weapon. So if you hesitate, *if* you fail to immediately drop below the barrel of the weapon, you're dead." He clapped for emphasis. "So move like you mean it. You understand me, Lee?" he asked, using her nickname.

Battles nodded. After three years of Krav Maga training, after reaching level four, she should not have hesitated. She knew better. "Understood," she said.

She could blame her hesitation on a rough day at work—a client court-martialed for juvenile crap, but that would be an excuse. She didn't make or accept excuses. The law, she'd heard it said, was a jealous mistress. Screw that crap. The law was a demanding bitch, but Leah had known that before she decided to pursue a career as a trial lawyer. As much physical time as her job took—and it took a lot—there were days when the law sapped her mental energy even more. Some nights she considered switching professions, doing something that allowed her to lock her work in a desk drawer at the end of the day and just go home. As much as she romanticized that lifestyle, however, she knew she'd become quickly bored. She loved the legal tactics and the legal strategy, seeing similarities between the law and chess, at which she excelled. You move and I counter. I counter and you don't? I win. This was especially true in trial, which she loved most about her job. Who wouldn't? Why even become a lawyer if not to try cases? Sure, it could be a major pain in the ass when you were trying to focus on something else—like your training, or *a freaking relationship,* but at least the law was consistent, which was more than she could say about the men she'd recently dated.

The daily mental stress the law inflicted was one of the reasons she enjoyed the physical exertion of Krav Maga, and why she worked hard to fit her classes into her schedule. She had little patience for a prosecutor if he pulled some crap that required her to miss working out. There'd be hell to pay, eventually. And she'd be the cashier.

She'd stumbled upon Krav Maga while attending the Naval Justice School in Newport, Rhode Island, following three years of law school. She'd wanted to both serve her country and try cases—real cases, criminal cases, not some bullshit money-judgment crap. The Navy's Judge Advocate General's program afforded her the opportunity to do both, right away—serve her country as a Navy lawyer and try cases. Yeah, some of the cases were penny-ante bullshit, but she was still standing before a jury making her arguments and cross-examining witnesses. You weren't going to get that at the big law firms, which promised a boatload of money but very little in the way of experience.

That was also what had drawn her to Krav Maga. It was not your typical workout. Krav Maga was serious, practical training on how to stay alive—throwing punches to the throat, kicks to the groin, takedowns. Developed by the Israel Defense Forces, it preached avoiding confrontation. It also preached that when confrontation could not be avoided, end the fight. In other words, make peace. When peace wasn't an option, kick ass.

This was something to get her mind off the law.

"Again," her instructor said.

She retook her position and her partner raised the replica gun. About to strike, she heard her phone ring above the grunts and groans of the other students. It wasn't her personal phone; she'd never bring her personal phone into class. This was the phone she carried when serving as the command duty officer. Her instructors acknowledged her unique situation, which placed her on call twenty-four hours a day when serving as the CDO. She apologized and excused herself, hurrying to retrieve the phone from inside her gym bag stuffed in the cubicles at the back of the room.

"This is Lieutenant Battles."

She listened to the caller and found herself conflicted. Sure, she wanted to finish her training, but she also could never turn down a good fight, and the one being explained over the phone sounded like it had the potential to be a brawl.

Tracy parked on a grass-and-gravel area abutting a chain-link fence not far from the intersection where D'Andre Miller had been run down. She couldn't help but think that the young boy had been so close to home, so close to being safe, so close to still being alive.

She stepped from the car and opened the gate to a concrete walk intersecting a neat but barren yard of crabgrass. Two steps led to a front porch and a maroon front door behind a screen. She pulled on the screen but found it locked. Not seeing a doorbell, she knocked and waited. A woman answered, but it was not Shaniqua Miller. The woman did not open the screen.

"Good evening," Tracy said. "I'm looking for Shaniqua Miller. Is she home?"

"What's this about?" The woman appeared youthful, dressed in a T-shirt and blue jeans. Tracy sensed from the resemblance that she was either Shaniqua Miller's sister or her mother. The woman looked at Tracy from behind round wire-rimmed glasses. Straightened hair framed her face and chin.

"My name is Tracy Crosswhite. I'm one of the detectives working D'Andre Miller's case. Are you his aunt?"

"His grandmother." The woman's back stiffened but her voice remained soft. "Is it important? Shaniqua's getting the boys ready for bed."

"It is," Tracy said. "I won't take up much of her time."

The grandmother frowned, unconvinced, then turned and walked away, not inviting Tracy inside, not opening the screen door. Tracy heard the woman call to her daughter. "Shaniqua?" The rest of her words were muted.

Sandy Clarridge, SPD's chief of police, had told the powers that be that he wanted an SPD presence involved in this case, and he didn't want that presence to simply be the Victim Assistance Unit. He wanted a detective to keep the family apprised of everything that transpired, in person, when possible. His desire had trickled down to Tracy's captain, Johnny Nolasco, and, ultimately, to Tracy, which explained Tracy's presence at the home.

"Who?" she heard a voice ask.

"One of the detectives."

"What does he want?"

"*She* wants to talk to you."

A pause. "Did she say why?"

"No. Just wants to talk to you. Said it was important."

"Hang on."

The older woman returned to the door. "She'll just be a minute."

They stood, uncertain what to say to each another, saying nothing.

Shaniqua Miller came to the door from the back of the house dressed in blue jeans and a T-shirt. She unlatched the screen door and opened it. A gold chain with a cross hung around her neck. She looked tired and worn-out, her eyes puffy. Her hair, also straightened, was clipped in the back, highlighting pronounced cheekbones and expressive eyes. "Can I help you?" she asked.

"Ms. Miller, we met the other night."

Miller did not immediately respond, as if trying to remember but not wanting to.

"I'm Tracy Crosswhite, one of the detectives working your son's case."

"Yes," she said, speaking softly. "I recall. You were in the street the night my son was run down."

"Yes, I was. I wanted you to know that we made an arrest tonight of the man who drove the car that hit your son."

Miller stared at her, saying nothing and revealing nothing. She showed no anger, no sadness, no joy or elation. Slowly, her hand reached up and her fingers found the cross around her neck. "You're sure?"

"We've positively identified his car as the car that hit your son," Tracy said. "And we've obtained a video of that man at a convenience store not far from the intersection and only a short time before the accident."

"What did he say?" Miller asked, fingers rubbing the cross.

"Initially he said his car had been stolen and he had not been in Seattle. Tonight, when shown the evidence, he chose not to say anything. He's requested a lawyer."

Despite the evidence to the contrary, Trejo had continued to maintain that the man in the video was not him. Then he went silent. Usually Tracy and Kins could get a suspect to talk, especially when they had video evidence to contradict his story. The suspect didn't always tell the truth, but they would usually, at least, try to explain the evidence. Perhaps Trejo had decided that he couldn't explain the video, and it was best not to say anything.

"Who is he?" Miller asked.

"He's an enlisted man."

"Army?"

"Navy. He's stationed on Naval Base Kitsap in Bremerton."

"What happens now?" Miller asked.

Tracy would return to SPD, where Trejo was being held prior to booking. "He'll be booked at the King County Jail. His first appearance will be tomorrow afternoon. We'd like you to be there . . . if you can."

Miller didn't answer right away. She looked past Tracy, her eyes losing focus. After a moment she reengaged. "What time?"

"Two o'clock."

She sighed. "I have to work. I don't have a choice. I still have two more boys."

"The hearing is for the court to determine whether there is probable cause to keep the suspect in custody. He won't enter a plea until the arraignment, which won't take place for about two more weeks." She paused, certain Shaniqua Miller was not interested in the criminal procedure. "Would you like me to explain the situation to your employer?"

"I won't get paid either way," she said.

Tracy nodded.

"What time did you say?" Miller asked.

"Two o'clock." Tracy provided the location of the district court on the first floor of the jail. Then she handed her a business card with her number and another card for the Victim Assistance Unit. "You can call me or you can call the number on that card. Someone has been assigned to keep you advised of and to explain the procedures as we go forward. They can also answer any questions you may have about the hearing or about the arraignment."

"I'll see what I can do," Shaniqua said. Then she stepped back and slowly and quietly closed the door.

—

Leah Battles clipped her shoes into the bike pedals, churned south on Westlake Avenue, and cut over to Fifth Avenue. She lived in an apartment in Pioneer Square, on the southern, or opposite, end of town. Not having to live on the naval base was one of the perks of being an officer. Tonight it had another perk. Laszlo Trejo had told her on the phone that he'd been placed in the SPD precinct holding cell in preparation for booking at the county jail. Both SPD and the King County Jail were located between her training class and her apartment, so she wouldn't be going out of her way to stop, speak to Trejo, and gather more information.

Battles knew it was not likely her officer in charge would assign her to be Trejo's defense counsel if she served as the command duty officer. Her role was to provide immediate legal support to the enlisted person arrested. Assigned defense counsel did not get involved with the arrests of Navy personnel, especially when the alleged crime occurred off base, and they didn't get assigned until ten days to two weeks *after* the arrest. Local police handled the booking. The suspect notified the command duty officer, who advised naval command of the details of the arrest, and it went through the proper channels. If deemed necessary, NCIS investigated, and, if the Navy took jurisdiction, charges were filed. Only then did Battles, as a defense attorney, get involved, and only if assigned to handle the case. Those instances were seemingly becoming more and more frequent since the airing of the documentary *The Invisible War*, recounting sexual assaults on female enlisted personnel throughout the armed forces. The public outcry had put commanding officers on military bases under intense pressure from Congress to clean up the military's problems, and every branch had become hyperaggressive about prosecuting cases. The Navy was no exception.

This case was not a sexual assault, but it sounded serious, and potentially embarrassing to the Navy. A hit and run of a twelve-year-old boy was tragic and, if proven, cowardly. Battles also knew that the Defense Service Office was understaffed, particularly in the current climate, and she was the senior defense counsel. Therefore, though serving as CDO, her chances of being named Trejo's attorney might actually *improve* if she was already involved, to a limited extent, which would be simple enough for her to accomplish.

And she wanted this case.

She wanted it very much.

At 8:30 at night, traffic on Seattle's surface streets wasn't an issue. However, the temperature remained butt cold and her sweat-soaked shirt further chilled her. By the time she reached SPD, her face felt numb and she was shaking beneath her workout clothes. She slid off the bike and locked it in a courtyard in front of the building. Yeah, like that made her feel better. Her first week in Seattle, she'd locked her bike in the rack outside her apartment building. She woke the next morning and found only the chain and the lock. Now, the bike came up in the elevator with her. If anyone complained, they could take the stairs.

Battles exchanged her bike shoes for flip-flops—which she wore with socks, a major fashion faux pas even for eternally liberal Seattle.

Inside SPD's building lobby, she made her way to a uniformed officer seated at a desk behind a sheet of bulletproof Plexiglas. He looked to be in his early thirties, about Battles's age, with his hair cut military short and a chest puffed up by a bulletproof vest fitted beneath his uniform. He looked up as Battles approached and dropped his gaze over her body.

"Good evening. I'm here to see Laszlo Trejo," she said. "I understand he was arrested this evening and is being held."

"I wouldn't know," the officer said. "If he was, you'd have to wait until he's processed over at the jail. But visiting hours are over." He smiled like a pubescent boy who'd seen his first picture of a naked woman. "Looks like tomorrow morning is the earliest you can see him."

She put her credentials up to the glass. "Despite my professional appearance, this isn't a social call to chitchat about the annual salmon run. Mr. Trejo called and requested legal counsel. I'm his legal counsel. I'd like to talk to him before anyone else does."

"You're a naval officer?" he said, eyeing the credentials and seeming surprised. "Lieutenant Battles?"

"That's correct. I'm also an attorney." She smiled again, though this time with a little more purpose.

"Well, Lieutenant, if he's still being processed, you're still going to have to wait until he's finished before you can talk to him." His smile broadened. "And, as an FYI, the salmon run is way up this year. I caught a couple kings this week."

Battles hoped that wasn't his best pickup line. "No kidding? I can't eat salmon. It makes me sick."

"That's got to suck living here."

"It does. Every social function I attend they put a big piece of fish on my plate. I end up giving it to my dates."

"Your dates must appreciate the extra piece." The officer grinned.

"They do," she said. "Until they realize it's the only piece they'll be getting that night."

Checkmate. Game over.

"So I'd appreciate it if you'd pick up that phone, call upstairs, and find out where my client is."

The officer sat back, no longer grinning. He gestured to some seats. "Take a seat, Lieutenant. It could be a long night."

Battles answered e-mails on her cell phone while she waited. After a few minutes, she heard the ping of an elevator door. A woman stepped around the corner, glanced at Battles, then looked at the uniform behind the desk, clearly confused. Perhaps she'd been expecting a man in a three-piece suit and tie rather than a bike messenger. The uniform nodded to Battles to dispel any doubt, and the officer stepped out from behind a security gate.

The Navy generously listed Battles at five foot six. This woman was a head taller, most of it legs. She had the blonde hair and blue eyes of one of those beach volleyball players in the Olympics with the ill-fitting shorts. Nobody had ever described Battles as having long legs, or guessed that she spent her days on a beach. She had her father's dark hair and dark complexion, especially when she tanned in the summers. She'd grown up on the East Coast.

This woman had "cop" written all over her—okay, the badge clipped to her belt near the gun was a giveaway, as was the fact that Battles was at Police Headquarters, but that wasn't what first struck her about the woman. What struck her was the woman's self-assured walk and demeanor.

"I'm guessing you're not Laszlo Trejo," Battles said.

"I'm Detective Tracy Crosswhite. Can I help you?"

"You can if you can conjure up Petty Officer Trejo and give me a room in which to talk to him."

Crosswhite looked only semi-amused. "And you are?"

"Leah Battles. I'm an attorney, a judge advocate from Naval Base Kitsap in Bremerton. Sorry, but I didn't get a chance to throw on my dress blues before I came down here. It would have avoided the confusion."

"Do you have some identification?" Crosswhite sounded skeptical.

Battles glanced at the uniform behind the desk, but he just smiled. Annoyed, she fumbled in her backpack and again produced her identification. "Do you get a lot of people pretending to be judge advocates asking to speak to clients?"

"No," Crosswhite said, taking the credentials. "Because we don't ordinarily let people see suspects. Neither does the jail, not after visiting hours."

Nice move. Battles liked her. She bet Crosswhite could play a mean game of chess. "But as an attorney, I can see a client whenever I wish."

Crosswhite didn't comment. She studied the identification. "This says Virginia. Are you licensed in the state of Washington?"

"I'm licensed in the United States Navy, which is sort of a global law firm, though I'm currently stationed at Naval Base Kitsap, in Bremerton, which is where Laszlo Trejo is stationed, which is why he called me, which is why I'm here, which is why I'd like to speak with him."

Crosswhite remained calm. "Is the Navy asserting jurisdiction?"

"I wouldn't know. What I know is that Mr. Trejo called the command duty officer, me. He advised that he'd been arrested, and asked for a lawyer. I'm that lawyer."

"You got here fast from Bremerton."

"I'm a fast swimmer."

Crosswhite smiled and handed back the identification. "You should have taken your time. You won't see Mr. Trejo until after he's booked."

"And miss out on all this fun we're having? I'm curious, Detective, what was Mr. Trejo doing over here at Police Headquarters?" Trejo had told Battles that he'd come over expecting to pick up his car from the police impound and that he had come over to Seattle to get it.

"You'll have to ask him."

"You didn't by chance bring him over under false pretenses, did you? Just to get him off base so you could arrest him?"

"Mr. Trejo doesn't live on base," Crosswhite said. "So I wouldn't need any false pretenses to arrest him. But again, you can ask him when you talk to him." She turned and started back for the security door.

"He asked to speak to an attorney," Battles said to Crosswhite's back. "I'd appreciate it if you'd let your brethren know that one detail."

Crosswhite didn't respond. She didn't turn. The security door buzzed and she stepped inside, letting the door shut behind her. The uniform leaned back in his chair with a satisfied smile.

Battles smiled too. She didn't mind a spirited opponent. She welcomed it. Competition brought out the best in her, and the interchange with Crosswhite just made her want the case more.

And she'd already wanted this case very much.

—

Tracy dropped her keys into the wood bowl on the antique farm table that she and Dan had purchased at an estate sale near the Canadian border. Beside the bowl, she'd positioned their wedding picture, framed and perched on a stand. Behind the table, two large windows offered plenty of light, though not at this early hour of the morning. The windows faced east, toward the horse pasture and tree-lined rolling hills, eliminating the need for curtains—unless your occupation was homicide detective and you spent much of your time hunting down the sick and depraved. She'd wanted window coverings. Dan didn't. They'd compromised. Dan put up outdoor floodlights with motion sensors. It seemed a fair solution, until the lights were repeatedly triggered by the many animals that ventured onto their property—squirrels, raccoons, deer, Rex and Sherlock, even Tracy's cat, Roger, who for the first time was allowed to go outside.

"Tracy?"

Dan came out of the bedroom wearing long pajama pants and a T-shirt from Boston University, his alma mater. Rex and Sherlock also padded out to greet her, tails wagging. She heard the television from the bedroom, which every marriage advice article said was a no-no, but there was no other place in the house to put it. Dan held a toothbrush and spoke through a mouthful of toothpaste.

"I didn't . . . ," he mumbled. "Hang on." He disappeared back into the bathroom. Tracy heard the water in their sink. Dan reappeared without the toothbrush. "I didn't hear you come in."

She rubbed the heads of both dogs. "We made an arrest in the hit-and-run case tonight and had to get him booked for the probable cause hearing tomorrow afternoon." She kissed Dan and stepped past him into the kitchen.

"The Navy guy?" Dan asked.

"Yeah." She opened a cabinet and filled a glass at the sink.

"You said you thought it was him."

She washed down two Advil with water, then said, "The video made it pretty clear."

"You have a headache?" Dan asked, leaning against the door frame.

"No, my shoulder is acting up." She'd hurt her shoulder just over two years ago when a stalker who'd made his way into her home in West Seattle tackled her from behind. The orthopedist said she'd partially torn the rotator cuff. If PT didn't solve the problem, she was looking at surgery and a six-month recovery. Or she could be like Kins and eat ibuprofen daily until the pain became unbearable.

"What did he say when you showed him the video?"

"He wanted to make a phone call." She retreated into their bedroom and sat on the bed, struggling to remove her boots.

"I assume that call was to a lawyer?" Dan grabbed each leg separately and helped pull off her boots.

"JAG officer from Bremerton," she said, shimmying out of her jeans.

"Really?" He sounded surprised.

"Yeah, why?" She stepped to the closet and hung her pants on a hook.

"JAGs don't normally get involved this quickly, especially defense attorneys. They usually have to run it up the chain of command first to determine if they're even going to take jurisdiction. Are they?"

"I don't know. I asked. She didn't know." She removed her shirt and bra and slipped on one of Dan's T-shirts embossed with a photo of Rex and Sherlock. It read: "We're not stubborn. Our way is just better." "But a JAG came to the jail to talk to him after he was processed."

"Sounds like they'll assert jurisdiction. If they don't, he'll plead. You have the video; what's he going to say?"

"At the moment, he isn't saying anything, not even about the video. I thought he'd try to explain it. Maybe he can't. I don't know." She brushed her teeth at the sink in the bathroom, then went back into the bedroom.

"You hungry? Want me to make you something to eat?" Dan asked.

"Thanks, but I grabbed a salad earlier and ate at my desk." Kins had also been sold on a salad, right up until he opened the takeout menu and ordered a pastrami sandwich. "Just tired."

Dan leaned against the bedroom door frame. "You okay?"

"Yeah, why?" She pulled back the down comforter.

"Dr. Kramer called the house phone to find out how you're feeling. There's a message for you."

Tracy stopped folding back the sheet.

"You're on Clomid?" he asked.

Tracy had not told Dan about the drug. She'd told him that Dr. Kramer had suggested that they just keep trying. She'd hoped that by taking the drug, she'd get pregnant, and she wouldn't have to admit to Dan that she was too old—that she was the problem.

"Is this one of your cross-examination techniques? Get the witness talking, then hit her with the question you're really interested in?"

"Don't do that," he said, his voice all business, his eyes fixed on her. "We talked about this; we talked about making a decision together."

"Yes, we did."

"But you excluded me anyway?"

Tracy sighed. "My chances of getting pregnant are very slim, Dan. It was either fertility drugs or a donor egg."

"What does that have to do with excluding me from the process?"

"I shouldn't have. Okay? I'm sorry." She started to climb onto her side of the bed.

"Then why did you?"

"Can we talk about this later?"

"No. You hid it from me. I think I have a right to know."

"I didn't hide it."

"You didn't tell me."

"I need to be at work early to prepare for the probable cause hearing," she said, flipping the pillows she didn't use onto the floor.

"I have a deposition to take."

"So let's go to bed and discuss it later."

Dan pushed away from the door frame. "Clomid has side effects; we talked about that."

"What, are you going to say my mood has been the shits?"

"I wasn't, but I could now."

"Very clever." She grabbed a pillow and stepped past him, deciding that she'd sleep on the couch in the living room.

"Hey, don't act like this is my fault. You should have included me. This is my child also."

She knew he was right, but she'd inherited her father's stubborn streak. "Yeah, well, it doesn't look like you're going to have to worry about that anytime soon." She grabbed a blanket from the reading chair and moved toward the couch.

"What does that mean?"

She turned and stopped. "It means I can't get pregnant," she said. "Okay? It means I'm the problem."

For a moment Dan didn't say anything, leaving Tracy to wonder what he was really thinking. Had he had his heart set on kids? Was he rethinking his decision to marry her?

Dan softened his tone. "I don't care about the baby. I care about you. I care about your health."

She sighed. "The doctor said the side effects are minimal. Mood swings and hot flashes. I'm fine. I'm sorry I didn't tell you. I should have."

Dan took a deep breath. When he spoke again, he was calm. He was always calm. Sometimes she wished he'd yell and throw things just so she could get angry at him. "Just tell me why you didn't."

She shook her head.

"What?"

She knew what she was about to say was juvenile and that too bothered her. But she'd wanted to have their baby, together. "You came back from the doctor all excited that day, pumping your fists and . . . I didn't want to disappoint you. I didn't want to be the reason we couldn't make a baby."

Dan let out a burst of air and moved toward her. He removed the pillow she'd been holding and put his hands on her shoulders. "I was excited because I thought you wanted a child."

"You don't?"

"Of course I do. But not if it means your health will be adversely affected. You're the most important thing to me, Tracy, not some child I don't even know. I'm sorry if I overreacted about the vasectomy. I was just playing up the situation. I thought it would make you happy if I showed a little more enthusiasm." He smiled, but she couldn't. "Hey, come on. We're physiologically different, Tracy. Hell, Mick Jagger just had baby number eight at seventy-three years of age."

"Is that supposed to make me feel better?"

"What exactly did the doctor say?"

"I'm on Clomid for fourteen days. If that doesn't work, we're looking at a donor egg. Or adopting."

"Okay, so—"

She pulled away from him. "I don't want someone else's child, Dan. I want *our* child. I want *our* baby." She was whining and she knew it.

Dan nodded. "Okay," he said softly. "Then we'll just keep trying and if it doesn't work, then we'll talk about that decision." He smiled and stepped toward her. She'd started to cry. "Hey. It's all right."

"No, it's not all right," she said, wiping her eyes, feeling overwhelmed. "This was not the life I was supposed to have, Dan. This was not the way things were supposed to turn out. I was going to have three kids. I was going to be a mother, go to PTA meetings and soccer games, help them with their homework, and sit down at the table and have family dinners." She exhaled, shaking her head. "What happened to my life? What the hell happened to my life?"

They stood, silent for a long moment, and Tracy realized she'd hurt him. "Dan, I didn't—"

Dan shrugged. "I was hoping you'd say your life turned out pretty well."

She felt nauseated, and it had nothing to do with Clomid's side effects. "I'm sorry. I didn't mean it like that."

He stepped back, away from her. "You don't think I felt the same way after my divorce? That I didn't wonder what had happened to my life? I had a wife, a good job at a good firm doing what I love. I drove a BMW and had season tickets to the Red Sox . . . and a boat. Then, in an instant, it was all gone. My ex-partner got my wife and the tickets and the boat, and I was back in Cedar Grove. You don't think I wondered where it all went wrong?"

She stepped to him. "You didn't do anything to cause it, Dan."

"Maybe I did."

"She cheated on you."

"Yes, but maybe because I wasn't around enough."

"Sometimes I wonder about that too," she said.

"What?"

"If I had just driven Sarah home."

He shook his head. "Sarah was killed by a psychopath, Tracy. He stalked her and he stalked you. And as terrible as it was, I'd like to think that maybe God spared you . . . for me."

She started to cry again. Dan always managed to say the right thing. Even when they'd been young, growing up friends in Cedar Grove, Dan found a way to say what Tracy needed to hear. It was a quality Tracy didn't possess—an ability to put things in perspective, to find something—if not positive then at least optimistic. After a long beat she said, "You're really hard to fight with, you know that?"

CHAPTER 14

There was no mistaking that Leah Battles was a JAG attorney Friday afternoon when Tracy followed Kins into the cramped district courtroom on the first floor of the King County Jail. Battles sat in the first bench, resplendent in a dress blue uniform with two gold stripes on the cuffs, and a patchwork of colored squares above her left breast pocket. She'd pulled her hair into a bun on the back of her head. On her lap she held a white hat with a blue bill, gold trim, and an eagle on the crown. Beside Battles sat another naval officer, an older man also dressed in blue.

"Looks like somebody came to play," Kins said. "I guess the Navy *is* taking jurisdiction?"

Tracy nodded, disappointed. "Looks that way."

"How do you think the family is going to take it?"

"I don't know. They were already guarded about the process, and I don't think this will help."

Trejo would not be formally charged this afternoon. The sole purpose of a first appearance was for the judge to determine if there existed probable cause to believe the defendant committed a crime. If so, Trejo would be held for an arraignment and a determination of bail, likely in two weeks. The delay was to give Tracy and Kins time to gather the evidence upon which the prosecutor's office would base any charges. The presence of the naval officers, in dress uniforms, gave Tracy serious doubt that would be necessary. The Navy looked ready to take jurisdiction.

Despite the relatively innocuous purpose of the first appearance, the two benches were full and more people stood in the back, almost all African American—relatives and friends of the Miller family. Tracy was pleased to see Shaniqua Miller among them. She stood beside her mother and a representative from the Victim Assistance Unit. They were listening to Rick Cerrabone. Shaniqua and her mother looked spent. They had a right to be.

Cerrabone made eye contact with Tracy and Kins, excused himself from the conversation, and nodded for the three of them to step outside. They found a cramped space in which to talk.

"Looks like they're going to pull this one," Tracy said.

"Dunleavy spoke with the Navy's senior trial counsel this morning," Cerrabone said, referencing King County prosecuting attorney Kevin Dunleavy.

"Is that him sitting in the courtroom beside Battles?"

"Who's Battles?" Cerrabone asked.

"The woman," Tracy said. "She came to Police Headquarters last night to talk to Trejo."

"Then I'm assuming the man next to her is senior trial counsel."

"Did he say they were going to pull jurisdiction?" Tracy asked.

"I haven't talked to him, but it sure seems likely, doesn't it?" Cerrabone tugged at the knot on his tie. "Dunleavy said the Navy is sending two investigators from NCIS to speak to you and review the evidence before they make a decision."

Tracy shook her head. "I had a case with them a few years back and I wasn't impressed then."

"Not a lot we can do about that," Cerrabone said. He checked his watch, which this afternoon was accompanied on his wrist by a black Fitbit. "Listen, if the Navy pulls jurisdiction, Dunleavy is going to want us to stay involved. The family is on edge, and given the recent climate, Dunleavy wants to be sure we continue to look invested."

"Clarridge expressed the same," Tracy said, "but how do you do that if they pull jurisdiction?"

"I charge Trejo with a hit and run and with running a red light. Even if the Navy takes jurisdiction, running the red light stays in play. So does your office."

"You're serious?" Kins said. "For running a red light?"

Cerrabone shrugged. "Running the red light is a civilian crime. So, if the Navy takes jurisdiction and we don't like the result, we maintain the right to try Trejo in superior court."

"Nolasco is not going to want to use his resources for running the red light. Not with the number of murders we've had already this year," Kins said. "Besides, what about double jeopardy?"

"It doesn't apply here," Cerrabone said. "But it's rarely an issue because the Navy isn't limited by the same sentencing guidelines we are. They can put Trejo away for a longer period than we can, if it comes to that. That's what I was just telling the mother and grandmother."

"How are they taking it?" Tracy asked.

Cerrabone shrugged. "I don't know. At the moment they're just holding on."

"Can't blame them," Tracy said.

"And I think they're distrustful of the system."

"I got that sense also when I went out to the house to tell them we'd made an arrest," Tracy said. "I don't think the Navy taking jurisdiction is going to help."

"It won't. I suspect they'll believe the Navy is taking the case in-house to protect one of its own. Dunleavy expressed the same concern and was told that if they pull jurisdiction, they'll quickly bring an Article 32 hearing to allay those concerns."

"A court-martial?" Kins asked.

Cerrabone shook his head. "No. An Article 32 is the military's equivalent to our convening a civil grand jury, except it's open to the public and to the media. Senior trial counsel said they can hold the hearing in two weeks. It might give the mother some assurance they're serious about prosecuting Trejo." Cerrabone looked at Tracy. "Dunleavy is going to push for you to be a witness with respect to what was found inside the car and how you secured the videotape. He wants SPD to continue to look invested. We'll just have to play this out." He flipped his wrist and again tugged at his sleeve, checking his watch. "We better get back in there."

Tracy and Kins followed Cerrabone back into the courtroom. He moved to be seated beside D'Andre Miller's mother and aunt. Tracy and Kins stood at the back. Though it was cold outside, the sheer number of bodies had warmed the courtroom and made it stuffy. An oscillating fan on the judge's desk struggled to circulate the air. Tracy felt like someone had turned on radiant heating, the warmth crawling up her body.

"Is it hot in here?" she asked.

Kins shrugged. "Not too bad."

Hot flash from the Clomid. Great timing. At least she hoped that's all it was. Her mother had gone through early menopause. That would end the baby discussion quickly.

At 2:30 p.m., Judge Milo Yokavich, who was said to be seventy-three but looked and moved as if he were 103, entered the courtroom dwarfed by two King County Jail correctional officers.

"Gringotts," Kins said.

Short, with wisps of hair, pronounced ears, and a crooked nose, Yokavich had been dubbed Gringotts, which was the Wizarding Bank in the Harry Potter books, by some heartless attorney who thought he looked like the head goblin.

Yokavich took the bench between the United States and Washington State flags and nodded to the clerk. She called case 17285 SEA, the State of Washington versus Laszlo Gutierrez Trejo. Yokavich had clearly adjusted his calendar to get the case heard first so he could clear the court for the remainder of the calendar.

Trejo entered from a door on the right dressed in red prison scrubs with the words "Ultra High Security" stenciled on the back. Cerrabone approached the desk and stood beside the two naval officers as Yokavich methodically turned the pages of the certification, taking several minutes to read it, though he had likely read it in chambers. When he'd finished, he flipped back to page one and set the pleading on his desk. "I've read . . ." He looked at the two naval officers, as if surprised by their presence. Then he said, "I've read the certification. Anything else from the state?"

"No, Your Honor," Cerrabone said.

"I find sufficient probable cause to detain this defendant." Yokavich looked to the officers. "Do either of you wish to be heard?"

The male officer nodded. "The defense wishes to be heard."

Yokavich nodded. "I thought you might." He sat back.

"Your Honor, my name is Captain Cameron Moore, senior trial counsel, United States Navy. This is Lieutenant Leah Battles, defense counsel assigned to Naval Base Kitsap in Bremerton, Washington, which is the defendant's base. As Your Honor is likely aware from the uniforms we're wearing, the defendant is enlisted in the United States Navy."

"It wasn't lost on me," Yokavich said.

"I wouldn't think so. Specifically, Mr. Trejo is a logistics specialist serving at Naval Base Kitsap. This morning I spoke with the King County prosecuting attorney about the possibility of the United States Navy asserting jurisdiction in this matter."

Yokavich looked to Cerrabone. "Counsel?"

"I am aware that the prosecuting attorney did receive a telephone call from Captain Moore, Your Honor. However, I'm unaware that any decision has been reached regarding jurisdiction. I was advised that Navy criminal investigators would be conducting a further investigation and a decision made upon completion of that investigation."

"So the Navy has not yet asserted jurisdiction?" Yokavich asked.

"Not yet. Not to my knowledge," Cerrabone said.

Moore spoke. "We are in the process of making that determination. As counsel represented, we have naval investigators assigned to this matter. Until we receive their information, Your Honor, I am requesting that Mr. Trejo be confined to the Northwest Joint Regional Correctional Facility at Fort Lewis, for his own safety."

"His safety?" Tracy whispered to Kins. "What is he talking about?"

Kins shook his head. "Don't know."

"Your Honor," Cerrabone said. "I'm sure the King County Jail can ensure Mr. Trejo has safe confinement."

"Why can't he be confined in the King County Jail?" Yokavich asked Moore.

"Your Honor," Moore said. "Mr. Trejo is an active duty service member and has served overseas during foreign campaigns on the USS *Stennis*, as well as at operating bases in Iraq and Afghanistan. He cannot be placed in general population because of the possibility of foreign nationals who would seek to harm him."

"Is he kidding?" Tracy said. "He worked in storage rooms."

"I don't think he kids," Kins said.

Cerrabone continued, "Until a decision has been made concerning jurisdiction, Mr. Trejo is in the custody of the King County Jail. That is where he has been booked and processed. If the Navy asserts jurisdiction, they can move him then."

"Your Honor, Mr. Trejo is also innocent until proven guilty. Since his safety cannot be guaranteed in a civilian prison, he should be allowed to exercise his right to be secured in the regional correctional facility on

Joint Base Lewis-McChord where he will be placed in pretrial confinement until such time as the Navy's investigation is completed. There is absolutely no prejudice to the King County prosecutor."

Maybe not, Tracy thought, but such a move would give the appearance of the type of preferential treatment by the Navy that concerned Shaniqua Miller and the rest of those gathered.

Yokavich gazed up at the ceiling as he considered the matter. Lowering his gaze to Cerrabone, he said, "I don't find any prejudice. Is there any prejudice?"

"It's an unnecessary step, Judge, and it's anticipating something that has not and may never occur," Cerrabone said. "That decision can be made if and when the Navy takes jurisdiction, which it hasn't. Until then, Mr. Trejo should be treated like any other King County defendant."

"We're here now," Moore said. "It avoids having to move Mr. Trejo, and it ensures his safety."

Yokavich nodded. "I'm going to grant the motion until such time as the Navy makes its decision."

"Dammit," Tracy said, loud enough that Kins turned and glanced at her. She noticed the majority of the crowd shaking their heads in resignation.

"If the Navy does not assert jurisdiction, we can revisit this issue," Yokavich said. "Until then, I am remanding the defendant to the Northwest . . . It's a brig isn't it?" He looked to Battles.

"You served, Your Honor?" Battles asked.

"Proudly," Yokavich said. "Petty officer second class."

Battles smiled and Tracy could see daggers in the eyes of those seated in the gallery.

"The brig is now called the Northwest Joint Regional Correctional Facility." Battles shrugged. "I think it sounds better to the politicians. Personally, I like brig."

Yokavich gave a thin smile. Tracy had never seen him smile. He looked like a schoolboy chatting up the best-looking girl in the class. "It's a mouthful, isn't it?"

"It is," Battles said.

"They better end this now or these people might riot," Tracy said to Kins.

"And with good reason," Kins said.

"Right." Yokavich looked to Cerrabone as if he'd forgotten he was there. "Anything else?"

"No, Your Honor," Cerrabone and Moore said in unison.

"Madam Clerk, call the next case," Yokavich said.

Tracy watched Battles walk with Trejo and the two burly correctional guards, bending close to whisper in his ear and pat him on the shoulder before he stepped through the door.

The victim's advocate present at the hearing was speaking to Shaniqua Miller and her mother, but they weren't paying her much attention. This had gone about as badly as Tracy could have predicted. Cerrabone turned and gave her an eye roll filled with disgust but otherwise held it together.

Battles and Moore started up the aisle to the exit. When she reached the doorway, Battles turned and looked back over her shoulder, her gaze finding Tracy, as if to drop a challenge of sorts.

CHAPTER 15

Del adjusted his suit jacket as he stepped from the elevator and made his way down the marble floor toward the courtroom of the honorable Deborah Kerr. He pulled open the large wooden door and slipped into a bench at the back of the sparsely populated gallery. Several jurors seated in the jury box on the front right side of the courtroom glanced at him, but only briefly. Their attention was fixed on Celia McDaniel. As Del had suspected, McDaniel was good on her feet, with an easy way about her and, today at least, a charming Southern drawl that was downright intoxicating.

After ten minutes, when McDaniel paused to change subjects, Judge Kerr looked up at the clock on the wall. "Counsel, perhaps this is a good place to break for the day?"

McDaniel glanced at the clock, though Del knew she'd break. The judge had just given her an opportunity to send the jurors home after a long day and long week. Only a fool would not accept. Celia McDaniel was no fool.

"That would be fine, Your Honor. With any luck, we might all beat the traffic home."

As the jurors gathered their belongings and filed out of the room, Del made his way to counsel's table where McDaniel was packing her materials into a Bekins box. She stopped when she saw him. He hadn't seen her since the coffee shop, when she'd left a coffee and two donuts on the table. Her upper lip curled, which he figured could be a smile . . . or a smirk.

"So, what brings you here so late on a Friday afternoon, Detective? Did you locate the drug dealer?"

Del would work with McDaniel to prepare charges, if and when he had the name or names of the persons who supplied Allie with the drugs that had killed her and potentially killed the others who had overdosed, but that was not his reason for being there.

"No, not yet." Del cleared his throat. "I came to apologize about the other day. I didn't know about your son and I said a few things that were . . ."

"Boorish?"

Del shrugged. "I was going to say insensitive, but boorish works."

She nodded. "Don't worry about it. I've heard a lot worse. What's the status of the information on the person who supplied your niece?"

He was glad to change the subject, though Allie's investigation had not been the reason for his visit. "I sent Allie's phone and computer to TESU yesterday for analysis. Melton is going to try to rush it for me."

"I understand from Funk that there've been more deaths."

"Two. Same scene. Appears to be the same product. I brought a sample for Funk to look at and hopefully analyze. He says it isn't black tar. It might be China white."

"That would be unusual on the West Coast."

"That's what Funk said."

"Did you notify the narcotics section?"

Del nodded. "They're talking to known users, and I heard they have bike cops out spreading the word. I was told that the case might be pulled from Violent Crimes . . . from me."

McDaniel thought about this. "Maybe with respect to determining what's in the product and where it's coming from, but not if we charge whoever is supplying it with a controlled substance homicide. That would be Violent Crimes jurisdiction."

"Thanks," he said.

She started to pick up the box, but Del put out a hand, wanting to discuss the reason for his visit. "I was hoping to maybe buy you a drink . . . as a peace offering for my boorish behavior."

McDaniel's brow furrowed. "Is this a pity drink, Detective?"

"No," Del said quickly, not expecting her response to be hostile. "No. Nothing like that."

"So you're just trying to clear your conscience because you feel bad."

Del rocked back on his heels, now completely uncertain of what to say. "I didn't think of it that way either."

McDaniel smiled. Her eyes glinted. "I'm just playing with you. Friday night after a long week, who can't use a drink?" She picked up the box. "But I never drink unless I'm eating, and I already told you I love to eat. Do you like Thai food?"

"Yeah," Del said. In truth, he wasn't a big fan but he wasn't about to say anything that could send the conversation off track. "Love Thai food."

McDaniel handed him the box. "Help me drop this off at the office," she said. "I know a great place downtown."

CHAPTER 16

Monday morning, Leah Battles unclipped her bike shoe from the pedal and pulled on the string around her neck. When riding to and from work, she carried her military ID in a clear slip holder beneath her riding shirt. She flashed the ID at the master-at-arms, or MA, working the Charleston Gate as she did each morning, and started to slip it back beneath her shirt.

"Hang on." The guard came out of the shack and walked toward her.

Battles had ridden her bike to Naval Base Kitsap every day for the past three years, rain or shine. Was she obsessive about it? No. She was frugal. She wasn't getting rich in the Navy, and owning a car in downtown Seattle without a designated place to park meant feeding an expensive garage. She'd rather feed herself. The cost of driving a car onto the ferry every morning and every night was also not inconsequential. A bike saved money, and provided at least some exercise for those days and weeks when work got crazy, as she sensed it was about to. The ferry terminal was just blocks from her Pioneer Square apartment, and it was about a two-mile ride from the Bremerton Ferry Terminal to the Charleston Gate.

And every morning she showed her badge to the MA on duty.

Unfortunately, while her routine remained consistent, the MAs did not. Some, like this lug nut making her take the ID out of the plastic slip, were anal about their job. Next would be a cavity search—of him, not her.

She fought the urge to say something sarcastic, tried not to become frustrated, told herself the MA was just doing his job, but she was also butt-ass cold and wanted to get inside, get coffee, and get warm.

"Do you have a chip reader or can I just slide the card in a slot?" she said, handing the MA her card.

The guard looked up, puzzled. "Excuse me?"

"I'd also like fifty dollars cash back and a couple of Powerball lottery tickets."

The MA didn't smile. Maybe he was practicing to be a member of the Queen's Guard at Buckingham Palace. His eyes shifted from the ID to Battles and back again. She smiled, wide.

He handed back the card, apparently not expecting the rank. "Thank you, Lieutenant." He even saluted.

Battles returned a halfhearted salute, slipped the ID into the sleeve, and tucked it beneath her top. She pushed away from the booth but didn't bother to clip her shoes back into the pedals—she could coast down the slope in the road—turned on Barclay Street, and cut across the parking lot to building 433. The last door on the right was the Defense Service Office, West Detachment Bremerton, or DSO—her home away from home. Like Naval Base Kitsap, which emerged from the reorganization of Naval Station Bremerton and Naval Submarine Base Bangor, the DSO had been reorganized from the Naval Legal Services Office (NLSO), which had provided both defense services and legal assistance—things like drafting wills, landlord-tenant contracts, and other exciting crap. The civil and criminal offices had been separated, and thank the Holy Trinity for that. Battles hadn't signed up to fight over who got what or who lived where.

Battles removed her bike helmet, entered the last four digits of her Social Security number on the touch pad to unlock the door and record her presence, and went inside the building. The warm air on her chilled skin felt comforting. Darcy, the receptionist, greeted her from her seat at the front desk, as she did every day. "What's up, ma'am?"

"Sun and sky, Darcy," Battles said, walking past. "I'll let you know when they aren't."

Battles walked to her office, which was just past the lobby, but before she could step inside, a voice called out from down the hall.

"Heard you had a busy weekend, Lee." Brian Cho, the prosecution's senior trial counsel at Kitsap, approached. He was grinning.

Cho had an office on the second floor near the courtroom. The fact that he was downstairs indicated he'd been waiting for Battles to arrive, or had seen her come through the Charleston Gate from his window. He wore blue-and-gray camos—what the Navy called NWU, which officially stood for "Navy Working Uniform," but which Battles unofficially dubbed "North West Ugly." Sailors referred to the uniforms derogatorily as "blueberries," and there had been talk the Navy was considering ditching them altogether; seemed they were unsafe to wear while fighting a fire. Flammable uniforms! Nice. Even the Secretary of the Navy was said to have taken a swipe at them. "The uniform provides great camouflage," he was reported to have said, "if you happen to fall overboard."

Battles ignored Cho because, well, he was Cho, and continued into her office to her desk. She turned on the Tiffany desk lamp that had once adorned her father's desk and tried to look busy. With no windows, the office had the charm of a prison cell, offering no natural lighting. It could feel claustrophobic, especially in the winter, when Battles often arrived before sunrise and went home after sunset.

Cho, not to be deterred by subtle rebukes, followed Battles into her office. "I heard about Trejo and the probable cause hearing."

With Cho, she straddled the fence between being collegial and unloading her Krav Maga training on his butt. A good-looking Asian man with a smile as dazzlingly white as the Mormon Tabernacle Choir, he didn't hide the cadre of women at his beck and call. He was also arrogant and sarcastic. And those were his good qualities. Battles surmised that if Cho had heard the news, it meant the head prosecutor had already prepared a situation report, or sit-rep, and had put that report on the desks of all the head honchos on base. They weren't wasting time, meaning they were likely taking jurisdiction.

"Then you know as much as I do." She dropped her bike helmet onto her desk.

"You moved awfully quickly; heard you met him at the jail."

She didn't take the bait. "He called. I had the phone and I was already over there." She kicked off her bike shoes. She kept her uniform and her black boots in her closet. Cho, however, didn't take the hint to leave.

"Where's Trejo now?"

"Lewis-McChord," she said.

"So we're taking jurisdiction?"

And there was the subject of Cho's interest. "Like I said, you know as much as I do at this point. We just tried to keep him out of the county jail."

"Enemy combatants?" Cho said, a hint of sarcasm in his voice.

"You know the drill."

"You talk to him?"

"Nothing specific," she said.

"I heard this one is coming back," Cho said. "That we're taking jurisdiction."

She didn't respond, picking up papers and pretending to read. "Wouldn't surprise me."

"You're bucking for it, aren't you?"

There it was—the purpose for his visit. "Was that part of the rumor too?" She set down the pleading.

Cho gave her a sardonic smile. He loved getting under people's skin. "Case of that stature would look good on the resume."

"Are you talking about yours or mine?" She moved toward the door; the women's bathroom might be the only way to ditch this dolt.

Still grinning, Cho cut her off. "My resume doesn't need any help, Lee," he said, letting the comment and his smile linger before he departed.

Battles shut the door, resisting her urge to call him an arrogant shit before she did, and made her way back behind her desk. On the wall, next to a framed Indian tapestry she'd picked up on a trip to Mumbai— "Join the Navy, See the World!"—hung her two Defense Counsel of the Year certificates. She'd worked hard for the acknowledgments, but Cho was right, the Trejo case could significantly improve her resume, not that she'd admit it to Cho. Cho was the only prosecutor to have beaten her, twice. She'd never beaten him. And while this one might be tough, she loved a challenge.

She left the fluorescent lights off, went back to her closet, and quickly changed into her uniform and black boots. She sat and went through the research she'd conducted over the weekend. Trejo faced a potentially long imprisonment. Under the Uniform Code of Military Justice, were Trejo to receive a general court-martial, a military judge or a jury could impose a sentence well in excess of ten years—the maximum civilian penalty. Given the current political climate since the Black Lives Matter movement, *and* given that Trejo had not stopped his vehicle, he was ripe for being made an example.

And that was what bothered Battles. Trejo didn't strike her as particularly dumb, or devious. He also had a wife to consider. So why'd he run? Trejo wasn't saying. He'd stuck to his story that he wasn't there, hadn't been in Seattle. He said the videotape that SPD had showed him wasn't of him. Maybe it wasn't. Since Battles hadn't seen it, she had no reason to doubt her client. She suspected command would call an Article 32 hearing, probably sooner rather than later. If Trejo wasn't in Seattle, the defense was simple. If he was, she'd need mitigating arguments—D'Andre Miller was hurrying to get home and not paying attention. It was dark out. Miller stepped off the curb without looking, leaving Trejo little chance to stop before striking him. Miller might not have even been in the crosswalk. Any number of things could have happened to explain the accident.

But not to explain the fact that Trejo had fled—if he'd fled.

Someone knocked on her door.

"Come in," she said.

"Lieutenant, may I have a word?"

Rebecca Stanley, Leah's officer in charge, or OIC, entered. Battles stood but resisted the urge to salute; the Navy was less formal than other branches of the military. A salute was only exchanged outdoors. However, Stanley had just recently been assigned to Kitsap and was a bit more formal than Leah's prior OIC. Battles didn't want to appear disrespectful, which was why she'd stood.

"Please," Battles said.

Stanley closed Leah's office door, turning gingerly to do so. It was a poorly kept secret at Kitsap that Stanley had injured her back while serving at a base in Kabul, Afghanistan, where she'd been assigned to help process the plethora of claims filed by Afghani civilians who'd suffered property damage or had lost loved ones during the United States's military mission. During one of those nights, Stanley's base had taken mortar fire, which wasn't unusual, though this time the accuracy of the attack had been. A mortar hit Stanley's room, throwing her from her bed and into a wall. She'd suffered a broken back and had to have several of her vertebrae fused.

Stanley looked up at the bank of unused overhead lights. "Is it always this dark in here?"

"I like to think of it as mood lighting," Battles said.

Stanley gave a polite smile and slowly lowered herself into one of the two cloth chairs. Battles sat behind her desk.

"The probable cause hearing has caused a bit of a stir around here this morning," Stanley said, getting right to the point.

"Thought it might."

"You met with Trejo?" she asked, her dark eyes fluctuating between dull and unexpressive, and piercing. She folded her dark hair behind her ears.

"Not to any great degree," Battles said, still positioning to get the case. "I got his call Thursday night. The King County Jail was on my way home from working out so I stopped off and told everybody he wasn't talking and to not even try." She shrugged, trying to make it appear as no big deal.

"I'm told NCIS is investigating the allegations, but there isn't a lot to do—no witnesses, a couple of videotapes. Forensics on the car are apparently inconsequential. I'm also told by senior trial counsel that the Navy will take jurisdiction."

"He indicated that at the hearing. I figured we would . . . under the circumstances."

"Trejo say whether or not he wanted civilian counsel?"

"He didn't, but I don't see how he's going to afford civilian counsel."

"And the videotape, what did he have to say about it?"

"He says it's not him."

"Have you seen it?"

"Not yet."

Stanley put her hands together, as if about to say grace at dinner. "Well, that brings it back to us."

"Yes, Captain."

"You want this case."

It wasn't a question. "I do."

"It has all the appearances of a dead-bang loser, unless Trejo is telling the truth and he isn't on the tape."

"Perhaps."

"You think you're up to it?"

"Absolutely."

"I've heard Cho has been assigned to prosecute Trejo."

Battles knew he'd been in her office for a reason. "Doesn't surprise me."

"He's never lost a felony case."

"There's always a first time." Battles sat back. "I'll go through the evidence and see how strong it is. If it's as strong as represented, Trejo might have to plea."

Stanley stood. "Sounds like you have it under control. Be sure you do."

"Captain?" Battles asked, puzzled by Stanley's comment.

Stanley braced her arms on the back of the chair and slightly pitched toward Battles. "Command is going to be watching this one closely, Lee. Cutting to the chase, it's ugly. If Trejo ran down that kid and fled, it's not going to paint the Navy in a very favorable light, and if the video is as damning as the police department contends, and Trejo won't own up to it . . ." She let that thought linger. "So make sure he understands the gravity of the crime and the gravity of the current political climate—were he to choose to fight the charges."

PART 2

TWO WEEKS LATER

CHAPTER 17

The odds hadn't been great, but that hadn't eased Tracy's disappointment. She wrapped the pregnancy stick in toilet tissue and discarded it in the garbage pail next to her empty prescription bottle of Clomid. Her fourteen days were up. She felt like an expired carton of milk. Dr. Kramer said she could still get pregnant, that the drug would remain in her system for a while, but he didn't sound optimistic when he said it.

Neither was she.

At least now that she was off the medication, maybe the hot flashes and mood swings would subside. Lucky her, she'd been one of the few to experience the side effects, and they'd nearly driven her crazy the past two weeks. She'd felt like she'd been sweating from the inside out. She'd kick the quilt off at night with her heart racing and her T-shirt damp. Poor Dan would wake up freezing. He finally got a separate quilt. During the days, she'd found excuses to step outside into the cold weather, but eventually even the weather stopped cooperating. It appeared winter had finally passed. Temperatures hovered in the midfifties, normal for the middle of March, though the increase in temperature had also brought three straight days of rain, a trend fore-casted to continue for the foreseeable future.

Tracy washed her hands at the bathroom vanity and considered her reflection in the mirror. The crow's-feet seemed more pronounced, and she could find strands of gray in her blonde hair. Her complexion, her mother's complexion, was no longer flawless; a few age spots had broken through. She'd never cared before. It hadn't been important. And she knew it wasn't the age that bothered her now. It was what the age represented. She felt it in her shoulder that ached and her knee that stung if she turned it the wrong way. Her eyesight, once 20/10 and her best asset for single-action revolver shooting competitions, had slipped to a mortal 20/20. She was nearing her father's age when he took his own life, unable to deal with the abduction of his baby, Tracy's younger sister, Sarah.

And she couldn't have a child.

Where had her youth gone?

She looked at the framed black-and-white photograph on the bath-room wall. Dan had hung it when they moved in, a surprise. Dan, Tracy, and Sarah, just children, sat in the limbs of the weeping wil-low tree in her parent's front yard. Why couldn't she remember that moment independent of a photograph?

She sensed her mortality, her place in the world, and the realization that there was no one to carry on her genetics, her family's legacy. The limb of her family tree would end with her.

Or maybe I'm still getting the damn mood swings because of the freak-ing Clomid.

She knew one thing. Standing at the sink ruminating on it wasn't helping.

"Tracy?" Dan called to her from the bedroom.

She gathered herself and stepped from the bathroom.

He lay in bed, propped up on pillows, reading a legal brief from behind round wire-rimmed glasses that, along with his long brown-gray curls, made him look studious.

"I'm glad you're home tonight," he said.

She'd come home early because she was testifying at the Article 32 hearing in the morning.

"Everything okay?" he asked.

She shrugged. "Negative."

"I'm sorry."

She shrugged again.

"Hey, we'll just have to keep trying."

She slid beneath the quilt on her side of the bed and inched across the mattress, close to Dan. He wrapped an arm around her shoulder. "You want to watch a movie?" he asked.

"I better not," she said. "I have the hearing at nine. The prosecutor is putting me on second, after the traffic collision investigator."

Dan made a face. "Are they going to allow you in the hearing before you testify?"

"I wouldn't think so, but the prosecutor said the evidentiary rules are relaxed, and the defense attorney apparently didn't object to my being present. And Clarridge and Dunleavy want me to accompany the family, so . . ."

"I'm still having a hard time believing it's gotten this far, with the video and all. I mean, what's he going to say?"

"Apparently he's maintaining that it isn't him on the video, that it's someone else."

"What are the chances of that succeeding?"

"I'd say about as good as the chances of me getting pregnant."

"Hey, we've got other options."

She didn't respond.

Dan rubbed her arm. "It's still early. Maybe there's something else besides television we can do."

She smiled, but she didn't feel like it. The failure on the pregnancy stick was still too raw. "You have to be pretty sick of me by now; I've been pushing you pretty hard these past two weeks."

"It's been a terrible ordeal," he said. "Ordinary men would have wilted under the intensity of your torture."

She looked up and kissed him. "You're a goober."

"Yes, but the law says I am now, legally, your goober."

Dan had always been goofy. Even as a kid, one of her best friends, he'd been goofy. Back then, she certainly hadn't thought of him as sexy, as she now did. Back then, he made her smile and he didn't care what others thought of him. Seemed he was never down, always optimistic. She'd called him "Mr. Optimism" once, but thought it sounded sarcastic. She didn't want to inhibit the thing that made him special, the thing she loved about him.

"Let's just get to sleep," she said.

He reached to turn off the light on his side of the bed but paused, looking down at her, hopeful. "You're sure . . . Sleep over sex?"

She smiled. "Sleep is like sex."

"How's that?"

"The less you have the more you crave it."

Dan laughed. "Who said that?"

"One of my academy instructors."

"Okay. Last chance, which one is it?"

She smiled and quickly lowered herself beneath the quilt. "Sleep."

He adjusted his pillows before turning out the light. Then he pulled Tracy close. After a moment he said, "I know your life didn't turn out exactly as you'd planned."

"That was the Clomid talking," she whispered.

"And I'd do anything to bring Sarah back," he said. She realized Dan was being serious. "But I'm glad you're here now, lying next to me. And I wouldn't have it any other way this night, or any other night for the next fifty years, what I know will be the best fifty years of my life."

"Oh, Dan." She rolled on top of him, pressing her lips to his. Amid her tears, she groped and felt for him and, eventually, found that love that had nothing to do with making a baby, but everything to do with needing him close, needing his optimism and spirit, needing to love him and to be loved by him—now, more than ever.

CHAPTER 18

Be careful what you wish for.

Leah Battles's mother used to caution her against pining for what she wanted and not appreciating what she had. Strange, then, that Leah would pursue a career in the law, a profession in which no truer words could be spoken. Over the years, Battles had pined for the big cases, the ones in which her client had something important to lose—like his freedom. When she worked those cases, her adrenaline pumped and her mind churned. It was a natural high and she loved it. But those were also the cases that kept her up late into the night and woke her early in the morning, unable to sleep. They consumed her.

Laszlo Trejo had consumed her.

Exhilarating one moment, the case and her client could be maddeningly frustrating the next. For two weeks, Battles had been getting to work by 7:00 a.m. and not making it home before midnight. She either ate and worked, or ate and slept on the ferry, putting those precious sixty commute minutes to use. Her exercise had become riding her bike to and from the terminals—except for one night when she absolutely had to relieve her stress or risk imploding. She left work early to attend her Krav Maga training.

The long hours became a certainty when Captain Peter Lopresti, Naval Base Kitsap's commanding officer, convened an Article 32 hearing, and made it clear this would not be the typical Article 32 hearing, which usually proceeded entirely on filed paperwork. Lopresti wanted an actual hearing, open to the public, with witnesses and summations. His reason was unspoken but transparent—he believed a strong showing by the prosecution could go a long way toward appeasing the public speculation that the Navy had taken jurisdiction to protect one of its own. That rationale also explained Brian Cho's over-the-top charging documents, which included the holy trifecta of hit-and-run offenses:

Unpremeditated murder [UCMJ Article 118(3)]

Involuntary manslaughter [UCMJ Article 119(2)]

Negligent homicide [UCMJ Article 134, para 85]

And, just because he was a putz, Cho had included a charge under UCMJ Article 111—usually reserved for occasions when the enlisted member was drunk but which included a charge for operating a vehicle in a reckless or wanton manner, resulting in injury. He'd also tacked on an assimilated charge under UCMJ Article 134 for wrongfully fleeing the scene of a crime. The prosecution did not have to prove each charge at the hearing. It just needed to put on enough evidence to demonstrate probable cause existed to proceed to a general court-martial against Laszlo Trejo for his alleged crimes.

The linchpin to each offense required Cho to demonstrate that Trejo had engaged in a dangerous act resulting in D'Andre Miller's death, thus showing a wanton disregard for human life. Speeding through an intersection against the traffic signal certainly fit that bill. The potential punishments for each offense varied greatly—from a conviction for unpremeditated murder, which could result in life in prison, to a finding of negligent homicide, which was punishable by one year in confinement.

If Battles had wanted a case in which her client had something to lose, she'd gotten it.

Be careful what you wish for.

Thanks, Mom.

Leah's plan—if the matter ever proceeded to a general court-martial—was to attack the first two charges with the most grievous sentences, then invoke her Catholic school education and pray, pray, pray for a conviction under either Article 134 or Article 111. Even that, however, would be a miracle to rival Jesus turning water into wine at the wedding in Cana. Battles had delved into the evidence, viewing the videotape first. That was really all it took to convince her that she could not win. No way. No how. No matter how she cut it, Laszlo Trejo was guilty, making the Article 32 hearing a mere formality to appease the public.

Once she'd reached this conclusion, Battles did what any good trial lawyer had to do. She'd sucked up her pride and brought all the evidence, and its consequences, to her client so they could discuss a plea.

Trejo wasn't interested.

He continued to maintain his innocence. He said he hadn't been in Seattle—that his car had been stolen. When Battles pressed him to explain the convenience store video, Trejo had simply shrugged and said, "It isn't me. It's someone who looks like me, but it isn't me."

Dumbfounded, Battles pointed out that Trejo was the same height as the person in the convenience store. She pointed out that Detective Crosswhite would testify that he'd been drinking a can of Red Bull when the Seattle detectives spoke to him, the same drink the man in the video had purchased at the convenience store. Battles explained that if the matter proceeded to a general court-martial, the jury would view the video and conclude Trejo was lying. She told him, bluntly, military jurors hated liars.

"It wasn't me," Trejo said.

She wondered if, perhaps, Trejo didn't understand the attorney-client privilege, if perhaps something in his naval training had led him to believe that Battles, a Navy officer, was required to divulge their conversations to persons higher in the chain of command. She explained that, though she was a Navy officer, she was first and foremost Trejo's attorney and that she could not divulge anything said between them—not to the other side, not to the judge, not to the independent investigator, not even to their CO.

"I wasn't there," Trejo said. "I didn't hit nobody."

Frustrated, but managing to keep her temper in check, Battles said, "I can't guarantee you I can do better than what they're offering."

"No plea," Trejo said.

That was the night she went to Krav Maga training and nearly killed her workout partner.

Someone knocked on her office door. She didn't need to ask who. No one else would be in the office this late. Brian Cho was taking pleasure goading her about Trejo's unwillingness to take a plea. Cho knew as well as Battles that command wanted the plea, that they didn't want the hearing, and they certainly did not want the court-martial to go forward and generate bad publicity for the Navy. The longer Trejo resisted, the more Cho insisted that Battles was not explaining the evidence in terms her client could comprehend, that somehow she wanted this case, despite it having every appearance of a dead-bang loser, as Stanley had said from the start.

Cho pushed open the door and stepped inside. Battles rocked back in her chair. She had the overhead lights off, her desk illuminated under the Tiffany lamp's green-tinted glass. Cho entered as if casing the joint for a burglary. He considered her paintings on the far wall like it was the first time he'd noticed them, though she'd hung them two years ago.

"That one of yours?"

Battles looked at the oil painting, an abstract inspired by a field of tulips she'd visited during a trip to the Skagit Valley Tulip Festival. "Yep."

"It's good," Cho said. "What is it?"

"Tulips."

"Huh." Cho took another second to study the painting before turning to Battles. "Have you talked with your client again?"

This guy was as subtle as a sledgehammer. "I did," she said.

"And?"

"He won't take the plea."

Cho lowered himself into the chair across from her desk as if to do so required great effort. The circle of light from the lamp barely illuminated him. "You know he's going down, Lee." He sighed, voice soft and sickeningly patronizing—as if she hadn't figured that much out for herself.

She suspected Cho had convinced himself that Battles wanted Trejo to turn down the plea; that her competitive nature wouldn't allow her to back down from the challenge of dethroning Cho from his unbeaten pedestal. Or maybe he was just worried that Battles had figured out how to keep the videocassette out of evidence and planned to surprise him at the court-martial.

She wished that were true. She'd never tell a client to turn down a deal simply to stoke her ego, especially when she wasn't making many friends in the chain of command. Rebecca Stanley had been in her office several times asking about the plea and why Trejo would not accept it.

Cho shrugged and pointed to the box of evidence on her desk. "The video confirms Trejo was in Seattle minutes before the accident. You have to know he's taking a fall. And when he lands, it's going to hurt you both."

Yeah, Battles knew. In fact, she was certain of it, but she wasn't going to let Cho see her sweat. "I guess that's why the horses actually run the race," she said.

"Huh?"

"Everyone can speculate on the winner, but until they run, nobody really knows the outcome."

He gave her a curious look. Then he smiled, another patronizing grin. "I think we do." He stood and walked to the door, turning to face her, as she knew he would. "This is a one-horse race." He pulled his blue-and-gray-camo hat from his back pocket. "See you bright and early."

He closed her office door. This time she didn't wait until she heard the DSO's front door open and close. She yelled, "Thanks, asshole."

She sat back, rubbed the fatigue from her eyes, and wondered out loud, "Why the hell am I still in the office?"

With the evidence stacked against her client, she'd even considered waiving the Article 32 hearing and proceeding to a general court-martial months down the road, likely sometime in the fall. Many seasoned attorneys would have employed that strategy. The extra time in the brig might convince Trejo to rethink his position, as well as diminish the considerable heat beneath the simmering public cauldron demanding justice.

But CO Lopresti *wanted* an Article 32 hearing, and he wouldn't be happy if Battles bailed out of his boat, though that wasn't why she was moving forward with the hearing. A seasoned defense attorney had once admonished Battles against waiving any proceeding in which she and her client stood to obtain free discovery. Because Lopresti was demanding a full show, Battles would have the opportunity to preview the prosecution's witnesses and evidence. There was little downside to having your opponent show his hand—even if only partially, especially since this indeed looked like it was headed toward a court-martial. Cho was also likely under orders not to hide the ball at the hearing, not with an anticipated crowd in attendance—all the more reason for her to go forward and find out what Cho intended and what the witnesses would say.

In other words, being in an Article 32 hearing was a little bit like being a gunslinger in a long-distance pistol shootout. You had no real expectation of hitting anything, but you paid very close attention to the bullets whizzing by.

CHAPTER 19

Early the following morning, Tracy set her coffee on the Formica table and slid into the leather seat across from Shaniqua Miller and her mother.

"Are you sure I can't get either of you a cup of coffee?" she asked.

They both again declined.

Their demeanor since they'd boarded the ferry had been polite but reticent. Neither had displayed much emotion or had said much, and Tracy had no doubt their reservation was with her and the judicial system. Tracy had not been able to offer any words to alleviate their concerns or to convince them that things would be different.

Shaniqua Miller, in a black suit and dark-blue blouse, folded her hands on the table. Her mother, seated beside her, also wearing black, directed her gaze out the ferry windows, which were spotted with rain. In the booths around them, D'Andre Miller's uncles, aunts, and the pastor from their church, also dressed in dark-colored suits and dresses, solemnly considered the heavy cloud layer, falling rain, and Elliott Bay's slate-gray waters.

It made Tracy think of Dan, how he liked to take the dogs for a walk on winter mornings and come back broadcasting a stilted local weather forecast. "This morning it will be gray, followed by more gray, with a burst of gray in the evening."

For Shaniqua Miller, less than a month removed from D'Andre's death, Tracy suspected from experience that her view of the world would be gray for quite some time. Following the disappearance and presumed death of her sister, Sarah, Tracy's world had become a black-and-white photograph, and it had taken nearly a year before even a glint of color pierced her bleak tapestry. Even now, more than two decades removed from that horrible event, there were days when the gloom descended—so heavy it was difficult for her to find the will to get out of bed, and nothing alleviated that sorrow.

So Tracy knew she could not say anything to the two women to minimize their distrust; nothing she could say to reassure them, calm their nerves, and alleviate their concerns. All she could do was act as a liaison between them and the judicial process, to be available to answer their questions, and to guide them if they needed guiding. So far they hadn't, or they hadn't wanted any. They had erected a curtain as thick as the cloud layer to protect against any more pain, and turned instead to each other and their unshakable faith in God for comfort. Tracy was not a part of their lives, and she could not pretend to be. And she had never received the gift of an unwavering acceptance of God's will. All she had to offer them was her experience, and her hope that the Navy had assumed jurisdiction to mete out punishment.

"I spoke to Brian Cho yesterday afternoon," Tracy said to break the uncomfortable silence.

"He called," Shaniqua offered, but did not elaborate on their conversation.

"He sounds well prepared for the hearing," Tracy said.

"But it's just preliminary," Shaniqua said. "He said there will still be a general court-martial, likely not for months."

"That's my understanding," Tracy said. "Unless Trejo pleads."

Shaniqua's mother gave an audible sigh and looked over the top of her round wire-rimmed glasses, but offered no words.

"What will be your role at the hearing?" Miller asked.

"I'll testify about what Mr. Trejo said when my partner and I interviewed him. I'll also explain where we found his car and the results of the interior search."

"The receipt you found," Miller said.

"Yes, and the evidence that someone tried to wipe down the car to eliminate fingerprints. I'll also testify about the cut on Mr. Trejo's forehead."

"But the hat he wore in the video, the prosecutor said it will prevent you from proving the cut occurred during the accident."

"Yes, but the blood found inside Mr. Trejo's car is circumstantial evidence that he was driving the car when it hit your son." She didn't want to overcomplicate things. "But really, the videotape from the convenience store should be enough for the preliminary hearing officer to find probable cause."

Shaniqua Miller's gaze drifted to the window. A seagull glided on the wind current created by the moving ferry. After a minute, she turned back to Tracy. "The prosecutor said Mr. Trejo will likely plead *after* the hearing?"

"He told me that also."

"Do you believe that?"

"I don't know," Tracy said. "I think it's possible the defense attorney might try to attack the video somehow and keep it out of evidence. It's the only thing I can think of for why Mr. Trejo hasn't pled."

"I keep thinking, if he was going to accept some plea deal, he would have done so already," Miller said.

Miller's mother raised her eyes and stared at Tracy. That had apparently also been on her mind.

Miller, no longer trying to hide her distrust, said, "I mean, he's seen the video, hasn't he? So why hasn't he admitted he's guilty? Why do we have to go through this hearing?"

"I don't know," Tracy said, and she didn't. In her experience, in a situation such as this, the defense counsel would be seeking a plea for her client. Maybe Leah Battles was waiting until after the Article 32 hearing. Or maybe she did have an argument to keep out the video and wanted to give it a try. There was no harm in waiting, hearing all the evidence, especially if her client was actually being recalcitrant.

"Cho said this is a big case for the defense attorney, that she may want to push her chances of defeating him," Miller said. "Did he tell you that?"

"He did," Tracy said.

The grandmother shook her head. Miller bit back a bitter grin. "It's all just a big game, isn't it?"

Again, Tracy had no words to console them. And, unfortunately, she knew firsthand that the judicial process would not bring them any satisfaction or relief. It wouldn't bring back D'Andre.

She only hoped Shaniqua Miller would find some closure from the proceedings.

—

Leah Battles had resisted the urge to sleep in her office, and thereby set a dangerous precedent for a profession that lawyers could so easily wed. She'd once known an attorney who took great pride in telling others he frequently slept in his office, seemingly oblivious to the fact that, at forty, he was also still single. Given her own ring-free left hand, and the lack of anyone even remotely considering adorning that finger, Battles didn't need any further help fueling the rumor mill inevitable for a woman in the military.

And no, she wasn't gay.

Not that there was anything wrong with that—to quote a famous Seinfeld proverb.

She'd caught the 11:40 p.m. ferry home, slept a few hours, then caught an early ferry back to the office. Now, at just before 9:00 a.m. it was show time, and she was dressed for it. Lopresti had let it be known that he wanted counsel in dress blue uniforms, no doubt to impress the crowd, including the press. As a result, Battles was as spit shined, though hopefully not as incompetent, as a young Demi Moore in the movie *A Few Good Men.*

She made her way out of her office carrying notes in the event that she opted to cross-examine any of the witnesses, and a few other materials. The evidence to be introduced was kept in the custody of the court reporter, and today was largely going to be Brian Cho's show.

She didn't have a long walk. The courtroom was one floor above, through metal detectors. This morning, with the anticipated crowd, several MAs would also be present, as well as brig chasers, or prison guards. It would make for a tight fit. The courtroom was not like some of the grandiose state courtrooms adorned with marble and mahogany and lit beneath hanging chandeliers. Far more functional than ceremonial, the Naval Base Kitsap courtroom consisted of a gallery of just four benches, two on the right and two on the left, which accommodated all interested spectators—with room to spare, in 99 percent of its cases.

Battles pulled open the door and stepped inside.

Not today.

The gallery overflowed, despite extra chairs, and the crowd made the room even smaller. With no exterior windows, the courtroom could quickly feel claustrophobic.

African American faces turned and considered Battles as she made her way to the railing separating the gallery. She caught sight of D'Andre Miller's mother, and, presumably, relatives and other supporters. They did not look happy to see her. The detective, Tracy Crosswhite, sat with them, as did Joe Jensen. Battles had seriously considered excluding both from the hearing until after they'd testified, just to screw with them, but she didn't see the point. She had the benefit of their official reports to keep them honest.

She walked the short aisle, pushed through the gate, and placed her materials on the desk to the right—dark wood but certainly not mahogany. Cho already sat at the desk on her left, his second chair occupied by Lindsay Clark, his assistant prosecutor and, according to rumors in the office, his latest conquest. They too were resplendent in their dress blues. Clark's job would be, no doubt, to hand Cho evidence and otherwise look competent. As Battles stepped past the lectern between the tables and settled at the table on the right, Cho glanced up, as if surprised to see her. Then, as if to say, *So be it*, he shook his head and refocused on the task at hand.

What's not to love about the guy?

Battles glanced at the empty jury box to her right. Today it would remain that way. At the front of the room, direct center, was the witness box. For some reason, the light oak chair, unadorned, always reminded her of Old Sparky, the electric chair in Stephen King's novel *The Green Mile*. To its left was the judge's bench; if elevated, it was a matter of inches, not feet. Recessed lighting spotted the United States and Navy flags, as well as two blue-and-gold disks hanging on the wall, the emblems of the Department of the Navy and the Judge Advocate General's Corps.

Battles continued to arrange her materials, not that she had much. She did not intend to call any witnesses or introduce any evidence. This was Cho's show. She was happy to just take it all in.

Free discovery. Never turn it down.

At minutes before nine, everything orchestrated, two brig chasers escorted Laszlo Trejo in from a door to the right of the bench. The murmurs in the gallery sounded like a low rumble. As instructed, Trejo seemingly took no note of them. He wore his work blues and looked like he'd slept little, bags beneath bloodshot eyes. Trejo, however, did not appear nervous, but that could have been because Battles had told him this was just a show for the court-martial, unless he pled.

Battles offered him the chair to her right, and he sat and faced forward, gaze alternately affixed on the tabletop or the blank wall behind the witness stand.

As soon as Trejo sat, the door to the left of the bench pulled open and the preliminary hearing officer, Sonya Rivas, entered in a black robe. Rivas, a lieutenant commander, was also a judge, which spoke to the seriousness of the allegations, and the Navy's concern that the proceeding be handled with the highest decorum. Today, however, Rivas would serve as the PHO, the preliminary hearing officer. Rivas and Battles had a good working relationship, but there would be no special treatment because they shared the same gender. If anything, Rivas was harder on female JAG officers. She knew they had to be better than their male counterparts. Nor would there be any sympathy toward Trejo because Rivas was Hispanic. The only colors Rivas saw were red, white, and blue.

—

Cho had told Tracy during one of their telephone conversations that Rivas was a good pick for the preliminary hearing officer. He described her as organized, thorough, and conscientious, but not sympathetic. She certainly seemed to be all business as she sat and looked out over the gallery, wasting no time getting under way.

"Let's go ahead and get started. This hearing will come to order." She turned to Trejo and Battles and introduced herself. "By order of Commanding Officer Peter Lopresti, I have been appointed the preliminary hearing officer under Article 32 of the Uniform Code of Military Justice. We are here in court to inquire into the truth of allegations set forth on the charge sheet, to examine those charges, and to secure information that will be helpful in determining the disposition of this case. Copies of the charge sheet and convening order have been furnished to the accused and his counsel by government counsel. Have you reviewed them?"

"Yes," Trejo said, voice so soft Rivas did not hear him. She looked up from her script—Cho had told Tracy the military was as big on scripts as it was on acronyms.

Trejo cleared his throat. "Yes, ma'am."

"Petty Officer Trejo, if at any time you do not understand what I am telling you, let me or your counsel know and I will explain it until you and I are both satisfied that you understand."

Rivas advised Trejo of the charges and said she would be making a recommendation to the commanding officer based on the evidence introduced at the hearing. "You do not have to make any statement regarding the offenses of which you are accused. You have the right to remain silent. You may, however, make a statement and present evidence in defense and mitigation so long as it is relevant to the limited scope and purpose of this hearing. If you do make a statement, whatever you say will be considered and weighed as evidence just like the testimony of any other witnesses. Further, any statement you do make may be used as evidence against you in a trial by court-martial. Do you understand my instructions?"

"Yes, ma'am," Trejo said.

Rivas continued, "I will now read the charges against you."

Battles slid back her chair, stood, and interjected, "We'll waive the reading, Your Honor."

Rivas nodded. "All right, thank you, Counsel." Rivas looked to Cho. "It is my understanding that the government intends to call three witnesses at this preliminary hearing: Seattle Police Department Traffic Collision Investigator Joe Jensen, Seattle Police Detective Tracy Crosswhite, and Archibald Issa, owner of a convenience store in Renton, Washington."

Cho stood, looking like he might bow. "That is correct, Your Honor."

"All right." Rivas looked out at the gallery. "Ladies and gentlemen, there may be testimony that is difficult for some, or all, of you to hear, or with which you don't agree. While I am certainly sympathetic to your emotions, I expect all parties to respect that this is a court of law. If you fail to do that, I have the power to close this proceeding. I sincerely hope that won't be necessary."

Rivas set down her script and addressed counsel. "Are there any other preliminary matters we need to take up before we begin the substantive part of the hearing? Defense?"

Battles and Cho stood. Speaking in turn, they responded, "No, Your Honor."

Rivas took a moment. Then she said, "Then the government may call its first witness."

CHAPTER 20

Battles listened as Brian Cho dispensed with the preliminaries quickly and efficiently, in part because Joe Jensen, his first witness, made it easy. Having testified in court on numerous prior occasions, Jensen was at ease with the process. The relaxed evidentiary procedure had also convinced Battles to object sparingly, knowing Judge Rivas would be inclined to allow the testimony and that objecting would largely be futile.

Battles had met and interviewed Jensen, so she knew what was to come. Jensen testified in a deliberate but down-to-earth tone that engendered confidence and honesty. His deep voice, graying red hair, and two-piece suit gave him an air of authority. It was like Cho had put a Boy Scout troop leader on the stand.

Cho quickly went through Jensen's current position with TCI, the fact that Jensen had been on call the evening of the hit and run, and the time he had arrived at the scene. Cho nodded to Clark, who fiddled with the keyboard of her laptop, and a grainy black-and-white photograph of the intersection, without the emergency personnel or the body, appeared on two flat-screen televisions. After establishing the picture was of the intersection and asking other foundational questions, Cho asked Jensen to point out the locations of the vehicles and the emergency responders upon his arrival, and anything else he'd seen.

It was a subtle way to get Jensen to share the location of the victim and the other things they'd found, like Miller's shoes and flip-flops.

Jensen said, "Near the body, a basketball lay in the gutter. Two Nike sandals were also in the street, and farther away, we located a pair of red Nike basketball shoes, laced together."

A woman in the gallery moaned as if stricken with pain. Battles did not turn her head or otherwise react. She had been expecting the testimony to evoke emotion from the gallery, and had given Trejo strict instructions not to respond to any comments or noises. However, she also hoped that the emotional nature of the testimony might get Trejo to rethink the latest plea deal. Trejo had not so much as flinched since sitting down. Battles wondered if he'd been medicated.

Jensen testified that the body was thirty-three feet from the intersection, which he said was significant because his working hypothesis was that the victim had been struck in the crosswalk, and that the car had been traveling south to north on Renton Avenue when it crossed the intersection at Henderson Street. "This appeared to be a wrap, where the victim wrapped around the hood, hit the windshield, and was projected forward."

"What did you do next?" Cho asked.

Jensen testified to his search for tire marks and not finding any.

"And in your experience, is the absence of tire marks significant?"

Battles wanted to object, but at an Article 32 hearing, only relevance and privilege objections applied. Cho was clearly asking Jensen to speculate. She knew Rivas would also give an expert investigator great leeway at the hearing.

"Normally, in a situation involving an impact, either with another car or, in this instance, a pedestrian, we will find tire marks indicating the driver of the vehicle tried to stop, or swerved. The absence of tire marks can be an indication that the impact was intended. It can be an indication that the driver didn't see the pedestrian—either because it was dark, the driver was distracted, had fallen asleep, or maybe was under the influence of drugs or alcohol."

Again, Trejo showed no emotion.

Cho established that the traffic lights at that intersection were working properly and that there was no surveillance videotape of the intersection from any of the businesses. In response to the next question, Jensen said, "Subsequently, we determined there was a traffic camera approximately one hundred yards west of the intersection controlled by the Washington State Department of Transportation, and we obtained a copy of that video."

"Before we get to that video, what else did you find of significance at the crime scene?"

Jensen discussed the car part found by the patrol officer. Cho signaled to Clark, who handed him the part, sealed in a see-through evidence bag. Cho handed the bag to Jensen, who testified that he took it to the Washington State Patrol Crime Lab, which provided him a serial part number and determined it had come off a Subaru. He also testified to taking it to a Subaru dealership and determining that the vehicle was black in color.

"It was from the front headlight and turn signal, on the passenger side of the vehicle."

Jensen testified that knowing the type of car, as well as its color, made it easier to go back through the video and locate the Subaru.

Cho set forth the groundwork for having the video played in the courtroom. Since Battles and Rivas had both seen the video, they knew it did not show the impact and would not be disturbing to the gallery. Cho asked Jensen to narrate the video. As he did, Battles heard more muted sobs behind her. Cho asked that the video be stopped when the dark vehicle appeared in the picture frame. He was milking this for all he could.

"The film is in black-and-white," Jensen said, "but we can see from this angle the light changes from the top light, red, to the bottom light, green, to allow traffic on South Henderson Street to proceed."

The car continued through the intersection without slowing, the impact with D'Andre Miller hidden by the angle of the camera.

Cho waited a beat. Then he said, "Were you able to determine the speed at which the car in the video was traveling?"

"Yes."

"Would you explain how you did that?"

"It's physics. The video is 30 frames a second. We measured the distance between the apartment building on the southeast corner and the closed restaurant on the northeast corner."

"How far was that?"

"That was 193 feet. It took 75 frames for the car to travel between those two points, or 2.25 seconds. If you divide the feet by the seconds, you determine that the car was traveling 77 feet per second. We know there are 5,280 feet in a mile, and 3,600 seconds in an hour. If you divide the first number by the second number, you get the conversion factor of 1.466 feet per second equaling one mile per hour. To convert 77 feet per second to miles per hour, we divided 77 feet per second by the conversion factor 1.466 and determined the car in that video was traveling at just over 52 miles per hour."

Cho took his time asking the next question. "Detective, what's the speed limit on Renton Avenue South at that intersection?"

"It's 30 miles per hour," Jensen said.

Cho let that thought linger. Trejo continued to stare at the wall.

Jensen testified about the patrol officers' discovery of the car in the backyard and his ability to confirm the car using the piece of the headlight cover found in the road.

"Did you impound the vehicle?" Cho asked.

"We did, and I sought a search warrant to search the interior."

Jensen spent time going through the search of the vehicle, the blood located on the driver's cloth seat belonging to Trejo, Trejo's fingerprints, and the DNA evidence. Cho asked that TCI's report be admitted into evidence, then discussed with Jensen the fact that the vehicle had been wiped down with an antiseptic wipe.

"What deductions, if any, did you make from that information?"

"In my opinion, the only reason someone would wipe clean the air bag and try to clean up the blood would be if they were trying to wipe away DNA evidence that they'd been driving the car when the air bag deployed."

"Did you find anything else within the car?"

"Yes," Jensen said. "We found a receipt in the backseat dated the night of the accident. It was for the purchase of two bottles of the energy drink Red Bull from a convenience store in Renton."

Cho established the date and the time of purchase and went through the steps to authenticate the receipt, sealed in an evidence bag, and introduced it into evidence.

"We ran the license plate and registration, and we were advised that the car had been reported as stolen by the owner the morning after the accident."

"And in your experience was that significant?"

Jensen grimaced and looked off before readdressing Cho. "It makes the hairs on the back of your neck stand up a bit—just the coincidence of it."

"And who was the registered owner of the vehicle?"

Jensen looked at Battles's side of the courtroom. "Laszlo Trejo."

CHAPTER 21

Del had received a call on his cell phone early that morning from Mike Melton, who said the Technical and Electronic Support Unit had successfully secured Allie's e-mails and text messages from her computer and her phone. Because the request for the information had been signed in under Faz's name, Del called him at home and asked if he'd take a drive with him to the Washington State Crime Lab.

Del picked him up.

"You spoke to Maggie?" Faz asked from the passenger seat of Del's Impala.

"I did."

"Is she still doing better?"

"Day by day. She made hamburgers and milk shakes for the boys, which thrilled them, and me. She's still not eating much, but it's better."

"Is she seeing the counselor?"

"Twice a week now."

"And you told her we got the e-mails and text messages off of Allie's phone?"

"She knows. She asked to see them when I'm through."

"She has a right," Faz said, nodding.

"Yeah, she does," Del said. "I just hope she can take it. I'm not sure I can."

A minute passed. KJR Sports Radio filled the silence. Faz said, "Have you seen that prosecutor again?"

Del looked across the car. "Celia McDaniel?"

"Yeah. The good-looking black lady."

Del smiled. "I just bought her a drink after work to make up for being rude."

"You didn't take her to dinner?"

Del shrugged. "Dinner and a drink."

"Sounds like a date."

"What date?" Del said, dismissing it. "I offered to buy her a drink. She suggested dinner because she doesn't like to drink on an empty stomach."

"So call her again. Make this one a date. See what she says."

"Who are you, Dear Abby?"

"I'm just saying it would be nice if every once in a while you came over to the house with someone Vera can talk to," Faz said.

Del sat back. After a few seconds, he asked, "You think she'd say yes?"

"Why wouldn't she?"

"I don't know. It's been a while, you know."

"What, since your divorce?"

"Since I've been on a date."

Faz waved it off. "Don't sweat it. You're like this car. You have some miles on the tires, but you take care of the exterior. You're still in good shape."

"I've lost ten pounds the past two weeks."

Faz moaned. "Don't tell me that. And don't tell Vera that. You lose weight and Vera's gonna make me lose weight. Why are you losing weight? You sick?"

"No, just trying to be healthy. Healthier."

Faz smiled. "You son of a bitch. You like this woman, don't you? That's why you're losing the weight."

"What, a guy can't lose weight for no reason?"

"Not when he's Italian, he can't. To us Italians, eating is like breathing. So unless you got a good reason, like a woman . . ."

"So, you think she'd say yes?"

"She said yes before, didn't she?"

"That was different."

"Why? You asked her for a drink and she upped the ante to dinner. Me, I don't see that as different. I see that as a woman saying yes."

"Maybe I'll call."

"Call her now."

"I ain't calling her with you in the car."

"So call after we get done meeting Melton."

"Maybe I will."

"Don't wait. Just get back and do it, first thing."

"I said I'd call."

"How are you fixed for condoms?"

Del faked a backhand. "I swear to God."

—

Mike Melton, director of the Washington State Patrol Crime Lab, was as much a dinosaur as Del and Faz. He'd worked at the lab for more than twenty years. Melton told Del he'd accepted the position of director for much the same reason he'd coached each of his six daughters in sports. "If anyone is going to screw them up, I'd rather it be me."

He was being modest. Three of his daughters had obtained athletic scholarships. The crime lab had also flourished under his leadership. Nearly as big as Faz and Del, Melton looked like a lumberjack more than a scientist. The detectives called him "Grizzly Adams" because of his close resemblance to the television actor on that show. He had wild brown hair and an equally thick beard, which was becoming more peppered with gray each year.

Melton kept an office on the first floor of the concrete building on Airport Way. While others in the building framed and hung their various diplomas, Melton displayed trinkets from past cases, like ball-peen hammers and baseball bats.

Del came to an abrupt stop upon entering Melton's office. The scientist had trimmed his beard and his hair, both of which now bordered on civilized. "Whoa," Del said. "You're really taking this director position seriously."

"You know me better. I'd never do this for a job. I'm marrying off daughter number four this weekend, and my wife said I needed to be presentable for the new in-laws."

"Bring them in here," Del said. "You're sure to scare them away."

"I bring in every one of my son-in-laws."

Del looked around the office. "Love what you've done with the place since your promotion."

"They keep threatening to move me. I told them to put my ashes on top of my computer and shut the door when I'm gone." Melton looked at Del. "You look like you've lost weight."

"Yeah, I've lost a few pounds."

"You look the same," Melton said to Faz.

Faz shook his head in disgust. "See what you've started," he said to Del.

"Very sorry about your niece," Melton said.

"Thanks. And thanks for expediting this."

Melton handed Del a USB drive. "The documents go back two weeks from the date you provided on the subpoena to the phone company. We pulled all the e-mails and text messages."

"What if she deleted a text or an e-mail?" Del asked.

"TESU pulled the current ones first and copied them over, then restored her backup. There weren't a lot, but there were some. You got them all."

"Thanks, Mike," Del said.

"Crappy reason to have to do it," Melton said.

CHAPTER 22

Leah Battles had been itching to cross-examine Joe Jensen. She wanted to establish not what he knew, but what he didn't know. She wanted to establish that he didn't know whether D'Andre Miller had crossed at the crosswalk, or whether Miller had been paying attention when he'd stepped from the curb or whether he had been distracted by the basketball. According to Terry O'Neil, who opened the rec center, Miller had had quite a night, the first time he'd been allowed to play. Maybe in his excitement he'd stepped off the curb without looking. Maybe he'd been listening to music on his headphones, also found in the street. It had been dark out and the clothing he'd worn had been dark. There were a number of points she could have scored on cross-examination, but it wouldn't prevent a judge from finding probable cause, and it would only educate Cho as to where she would attack his witnesses and allow him to better prepare for the court-martial. As hard as it was to remain silent, she knew that sometimes the best thing to say was nothing at all.

"No questions," she said, and Rivas dismissed Jensen and called for a short break.

Tracy Crosswhite made her way to the witness stand after the break. This morning she dressed like a lawyer, wearing a blue suit, but she still had the unmistakable demeanor of a cop. She did not look the least bit intimidated. Battles had done some research on Crosswhite in preparation for the hearing and found that the two women had a few things in common. Battles had also grown up in a small town, though on the East Coast. Her parents didn't have much money—not the kind that can make a difference in a kid's life. So whatever Battles was to achieve, she was going to have to earn. Chess had provided her with scholarship money and that same swagger she now detected in Crosswhite. Battles surmised that it came from the single-action shooting competitions at which Crosswhite apparently excelled. Battles knew you didn't get that self-assurance by just getting up every day and driving into an office. It came from competition, from putting yourself at risk of losing, then winning anyway.

After swearing Crosswhite in, Cho made short work of establishing her credentials, background, and her presence at the hit and run.

"So your initial impression was the same as Detective Jensen's?" Cho asked. He glanced at Battles, tweaking her for not moving to exclude Crosswhite from the courtroom during Jensen's testimony, and perhaps pimping her to object. She ignored him.

"It appeared to have been a hit and run," Crosswhite said.

Crosswhite then testified about the meeting the following morning at Police Headquarters with Detective Jensen at which he'd advised them of the Department of Transportation video of the Subaru and how they'd been able to get the information out to the officers on morning roll call.

Cho moved forward quickly.

"Can you tell us what you did next?"

"I was in the office later in the day and received a call from Detective Jensen. He said that a woman had reported a car in her backyard that fit the description of the car we were looking for."

"Can you tell us about your trip to that site?"

Crosswhite did.

Cho went through the car part matching the damage to the car, and how Jensen had linked it to Trejo, who had reported the car stolen that morning. Then he asked, "Did you have any initial reaction to that news?"

"Well, given what had transpired, I wondered if the report that the car had been stolen was legitimate. It seemed too convenient. I thought it was worth exploring further."

Battles made a note to attack Crosswhite on cross-examination at the court-martial and to insinuate that her and Jensen's investigation had been colored by the fact that both believed Trejo had lied before ever speaking with him.

Cho methodically went through the meeting between Trejo and Crosswhite and her partner, Kinsington Rowe. "What did he tell you happened to his car?"

"He reconfirmed that his car had been stolen and said he had reported it to the Bremerton Police Department."

"Anything else of significance that you noted during that conversation?"

"Mr. Trejo was drinking from a can of Red Bull, an energy drink. He also had a cut on his forehead, which he'd bandaged."

Crosswhite testified as to what Trejo had told her and Kins about how he had hurt himself on the corner of a kitchen cabinet. She said that, later, when confronted with the evidence of blood inside the car, Trejo said he'd thought he'd stopped the bleeding, but that he'd gotten blood on the seat and tried to clean it.

Which would be logical, Battles noted for cross-examination. She also noted that head wounds bleed a lot. She was practically sitting on her hands to avoid objecting.

Crosswhite was clearly a seasoned witness, testifying to questions from Cho about TCI finding a receipt from a convenience store in

Renton for the purchase of two energy drinks within a half hour of the accident. It was all foundational, laying the groundwork to introduce the evidence most damaging to Trejo: the convenience store security tape.

As Cho spoke, Battles noticed Lindsay Clark looking through the box of evidence on the courtroom floor and searching counsel's table.

"Your Honor—" Cho paused when he noticed Clark gesturing to him. "Excuse me, Your Honor, if I may have a moment to confer with co-counsel." Cho walked to Clark and turned his head to engage in a whispered conversation. He looked perplexed then began digging through the evidence box. A moment later he approached the court reporter, Bob Grassilli, who Battles knew well. Cho said something inaudible. Grassilli began to look around his desk.

Cho said, "Your Honor, I wonder if we may have a brief recess to secure a piece of evidence."

Rivas looked at the clock on the wall. "This hearing will be in recess. How long do you need?"

Cho said, "Just a few minutes, Your Honor."

The murmur in the crowd increased as the court reporter quickly left the room followed by Cho and Clark. Battles stood to stretch her legs and turned to Trejo, but her client remained seated, facing forward. She was about to talk to him when she noticed Detective Crosswhite looking from her chair to the gallery, to where Joe Jensen sat. Crosswhite gave him a curious shrug.

CHAPTER 23

After picking up Allie's computer and phone records, Del dropped off Faz at the office but didn't stay. He knew he couldn't get anything done with the information in his briefcase. He drove home.

Following his divorce, Del had rented a home on Capitol Hill from a friend who'd been relocated to Portland for her job but intended to move back to Seattle after she retired. At least that's what she'd said. The neighboring homes had all been remodeled, some more than once, but little had been done to the 1930s Craftsman, which meant it had a lot of charm and needed a lot of upkeep. In exchange for reduced rent, Del took care of the property, fixing what broke and performing needed maintenance. He even tended to the yard, though it wasn't much. He could mow the front and back lawn in under a half hour.

A reduced rent was the only way Del could afford a home in what was one of Seattle's more desired neighborhoods. Atop a steep hill just east of downtown, the home had sweeping western views across the I-5 freeway to Seattle's skyscrapers, Elliott Bay, and across that body of water to Seattle's islands and the distant Olympic Mountains.

Del parked the Impala on the dirt-and-gravel drive he'd made along the side of the house; he wasn't about to park his baby in the street. As soon as Del reached the top step, his Shih Tzu, Santino, leapt onto the back of the couch, as he did each night when Del got home from work. "You're nothing if not consistent," Del said, looking through the window. "But you can't tell time for shit."

Santino's body wagged furiously as he alternately bolted onto the top of the couch, standing on his hind legs to tap at the window, and ran to the front door. Del had bought Santino, or "Sonny," for his wife, thinking a dog would keep her company during the nights Del was on call, but in the end, she liked the dog almost as much as she liked Del. Sonny knew it too, which was why he preferred Del. Shih Tzus were apparently an extremely smart breed.

"Okay, okay," Del said, opening the door. Sonny jumped and spun on his hind legs like a top. Brown and white, his hair was short and curly, unless Del gave him a bath. Then he looked like an exploded cotton ball. Del had named him after the high-strung brother played by James Caan in the *Godfather* movies—the greatest movies ever made.

Del picked up Sonny from the ground, scratching him under the chin and letting him lick his face. "I've barely been gone an hour. I hope you didn't drop any bombs in here."

Santino didn't always make it out the dog door Del had installed at the back of the house, especially on days like today, when it rained. Del did a quick survey of the kitchen linoleum and determined the coast was clear. "Good boy." He grabbed a dog treat from a box on a shelf in the kitchen and put Sonny down. "You ready?" Del pointed his finger at Sonny, like a gun. "Bam!"

Sonny dropped onto his back, paws in the air as if he'd been shot. "Up," Del said. Sonny sprang to his feet and took the dog treat from Del's hand. "Good boy."

As Sonny crunched on his treat, Del considered his phone. He'd called Celia McDaniel the night before but got her voice mail. She hadn't called him back. "No sense sitting around like an eighteen-year-old virgin," he said to Sonny.

He stepped into the den at the back of the house—his man cave. It had a television—an old-fashioned picture tube—but Del rarely turned it on. An assortment of fiction and nonfiction books filled the floor-to-ceiling bookshelves, including Del's not inconsequential collection of Civil War books. He'd read the biographies of the central players in the conflict, Robert E. Lee, Stonewall Jackson, Ulysses S. Grant, and Joshua Chamberlain. He'd also collected a few artifacts and some tourist trinkets from Gettysburg and Antietam, as well as the other battlefields he'd visited. On the wall above the couch hung a framed map of the courthouse at the Battle of Appomattox, where Lee fought his last battle on April 9, 1865, before he surrendered, ending the war.

Del sat on the leather couch facing a bay window with a million-dollar view of the city, powered up his laptop, and inserted the USB drive Melton had provided. He clicked on the file for Allie's e-mails and pulled them up. Seeing Allie's name, however, pierced him like a sharp knife, and he had to remove his hands from the keyboard and sit back, fighting his emotions. He took several deep breaths, composed himself, and started through the e-mails. There weren't many; kids today e-mailed about as often as people sent handwritten letters. They texted. They Snapchatted. They did something his nephews called "My Story."

Most of Allie's e-mails were school and work related. He skimmed them, paying more attention as he neared the date of her death. He paused on an e-mail dated two weeks before Allie died.

> Hey, how come U didn't text me back? I heard U were
> back from the prison. Did U escape? HaHa. How come
> U haven't called? I'm using e-mail in case your mom
> took your phone.

Del looked at the message header. The e-mail was from someone called J-Man, e-mail address: jman@cdrpm.net.

The next day, after Allie had still not responded, J-Man sent a second e-mail.

> U avoiding me? Been thinking about u non-stop since
> u left!!! U just disappeared. WTF? Really want to see u.

Again, Allie did not respond.

Del continued through her e-mails, finding several more from the same address. After J-Man's fifth e-mail, Allie finally wrote back.

> Sorry. Mom has my phone so didn't see any texts.
> Crazy busy. Um . . . I don't think we should see each
> other. It would be too hard. Not going to school this
> semester. Working. Ugh! Finishing up this summer at
> home and going to Gonzaga. U take care. Al

J-Man immediately responded, ignoring the statement that they not see each another. He clearly did not get the hint.

> Glad U're still alive! Bummer about U're phone. Ran
> into TC. Said you were kickin it, working. No partying?
> Man, I couldn't do it. Me? Just chillin and hangin with
> TC. So U saving up for college or a car? A car I hope!
> Lasts Longer! HaHa.

Allie responded.

> No Car. ☹. HaHa. Just keeping busy. Getting my mind
> right. Yeah, TC said she saw U. Said you were in a 'ship.
> TBH I'm happy for you.

J-Man again responded at 11:54 p.m.

> No 'ship, man, except to my music. That's B-S!

Del deduced "'ship" to be short for "relationship," and TBH to
mean "to be honest." He was betting J-Man's "'ship" with TC lasted as
long as Allie's stint in rehab.

J-Man continued, We were all just hanging. SRSLY!

Allie's response was apologetic, and the tone made Del sick to his
stomach. He suspected J-Man had an ulterior motive.

> Sorry. Didn't mean A/T. Didn't expect U to wait around
> for me.

J-Man wrote: We should get together. When u around? U got
your phone back?

> Tomorrow?

Allie responded immediately. NAGI. Family keeping close watch
on me. And my uncle is a cop with a gun. HaHa.

J-Man persisted. Del had a sense J-Man was an addict looking for
a score more than a relationship. He fought to keep his anger in check,
but a part of him wanted to find J-Man and remove his fingernails one
by one.

No biggie. I've missed U. Nobody gets me like U, Al.
Sad since U left. Lonely. (:

This time Allie did not respond and Del could almost hear the debate raging in her head.

J-Man e-mailed again to ask, WYCM?

Don't do it, Del thought. *Don't you call him.*

Again, it took some time before Allie replied. Her response broke Del's heart.

Tomorrow. WCY.

CHAPTER 24

After several long minutes, the door to the left of the bench opened, and Tracy watched Cho, Clark, and Grassilli return. Unlike that morning, when Cho had looked relaxed and confident, he now looked concerned—more than concerned. He looked upset. Clark looked like a deer in headlights with her eyes fixed on an imagined oncoming car. Grassilli, the court reporter, also looked unsettled. Upon getting to his courtroom desk, Grassilli again searched it and the surrounding area. Cho went through the box of evidence and searched counsel's table.

"Counselor, are you ready to move forward?" Rivas asked.

"Your Honor, we seem to have run into a bit of a snag. We're having difficulty locating a piece of evidence."

"What piece of evidence?" Rivas asked.

Cho said, "The video from the convenience store."

"What do you mean? It's missing?" Rivas asked. Her eyes shifted between Cho and Grassilli, who kept custody of all evidence to be presented at an Article 32 hearing.

Tracy looked to the gallery. Shaniqua Miller dropped her gaze, then her head. Her mother, seated beside her, closed her eyes, and looked to be breathing deliberately. This was their worst nightmare.

"I mean we had it, but . . ." Cho looked and sounded out of breath. "It appears to be missing."

"When did you last see it?"

"We checked out the materials from NCIS lockup yesterday afternoon in preparation for this hearing."

"And then what?"

"We checked everything back in."

"And that was the last time you saw it?"

Cho seemed to give this a moment of thought. "No," he said, as if remembering something. "It isn't." He turned and looked at Battles. "The last time I saw the tape was last night before going home. It was on defense counsel's desk."

The members of the gallery, initially stunned or uncertain, began to understand the ramifications of what was transpiring, and to verbally protest. For a group predisposed to believe the Navy would protect one of its own, the lost tape was no accident; it was a deliberate attempt to subvert justice, and Cho had placed Battles at the center of their ire. Several stood, shouting and pointing at her. The MAs stepped between the spectators and the railing. Two brig chasers quickly moved to remove Trejo from the courtroom.

"I'll speak to counsel in back," Rivas said over the growing discontent.

———

Del looked through the remainder of Allie's e-mails, but found little of interest. He knew that once Allie got her phone back, like most teenagers, the majority of her communication would be either text messages or through her Instagram account. Sonny trotted into the room, jumped onto the couch, and looked up at Del as if to ask, "What are you doing?"

Del moved the newspaper and Sonny dropped into a ball at Del's side, his usual resting place. "Eating and sleeping," Del said. "Not a bad life."

He pulled up Allie's Instagram account. As he proceeded through it, he felt like he was trying to decipher a foreign language laced with photographs, mostly selfies of Allie, and symbols like smiley faces. He could see her transformation from the sweet girl he'd known to the junkie. In some of the pictures she was so thin she was almost unrecognizable, her nose and chin pointed and pronounced, sunken cheeks, and hooded eyes. Some messages were nonsensical, or simply acronyms that Del could not decipher. *GLHF. IANAL. FWB.*

He scrolled quickly through them, looking for the date after Allie's e-mail conversation with J-Man. He found one dated the following morning. J-Man had immediately contacted her. "Relentless little prick," Del said.

J-Man: KKUT.

Del had no idea what that meant, but it was accompanied by a selfie of J-Man. He had shoulder-length, greasy brown hair, blue eyes, and a wispy goatee. He wasn't what Del had expected. He'd expected a slimy punk, someone at whom he could direct his anger. J-Man looked like a kid. Del remembered Allie's counselor's comment that so many addicted were "good kids, from good homes."

Allie: I'm here

Allie included a picture of herself. She smiled, though it looked tentative, even a bit scared.

J-Man: There U R. Wow. Too Long!

Allie: IKR?

J-Man: So we getting together 2day?

Allie: Have 2 work

J-Man: Where? I'll stop by

Allie: Can't. No friends allowed. Boss is a Nazi.

J-Man: What time u get off?

Allie: 7

J-Man: Drive u home?

"This guy don't freaking quit," Del said, causing Sonny to look up at him from the couch.

Allie: Fam home

This time J-Man sent a picture of himself with his eyebrows raised, some silent communication—maybe looking to get high, or to have sex. Forget the fingernails. Del wanted to snap every one of this guy's fingers.

Allie: NAGI

When J-Man didn't respond, Allie asked: RUOK?

J-Man: Hard. I really loved U . . . Still do.

"Are you freaking kidding me?" Del said. Based on the content of the subsequent text messages, some time passed with no response from Allie. Del silently prayed she hadn't, that somehow this had all been a big mistake. He looked up at the far wall, at the crucifix that had once adorned the bedroom wall in his mother's house in Wisconsin, and he made the sign of the cross, not for him but for his niece.

J-Man: U Still there?

Allie: Got to go

Later that night, after Allie got off work, the messages from J-Man started again. Del could feel his anger starting to boil. Several times he had to stop reading and set the computer aside. He went to the windows, watching the cars on the freeway. He knew where J-Man's conversation was headed and he wondered if the outcome could have been different—if J-Man had stopped texting Allie, if Allie had not responded, if Del had smashed her phone or if he'd found J-Man and smashed him.

He went back to the computer.

J-Man: U home?

Allie: Yes. WRU doing?

J-Man: Kickin it. WTPA?

Del deciphered this to mean, *Where's the party at?* J-Man sent a picture. He was clearly high.

Allie: R U hi?

J-Man: SMH Maybe. LOL

Allie: Thought u quit?

J-Man: New stuff SRS shit

Del's interest was piqued. J-Man included another photo. He looked like a clown, goofy smile, eyes half closed. A young girl, Allie's age, also high, leaned into the picture beside him.

Allie: U're with TC?

J-Man: U Should come

Allie: Did U 2 hook up?

J-Man: HaHa

Allie: Thought you said you didn't?

J-Man: It's all good. We just hanging. Come by.

Again, minutes passed before Allie answered.

Allie: Can't

J-Man: IU2U

Del felt sick to his stomach. He deciphered the code to be *It's up to you.* He had to force himself to sift through the continuing dialogue, which seemed nearly nonstop over the next three days and nights. J-Man had been relentless, telling Allie he loved her and touting the quality of the heroin, wearing her down. Allie had continued to resist, but maybe only because she didn't have access to a car. Eventually, she broke, and J-Man's motives became clear.

Del read the conversation he'd dreaded the most, the night before Maggie found Allie.

J-Man: Pic U up from work?

Allie: K

J-Man: Lookin' 4-word to seeing U!!!

Allie: We can go 2 my house.

J-Man: What about Fam?

Allie: Out late

J-Man: Sweet. Maybe we can put all that money you're making to good use

And there it was.

It wasn't love. And it wasn't friendship. It was what the counselor had told Del and Maggie. J-Man was no different from all the other junkie losers out there. It was money. It was about buying the next hit, and he didn't care where the money came from, or how he got it, so long as he got it.

Allie's final text was like a knife to the heart. Between her addiction, the draw of the heroin, and J-Man's relentless badgering, she'd never stood a chance.

Allie: Maybe

Del shut his eyes, tears wetting his cheeks. He let out a held breath and it shuddered in his chest. His cell phone rang. Initially he couldn't find it. He reached below Sonny to retrieve it.

"Yeah," he said, thinking it was Faz.

"Yeah? Is that how you answer your phone?" The voice was light.

Del pulled back his phone to check caller ID, which said "Unknown." He cleared his throat. "Celia?"

"Obviously not who you were expecting?"

"I thought it was my partner." Del checked his watch. He had a couple hours before he needed to get back to the office. "We got the e-mail and text messages off Allie's phone and computer, and I decided to look at them here at home."

Celia was momentarily quiet. Then she said, "Are you all right?"

"Yeah," he said. "I'm all right."

"I'm just returning your call from last night," she said. "Why don't I call back later?"

"No, it's fine," Del said. "I was just wondering if . . . maybe you'd like to get a bite to eat again."

"I'm in trial, and . . . It doesn't sound like you'll have any nights free until the end of your night shift this month."

Del noted what she hadn't said. She hadn't said she wanted to go to dinner. "Sure," he said. "Yeah. I guess that would make it tough."

"I give my closing argument tomorrow morning," she said.

"Good luck," he said. "You'll do great. The jurors love you."

"You sure you're okay, Del?"

Del wasn't sure. "Yeah. Yeah, no problem. I'll give you a call, maybe when both our schedules calm down."

———

As Battles followed Cho and Clark out of the courtroom, she heard the crowd behind her continuing to protest. At the end of the hall they entered a cramped office Rivas had commandeered for the hearing. It contained an austere metal desk and metal shelving with just a few books. Rivas moved behind the desk. Battles stood on the far left next to the shelving. Clark and Cho stood to her right. The court reporter, Bob Grassilli, stood closest to the door.

"Let's go through this again," Rivas said to Cho, trying to bring calm to a tense situation. "You checked out the videotape from lockup when?"

"Yesterday afternoon." Still seething, Cho looked as though ants were crawling over his skin. "We were preparing for this hearing."

"And you're sure you signed it back in?"

"Yes. We signed in the evidence box, not just the videotape. The sign-in log will confirm it."

Cho looked to Grassilli for confirmation. He had a copy of the sheet and reviewed it. "That's correct, Your Honor. They signed the box back in at five thirty-two p.m."

"Was the tape in the box at that time?"

"I assume so," Cho said.

"You don't know for certain."

"It was in the box when we went over the evidence so, yeah, I'd say it was in the box when we returned it."

Rivas turned to Battles. "You had the tape last night?"

"I had the same box of evidence," she said, trying not to look or sound guilty. "I signed it out and asked that it be brought to my office just before Bob went home, but I don't specifically recall seeing the tape."

"Meaning what?" Rivas asked.

"Meaning I didn't look at the tape last night. There was no reason to view it again and, besides, I didn't have a television to play it."

Rivas turned again to Cho. "I thought you said the last time you saw the tape was last night?"

"The box," Cho said, his gaze intense. "I didn't see the tape specifically, but I saw the box on her desk last night. Where else—"

Rivas cut him off, looking again to Battles. "Did you return the box?"

Battles nodded. "I brought it back and left it on Bob's chair. He'd already left for the day."

"So it wasn't logged back in?"

Grassilli shook his head.

"But I did return it," Battles said to Grassilli. "You had the box this morning, right?"

"I had the box," Grassilli said.

"But not the tape," Cho said.

"I returned the box," Battles said. "We don't know about the tape, whether it was in the box."

"And the tape isn't in your office?" Rivas asked Grassilli.

"Not that I can find."

"And it wasn't in the box this morning?"

"No," Clark and Cho each said.

"And it isn't in an office somewhere, got misplaced?" Rivas asked.

"Not that I'm aware of," Cho said.

"I didn't take it out," Battles said.

"Check," Rivas said.

They agreed they would.

"Is there a copy?" Rivas asked Grassilli.

Grassilli sighed. "It was a VCR tape, Judge. We're not equipped to copy that here and it was in use by counsel preparing for this hearing, which, as you know, was being expedited. We were going to send it out after the hearing."

"There's no copy?" Rivas looked to Cho, her voice rising in both pitch and volume.

"No," Cho said. He rushed to confirm what Grassilli had said. "The equipment used at the convenience store was outdated. We couldn't copy it here and it was in use . . . I intended to send it out to be copied after the hearing."

"What about the Seattle Police Department? Did they keep a copy?" Rivas asked.

"I doubt it," Cho said. "We took jurisdiction almost immediately."

"Well, I think you better find out."

"I will," Cho said, not sounding optimistic.

Rivas looked at Grassilli before making a pyramid with her hands and putting her fingers to her lips, perhaps thinking, but not saying, what everyone in the room was also thinking. This was a significant problem for the prosecution to overcome, especially at a subsequent court-martial, which required a higher degree of proof of guilt.

"Your Honor," Cho said, "I can prove the existence of the tape through Archibald Issa, the owner of the convenience store, and both he and Detective Crosswhite could testify to having seen Laszlo Trejo on the tape."

Rivas shook her head and lowered her hands. "Without the video-tape, any further testimony by Detective Crosswhite related to that tape could not be effectively challenged by Mr. Trejo and his counsel. I won't allow it. And I can guarantee you that, at a court-martial, a judge would find that the lack of the video impedes Mr. Trejo's Sixth Amendment right to confront and cross-examine not only Detective Crosswhite but Mr. Issa, and anyone else you might put on the stand."

"We could call Mr. Issa to establish that he recalled Mr. Trejo being in his store," Clark said.

"Does he specifically? Does he independent of the tape? Or would that only be because he received a telephone call and subsequently viewed the videotape? That was—what, nearly three weeks ago now? Does he remember any other customer?" She shook her head, her voice becoming more emphatic. "Even if he recalled the defendant in his store, the best evidence is missing. You have the same problem. And given my understanding that the videotape will tie together all the other evidence—like the significance of the store receipt found in the car— you might get by this hearing, but you won't get by any subsequent court-martial where the rules of evidence and the burden of proof are strictly enforced."

Cho pointed his finger at Battles. "There is no dispute the prosecution logged the evidence back in yesterday afternoon and no dispute that she requested and had it in her possession after that. She just said she clearly had it last. That is not debatable."

Battles shook her head. "I said I don't recall viewing the videotape, and I resent the insinuation. I brought the box back to Bob's office."

"The log-in sheet doesn't confirm that," Cho said.

Rivas looked to Grassilli, who reluctantly shook his head. Battles could see that she had put him in a bad spot and she regretted having done so.

Cho faced Battles, Grassilli now between them like a promoter between two fighters at an upcoming fight press conference.

"I left the box on Bob's chair," Battles said. "Maybe the tape didn't get put back in the box."

Cho spoke through clenched teeth. "This is the slimiest thing—"

"Enough," Rivas said. Cho turned away, his head cocked at a defiant angle. It felt like someone had suddenly sucked all the air out of the room and no one could breathe. "Unfortunately, Lieutenant, the prosecution has an absolute duty to preserve evidence."

"And we did!" Cho snapped. "The log shows that we did. Since defense counsel had the evidence last, the presumption that the evidence has somehow been lost or destroyed rests with her, and all negative inferences should be construed against the defendant."

Rivas shook her head. "That's for another hearing," she said. "Regardless, you have the same problem; no court will court-martial a defendant based on the *alleged* improprieties of his attorney. Since Mr. Trejo was sitting in the brig at JBLM, he clearly had no involvement. As I said, you might get by here, at an Article 32 hearing, but the court-martial is another story altogether."

Rivas paused, perhaps thinking of the political ramifications that could unfold if the prosecution did not find the tape. She shook her head as if to shake the thought. "I'm going to give the prosecution twenty-four hours to come up with the tape or an explanation for its disappearance. I will keep the Article 32 hearing open until then. If the tape cannot be found, I will make my decision on the evidence I have before me. If you wish to bring a motion that the presumption of wrongdoing should shift to defense counsel, you can do so. In the interim, I'd get on the phone with Seattle PD. And, I would check all of your offices."

Cho and Clark followed Grassilli out of the room. Battles let them go before she started to leave. "Lieutenant Battles," Rivas said.

Battles stopped and turned back, already certain of what Rivas intended to say. The box of evidence was in her possession last, and the ramifications of the tape having gone missing would also rest with her.

"I would seriously consider new counsel for Mr. Trejo," Rivas said, "and perhaps for yourself."

Battles hurried into her office and shut the door. It didn't stay shut for long.

Brian Cho stormed in without knocking. "Is beating me so important that you would risk your career?"

Battles faced him. "Get over yourself. This isn't about you."

Cho took another step forward, the two now just inches apart. "You're damn right it isn't about me. It's about you. Big-time. We're going to bring that motion, and after I intend to drop an e-bomb in DC. It isn't going to just be Trejo who's looking at a court-martial."

An e-bomb was an ethics complaint filed with the JAG office at the Pentagon in Washington, DC. Such a threat was not levied lightly nor taken lightly. The JAG officers who did the investigations were referred to as "coneheads" because, while bright, they usually had little common sense and zero sense of humor.

"Bring it!" She stiffened. If Cho was looking to intimidate, he'd picked the wrong person. "I didn't take the Goddamn tape," she said. "And when you find it on your desk, or in Clark's bed, you can take your apology and shove it up your ass."

Cho looked like he was about to react. Battles hoped he did. She'd bust his nose and send him out the door, walking bent over for a week, before he laid a hand on her.

"Counsel." Rebecca Stanley stepped into the office. Cho quickly stepped back. "Is there a problem?"

"No, ma'am," Cho said.

"Then I think you should be spending your time searching for that videotape, don't you?"

Cho nodded. He looked like a teakettle about to spout as he stepped from the office into the hallway.

"Lieutenant?" Stanley said.

Cho turned back, his jaw undulating.

"Close the door, please," Stanley said.

Cho reached and pulled shut Battles's door, giving her a final glance.

After a beat, Stanley turned and addressed Battles. She spoke calmly. "You want to tell me what happened?"

Battles shook her head. "I don't know what happened."

"You had the box of evidence last?"

"I had the box brought to my office last night. Bob said it had the significant pieces of evidence and it seemed easier to just log out the entire box."

"He delivered it to your office?"

"Yes."

"And you returned it?"

"Last night—probably around eleven."

"But Bob wasn't there."

"No. I left the box on his chair. I've done it before."

"Maybe, but that isn't procedure, Leah. The court reporter takes physical custody and is responsible for all Article 32 evidence."

"I know."

"You put Bob in a bad position." Stanley exhaled. "And you don't know whether the tape was in the box?"

"I don't recall taking the tape out of the box, and I certainly did not view it last night."

"Did you see it?"

"Not last night."

"So you don't know."

"I can't say for certain I saw it, no."

Several seconds passed. In a solemn voice, Stanley said, "But you were the last person to have the evidence box."

Battles took a moment, thinking back to the prior night, to Cho pimping her in her office, and the evidence box sitting on her desk. She measured her response. She knew she'd have to measure all her responses from this point forward.

"I was the last person to have the evidence box," she said.

Stanley dropped her hands. "Then you better hope Cho finds that tape, Leah. You better hope this was all just a big misunderstanding, because Lopresti wants somebody's ass to run up the public flagpole, and if he can't have Trejo's . . ."

Stanley let the thought, and the alternative, linger unsaid, but both women knew whose ass Lopresti would hang from the flagpole and it wasn't Stanley's.

Del stepped into the elevator at Police Headquarters at the end of his shift tired and emotionally spent. After going through Allie's e-mails and text messages, he'd gone to work; he needed the diversion, and work had always provided it. Tonight, however, had been slow, leaving him time to think about Allie's text messages and what might have been had he destroyed her phone when she went to rehab.

He'd decided to wait before telling his sister about the contents of the e-mails and text messages. He would stop by her house and talk to the twins before work tomorrow and ask if they knew about J-Man, or at least whether they knew his real name.

He stepped from the elevator and started across the secured parking structure where the detectives kept their personal vehicles and the department kept its pool cars. Pigeons pranced and cooed in the concrete rafters. Spiked fencing had not deterred them, nor had the persistent drone of the cars on the adjacent I-5 freeway. Most of the detectives' personal cars were gone, but Del wouldn't have missed her if the lot had been full.

Celia McDaniel leaned against the trunk of his Impala looking like a catalogue model. She was dressed in blue jeans with knee-high black boots, a white silk shirt beneath a jean jacket, and a black-and-white scarf fashionably draping her neck.

Del stopped cold, confused to see her here, at this hour of the night. His tired mind tried to determine some reason she'd be present.

"Celia? What are you doing here?"

"I figured this was your car." She pushed away and admired the Impala. "You really are old-school, aren't you?"

On the car's trunk he noted a wicker picnic basket. "In some things, I guess."

"I like that," she said. "I'm old-school also." Her smile had a warmth and a genuineness to it Del had not experienced in years.

"You," he said, "do not come across as old-school."

"No?"

"You look like you're twenty-eight."

Her smile broadened. "One of the advantages of being black. We don't crack."

"Excuse me?" He had to stifle a laugh.

"Black don't crack; you've never heard that before?"

Del blew out a breath, unsure what to say.

"I'm forty-one," she said. "But my skin says I'm twenty-eight. No wrinkles. My mother and I used to get confused for sisters. It bugged the hell out of me until I realized I'd someday be in my forties."

"Ah," Del said, understanding. "My mother and I were never con-fused for sisters."

Celia laughed, lifted the basket, and approached. They stared at each another, like two high school kids.

"I don't have anything more on Allie's dealer—an e-mail address, but not a name."

"You'll get there." She lifted the picnic basket. "I figured you hadn't eaten."

"It's twelve thirty at night."

"I know. I thought you said you get off at twelve. What do you people do for half an hour? I figured you'd be running out of there like the place was on fire."

It dawned on Del that McDaniel's presence had nothing to do with Allie's case. Celia knew he'd had a hard day going through Allie's computer and phone records, and she'd gone to a lot of trouble just to make him feel better, to let him know that she cared. "Faz was waiting for his wife . . . Wait, what about your trial?"

"I'm no longer in trial. Shortly after getting off the phone with you, I received a phone call from the defense attorney accepting my last plea deal. We went back to court and put it on the record."

So she didn't have to work.

She lifted a blue-and-white-checkered dish towel covering the basket's contents. "Now, nothing special—some French bread, prosciutto, salami, cheeses, and an assortment of olives."

"Wow. It doesn't get any more special," Del said, not even glancing at the basket's contents.

"I figured Italian was a safe bet. We don't have anything to drink, though. I'm hoping you have a good Italian wine to go along with it?"

"I bet I could find something," he said.

CHAPTER 25

The following morning, Leah Battles thought the MA at the Charleston Gate took twice as long as necessary to consider her identification card, though she realized it could just be her paranoia in the aftermath of the Article 32 hearing. Word spread like a wildfire across a naval base, and no doubt everyone was talking about the missing videotape and speculating over what had happened to it. That was the reason Battles got up that morning to go to work, as scheduled. Her mother had once told her, during Battles's high school years, that her absence spoke volumes, and so did her presence. She intended to be present.

When she entered the front door of the DSO building, Darcy, the receptionist, and two people standing at her desk turned to Leah. They looked as if they'd been caught. Their conversation ceased, and the other two slowly turned and walked away. Battles nodded to Darcy and continued toward her office, waiting for Darcy's customary greeting. It never came.

She slipped into her office and shut her door, taking a moment to consider her surroundings. Her office décor was just the right mix of work and home, and it had always been a sanctuary, a place where she felt grounded. Today, however, it felt foreign, isolated, and claustrophobic. She wanted to turn and leave, but she knew she couldn't make it that easy on them. Instead, she turned on the overhead fluorescent lights, hoping their brightness would remove some of the impending gloom, and changed into her working blues.

Sitting at her desk, she hit her keyboard, received the customary prompt asking for her name and password, and typed in both. While the computer booted up, she finished changing into her blue work uniform and black boots. Then she unlocked her desk drawer where she kept her active files and pulled it open. The drawer was empty. She looked at her computer monitor. The system did not recognize her name or password.

She swore under her breath and typed in her name and password a second time, though the empty desk drawer made it clear she hadn't made a mistake. Again, the screen refused her access. She rocked back in her chair, processing what had happened. She'd never heard of a defense attorney having her files yanked so quickly. The attorney-client privilege mandated that an attorney's clients had to release the attorney. There was only one likely explanation. They'd locked her out and taken her files.

So much for being present.

A tentative knock on her door diverted her attention. "Come in," she said.

Darcy poked her head into the room with a tentative smile, the kind normally reserved for funerals. "What's up, ma'am?" she said softly.

Battles almost said, "Not me for promotion," but she wasn't about to act defeated. She returned the smile. "Sun and sky, Darcy. I'll let you know when they aren't."

Darcy stepped in and closed the door.

"How're you doing, ma'am?" Darcy asked. Enlisted personnel always used "ma'am" as a sign of respect when addressing female naval officers.

"I'm doing fine. Thanks for asking. What's the status of the rumor mill out there?"

Darcy stepped to the corner of Battles's desk. "Everyone is talking about what happened."

"So what's the verdict? Am I guilty?" The unwilling computer and empty desk drawer seemed to answer that question.

Darcy grimaced.

Battles managed another smile. "Don't worry about it, Darcy."

"I don't believe it, ma'am," Darcy said quickly. "I didn't believe it when I heard it and I still don't. I wanted you to know that."

"Thank you. I appreciate it."

"So, you'll still be coming in?"

"Until they tell me otherwise," she said, which they could do any minute now.

"Then you'll let me know if the sky is falling."

"Count on it."

Battles's desk phone rang.

"I'll let you get back to it then," Darcy said. She smiled as she pulled open the office door, but the smile had a sad quality to it, like she was looking at a death-row prisoner a final time before her execution.

Battles looked at the clock on her wall: 9:01. Darcy might very well be right.

—

With two nine-year-old boys in his sister's house, Del doubted there were many secrets, especially about who was dating whom. He was right. Mark and Stevie quickly pegged "J-Man" to be Jack Welch, a senior at Ballard High School, who they said had been sniffing around Allie for six months.

"He's a loser," Stevie said, dismissing Welch with a wave of his hand. "He's in a band."

"They suck," Mark said, eyes widening. "We saw him play once at a talent show at Allie's school. He was like . . ." Mark jumped off the couch, furiously strumming the imaginary strings of an air guitar and bobbing his head so hard Del thought it might snap.

"It was insanely awful," Stevie agreed. "The singer was so bad, you couldn't even understand him." He too went into a furious imitation, grunting and mumbling his words.

"When's the last time you saw him over here?" Del asked.

"Mom doesn't let him come over here." Stevie emphasized his words. "She hates him."

"He's a loser," Mark said again and slumped down onto the seat cushions.

Del suspected as much, but at least J-Man now had a name.

—

Battles sat across the desk from Rebecca Stanley, who kept an office just down the hall. Stanley had the look of a mother whose daughter had been invited to her first prom, but by a young man she didn't care for. Battles decided to take the same approach she'd taken when she'd been called in to the Dean of Students's office at her Catholic all-girls high school. She wasn't about to start defending herself until the charges and the supporting evidence were spelled out.

"Did you pull my files?" Battles asked.

"I did."

"All due respect, but the clients I have been defending need to be notified and—"

Stanley raised a hand. "They were, and they've each agreed to seek new counsel. I apologize, Leah, but these are unusual circumstances. I talked with the CO late last night."

"And?" Battles said.

"I told him it was not within your character to do what you have been accused of doing. I also want you to know that my opinion might not matter much."

Battles knew the loss of the tape would cause significant interdepartmental stress, and Stanley had a duty to run the department. "So Brian filed papers?" she asked.

"He dropped an e-bomb this morning, and I think we can expect that things will go nuclear. Cho is under considerable pressure, because of the nature of the crime, to court-martial Trejo. The loss of the tape . . . The CO said we can expect an investigation. I'm told that NCIS will be brought in to interview everyone."

Battles nodded, but did not speak.

"Look, an Article 32 is supposed to be just a stepping stone, but Lopresti built it up to be something much more for the public and the media. He was hoping it would force a resolution and mollify public outrage. Now it's blown up in his face, and he isn't happy about it."

"Trejo wouldn't plea," Battles said. "I explained everything to him, the charges and the likely ramification of those charges. I went over the evidence with him, showed him the videotape. I even told him that I couldn't beat the plea he was offered. He wouldn't take it."

"You spoke to his wife?"

Battles nodded. "She said he was home, but I believe she's standing by her husband."

"He told her to say he was home," Stanley said.

"I think so."

"He couldn't have somehow known that the tape would go missing, could he?" Stanley's eyes narrowed and her brow furrowed.

Battles sat back in her chair. "Nothing I said would have given him that impression."

"Well, we now have a massive headache and the public wants the Navy's head on a stake."

"And Lopresti needs a designated head, and I'm it. I get it." Battles had had difficult cases before, but she'd always had the safety net of knowing she could walk away after doing her job. This was different. This time, she was the person with much to lose. "But if it's all the same to you and the CO, I intend to keep my head."

"I hope you do," Stanley said. "Lopresti asked that I pull and review the security tape for the DSO night before last. I'm to report to him in about an hour and tell him what the tape reveals."

Battles knew the security camera was positioned over the front door to cover the interior lobby. She suspected Stanley had not elaborated on the tape's contents because it didn't help Battles.

"Can I see it?"

Stanley nodded. "I don't see why not."

It took Stanley a few minutes to load the security feed onto her computer. She pivoted the monitor forty-five degrees so they could both watch. The black-and-white camera captured anyone who entered and exited the building. The angle, however, meant the viewer was looking at the top of people's heads as they entered and exited the front door. If they entered the building wearing their baggy blueberries and cap, everyone looked similar.

"I asked for a copy of the tape from ten p.m. to six a.m. the following morning," Stanley said.

Neither woman intended to watch the full eight hours. Stanley hit "Fast Forward." At 10:31, Brian Cho came down the hall and stopped outside Battles's office. Cho knocked before entering, and closed the door.

"That's when Brian came down to find out if Trejo was going to plead," Battles said.

"When he saw the box of evidence?" Stanley asked.

"I still had it," Battles said.

At 10:37 p.m. Cho reemerged, pausing outside Battles's office door. He looked to be smiling. In his hands he held his hat, what the Navy referred to as his "cover." Then he shook his head, put on his cap, and exited the building.

"What was that?" Battles asked. "Was he smiling?"

"I don't know." Stanley glanced at her before returning her attention to the computer. She hit the "Fast Forward" button again.

At 10:49, Battles exited her office carrying the evidence box, the top affixed and in place. She carried the box away from the camera, toward the stairs leading up to Bob Grassilli's office on the second floor just across from the courtroom.

"That's when I took the evidence box back," she said.

"Unfortunately, there's an argument that the tape isn't in the box," Stanley said.

On the tape, Battles returned to her office. Several minutes later, she came out dressed in bike clothes and wearing her backpack as she strapped on her bike helmet.

"The backpack doesn't help either," Stanley said.

No one else entered or exited the building until 11:03 p.m., when the civilian janitor pushed in a rolling garbage can. Stanley hit "Fast Forward" and the janitor's movements looked a bit like a Charlie Chaplin movie.

"Can you slow it down?" Battles asked.

Stanley did.

The janitor walked behind the reception desk, then in and out of the ground-floor offices, emptying their garbage cans. After doing so, he departed the building, presumably to discard the garbage, which would be incinerated. Stanley again hit "Fast Forward," stopping the tape when the janitor returned carrying a vacuum and a bucket of cleaning supplies. He set the vacuum in the entry and took the cleaning supplies down the hall, to the bathrooms. Stanley advanced the tape, slowing it when the janitor returned, placed the cleaning supplies on the reception desk, and started vacuuming. When he'd finished, he exited the building, this time for good.

No one else entered or exited until office workers arrived the following morning—Cho had been one of the first at 7:15 a.m. He walked through reception and down the hall to the stairs leading up to his office on the second floor.

Battles arrived a half hour later.

The tape ended. Battles sat back. "Cho's office is on the second floor, close to the court reporter."

"Yes, but he left before you brought the evidence back," Stanley said.

"But if the tape wasn't in the box . . ."

Stanley shook her head. "That's a hell of a risk—that you might look for the tape and not find it—and we don't have any information to confirm that was the case." Stanley readjusted her monitor back to its initial position. "NCIS spoke with the janitor. He doesn't recall any videocassette on your desk or on the floor, and he said he wouldn't have touched anything even if it was there."

Battles nodded. "So where do we go from here?"

Stanley shrugged. "Trejo has asked for new counsel. I've assigned Kevin Cipoletti." Cipoletti used the office across the hall from Battles. "It's for the best, Leah, under the circumstances. If they reconvene the Article 32 hearing, you can't very well be Trejo's counsel, not to mention the ethics investigation is going to keep you busy."

"Do they intend to reconvene the hearing?"

"I don't know, but I understand Cho is going to argue that he can use other evidence to at least establish probable cause. He might be right, but that decision will be for the preliminary hearing officer to decide. I'm scheduled to have a conference call with Lopresti and senior trial counsel later this morning. I don't know what the outcome will be, or if they've even had time to make that decision."

"You mean regarding the ethics investigation?"

"Among other things," she said. "But I'm not sure they'll stop there, Leah. If they get that far, and there's no better explanation for the tape having gone missing, they could seek to court-martial you for dereliction of duty and obstruction."

And in one fell swoop wipe away all the reasons Battles had joined the Navy, to make some money, to try cases, and to serve her country and earn a pension. She exhaled. "And until then, what am I supposed to do?"

"Until that decision has been made, you can either work desk duty or take an accrued leave of absence. Given the climate around here, the latter might be worth considering. You don't need to tell me your decision now."

"That's not a problem," Battles said, thinking again of her mother's admonition about not being present, and what it signified. "I have no intention of taking a leave of absence. If I have to twiddle my thumbs at my desk, then so be it. But I intend to show up here every day, until someone tells me not to."

When he arrived at work, Del ran Jack Welch through the system. Welch had turned eighteen years old during the school year, an adult. He had no prior arrests. Faz had looked him up on Google and found a Facebook page. Welch played guitar in a band called CHAOS. In his posted pictures, he looked a lot like the drug addict in the pictures in Allie's text messages—so rail thin it was a mystery how he was still alive.

"Listen to this crap," Del said to Faz. Noise burst from his computer speakers. It sounded like cats walking over guitar strings. "Apparently that's music." He shut it down. "And here I thought Stevie and Mark were making it up when they said the band was bad. Hell, they sounded better than the band."

Del also determined that Welch lived at an address not far from Allie's home. He wanted to pick him up outside of the high school and bring him downtown for questioning.

"You're inviting unnecessary problems," Faz said, rocking his chair away from his desk. "Let's pick him up at his home. Maybe he's willing to talk. Maybe his parents will talk."

Del paced the workspace in the center of the A Team's four cubicles. Tracy was not yet in, and Kins was out on medical leave, finally having his hip replaced. "He's over eighteen. We don't have to go through his parents."

"If he asks for a lawyer, or his parents get him a lawyer, we won't get squat out of him," Faz said. "Let's hope he's scared. Wouldn't you have been at eighteen? Look, a lot of these parents know each other. They knew Allie. I say we use his parents rather than fight them. He's not the guy you're after, Del. You want his dealer, and whoever his dealer is buying from."

"And if the parents won't cooperate?" Del asked.

"Then we take your approach, assuming we can prove he supplied the drugs. We have enough to at least bring him in and question him."

"Fine, but if he provided Allie with the heroin that killed her, I'm going to see that Celia McDaniel charges him with a controlled substance homicide."

"One step at a time," Faz said. "First, let's see if he talks."

"See if who talks?" Tracy dropped her backpack on her chair.

"The kid who supplied Del's niece with the heroin," Faz said.

Tracy looked to Del. "You found her dealer?"

"I found the guy who knows her dealer."

Faz looked like he'd been struck by a thought. "Wait, what are you doing here? Did you finish the Article 32 hearing in one day?" He sounded skeptical.

"You could say that," Tracy said. "You remember that videotape Kins and I got from the convenience store?"

"The one that showed Trejo buying the energy drinks?" Faz asked.

"It's missing."

"What do you mean, 'missing'?" Del said.

"I mean the Navy prosecutor can't find it. Neither can the court reporter who is responsible for keeping all the evidence."

"Someone stole it?" Del said.

They both started to interrupt but Tracy cut them off. "It gets better. The defense attorney was the last person to have the evidence. And no one has a copy."

"We don't have a copy?" Faz asked.

Tracy shook her head. "We never got that chance, not after the Navy asserted jurisdiction so quickly. We turned over what we had. The prosecutor said he was going to make a copy after the hearing."

"So what happens now?" Faz asked.

"Good question. The preliminary hearing officer gave the prosecutor until end of today to find the tape."

"Then what?"

"Don't know."

"You think Trejo could walk?" Faz said.

"I don't know, but that tape is a key piece of evidence. Without it, I'm not sure the prosecution can place Trejo in Seattle at the time of the accident. If they can't, I don't see how they can prove he was driving the car."

"The defense attorney . . . what was her name?" Faz asked.

"Battles. Leah Battles," Tracy said.

"What does she say?"

"She doesn't deny she had the evidence brought to her the night before the hearing, but she can't say for certain that the tape was or was not in the box. It might have been, but she said she didn't take it out of the box that night. She says she put the box on the court reporter's chair late the night before the hearing, long after he'd gone home."

"Sounds like bullshit," Faz said.

Tracy shrugged. "Maybe, but given the potential consequences, why would she do it?"

"She couldn't win with the tape," Faz said. "I don't think she could, but she's no dummy—aggressive, yes, but not stupid. She had the evidence brought to her office and the prosecutor saw it there that night when they talked. If she was going to do something like this, wouldn't she have been a little more discreet about it?"

"People do stupid things all the time," Del said. "That's what keeps us in business."

"But this wasn't a spur-of-the-moment action. She would have had time to think about it. What could she have hoped to gain?"

Faz said, "If she didn't take it, then who did?"

"And why?" Del said. "I don't know, Tracy. Seems like she's the one with a motive."

"To answer your first question—who could have taken the tape, I'm assuming anyone with access to the court reporter's office," Tracy said.

"Which is who?" Faz asked.

"I don't know yet, but apparently he doesn't lock his office."

"So anyone, then," Faz said.

"Anyone with a reason," Del said.

Tracy checked her watch. "I've got a meeting with Clarridge, Cerrabone, and Dunleavy to discuss SPD possibly reasserting jurisdiction."

"They're not going to do that, not without the tape," Faz said.

"I don't think so either." Tracy paused, thinking. "I want to talk to her. I want to talk to Battles, find out what she knows."

"Why would she talk to us?" Del asked. "Especially if she did take the tape."

"Maybe she won't. But if she didn't take it, then we have the same goal."

"D'Andre Miller's family is going to go crazy," Faz said.

"They already are," Tracy said. "The hearing got out of control, and the mother looked at me like she'd expected something like this all along." She checked her watch again. "I'm not looking forward to briefing Clarridge and Dunleavy. They're going to be pissed. But I'm really not looking forward to talking with the family."

CHAPTER 26

Jack Welch lived on a street much like Allie's—single-family houses in a middle-class neighborhood with modest yards and foliage. Cars parked along the curbs left barely enough room for a single vehicle to pass. People in these homes weren't supposed to have sons and daughters hooked on heroin. The junkies were supposed to be downtown, living in dark alleys and abandoned buildings, sleeping on soiled mattresses amid garbage and rodents. Del thought again of what Celia McDaniel had said, about the epidemic, about the drug cartels plowing their pot fields and planting poppy fields, and about the easily obtainable opioids. He thought about the counselor's statement that addicts now were good kids from good families, and easy pickings for those cartels. It made him shudder.

At 5:30 p.m., dusk had descended over the neighborhood and a light wind rattled the leaves of the trees in the front yards. Faz parked the Prius to the south of a concrete walk and shut off the engine. He and Del sat watching a yellow, two-story A-frame house. Lights inside the house indicated someone was home.

Del spit a spent sunflower shell into a cup. It made him feel like he was twelve again, playing Little League baseball. A friend had told him that he'd lost thirty pounds eating sunflower seeds when he watched TV, rather than potato chips and Oreos. Del saw the pack of seeds at his sister's and decided he'd give it a try. He was pleased to find that the seeds weren't like the seeds he'd eaten as a kid. Those were a single flavor—salted. These seeds were barbecue flavored, but Stevie said they also had cracked pepper, ranch, and others.

Faz looked over at him. "You're still on that diet, huh?"

"Just watching what I eat," Del said, cracking a seed, his gaze on the house.

"Smells like barbecue in here."

Del held up the bag. "They got ranch and dill now too."

"Terrific. I hope the birds in the backyard appreciate them." A moment passed. "Did you call that prosecutor?"

Del spit the shell of a seed into the cup while staring at the house. "I did."

"So you're going to see her again?"

"I saw her last night," Del said.

"Last night . . . You worked last night."

"She met me after work."

"No kidding. How'd it go?"

"It was nice." Del spit another shell into the cup. "She brought prosciutto and salami, French bread, a little cheese."

"You're killing me. Really?" Faz said.

"Really."

"Where'd you go?"

"My place."

Faz nodded, a grin on his face. "Good for you, Del."

"Yeah. We'll see where it goes." It had gone well—easy and comfortable. Del had been worried, but Celia had made it clear she had no expectations other than his companionship. He'd been able to relax and enjoy the evening.

"What?" Faz asked.

"What?" Del said.

"Something bothering you?" Faz asked.

"No."

"You don't seem all that excited about it."

Del blew out a breath. "I don't know. It's just . . ." He kept his gaze on the home. "It's been a long time, you know."

"Since you dated?"

Del looked at Faz. "Since I slept with anyone."

"Oh," Faz said. A beat passed. "Hey, it's like riding a bike."

"Yeah, but I mean, what if the bike gets a flat?"

Faz gave him a look. "Did that happen?"

Del shook his head. "No. No, nothing like that."

"You worried about it?"

"I don't know. I mean . . . Yeah, I guess maybe I am." He was. He hadn't slept with anyone since he and his wife had separated.

"Listen. They got all kinds of pills now. If it's an issue, you talk to the doctor."

"You ever have that happen?"

"Me? Hell, I've been married twenty-eight years. What's the line from that movie? 'I get hard when the wind blows.'"

"Eddie Murphy—*48 Hours*."

"Listen, don't worry about something that hasn't happened yet. It hasn't happened yet, right?"

Del shook his head. "I'm just talking hypothetically." He set down the cup of spent seeds. "Come on. Let's go see if Jack Welch is home."

"Hold on," Faz said.

Del kept his gaze on the house. He thought for sure Faz would ask for details about the remainder of his night with Celia McDaniel. She'd stayed—Del wasn't about to send her home at four in the morning, but they hadn't slept together, though there had been some physical contact. They'd shared the same bed.

"You're going to let me take the lead, right?" Faz asked.

Del looked at him. "What? Yeah. No worries."

"Del."

"I'm good, okay? You can take the lead. I'm fine."

"You don't look fine. You look on edge."

"No, I was just . . . I'm fine. Okay? How long have I been doing this? Let's go see what he has to say." Del pushed out of the car.

A leaning white picket fence surrounded an oak tree and small patch of lawn. A grass-and-gravel driveway ran along the left side of the property. At the back was a two-story garage with a window over the garage door. A staircase rising along the north side of the building indicated someone lived in the second story. Faz caught up to Del as he stepped through an opening where the gate to the picket fence had once swung, but the gate now leaned up against the trunk of the oak tree. To Del, the damage to the gate looked like more than wear and tear. It looked like someone had kicked the gate off its hinges.

Del climbed three wooden steps to the front door. The porch light, a bare bulb, was too bright for the overhead socket and emitted an annoying buzz. He heard the television from inside and smelled something cooking. He knocked.

A young girl pulled the door open. Small, with straight blonde hair down her back, she appeared to be nine or ten, about Mark and Stevie's age. Del took a deep breath. As much as he wanted to wring Jack Welch by the collar, this was a family—probably one that had suffered as much as Maggie and the twins.

"Hi," Faz said. "Is your mom or dad home?"

The little girl turned her head and yelled toward the interior of the house. "Mom! There's someone at the door."

A woman came quickly from the back of the house. She had a dish towel in hand but wore business attire—cream slacks, black pumps, a blouse. Given how quickly she'd come to the door, she probably had admonished the little girl about opening the door to strangers. *Good kids from good families,* Del thought.

When she saw Del and Faz, the woman came to an abrupt stop. She looked as if she'd started to melt. Her body sagged, her shoulders slumped. She dropped the towel. Her face took on a deeply pained expression.

"Go to your room and read," she said to the little girl in a voice so soft Del almost couldn't hear her.

The girl didn't argue or ask questions. She'd been through this before. She disappeared down the hall. The woman waited to speak until she heard a door close. She approached them, tentative, her arms wrapped around her. "Is he dead?" she asked.

Del and Faz hadn't even had the chance to show the woman their identification and badges. "Are you Jack Welch's mother?" Faz asked.

She sighed. "Yes. I'm Jeanine Welch. Are you here to tell me my son is dead?"

"No," Faz said. "We just want to talk with him."

She let out a held breath. Her knees folded and she stepped back, collapsing onto a coffee table.

"Are you all right?" Faz asked.

Jeanine Welch exhaled another deep breath and squeezed her eyes shut, as if light-headed or fighting a headache.

"I take it your son's not home?" Faz asked.

"No," she said, her head still lowered and her voice soft. "He's not."

"Do you know where he is?" Faz asked.

With another breath she looked up at them. "What?"

"Do you know where he is?"

"He called me at work earlier today. He said he'd be home. I don't know what that means. He didn't come home last night."

"May we come in?" Faz asked.

"What is this about?" the woman asked.

"Allie Marcello," Del said.

Her brow wrinkled. "From school?"

"Yes," Del said.

The woman's eyes shifted between Del and Faz. "What about her?"

"She overdosed," Del said. "She's dead."

"I know," the woman said. "I went to her funeral. I saw you there," she said to Del. She sounded defeated but managed to stand. "Why do you want to talk to Jack?"

"We'd like to ask your son what he knows about her death," Faz said.

"Do you think he had something to do with Allie's death?"

"We think he might have information related to her overdose," Faz said.

The woman digested that for a moment. Then she said, "Come in."

They entered and closed the door. The front room was quaint but tired. A worn couch and chair faced a television. The couch had a blanket on it and an open newspaper. Del wondered if the woman had slept there, waiting for her son to come home; a similar blanket and newspapers had lain across his sister's couch many recent evenings. Magazines lay scattered across a coffee table, along with an unopened newspaper still in its plastic sleeve. The woman quickly cleared the couch and used the remote to shut off the television.

Del and Faz sat. She dumped the blanket and newspapers behind the couch and picked up the dish towel. "Sorry for the mess," she said, moving to the chair.

"You should see my house." Faz smiled politely. "When my son was home it looked like a tornado ran through it."

She slumped into the chair.

"Why did you ask if your son was dead, Mrs. Welch?" Del said, gently prodding her.

She shrugged, then sighed. She looked to be fighting tears. "I've been expecting a call or knock on the door for some time."

"What's he addicted to?" Del asked.

"Heroin," she said. "For about a year now." She shrugged again and blotted the corners of her eyes with the dish towel. "I can't control him. I've considered kicking him out, but . . . he's my son. I worry about my daughter, about his influence on her."

"You said he didn't come home last night?" Faz asked.

"No," she said.

"Do you know where he stayed?"

"I don't know where he goes anymore." She looked and sounded tired. "I've given up trying to keep track of him."

"He still lives here, though?" Faz asked.

She shrugged as if to say, *What am I going to do?* Then she nodded. "Yes. He lives above the garage."

With time to consider her, Del realized Jeanine Welch was still young, probably Maggie's age, early forties. She was also attractive, tall and thin, her hair the same color as her daughter's but cut shoulder length. She carried herself, though, as Maggie carried herself, as if burdened by a huge weight, one that had shaved years off her life.

"He's in a band," she said. "They practice there . . ."

"How did you find out about the heroin?" Faz asked.

"I've found things in his room. Syringes, spoons." She shook her head. "He started smoking pot in the eighth grade. It got worse from there. I think others in the band may have got him started on the heroin."

"Did you know Allie well?" Del asked.

The woman nodded. "Pretty well. She'd come over here every so often to listen to the band and they'd all go up in Jack's room above the garage. She was a nice girl, Allie. It was so sad, what happened to her."

"What about Jack's father?" Faz asked. "Is he around?"

She smiled, but it had a sad quality to it. "Depends on what you mean by 'around.' He gets the kids Wednesday nights and every other weekend. Jack stopped going about a year ago and now his father can't force him so it's just my daughter."

"How long have you been divorced?" Del said.

"Seven years," she said.

"Do you know Jack's group of friends?" Faz asked.

"Some."

"Do you know who's supplying him with the heroin?" Faz asked.

She shook her head. "No. Like I said, maybe the band, but it seems it's everywhere now." Her voice cracked but she caught it. "I don't know what more I can do. If I kick him out . . . then what?" She took a moment to regroup. "But I had to get him out of the house, at least . . . for my daughter." She blotted her eyes again. Then she asked, "Why do you want to talk to him about Allie?"

"We believe Allie took a very potent form of heroin. We're trying to find out where it came from," Del said.

"Do you think Jack gave it to her?"

"We just want to find out what he knows," Faz said. "Do you have access to Jack's room above the garage?"

"I did, but he put a lock on the outside. I asked him to remove it, but . . . I don't know the combination."

Del leaned forward. "Has your son ever overdosed?"

"Twice," she said without hesitation.

"Recently?" Del asked.

"The last time was about a month ago. His friends . . . They brought him to the hospital and they treated him and let him go. They said they couldn't keep him."

Faz said, "Does your son have a cell phone?"

"Yes," she said, sounding somewhat confused by the question.

"Is it his phone or did you purchase it for him? Is it your plan?"

"It's a family plan." She chuckled. "Jack doesn't have the money to afford to buy lunch at school."

The comment further confirmed Del's conclusion that Jack had used Allie for her money. "So the phone bill is in your name."

"Yes. Why do you ask?"

"We'd like access to Jack's text messages and Snapchats," Faz said. "We'd like to find out who he's been talking to—who his supplier is."

"What can you do about it?"

"Shut him down," Faz said. "They've had multiple overdoses recently and we're trying to keep that number from increasing."

"My God," she said softly.

"We're concerned that more people could die unless we can find out the source of the drug. Can you get access to Jack's phone?"

"I suppose so," she said. "I've never done it before though."

Del rattled off a ten-digit number.

"That's Jack's number," she said.

Del pulled out a folded sheet of paper authorizing the phone company to release Jack's cell phone records and handed it to her. She looked at it a moment. "I don't—"

Del handed her a pen. "It just allows us access to Jack's cell phone, to determine who he is communicating with."

She took the pen, considered the document briefly, and scribbled her name. Then she handed both back to Del. He gave Faz a subtle nod. They had what they needed. Faz handed Jeanine Welch a business card. "We'd like to talk to your son. It's not our intent to embarrass him, or you, by picking him up at school. If he comes home, that's my number."

The woman leaned forward and took the card. "Can you lock him up?"

"What's that?" Faz asked.

"Can you arrest him? Put him in jail? Maybe he can get some help. I don't know, maybe it will scare him enough to get help. I don't know what else to do." She sounded very much like Maggie. "Every time the phone rings or there's a knock on the door . . . I expect it to be someone coming to tell me my son is dead."

CHAPTER 27

Tracy pulled to a stop outside a brick apartment building on King Street near the train station in Pioneer Square. According to a DMV search, Leah Battles lived in one of the units. At six stories, the building was one of the tallest in the area. Most were one and two stories, with an assortment of shops and restaurants on the street level. Bars, music venues, and art shops attracted many of Seattle's young, along with a number of its homeless and mentally ill. Early evening, music filtered from one of the stores and people walked the streets, some on their way home from work, others looking like they were getting a jump on the upcoming weekend.

Earlier that afternoon, Tracy had met with Rick Cerrabone, Sandy Clarridge, and Kevin Dunleavy. They'd expressed concern over the news about the missing videotape. Dunleavy explained that the Navy's senior trial counsel had called to advise that they had been unable to locate the video, and that they were proceeding with an ethics inquiry against Battles. He explained that, depending on the outcome of that inquiry, a court-martial for dereliction of duty could be imposed. He also said Battles no longer represented Trejo, and that they were awaiting the preliminary hearing officer's determination on probable cause to continue holding him. Dunleavy explained what everyone in the room understood. If the PHO punted and King County reasserted jurisdiction, they faced similar problems bringing an action against Trejo. In a superior court, the standard to convict was beyond a reasonable doubt, a much more stringent threshold than probable cause. Without the videotape, their case had become significantly weaker. Tracy got the sense from the discussion that it was unlikely the powers that be would take back jurisdiction, though no one in the meeting said that out loud. She understood their reasoning. Why put your head in the lion's cage if you knew it was going to be bitten off?

Tracy pushed out of her car and approached the apartment building's overhang. The night air had a bite to it, though not nearly as cold as earlier that month. Antique streetlamps lit the dampened sidewalk, and the air had a musty smell of impending rain. She located the name Leah Battles on the apartment registry and pushed the buzzer. No one answered. She tried again with the same result.

"You looking for a restaurant recommendation?" Battles climbed off a bicycle in attire similar to what she'd worn to the jail the night Trejo had been booked. She pointed. "Good idea to wear that gun, though this neighborhood isn't too bad." Battles sounded out of breath. She removed her bike helmet. Her dark hair was pulled back in a tight ponytail, her cheeks flushed.

"I was hoping we could talk," Tracy said.

"Why would we do that?" Battles sounded more curious than adversarial.

"Because I think we both want the same thing."

"You want to win the lottery and move to a yacht in the Mediterranean?"

"That would be nice," Tracy said. "Though the grass isn't always greener."

"You see any grass around here?" Battles looked at the pavement. "What do we both want?"

"Can I buy you a cup of coffee?"

Battles gave her an inquisitive stare. "A cop springing for a cup of coffee? Okay, I'm interested. Let me get my bike indoors. I lock it up out here and I'll be lucky if they leave a spoke."

Minutes after she went inside, Battles emerged without the bike, the helmet, or her shoes. She clutched Kleenex and wiped at her nose. She wore Birkenstock sandals with white socks. "I like to make a fashion statement when I go out," she said. "The guys dig it." She looked around the street. "So where do you want to go?"

"Your neighborhood," Tracy said. "Pick a place and I'll follow."

"Okay." Battles gave it some thought before leading Tracy around the block to Zeitgeist Coffee on Jackson Street. Battles ordered an iced coffee. Tracy ordered a decaf; she had enough trouble sleeping without caffeine in her system. "You want a bite to eat?" she asked.

Battles smiled. "This is beginning to feel like a date."

Crosswhite held up a hand. "Married."

"Yeah? Does he have a friend?"

Battles picked up her coffee and headed to one of the tables. Halfway across the shop she stopped to consider a dictionary open on a stand near the door. She scanned the words with her finger. "'Intriguing,'" she read out loud. "'Arousing one's curiosity or interest. Fascinating.'" She looked at Crosswhite. "Prophetic."

They took their coffees to an isolated table near a brick wall. Overhead, a white sculpture depicting clouds hung from an unfinished ceiling of beams, ductwork, and cables. Tracy removed her jacket and the two women sat in chairs across the table from each other. "You were out for a ride?"

"No," Battles said. "The bike is a means to an end. I train on the north end of the city, and a car in this town is too expensive."

"What are you training for?"

"Nothing in particular. I take a class called Krav Maga. Have you heard of it?"

"Not in any detail. Isn't it Israeli commando fighting?"

Battles explained the development of the training and Tracy could sense her pride discussing it.

"Sounds practical," Tracy said.

"In theory." Battles sipped her drink. "But executed the right way, it's disabling." Battles set her cup on the table and leaned back in her chair. "Your meeting. Your agenda."

"I don't think you took the video."

Battles gave a thin-lipped smile. "Unfortunately, you'd be in the minority."

"There's nothing in it for you to gain."

"My client walks free and I'm the big winner."

"And you're prosecuted."

"Potentially."

"Potentially," Tracy agreed. "I don't see that as a fair trade—at least not one that benefits you."

"I don't know. I lose my law license, I'm dismissed, and I lose my pay—which is to say, I lose pretty much all the reasons I joined the Navy."

"And you're too smart to do something that stupid."

Battles sat forward. "You sure this isn't a date? You're a lot nicer than some of the men I've gone out with."

Tracy smiled. She was glad to see Battles hadn't lost her edge. "So, will you talk to me?"

"I can't talk about my client. Former client."

"Understood."

"Let me ask you a question first." Battles sat up. "You don't have jurisdiction and I'm sensing Seattle PD won't be anxious to get back a dead-bang loser with the potential to incite the masses."

"You may be right."

"So why are you here? Why do you care?"

Tracy gave the question some thought. She'd made a ride out to Shaniqua Miller's home after the meeting with Cerrabone, Dunleavy, and Clarridge. Miller had been polite, but clearly wasn't interested in discussing the matter in detail with Tracy, whom she viewed as part of the justice system—which she now distrusted more than ever—and therefore part of the problem.

"I care about that boy," Tracy said. "I care about a mother who may have to live the rest of her life without any answers."

Battles sipped her coffee. Her gaze drifted out the plate-glass windows at the fading daylight and the streetlights illuminating the trunks and leaves of the trees in the sidewalk. An old-fashioned trolley car rumbled past the coffee shop, clanging as it went. She reconsidered Tracy. "Defending the wretched isn't always the most popular position," she said. Then, more subdued, she said, "Go ahead and ask your questions."

Tracy gathered her thoughts, though she'd known where she'd start if Battles consented. She had snippets of what had happened from being present at the hearing and from her meeting that afternoon. She wanted to see how Battles reacted to being accused. "You were looking at the evidence the night before the hearing?"

"I was reviewing some of the evidence, but not the tape. I didn't take it out of—Actually, I don't even know if it was in the box at that point. But I do know that I didn't look at it then. Why would I? I'd already looked at it. I won't say what was on it or what I thought of it, but I pretty much knew it wasn't going to change by looking at it again. Besides, I didn't have a television to play it."

It sounded plausible to Tracy. "Fair enough. What did you do with the box of evidence when you'd finished with it?"

"I took it back to the court reporter and left it on his chair. Ordinarily he signs it back in, but he's a civilian and he was long gone by then. I've done it before. We operate on the honor system." She raised her fingers in a Girl Scout's salute.

"Is his office in the same building?"

"It is. He's located on the second floor across from the courtroom."

"Where's Cho's office?"

Battles smiled. "Second floor, just down the hall from the court reporter."

"What time did you return the box?"

"After Cho left my office, if that's where you're headed, between ten forty-five and eleven p.m."

"Cho came to your office?"

"On his way out the door to go home."

"And you still had the box of evidence?"

"Yes."

"Did you see him leave?"

"The building? Only on the security tape."

"Your building has a security camera?"

"Inside the door, positioned to view the lobby."

Tracy hadn't thought of security for the building. She made a mental note to get that video. "How do you get in? Is the door secure?"

"Always. You punch in the last four digits of your Social Security number. If it recognizes your digits, you get in. If it doesn't, you don't."

"Where is that record kept, the record of acceptable Social Security numbers?"

"There's a security office on the first floor, just down the hall from me. I assume they have it. They also keep all the surveillance videos."

"For how long?"

"I don't know. Never been an issue before."

"Is that where the tape for that night is kept?"

"Yes, but my OIC has a copy."

"Your OIC?"

"Officer in charge. Rebecca Stanley."

"And you've seen that tape."

"I have."

Tracy looked for some tell from Battles as she spoke. "What time did you leave that night?"

"The building? Shortly after Cho. The last ferry departs at eleven forty. It takes me about ten minutes to ride my bike from the office to the Bremerton Ferry Terminal. So I returned the evidence to the court reporter's office and left the building right after that."

"You should have just slept at the office."

Battles held up a bare left hand. "Did I mention that I'm still single and not looking to die alone?"

"Did anyone see you return the box?"

"No one else was in the building, at least not that I'm aware of."

"Okay," Tracy said. "And to your knowledge, no one came into the building after you?"

"Just the janitor. He's on the tape."

"Is the company military or civilian?"

"Civilian."

"Anyone talk to him?"

"I assume NCIS. They're talking to everyone, including me."

Tracy made a mental note to determine whether NCIS had typed up their interviews.

Battles said, "So it seems someone removed the tape before I checked out the box, or got in early the following morning, saw it on the court reporter's chair, and removed it."

"Cho?"

"I don't know, but if I had nothing to gain by taking the tape, he really had nothing to gain. Not having the tape hurt him."

"And it would be risky to remove the tape before you had checked out the box?"

"You mean because I could have noticed it was missing? My OIC said the same thing. Seems to make the most sense, but like I said, no one came in or out of the building after me except the janitors."

"Who has access to your offices?" Tracy asked.

"Other than the janitors?" Battles shrugged. "Everyone with an approved Social Security number."

"How many would that be?"

Battles scoffed. "A lot." She became more pensive. "Not a bad thought to get that list, but aren't you ignoring the same question you asked me?"

"Why would someone do it?"

Battles nodded.

Tracy didn't know, but she'd get the printout of the codes entered for that evening anyway.

—

Jeanine Welch walked Del and Faz down the porch to the broken front gate, her arms folded tight across her body to ward off the chill. Dusk had given way to night. The sporadic streetlamps spotted the sidewalk in pale yellow light, and an array of cables and wires stretched between telephone poles and the houses on the block. Somewhere down the street two boys shouted, likely rushing to finish a game on their small patch of lawn before darkness enveloped them.

Welch paused at the gate, or where the gate should have been. "He kicked it off its hinges when he left a few nights ago." She sounded weary. "He wanted money. He said it was to buy a new amplifier, but I've come to know better than to give Jack any money." She turned back to her home. "I used to have more things, but anything I have of value he steals and sells. He sold the jewelry I'd inherited from my mother, our toaster, televisions, his sister's bike. He denies it, but I know he did."

Del reached inside his pocket and pulled out a packet of business cards. He handed one to Jeanine Welch. "Allie was my niece," he said. "That's why I was at the service."

Her hand stopped, as if the card might bite. "I'm so sorry," she said. "If there's ever anything I can do."

She nodded and tentatively took the card.

Del heard the heavy bass beat of muffled music. A late-model Honda Accord sped around the street corner, nearly hitting one of the parked cars, and jerked to a stop at the end of the driveway.

"That's Jack," Welch said, sounding somewhat hesitant.

Jack took one look at Faz and Del talking to his mother and quickly threw the car into reverse, grinding gears as he did.

"He's running," Del said, moving to the passenger door of the Prius. Faz hurried around the hood to the driver's side.

The Honda stuttered and stalled in the street. Jack restarted the engine, struggled to find the right gear, and lurched forward.

Faz started the Prius and dropped it into gear. They wouldn't break any land speed records, but that was a good thing. They wouldn't engage Welch in a high-speed chase, if that was his intent. Regulations forbade it, and they didn't want to see anyone injured unnecessarily.

The Accord turned right at the stop sign without so much as a pause.

Faz pumped the brakes, slowed at the corner to ensure no cars were coming, and turned to follow.

"Left at the next corner," Del said. "He ran another stop sign."

"See if we can get some help before he kills someone. Right taillight is out," Faz said.

Del picked up the microphone and called in the make and model of the Honda, its license plate, and their current location and direction. If Welch took an on-ramp onto the freeway, they'd alert the highway patrol and turn the chase over to them.

Parked cars whizzed past their windows. Faz glanced down at the dash—fifty miles per hour on a residential road. His eyes searched for cars pulling from the curb or backing down driveways, and for kids on the sidewalk.

"Any help?" he asked Del.

Del continued to provide their location on the radio. "There's a patrol unit close by," he said to Faz.

"I'm going to slow down and back off. Maybe he will too. He's making another turn," Faz said.

Del called it in.

Up ahead, what Faz had feared came to sudden fruition. As the Honda accelerated, a red truck backed quickly down a driveway.

"Hang on," Faz said.

The Honda's single taillight illuminated and its brakes screeched. The hood dipped low and struck the rear panel of the truck with a loud bang of crumpled metal and shattered glass.

"Call for an ambulance," Faz said, but the Honda's driver's-side door pushed open and Welch scurried out. "This guy is like a freaking cat."

"I'm on it." Del pushed open his car door, giving chase.

Welch sprinted across several front lawns, then turned down a driveway. Del wouldn't catch him; his prime was well in the past, but having lost fifteen pounds, he felt good just keeping up. Welch scaled a fence along the side of a house and scurried over it. As Del looked for a gate latch, a floodlight illuminated on the corner of the house and a big dog barked and growled. Hands reappeared atop the fence, followed quickly by Jack Welch's head and shoulders. The boy looked panicked. He lifted a leg over the fence and flopped hard on the grass-and-concrete drive. His lower pant leg had been ripped. Del put a knee in his back and snapped cuffs on each wrist. A man came through the gate carrying a baseball bat. "SPD," Del said, fishing out his badge from his pocket and holding it up for the man to see.

Then he turned back to Welch. "You have the right to remain silent."

CHAPTER 28

Del and Faz opted not to take Jack Welch to jail and instead stuck him in one of the interrogation rooms. At his desk, Del called Celia McDaniel for advice.

"The statute clearly provides that to convict a driver you needed to be in uniform and the car equipped with lights and sirens," McDaniel said over the speakerphone.

Faz shook his head. "If Welch gets a criminal defense lawyer worth his weight in salt, he'll know we didn't meet any of those criteria, or he'd find out quickly enough. You have any advice?"

"You could book him for reckless driving or reckless endangerment, but those are misdemeanors with unlikely jail time and a minimal financial penalty. Even if Welch couldn't pay, all it would mean is he'd be cleaning up garbage along the freeways."

"But Welch doesn't know the law," Faz said. "And his mom isn't likely to bail him out."

"Doesn't sound like he's on speaking terms with his father either," Del agreed. So they had some leverage, at least for now. "Sounds as though we'll get more bang for our buck if we question him before we book him. Frankly, I don't give a rat's ass about a charge of eluding a police officer or reckless endangerment. I want to find out what Welch knows."

"If he asks for an attorney, all bets are off," Celia said.

"So we take that chance," Del said.

They thanked her and disconnected.

The windowless interrogation rooms on the seventh floor of Police Headquarters weren't a lot of fun to sit in alone, and they got considerably smaller, and uncomfortable, when both Faz and Del squeezed their hulking frames inside. They took pride in making the room feel as small as possible, and they excelled at it.

They let Welch stew while continuing to debate their dilemma, observing him from behind the one-way mirror in the viewing room. Welch might have been eighteen years old, but he didn't look it. "He looks sixteen, at best," Del said.

Five feet seven inches, small boned, and rail thin, Welch couldn't have weighed 120 pounds fully dressed. "I got coatracks weigh more than him," Faz said.

Welch wore an unbuttoned, long-sleeve flannel shirt, likely to hide the track marks on his arms, and a black T-shirt with a picture of the Seattle grunge band Nirvana. His hair touched his shoulders and looked like it hadn't been washed in weeks. He kept his head tilted, looking out from behind bangs. "He thinks he's Kurt Cobain," Faz said.

"Who?" Del said.

"His shirt. That's the singer who had the drug problem. He shot himself two decades ago. Antonio listened to that crap."

"I've got enough trouble keeping current," Del said.

"You never had a teenage boy at home."

"If this guy is the type of boy I'd have, I'll take Sonny. At least his hair is short, he bathes, and he comes when I call him."

It pained Del to think this was the guy Allie had been dating, that she thought so little of herself. But he again suspected, based on what the mother had told them about Jack's need for money, that his relation-ship with Allie had not been based on mutual attraction but on mutual need—what Oprah, or Dr. Phil, would call "codependence"—a mutual need for heroin.

"You think he's high?" Del asked.

"Hard to tell," Faz said. "Left leg is doing a hell of a jig under the table, though. Based on what the mom said, he might be coming down after a binge." Faz paused and turned from the window, facing Del. "Listen, why don't you let me handle this one on my own, at least to start. Let's see what he's going to say."

"I'm good."

"Del—"

"I'm good." He looked Faz in the eye. "Seriously, I'm all right. I understand what we're trying to get out of this guy and I'm not going to screw that up."

"You'll let me take the lead, right?"

"I understand."

"So how do you want to play it?" Faz asked.

"Same as always," Del said. He pulled open the door to the room and stepped into the hallway. "I'll be the hard-ass. Comes naturally."

Faz followed Del around the corner. Del pulled open the door to the interrogation room and Welch glanced up at him through his long hair. Faz picked up a chair from the hall and made a production of fit-ting it into the room and setting it beside the other chair. He and Del sat shoulder to shoulder and leaned across the table, further closing the space with Welch. The young man pulled back as far as the chain, attached to handcuffs on one end and hooked to an eye bolt in the floor, would allow. If Welch hadn't been claustrophobic before, he was one step closer now. The leg kept shaking.

"You're sure you don't need any medical care?" Faz asked.

Welch shook his head.

"Is that a no?" Faz asked.

"Sit up," Del said, voice harsh. Welch turned his head and looked at him. "I said sit up or we're finished here. We take you to jail and we book you on a whole host of charges—eluding arrest, driving under the influence, dangerous and reckless driving and, while we're at it, how does controlled substance homicide sound to you?" Del waited a beat before adding, "We're not talking about the penny-ante, bullshit charges that allow you to walk out of here and go home to Mommy. We're way past that, Jack."

Welch flipped his hair from his eyes and looked from Del to Faz. He sat up. "Homicide?" He sounded confused, voice hoarse. "I didn't kill anyone."

"No? Does the name Allie Marcello ring any bells?" Del didn't give Welch time to answer. "We have e-mails, text messages, and Snapchats that prove you pressured Allie Marcello to buy and use heroin the night of her death. She was clean, J-Man." He emphasized the e-mail name, saying it with sarcasm. "She'd been clean for almost two months until she came home and you started in on her."

"I didn't sell her any heroin," he said, stuttering. "I wasn't even there."

"You're lying," Faz said, voice calm. "And we know you're lying."

"I just told you, genius, we got her phone and her computer, and your name is all over both. What, do you think we're stupid?" Del let that thought linger a few moments.

Faz reengaged. "So let me lay this out for you, Jack. Controlled substance homicide isn't one of those arrests where you're out tomorrow. The prosecutor charges you—that's about two weeks from now, and if you can't make bail, and I doubt you can, you're going to be locked away until trial, which no one is going to rush. Probably take place a year from now. After you're convicted, and you will be convicted, you're going away for a long time."

Jack Welch looked like he was about to say something, but Faz cut him off—and Del knew it was deliberate, in case Welch had been about to ask for a lawyer. Faz spoke patiently, like the times Del had been present when Faz spoke to his kids about some dumb thing they'd done. Vera made him soften his tone. "We want to find out what happened to Allie Marcello, Jack. We want to find out where she got the drugs. You were her friend."

"I was her friend," Welch quickly agreed.

"And you were with her when she overdosed," Faz said.

"No. I wasn't there. I left."

"But you were with her when she shot up the heroin," Faz said.

"I was there, but I didn't take any."

The lie was unraveling, one thread at a time. Del exercised discretion. "She'd been sober, hadn't she?"

"I don't know."

He leaned in closer. "Yes, you do. Her family sent her away. She'd been in Eastern Washington at a rehab facility. You e-mailed her because you couldn't text her. She didn't have her phone."

Faz slid several of the e-mails Del had printed across the table. Welch flipped his hair out of his eyes and looked down at them, but did not pick them up. "When she got her phone back you continued pressuring her to see you."

"No, that isn't true."

Faz slid more of Allie's text messages across the table. "She finally gave in."

"Her mother found her in her bedroom," Del said. "Her last text indicates you were with her that night. So don't tell us you weren't there because we already know you were."

"You needed her," Faz said. "You needed her money to make the buy." Faz tapped the papers. "We want to know where you got the heroin."

Welch inhaled and leaned away from the table, blowing out a breath. He started to cry. "She took too much. I told her she took too much. But she was fine when I left. I swear she was fine. She was snoring."

Snoring was not a good sign, Del knew. Snoring was an indication that her respiratory system was struggling, that fluid was building up in her lungs.

"We want to believe you," Faz said, calm. "But we can't prove it unless we know where you got the heroin."

Welch's chest shuddered. "She bought it. She bought it from this guy. I don't know who he is."

Del looked at Faz, shaking his head. It was time to amp up the pressure. "We're not going to get any straight answers out of this guy. I'm going to call the prosecutor and get him booked." Del stood and pulled open the door, shoving the chair into the hall and stepping out. The wall rattled when he closed the door.

Del moved quickly around the corner and slipped into the room with the one-way mirror in time to hear Faz sigh as if he wasn't sure what to do. Faz spread his hands wide, then clasped them in front of him. "Here's the problem I'm having, Jack." He nodded to the papers on the table. "All those e-mails and text messages, they confirm you were with Allie the night she died."

"I was; I told you I was."

"They also confirm that you, not her, know the guy who sold the two of you the heroin. I don't come up with a name of that guy then I got one choice where to go. Her family is going to want accountability, Jack. They're going to want someone held accountable for their daughter's death." Faz pointed across the table. "You're that guy. My partner's right, Jack—this is no longer just a possession charge. Controlled substance homicide is a felony. You go to prison when convicted of a felony. That's after a trial, which will make all the newspapers and social media. Are you willing to throw away years of your life for some dope dealer?"

Welch didn't immediately respond. Faz sat back, and Del knew Welch was letting those final words rattle around in his head. If Welch had a brain, he'd recognize that Faz was suggesting an out, an alternative to a long jail sentence.

Finally, Welch said, "What will happen to him?"

Bingo, Del thought from the other side of the glass. Now to reel him in.

"This guy a friend of yours?" Faz asked.

Jack said, "Hypothetically . . . I mean, if I knew him. What will happen to him?"

Faz shrugged. "I can't say for certain, Jack, but I can say that, if he cooperates, the judge would look more favorably on him than he's going to look on you if you don't provide a name."

"Can I call him? Can I talk to him?"

Faz shook his head. "It doesn't work that way, Jack. You give me his name and I'll bring him in. You don't even have to be involved."

"But he would know, right? He'd know that I'm the one who told you."

"We don't have to use your name. We can say we found his name in Allie's contacts. Had she bought from this person before?"

Welch nodded.

"So his name is probably in her phone contacts. We could say we found his name in her phone."

A nice move, Del again thought. Let the kid think he could hide his involvement.

Jack gave this some additional thought. When he stared at the tabletop, Faz glanced at the one-way mirror, knowing Del stood watching and listening on the other side.

He reengaged Welch. "What are you afraid of, Jack? Has this guy threatened you in some way?"

Welch shook his head. "No."

"So, he's a friend of yours?"

"Yeah."

"You know what, Jack? I don't think he's your friend." Welch looked up at him. "You have to ask yourself, would this guy go to prison for you if the situation was reversed?"

Jack shook his head and wiped at his nose with the cuff of his shirt.

"So what are you so worried about?"

"He runs the band."

"Excuse me?"

"He runs CHAOS, our band."

Del couldn't believe the kid's logic, or lack thereof, but then the stupidity of teenagers had always amazed him. Jack Welch was facing years in prison, and what was foremost on his mind was whether he'd be kicked out of some garage band.

"And what, you're afraid you'll be out of the band?" Faz asked, again keeping his voice calm and understanding.

Welch nodded.

Faz cleared his throat. "I want you to think about this, Jack. Okay? Follow along with me here. If you protect this guy, and you go away to prison for, say, five years, do you think he's going to hold your place in the band until you get out?"

Welch looked up when Faz said "five years." Faz leaned forward and arched his eyebrows to drive home his point.

"No," Jack said, soft and tentative.

Faz gave a closed-lip smile, shaking his head. "There's not going to be any band, Jack. Not with you in it."

CHAPTER 29

D an called the months that Tracy worked the night shift "vampire time." If he was busy at his law firm, as he was now, they could go days without seeing each other in daylight. This was one of those months. Tracy's day off, midweek, she'd slid out of bed after Dan was already long gone. He'd left a note that he'd be in a deposition most of the day. Tracy ran errands, then drove across the 520 bridge to visit Kins in Seattle.

She'd received daily phone updates on his progress from Kins or his wife, Shannah. Kins had been out of bed and walking the day of his surgery, and he left Swedish Hospital and went home the following day. Though he lived in Madison Park, an expensive Seattle neighborhood, Kins called it "Kinsington Estates." His house was accessed just over a cement bridge so narrow it could only accommodate a single car—not that traffic was a problem. Once across the bridge, there were only two homes before the start of the Seattle Arboretum—Kins's three-story white colonial and a Spanish-style manor with an orange tile roof and leaded-glass windows. Tracy had always admired the second house, but the owners would never sell. The two couples were the same age, with children close in age, and shared the same interests. According to Kins, life couldn't possibly get any better.

Kins's home was classic colonial architecture with a large dining room, living room, and small kitchen on the ground floor, and a large master bedroom, one bathroom, and two small bedrooms on the second floor—not exactly functional for three boys. Kins had spent much of his free time during the early years building out the daylight basement: adding bedrooms, a large bathroom, and a rumpus room with a pool table, sofas, and a television. A back door led to the arboretum, 230 acres of lawn and exotic plants and trees almost big enough to accommodate his three boys.

Tracy parked in a cutout in front of Kins's home and accessed the yard through a green gate. She carried a stack of magazines and several books the office had cobbled together to keep Kins occupied during his recovery. That was a tall order. Kins had a kinetic energy much like his sons. Keeping him immobile to allow his hip healing time would be a real chore for Shannah.

Shannah answered the door, but Kins called out immediately, expecting Tracy. "Crosswhite? Took you long enough. I'm dying in here and the office doesn't even bother to comfort me."

Shannah rolled her eyes. "He sounds like he's dying, doesn't he? I'm the one dying." She looked at the stack of reading material. "Thank God. That should last him at least a day or two."

Shannah and the boys had moved a bed into the living room so Kins wouldn't have to immediately climb the narrow stairs up to their bedroom.

"Well, I can see you're a good patient," Tracy said, walking in.

"I'm going stir-crazy and I've been home less than forty-eight hours."

Kins hadn't shaved, and it reminded Tracy of when they'd first met. He'd worked undercover narcotics and had grown a wispy goatee and long hair, earning the nickname Jack Sparrow after the Johnny Depp character in the *Pirates of the Caribbean* movies.

"I'm making lunch, Tracy. Can you stay?" Shannah asked.

"I'm not sure I want to." She cocked a thumb at Kins. "Does he have to be here?"

"Not if you put a pillow over his head when I leave the room."

"You know I could get this kind of love at the office from Del and Faz," Kins said.

"Maybe, but they definitely wouldn't share their lunch," Tracy said.

Shannah departed for the kitchen. Tracy pulled over a chair and sat at the side of the bed. "The office put this together for you." She placed the reading material on Kins's bed. Soft music played from a black speaker. "So how are you doing?"

"The drugs are making me tired and loopy, but I've already started to wean myself off them. Just don't like the way they make me feel."

"And the pain?"

"Surprisingly little," he said. "Everyone was right. I should have had the surgery two years ago. How's work? Did they move anyone in to take my place?"

"Ron's helping out," she said, referring to Ron Mayweather, the A Team's fifth wheel. "We're doing okay."

"What's happening with D'Andre Miller and Trejo?"

Like most detectives, Kins didn't like to feel out of touch and had a subconscious desire to be needed.

"How much medication are you on?"

"Why, something bothering you?"

"Something's not right about this whole thing," Tracy said. "Something about Trejo has been bothering me from the start."

"Like what was he doing in Seattle in the first place?"

"That, for sure. But if he hit D'Andre Miller accidentally, why wouldn't he own up to it?" Tracy said.

Kins called out, "Alexa, off." The music from the black speaker tower stopped. "My latest toy from Amazon; the boys steal it when they have friends over." He adjusted in the bed. "People do stupid things for stupid reasons all the time. I should know, with three sons. I think they get caught up in the moment and then it's like a fly in a spider's web. They can't get out."

Shannah entered the room carrying a plate with two sandwiches, iced tea, and cherry tomatoes. She set everything down on the coffee table. "Okay, I'm out. The boys have soccer practice so it will be a two-hour reprieve . . . I mean two hours of drudgery."

"Funny," Kins said. "You're a regular Conan O'Brien."

"You need anything while I'm out?" Shannah asked, bending down to kiss him.

Kins smiled. "Potato chips?"

"Nice try." She kissed Kins, said good-bye to Tracy, and departed out the front door.

"Are you dieting too?" Tracy asked.

"I'm going to kill Del. He called the other day checking on me, and he and Shannah talked for half an hour. He says he's lost fifteen pounds."

"Might be more than that now. He looks good," Tracy said.

"Yeah, well, so now Shannah is telling me this would be a good time to get healthy."

"Might be." Tracy picked up half a sandwich and started eating. After a minute she said, "Let's assume Trejo isn't stupid. Let's assume he couldn't stop."

"You mean his brakes were out, something like that?"

"I mean what if he was doing something illegal, something that could have got him in bigger trouble if he'd been caught."

"Bigger trouble than running a kid down?" Kins popped a tomato into his mouth.

"What if he'd been drunk or high when he hit the kid?"

Kins gave it some thought. "It would explain why he abandoned the car."

"But not necessarily how he knew the lot was there. The easement looks like a driveway."

"You'd drive right past it unless you knew about it," Kins agreed.

"And he said he was from San Diego and didn't get over to Seattle often."

"So he either already knew about it . . . somehow, or someone let him know about it," Kins said.

Tracy took another bite of her sandwich. "He also had to know we would figure out his car wasn't stolen." CSI had not found any marks on the ignition switch and nothing untoward with regard to the wires underneath the dash to indicate a theft. "Which is why he concocted that story about keeping a hide-a-key under the back bumper."

"No real way to disprove it," Kins said.

"No, there isn't. But again, doesn't it indicate someone thought this through? It seems a bit more sophisticated than I'd give Trejo credit for," she said.

"Like the interior of the car being wiped down, including the air bag," Kins said. "It sounds like a lawyer, Tracy."

Tracy sipped her iced tea. "Someone who knows about liability and evidence for sure," she agreed.

"Battles?"

"Maybe. But I keep thinking, what does she get out of it?" She finished her half of the sandwich and wiped her hands with a napkin. "I could make an argument why she might take the videotape, but that doesn't get us to who helped Trejo hide the car and get home that night."

"She lives in Seattle," Kins said.

"I know, but I just don't see her putting her career at risk for Trejo."

"Maybe he has something on her, something to blackmail her."

"Maybe."

"Or it could be more than one person," Kins said.

"Could be." She set down her glass, thinking. "Something else, something I noticed when all the crap was flying around the courtroom about the tape being missing—Trejo never flinched."

Kins reached for another half sandwich. "What do you mean?"

"I mean he just sat there, staring straight ahead, like he didn't understand what was happening."

"Maybe he didn't."

"He had to understand. Everyone else in the courtroom understood. Cho said it right there—they couldn't find the tape."

"But he showed no reaction?" Kins said.

"Wouldn't he? Confusion? Joy? Bewilderment? Something?"

"Could he have been medicated for the hearing? Maybe the stress was too much and they had him on something." Kins set down his sandwich.

"Maybe," she said. "Or maybe he knew it was going to happen."

CHAPTER 30

Nicholas Evans was a high school graduate, bass player in the heavy
metal band CHAOS, and heroin dealer.

"Quite the resume," Del said to Faz.

After reviewing the text messages on Jack Welch's phone, they had the
evidence they needed to establish that Evans sold Allie and Welch the heroin that killed her. Welch had texted Evans the afternoon of that final day.

Looking to score some shit. Have the money.

It took Evans a half an hour to respond. Later today, bro.

When Welch didn't hear from Evans, he contacted him again late
in the afternoon. Dude, my friend and I are ready whenever you are.

Evans responded. Chill, bro. I'm working on it.

Finally, at five in the afternoon, Evans contacted Welch. BK on
Aurora. 20 minutes.

Welch then texted Allie the messages Del had seen on her phone,
but which now had a much better context. Score! Need to be there
in 20. I'll pick you up.

Allie, however, continued to express reluctance. **Not sure home by then. Just go w/o me.**

Del sat back from his computer. Tears filled his eyes. Allie had been so close to just going home, so close to staying alive, but Welch didn't have the money for the buy, and like most addicts, he wasn't about to let it go.

I'll pick you up. Can't miss out. He has other buyers. Srsly. This stuff is sweet.

Allie's response, so simple and so sad, might have expressed more about the hold heroin had on her being, the life-and-death daily struggle she fought, than anything else she could have said.

K.

Faz contacted Narcotics and asked whether they had any information on Evans. Surprisingly, they did not, despite several detectives working undercover in Seattle. They were certainly aware of several suspected dealers, but Evans's name was not among them. Given that Evans was not peddling black tar but rather a high-grade heroin, or one laced with something deadly, they speculated that he could be a lone wolf, keeping a low profile to remain off all the radars. Del asked that he and Faz be kept advised.

Del and Faz had located Evans in an apartment in Green Lake and brought him, without incident, to the King County Jail. Evans wasn't a high school senior, like Welch. He was twenty-two, and at the moment he was acting like a tough guy, professing an unwillingness to talk to them, except to say he wanted a lawyer. So be it. Late on a Friday afternoon, Evans wasn't getting out of jail until, at the very earliest, a probable cause hearing the following Monday. Celia McDaniel would handle that hearing and told Del that, realistically, Evans's bail would be set at $50,000.

She could try for more, argue the gravity of the situation, the deadly nature of the drug Evans was peddling, but they could only link him to Allie's death at this time, and they were still awaiting the toxicology analysis on the heroin Del had found in his niece's bedroom.

"The smart move," she'd said over the phone, "is to keep the amount of bail within a ballpark that a judge will feel comfortable imposing."

That meant that, with a $5,000 payment to a bail bondsman, Evans would walk from jail. But Del didn't think so.

"Play it as you ordinarily would," Del said. "I suspect from my view of the shit-hole apartment Evans lived in that he's a lot like Welch, and has worn out his welcome at home. I don't think Mommy and Daddy will be eager to dig up the cash necessary to bail him out."

And that would give Del the weekend to put together the evidence needed for the charging documents. It was definitely a step in the right direction, a step toward determining who was supplying the drug that had killed Allie and maybe several others, but the closer Del got, the further away he felt from any form of satisfaction or closure. He kept thinking of what Celia had told him, about the three or four dealers who'd be waiting in the wings to fill any gap in the supply chain, about how her conviction of her son's dealers had brought her little satisfaction.

"Revenge," she'd told him, "is a poor substitute for a son."

Del kept telling himself that he had a job to do, that he was a cop, that others might also be out there dying, and that he had been tasked with putting a stop to it. But he also couldn't ignore the truth in Celia's words. He wondered, when it was all finished, when he had found those who had supplied Allie, when they had been prosecuted and put in jail, whether he would feel the same as Celia, and, more important, whether his sister would too. He wondered if his burning desire to bring those responsible to justice wasn't actually about his sister at all, but about his own burning desire for revenge. And he wondered whether, in the end, revenge would be just as hollow a substitute for a niece . . . and certainly for a daughter.

CHAPTER 31

Friday afternoon, when Tracy walked into the conference room, Cerrabone and Dunleavy sat waiting. Her captain, Johnny Nolasco, and Chief of Police Sandy Clarridge would also join the meeting. "How's Kins?" Cerrabone asked as she entered and sat.

"He's doing well," Tracy said. "I just saw him. It's pretty amazing what they can do now. He calls in several times a day just to drive us all crazy."

"How's the pain?"

"Mine or his?" They laughed. "It was either surgery or replace his kidneys from all the ibuprofen he was taking," Tracy said.

Clarridge entered the room followed by Nolasco, who shut the door.

Once they were all seated, Dunleavy led the meeting. "We received a call today from the Navy's senior trial counsel. Trejo is going to be released in a couple of hours."

"Is the case coming back?" Clarridge asked.

Dunleavy shrugged. "That decision has not been formally made yet, but I suspect that, absent the videotape, the Navy's case got a lot more difficult, especially if it proceeds to a court-martial and a reasonable-doubt standard. Trejo and his counsel will scream about the missing tape and his inability to confront witnesses. I'm not sure the prosecution can overcome it. I'm not sure we could either."

"And I'm dead certain the community will not be satisfied with that answer," Clarridge said, growing red in the face.

"At the moment the community is upset with the Navy," Dunleavy said. "I'm not sure we want to step into that mess and give them the opportunity to direct their ire at us, especially if we can't convict. I'm told the Navy is going to go after the defense attorney on an ethical investigation and, depending on the outcome, may court-martial her for dereliction of duty, among other things."

"So they got their scapegoat," Nolasco said.

"What do you think?" Clarridge looked across the table to Tracy. "Could she have taken the tape rather than it just being misplaced?"

"Could she have? Sure," Tracy said. "She certainly had access to it. Did she? That's a more difficult question. I don't know. What we do know is whoever helped Trejo definitely knew about evidence, the significance of it anyway. Not many people would have thought to wipe down the air bag."

"It's on every cop show on television," Nolasco said. "Let's not get carried away here."

"The air bag?" Tracy said. "I must have missed that show."

"They might have wiped the air bag in the process of wiping down the car," Nolasco said. "I could see Trejo being at least that smart, or lucky."

"Maybe," Tracy said. "But would he have known that without the tape all the other evidence becomes circumstantial?"

"He might not have been thinking that far in advance," Nolasco countered. "Like I said, blind luck. It does happen. Think of it another way—why would the defense attorney do it? What did she hope to gain?"

"According to the prosecutor, she had a competitive streak, didn't like to lose," Cerrabone said.

"I agree with the captain," Tracy said.

"Anybody taking notes? That might be a first," Nolasco said.

"We're talking about a court-martial, loss of pay, dismissal . . . That's an awful lot to give up just to get a win, especially under these circumstances," Tracy said. "The alternative is Trejo may have some information detrimental to her or her career."

"Blackmail?" Clarridge asked.

"I'm just trying to think of all the possibilities."

"Do we know what she says happened?" Clarridge asked.

Tracy nodded. "I spoke to her last night. She says she had the evidence box the night before the hearing but isn't certain the tape was in the box. I think it had to be."

"Why?" Clarridge asked.

"Because it would have been too big a risk for someone else to have taken it before she had the box."

"So it disappeared while she possessed the box," Nolasco said. "That's evidence she took it."

"Yes, but she says she'd already looked at the tape and didn't see the need to look at it again that night, nor did she have a television to view it."

"Sounds like convenient bullshit," Nolasco said. "If she already watched it, she knew Trejo was screwed. She didn't need a TV to watch it again before she got rid of it."

"Maybe not," Tracy said. "But again, it's a hell of a risk to take the tape when everyone knows you were the last person to check out the evidence." She could see the others agreeing with her. "It makes more sense to take the tape after she returned the box to the evidence room."

"Maybe she did," Nolasco said.

"Maybe," Tracy said.

"Or maybe the tape was simply misplaced," Dunleavy said.

"NCIS interviewed the janitors," Tracy said, "and the one who cleaned the first floor, and her office, doesn't recall seeing any tape. He also said it goes against their company protocol to disturb anything in the offices. All they really do is empty the garbage and vacuum."

Clarridge intervened. "Okay, so assuming it was in the box when Battles returned it, who else had access to get it?"

"Anybody with access to the court reporter's office," Tracy said. "It's just across the hall from the courtroom. The prosecutor's offices are also on that floor. However, from what I'm told, anyone coming into the building has to enter the last four digits of their Social Security number. So there'd be a record of who went into the building."

"Could it have been Cho?" Clarridge asked. "Could he have taken it before he left?"

"He could have, but I can't think of any reason why the prosecution would take it. The tape helped them," Tracy said.

"Anyone else?" Clarridge asked.

Tracy shook her head.

"So either it was misplaced and lost," Nolasco said, "or Battles took it."

"Even if we reach that conclusion, it doesn't answer the other questions, like who helped Trejo hide his car and get back to Bremerton that night."

"They don't have to be related," Nolasco said. "It could have been his wife. What does she say?"

"Exactly what Trejo says," Tracy said. "He was home that night."

"So she's lying for him, and Battles miscalculated the ramifications," Nolasco responded. "Let's not overthink this. We have enough on our plate as it is. If we get back involved, let TCI handle the investigation."

"How long will it take the Navy to make up their mind if they're going forward or not?" Clarridge asked Dunleavy.

"The preliminary hearing officer isn't saying they shouldn't go forward with a general court-martial, but she also didn't mince her words:

the case is significantly weaker without the tape, and the defense will surely exploit that weakness," Dunleavy said.

"So Trejo just waits for the court-martial knowing the prosecution can't meet the more stringent guilty standard," Cerrabone said.

"That appears to be the Navy's thinking as well," Dunleavy said.

Clarridge sat back, biting his lower lip. "What can we charge him with, if we were to take back jurisdiction?"

"Absent the tape?" Dunleavy shook his head. "I'm not sure we can get anything to stick. He says he wasn't there. Everything we would put forward would be circumstantial. The defense would almost certainly win a motion to exclude any mention of the tape, given that they can't effectively cross-examine any witness who would testify that they viewed it. If the Navy is expressing reluctance to move forward—and they routinely take weaker cases to trial—I'm not sure we would want to do anything, especially in this particular climate," Dunleavy said.

"I agree," Nolasco said. "Better we stay out of it and let the Navy take the heat."

"And what about that little boy, that mother?" Tracy said.

"It's tragic," Dunleavy said. "No one is saying it isn't, but I'm not certain there's anything we can do about it."

"If I may," Tracy said. The others in the room looked at her. "I was in the courtroom when the tape went missing. I was on the witness stand, facing the audience. I saw Trejo. I watched him. He had no reaction to the news."

"So what are you saying?" Clarridge asked.

"I think he knew the tape was not coming in. I think he knew he was going to walk."

"What you think is not—" Nolasco began before she cut him off.

"He was definitely in Seattle that night," she said. "That's a fact. I saw the store receipt and I saw the video. Forget whether we can prove it for the moment. He was there. He ran that kid down. And, he had help after the fact."

"How do you know that?" Dunleavy asked.

"Because someone had to help him stash his car in the vacant lot behind that woman's house—"

"Maybe he knew it was there," Nolasco said.

"Maybe. But then how did he get back to Bremerton without his car? He didn't take a cab and he didn't swim." Before Nolasco could protest, she said, "Look, if someone took that tape it makes these other factors, the vacant lot, Trejo getting back to base, a lot more relevant. It would mean that someone went to a lot of trouble to make sure Trejo would get off. And if they did, the question is, Why? Either Trejo was important to someone, or he had some leverage over them."

"A lot of ifs," Dunleavy said.

"I don't disagree, but I think we owe it to that mother and to that boy not to just walk away."

"So what are you proposing?" Clarridge asked.

"We still technically have jurisdiction, if the Navy punts, right?" She looked at Dunleavy. "There's no double jeopardy here. We could still try him for the same offenses."

"Didn't we just all agree that's the one thing we don't want to do?" Nolasco said.

"I agree with your captain, Detective. I'm not sure we want to dive back in without the evidence to support the charges," Clarridge said.

"I'm not saying we prosecute him. I'm saying we make it look like we're going to prosecute him." She looked to Dunleavy.

"You're saying, if others helped Trejo, we make it appear that we are going to prosecute him and hope that when he's out of the brig, he makes contact with whoever it is that helped him?"

"Trejo is getting out this afternoon," Cerrabone said. "We could call a press conference for the same time and put out the word that we are seriously considering prosecuting him. Make him think he isn't out of the woods and see what he does. See if he runs to anyone."

"You want to put a tail on him?" Clarridge said.

"We could alert the Bremerton Police Department," Nolasco said. "Have them tail him."

"I'd prefer to tail him myself," Tracy said. "I know where he lives and I know where he works. I've been to his apartment, and I know the layout of the complex, the type of car he drives, and where he parks. This way we can also keep it internal."

"We got enough on our plates," Nolasco said again.

"We keep Bremerton out of it," she said, "and nobody knows we never intended to prosecute him."

Clarridge looked to Dunleavy. "Do you see any problems?"

Dunleavy shook his head. "No." He looked at Tracy. "Other than that you could be in for some long nights."

"Kins is already out of commission," Nolasco emphasized. "We're shorthanded."

"I don't need anyone else," Tracy said. "I can spend the night over there, and in the morning I can use the time to talk to the janitorial service and get a copy of the security tape for the DSO building for that night."

Dunleavy looked around the table at the others. "I don't think it could hurt."

"It's worth a shot," Cerrabone said.

They looked to Clarridge. After a moment of thought he said, "Then let's get started on a statement to the public that might make Trejo react."

CHAPTER 32

Tracy took one of the pool cars and crossed Elliott Bay on the ferry. The winter chill had given way to spring rains—but not the traditional on-again, off-again Seattle sprinkles; these rains swept in like East Coast storms, releasing a downpour, subsiding, then hitting again with another fury. Exiting the ferry, Tracy drove to Jackson Park, arriving at the apartment complex after dark. She knew from her prior trip that Trejo lived in an apartment building located on a street corner. If she parked on the street perpendicular to Trejo's complex, a sloped lawn provided some protection from nosy neighbors. So would the heavy rains.

Once situated, she saw no late-night dog walkers or joggers, and no athletes played on the basketball or tennis courts. The location afforded her a view of Trejo's walkway, which descended a couple steps to his front door. The Subaru was parked in its designated parking stall, the front fender still dented, though the windshield had been fixed. If Trejo left the apartment Tracy would see him. And there were only two ways to exit the complex by car, neither of which would be difficult to follow—if Trejo went anywhere.

Dunleavy had issued his statement at just after 5:30 p.m., timing it with Trejo's release. He made it emphatic, without promising anything, saying that SPD would review all of the evidence with an eye toward charging Trejo. Tracy thought the wording was strong enough that, if Trejo was going to act, he would do so. She hoped she was right about someone providing Trejo assistance after the accident. If she was, she suspected that person or persons would not want to have discussions with Trejo over the telephone, but rather would choose to meet in person. She'd find out one way or another soon enough.

She sat eating a protein bar and listening to the rain beat on the roof of the pool car. At just after 9:00 p.m., the porch light over Trejo's front door illuminated. It could have been a timer. Tracy sat up, watching through a sheet of rain. The door to the apartment opened, light spilling from the apartment onto the front walk, and Trejo, she assumed, hurried out and down the walkway. He was the right height, but the person had a hood over his head to protect him from the rain, and he was jogging away from her, toward the Subaru. She had little choice but to assume it was Trejo and follow.

She pulled down the bill of the Mariners baseball cap she'd taken from Kins's cubicle and started the car. She kept the lights off and made a U-turn, then a left at the corner, driving on the street parallel with the back of Trejo's apartment complex. Up the hill, through the rain, she saw the lights of the Subaru brighten. The car backed out from the carport and drove toward the first of the two exits. Trejo, if it was him, turned left. One street below, she followed.

Trejo wound his way through the complex toward the exit and turned north onto State Route 3, a four-lane road with a grass-and-dirt center divider. Moments later, Tracy reached the intersection, turned on the car's lights, and followed. SR3 was not heavily populated, especially on a miserable night. The persistent rains and darkness would help to conceal Tracy's car, but she kept her distance and tried to blend in with the few cars on the road.

Five minutes into the drive, Trejo took the exit for Newberry Hill Road. Long and flat, the exit allowed Tracy to keep an eye on the Subaru without getting too close. Trejo merged right. Tracy hoped to get behind another car, but did not see any headlights approaching when she stopped at the bottom of the exit. Not wanting to get too far behind and risk losing Trejo at another light, she turned right and followed. Newberry Hill was two lanes, one in each direction. At a bend, the road became Silverdale Way, and passed large single-family homes on the shores of Dyes Inlet. Tonight the water was a dark ink color with whitecaps churned by the wind and rain.

As the Subaru approached Bucklin Hill Road, the first major intersection, it slowed for a red light. Rather than get too close, Tracy turned into a strip mall with a large parking lot and continued across it. She exited onto Bucklin Hill, again behind the Subaru, when its taillights brightened unexpectedly and the car slowed and again turned right, this time onto an unmarked road. Signage indicated this was an access road to Old Mill Park, a dead end.

Tracy drove past the park entrance in case Trejo suspected he was being followed and was using the park to double back, or just taking precautions. Instead, she turned left into a shopping mall across the street and parked in a stall that allowed her to watch the entrance to the park. If Trejo exited, she'd see the car. When the Subaru did not emerge, she shut off the engine and pushed open her car door. She quickly slipped on her raincoat and pulled the hood over the baseball cap as she hurried to the sidewalk along Bucklin Hill Road. She let traffic pass and cut across the first two lanes to a center island. She waited again for an opening in traffic before jogging across the two westbound lanes to the park entrance. Water dripped from the bill of her hat and the rain, whipped by the wind, made it difficult to see. She picked up her pace down the access road. The Subaru was the only car parked in a dozen stalls. Trejo was not in it. Neither was anyone else. Just past the stalls she came to a concrete-block public restroom. She tried the door and found it locked.

She crept past the building to a fork in the dirt paths. One proceeded straight. The other branched off to her left. She had no idea which path Trejo had taken or where either trail ended. In the dark, with the heavy rain, she doubted she'd be able to pick up his footprints, but that was not her biggest concern. She had hoped Trejo would drive to an apartment or to a home, which would allow her to get an address and determine the owner. Alternatively, she had hoped he'd meet someone in a public setting, like a restaurant, where she could get a visual ID on the person. An outdoor meeting had not entered her mind. If this were some type of setup, she'd be walking into it blind.

CHAPTER 33

When Faz turned the street corner, Del saw patrol vehicles from the North Precinct blocking the road, and officers in rain gear redirecting traffic. He felt sick. The lights on the patrol cars illuminated the night in mournful strobes of red and blue. Del and Faz had been at Shawn O'Donnell's finishing dinner when Del's cell phone rang. Jeanine Welch had received the call that she'd been dreading for years.

A fire engine was parked at an angle in the street just behind an ambulance and the medical examiner's van. Most of the activity centered on the garage at the back of the property, more specifically on the apartment above it.

"Hopefully the weather will keep the neighbors inside," Faz said.

"I doubt it," Del said. "This is like the circus coming to town." He was right. A closer inspection revealed people already standing in the street dressed in rain gear and holding umbrellas, or looking out from the covered porches of their homes. But the invasion of Jeanine Welch's privacy was not what was foremost on Del's mind. Foremost was Stuart Funk's warning of a highly potent heroin on the street.

Del lowered the window to speak to the officer directing traffic, and the rain spit at him through the gap. The officer, in full rain gear, bent down close to the gap. Del badged him. "Looking for the sergeant in charge," he said.

The officer pointed to a Hispanic officer standing near the garage, then stepped to the side to allow them to enter. Once parked, they exited, pulling long raincoats tight and opening black umbrellas.

"Violent Crimes?" the sergeant said when Del and Faz introduced themselves. "This is an overdose."

"We got an ongoing investigation," Del said. "Where's his mother?"

The sergeant gestured to the back of the house. Rain dripped from the brim of his hat, which was covered in plastic. "She's inside. I have an officer getting a statement."

Del looked at the house, knowing it would never be the same. "Is the daughter home?"

"No. The mother said she sent her to a friend's house when she got the call at work."

"When was that?"

The sergeant talked over the rain and wind, which had picked up in intensity. "About an hour, hour and a half ago. A friend came by and found them."

"Them?"

"Young man and young woman."

Del looked to Faz, then back to the sergeant. "Where's the person who called?"

"Gone. Anonymous, apparently. No one here when the patrol units arrived. Medical examiner is in there now; said this is the twelfth or thirteenth OD already this month. It's becoming an epidemic."

Del thought of Celia McDaniel's admonition in the donut shop. "It already is an epidemic," he said.

A yellow light illuminated the staircase leading up to the apartment. At the landing, Del and Faz shook out their umbrellas and leaned them against the side of the building. They signed a log-in sheet presented by an officer at the door and stepped inside a twenty-by-twenty-foot room humid from the rain-soaked bodies huddled inside. Condensation covered the windowpanes, and the air held the pungent, sour smell of cigarettes. Clothes lay in heaps. Unwashed kitchenware, spent soda, beer cans, and other items lay strewn about the furnishings, which were sparse—a lone chair for sitting, no television or stereo. Del recalled Jeanine Welch telling them that Jack sold whatever he could in his never-ending quest to get high. He suspected the room had become little more than a place where Jack Welch crashed.

The assembled men and women, Funk included, were gathered around a mattress on the floor beneath a sloped ceiling, the night sky visible beyond two skylights. A young woman lay on her stomach, fully clothed, with her head tilted awkwardly off the edge of the mattress. A puddle of spit pooled on the floor. Jack Welch lay beside her, on his back. His drug-ravaged body looked as small and thin as a little boy's. His eyes remained open, as if admiring the distant stars through the skylights. The friars had taught Del to believe that those he loved would be waiting at his death to welcome him into heaven. Del had always doubted the stories, until Allie's death. It was easier if he believed that his father or mother had greeted Allie, and that she'd be taken care of. He hoped so.

Hope became something to cling to when there was nothing else but despair.

On a wooden crate beside Welch's bed, an alarm clock and pack of cigarettes sat amid the drug paraphernalia—a burnt spoon, several syringes, lighters, and a plastic bag containing a powdery substance that, upon initial review, closely resembled in color and consistency the substance Del had found in Allie's room. The fact that the anonymous caller, likely another junkie, had not taken the bag might have been most significant. The ramifications of its contents were right there—two dead bodies.

Funk noted Del's and Faz's presence and stepped away from the bed to speak to them. He kept his voice soft. "How'd you hear?"

"He went to school with Allie," Del said. "The mother called. We came out to talk to her the other night. He was with Allie when they bought the product that killed her."

Funk grimaced and readjusted his glasses. "Then that's a problem. This is not black tar. I don't know what it is, going to have to wait until the toxicology lab tests it, but I'd venture to guess from the lack of any smell that it's China white, or something close to it, highly potent, or cut with something like fentanyl."

"What do you mean the lack of any smell?" Faz asked.

"Most street heroin has a smell, like vinegar, because the producers don't care about getting it beyond ninety percent pure. The other ten percent is usually some kind of un-reacted acetic acid. Really pure heroin doesn't have that smell."

"Do we know who the woman is?" Faz asked.

"We found her purse on the counter. Her name is Talia Crenshaw."

"TC," Del said.

"What's that?" Faz asked.

"She was in a picture with Welch. Allie called her TC. Welch was dating her when Allie went into rehab."

"Can we tell if it's the same stuff that Allie used or any of the other overdoses?" Faz asked.

"All I can tell you at this time is it's definitely not black tar," Funk repeated. "But I'd say it's likely we're talking about the same product. We're going through all the proper channels to warn people on the street. We don't have a choice, not with people dying."

Del and Faz asked additional questions, requested that they be kept posted on any toxicology results, then let Funk do his work. Outside they gathered their umbrellas and went back down the stairs.

"I'm not looking forward to this," Del said, making his way toward the house and a conversation with Jeanine Welch. When last they'd spoke, Welch said she'd been resigned to Jack's death, but Del knew from experience there was a big difference between speculation and reality. Looking into your child's eyes, knowing you would never again see in them the glint of life, was the harshest kind of reality, and there wasn't a faith in the world that could ease that pain.

—

Tracy chose the trail that proceeded more or less straight, though in the darkness and blanket of rain, she was walking blind. Swaying trees and thick brush lined the path, and the winds carried the briny smell of wetlands. Though she was just a stone's throw from civilization, she could not hear anything over the howling wind and rain, and the pounding of waves on the shore. Puddles had begun to overwhelm the path and to penetrate her leather boots, saturating her socks.

She continued until she neared the end of the stand of trees, about twenty feet from the beach. She saw the iridescent glow of the surging white foam crashing onto the rocks and sand, and scattered bleached logs, strewn like the discarded bones of a whale. She did not see Trejo or anyone else. To her right was a V-shaped Best Western hotel. She quickly dismissed the possibility Trejo had gone there. If he had, why wouldn't he have parked under cover, protected from the rain? It was more likely Trejo had taken the other path.

She'd chosen incorrectly.

She walked along the beach toward where the other trail ended, mindful of her footing on the beach logs and scraps of wood. The rain intensified and she lowered the bill of her hat to deflect it, struggling to see. She slipped but managed to remain upright. Water seeped through crevices and she felt her shirt sticking to her back.

As she neared where the second footpath intersected with the beach, she heard a muffled pop and saw a blue-white light flash in the trees. Gunshot. She dropped to a knee and removed her Glock. She watched and listened for nearly a minute, then dismissed the thought that anyone had been shooting at her. If someone wanted her dead, they could have easily stepped from the brush and put a bullet in the back of her head.

She stood and hurried away from the water into the stand of trees where she had seen the muzzle flash. The saturated ground clung to the soles of her boots, making a sucking sound with each step. The trees, at least, provided some relief from the rain and allowed her to push back the hood of her raincoat and to raise the bill of her hat. As she made her way through the trees, she again stopped to consider her surroundings. She saw no one and heard only the gusting wind and beating rain. She followed the trail for another twenty yards, until she saw that someone sat at one of two picnic tables in an open field and again dropped to a knee. The figure, slumped over the table, wasn't moving. Tracy waited a full minute before proceeding forward, gun drawn.

As she approached, she stepped to her right to get a better angle in case the figure suddenly sprang to life. It didn't.

She recognized the jacket.

A step closer and she saw the face—Laszlo Trejo. On the other side of his body, a handgun rested on the table near his left hand.

—

Del had called the King County Jail on the drive back from Jeanine Welch's home, after spending time with her, knowing what she was going through. He asked that Nicholas Evans be escorted through the underground tunnel to the interrogation room. He didn't care what time of night it would be when they arrived. He and Evans had things to discuss. If Evans continued to choose not to talk, then he could listen.

Evans turned his head to look at Del and Faz as they entered the interrogation room. This time neither carried a chair. Behind the one-way glass, members of the narcotics unit sat observing Evans, eager to hear what he had to say, if he said anything at all.

Evans's eyes followed them. He looked uncertain and uncomfortable but fought to maintain the tough-guy persona. Del knew tough guys. He'd grown up with some tough guys in Wisconsin, and he'd arrested more than a few in his day. This guy was no tough guy.

Evans sat back as far as the long chain that extended from his handcuffs to the eyebolt ring in the floor would allow. Portions of the tattoos on his chest and arms peeked out from his red jail scrubs—a cross on his right forearm, several tombstones—each with a name—on his left. Del wondered if they were the names of friends who'd died. Evans would need room for at least two more. The upper half of the word CHAOS extended across the base of his neck from collarbone to collarbone, like a necklace. He'd pulled his shoulder-length, curly blond hair into a bun that made his already thin, feminine features more prominent. Time in prison would be a bitch for this guy, and he'd be the bitch.

"I'm not speaking to either of you." Evans dropped his chin and refused to meet their stares.

"Then you can listen," Del said, voice calm and deliberate, as if he had all the time in the world. "We just came from Jack Welch's home."

Evans peeked but kept his head turned to the side.

Del said, "CHAOS is going to need a new guitar player."

Evans turned toward them, concern in his face.

"Let me paint you a picture," Del said, resting his palms on the table and leaning down into Evans's personal space. "Jack was lying on his back on his mattress. His eyes were open and he was staring up through skylights. Beside him lay a young woman with her head over the side of the bed, foam spewing from her mouth onto the floor. On the dresser we found used syringes, a blackened spoon, some BIC lighters, and a small bag of heroin." Del waited, letting the uncomfortable moment grow. Evans stared at the tabletop, his gaze unfocused. "You're selling death," Del said. "More than ten people we know of have died from the shit you're selling." Del didn't know, not for certain, but then neither did Evans.

Del pushed back from the table. "So let me tell you how this is going to go. The prosecutor will charge you with a controlled substance homicide and try you separately for each death. The penalty is a ten-year sentence, each to run consecutively. That's ninety to one hundred years, Nick. You'll never get out. And a guy like you . . ." Del shrugged. "So you go ahead and be a tough guy, and you tell us you're not going to talk to us. You go right ahead. But we aren't coming back again."

Evans sat back. His right leg bounced, making the chain between his legs rattle like he had loose change in his pocket. His head bobbed to a different beat—out of sync with his leg, and he looked to be having trouble catching his breath, breathing in deeply as if trying to ward off hyperventilating. "I need a lawyer," he said, voice cracking.

"Okay." Del looked to Faz, who shrugged. "Let's go."

Evans quickly stopped them. "No! I mean . . . I need a lawyer to structure a deal."

"A deal?" Del said. "Why would we make a deal with you?"

"Because I know some things." Evans stumbled over his words, speaking in a rush. "I know . . . I know where the drugs are coming from."

"The drugs are coming from you," Del said. "We have text messages and e-mails confirming . . ."

"No," he said, shaking his head. "What I mean is, I know where they're coming from . . . I could tell you where I'm getting them. You'd want to know that, right?"

Bingo, Del thought. "Okay, be my guest. Tell us. Where are they coming from?"

Evans shook his head. "That's why I need a deal. That's why I need a lawyer."

Del nodded to Faz to proceed.

"We have families to think about here," Faz said. "They're going to want to see someone punished for their child's death. What are we supposed to tell them?"

Evans didn't have an answer. His legs continued the jig, the left leg now accompanying the right.

"You see the problem?" Faz said. "So if you want a deal, you've got to give us something to take to the prosecutor, because I can tell you he's not going to be inclined to make any kind of a deal with someone who's selling death."

"I didn't know it was killing anyone," Evans said. "I didn't know that."

"It doesn't matter," Del said. "It's one of the hazards of selling heroin."

They sat in silence for almost a minute, Evans looking uncertain, chewing on his bottom lip. Finally, he said, "What if I told you that I know something about that guy, the one you arrested a couple weeks ago?"

Del frowned. "You're going to have to be a little more specific than that, Nick."

"The guy who was involved in that hit and run, the guy who killed that black kid in Rainier Beach."

CHAPTER 34

Nicholas Evans looked up at Faz, who now sat beside Rick Cerrabone in the interrogation room. Del was in the adjacent room behind the one-way glass, listening and watching with Celia McDaniel and the narcotics detectives.

Upon Nicholas Evans's revelation, Del and Faz had called Cerrabone and Celia at home and told them, "We got a drug dealer in the interrogation room. You're going to want to hear what this guy is telling us." Del also tried to call Tracy, but she did not answer her cell.

Faz made the introductions. Cerrabone, in a striped button-down shirt that he'd likely worn to work that day, looked tired, but he always looked tired, the bags under his eyes like spent tea bags. Balding, he combed his hair straight back from his forehead. They said sixty was the new forty, but for Cerrabone and a lot of trial lawyers, forty looked to be sixty.

"I'm told you might have information on a hit and run in Rainier Beach," Cerrabone said.

Evans nodded. "But I want a deal. I won't testify or put anything in writing unless I have a deal."

"I understand," Cerrabone said, calm and matter-of-fact. Making no promises. "But I need to know a little more about what you told Detective Fazzio before I can consider anything."

Evans gave this some thought. He sat forward, as if imparting a secret. "You guys arrested a guy in Rainier Beach for a hit and run. He was in the Navy, right?"

"That's right," Cerrabone said.

"Well, I know what he was doing in Seattle that night."

Cerrabone didn't react. Neither did Faz. When Evans didn't continue, Cerrabone said, "How do you know what he was doing?"

"Someone told me."

"Someone?"

Evans sat back, smug. "Yep."

"Who?"

"A guy who would know."

Cerrabone frowned. He glanced at Faz. This was all part of an act. He shrugged. "'A guy who would know' really doesn't tell me anything, Detective." He spoke to Evans. "If you don't have personal knowledge it's called hearsay, and hearsay evidence isn't any good to me because a judge won't allow it in court. It isn't considered reliable." He spread his hands as if to say, *What am I going to do?*

Evans hesitated again, thinking. Then he said, "It's the guy who supplies me the heroin."

"He's your source?"

"Yep."

"Okay. Again, Nick, look at it from my perspective. A judge, or a defense attorney, will say that I took the word of a drug dealer looking to make a deal about another drug dealer. Do you see the problem? The story of the young boy killed in the hit and run has been in the newspaper and on the evening news. He'll say you could have just read about it and made the whole thing up. And that's just not going to get me very far."

Evans pointed to Faz, seemingly alarmed that his big news might not be his ticket out of trouble. "What if I tell him? Then he can find out if it's true or not, right?"

"Maybe," Cerrabone said. "What did your supplier tell you?"

Evans licked his lips. "He asked if I'd read about the Navy guy who'd got busted for hit and run. I said I hadn't heard anything about it. That's when he told me."

They were going in circles. Cerrabone, after a breath, said, "Told you what, exactly?"

Evans squinted as if looking into a bright light. "Do I have a deal?"

"I don't know. You really haven't told me anything yet."

"So this guy that sells, he asked me whether I knew about the Navy guy, and I said no. Then he said that the Navy guy was delivering over a pound of heroin when he hit that kid."

"Delivering?" Cerrabone said.

"That's right."

"From where?"

Evans shrugged. "I don't know, but he was definitely this guy's supplier."

CHAPTER 35

Tracy sat in a room at the Bremerton Police Department on Burwell Street, just after midnight. She'd been to the Bremerton station on one prior occasion, seeking support for the execution of a search warrant in a homicide case. The red brick-and-metal building took up half a city block, including a fenced-in area for police vehicles—part of a weird zoning mix of residential homes, apartment buildings, and parking lots. She looked and felt like a sodden cat, her clothes still damp. She'd called in Laszlo Trejo's body, then waited several hours while the coroner and detectives completed their work.

A secure door opened, and a man, perhaps five nine, midfifties, his hair slicked back and graying at the temples, entered. Despite the hour, he looked fresh in a button-down, the cuffs neatly folded up his forearms, revealing a silver watch, silver-and-turquoise band, and wedding ring. He had not been one of the detectives at the site. Tracy figured him to be a sergeant.

"You must be Crosswhite?" The detective offered a hand and a confident smile. "No one else would be out this time of night or in this weather. John Owens," he said. "Come on back." Tracy followed him through the door. "It's a late night for me, but it has to be a very early morning for you," Owens said.

"I'm working the night shift," she said, though she no longer knew what shift she was working.

"On Bremerton?" Owens glanced back over his shoulder as he worked his way down a hall. Police could be territorial, and Tracy knew that foremost on Owens's mind was the reason for SPD's presence at a crime scene in his jurisdiction, and why he hadn't received any notice. He stepped into a small office with a cluttered desk and pointed to a round table. "Make yourself comfortable." He held up a mug and a pot of coffee. "Coffee? Just made it."

"Sure," Tracy said. She accepted the coffee, the mug warm in her hands, and sat at the table. Above her she heard the low hum of the air conditioner and felt a brush of cold air from a vent. She noted several framed certificates on the wall, one bordered in navy-blue and gold, an honorable discharge from the United States Navy.

"You served," she said.

Owens glanced over his shoulder as he poured himself a cup of coffee. "I did. Thought about making a career out of it but decided I'd rather be a cop. Ironic that I would end up here where the naval base dominates."

Tracy adjusted her chair so the vent was not blowing on her.

Owens joined her at the table. "You said you guys were interested in Trejo in a hit and run in Seattle?" He'd talked to his detectives.

"That's right. A twelve-year-old boy."

"I recall that case, but I thought the Navy took jurisdiction?" Again, the question was pointed.

"They did," Tracy said. "And it appeared to be open-and-shut until a key piece of evidence disappeared at the Article 32 hearing."

Owens sipped his coffee. Then he said, "Trejo's Article 32 hearing was also prominent in the local newspaper. I guess what I'm more confused about is why an SPD homicide detective is here, now, if SPD didn't have jurisdiction. Trejo's death is our jurisdiction."

"The powers that be wanted us to keep a hand in this case since it looked like it could come back."

"Okay. So why are you here now, this time of night . . ." He checked his watch. "Morning?"

"We were told Trejo was going to be released from the brig this afternoon. The DA in Seattle decided to issue a statement to the effect that we intended to pursue charges."

Owens squinted, as if trying to understand. "Do you?"

"That isn't for me to decide," Tracy said, not about to throw anyone under the bus. "We were hoping that by issuing a statement, Trejo might react."

"Well, you got that wish." Owens sipped his coffee and set down the mug. "What were you hoping he'd do?"

She shrugged and explained her hypothesis that someone had helped Trejo ditch his car and get back to Bremerton.

"So, what, you thought he might run to someone?"

"He couldn't while he was in the brig, so, yeah, I thought it possible he would meet that person as soon as he was out."

"You have any other evidence to support that theory?"

"He's dead, isn't he?"

Owens's eyes narrowed. "My detectives said you don't believe it was a suicide."

"Like I said, given everything else that has transpired, it seems doubtful."

"It was his gun."

"But you didn't recover a bullet, did you?"

"That isn't unusual, given the location of death. It could be lodged in a tree somewhere." Owens sat back.

"But without the bullet you can't definitively say he was shot with his gun."

"Look, Crosswhite, this is all very interesting, but in my experience, things are often exactly what they look like. He ran over a twelve-year-old boy, the guilt and shame built, and he shot himself. That could get to anyone."

"Maybe. But the security tape did go missing."

Owens paused. "Tell me again what you saw tonight."

Tracy went through her surveillance on Trejo, how she'd picked the wrong trail, the shot she'd heard, and the blue-white flash of the gun that drew her, ultimately, to the body.

"But you didn't see a person who might have shot him."

"No. But I'd ask his wife whether Trejo was left- or right-handed." Trejo had drunk the Red Bull from a can in his right hand. "The gun was on the table near his left hand."

"Okay, so assuming he didn't kill himself, who's the mostly likely suspect? His defense attorney?" Owens picked up a sheet of paper, reading from it. "Leah Battles?"

"At this point I think everyone's in play."

"Everyone?" Owens shook his head. "You said something about forensics?"

Tracy nodded, but the lack of sleep was setting in and she did not feel like she was speaking clearly. "The inside of his car was wiped clean . . . with an antiseptic wipe, including the air bag, which was the best source of DNA for whoever was driving the car at the time it hit the boy."

Owens sat back and sipped his coffee. He said, "Battles is a lawyer, she knows evidence, and according to my detectives, you said she lives in Seattle."

"Pioneer Square."

Owens nodded. "So she could have helped him that night, if anyone did. And she could get to him in the brig, right, to talk to him?"

"She could."

"And as a JAG, she would have known that you still had jurisdiction over him in Seattle. *If* she were somehow involved, which I'm not convinced she was. It sounds to me like you're fishing and not getting a lot of strikes."

Tracy gave the last comment some thought. "Your detectives spoke to his wife?"

Owens nodded. "She said he left the house just after nine to pick up some groceries."

"Was that something he did regularly or did he get a phone call?"

"She didn't know."

"We need to check his phone."

"I got guys already on it."

"Did she say whether he was right- or left-handed?"

"I'm not sure my detectives asked, but we will."

After a beat Tracy asked, "How's she doing?"

Owens gave another shrug. "About as well as you'd expect for a woman who just lost her husband violently and unexpectedly." Owens scowled. His voice changed. "I don't appreciate being left in the dark on this. If you intended to pursue the hit and run over here, I would have liked a little heads-up. Maybe this could have been avoided."

Tracy nodded, but she wasn't about to apologize. Her cell phone rang, which was odd, given the hour. She checked caller ID. Del's cell phone. He'd called her earlier, but she couldn't take his call at the time. She excused herself, stepped into the hall, and explained where she was and what had happened.

"Then that's a problem," Del said.

CHAPTER 36

After speaking to Tracy, Del went home, feeling both physically and emotionally exhausted. He drove the Impala far enough forward for the second car to pull into his driveway. Celia McDaniel lived thirty-five minutes away. At three in the morning, that was too far to be driving home. At least that's what Del told himself when he'd invited her to spend the night. She winked and told him she'd brought a change of clothes.

So she'd been thinking about it also. He felt both excited and anxiety stricken.

On the drive home, Del kept his mind occupied by contemplating Tracy's news that Laszlo Trejo had been shot in the head. It certainly seemed to jibe with what they'd learned that night from Evans—that Trejo had been delivering heroin. Free from the brig, somebody saw Trejo as a liability, especially after SPD and the prosecuting attorney put out the statement that they intended to go after him. The best way to keep that from happening—to keep Trejo quiet—was to put a bullet in his head. Someone had succeeded.

Del and Tracy had speculated on what this would mean to D'Andre Miller's family, and about how the conspiracy theorists would start crying foul and speculating that the Navy was somehow involved—that Trejo had been killed to hide a secret. Del and Tracy doubted the heroin had anything to do with the Navy, as far as they could tell, anyway. Still, they couldn't deny that Trejo's death muddied the water—"bloodied" might be the better word.

Del exited his Impala and met Celia, who was opening the back door of her Honda. "Let me help with that." He carried her overnight bag and led Celia up the front steps.

The heavy rains and wind had passed, leaving a partially cleared sky with billowing clouds and gaps of silver moonlight.

"You're tired," she said.

Del had pulled down the knot on his tie and unbuttoned the top button of his shirt. He carried his sport coat over his arm. "Yeah, I'm beat. Night shift gets harder every year. But this has got to be really late for you."

"Why do you and Faz still wear ties, Del?"

Del shrugged as he flipped through his ring for the key to the deadbolt. "I do it out of respect for the justice system," he said. "Faz? I think he's too cheap to buy another set of clothes."

She smiled and looked at the window. "Sonny must be going stir-crazy."

"I got him out for his walk earlier," Del said, "but yeah, I'm sure he is."

When Del inserted the key in the lock, Sonny came running. Time was inconsequential to him. He leapt onto the back of the couch and furiously pawed at the window.

"Okay, okay," Del said. "Don't break the glass."

Del opened the door and Sonny bounded from the couch to the front hall to meet them, dancing on his hind legs. He toppled over onto his back, rolled, and got right back up again. When Celia bent to greet him, he ran from her—down the hall, into the kitchen, and back out the door into the living room, a loop. After three circles he came back exhausted, his tiny tongue hanging out of his mouth, panting.

"Let me get him a treat to calm him," Del said. He put her overnight bag down at the foot of the stairs. Celia followed him into the kitchen, the heels of her shoes clicking on the parquet. "You want a glass of wine?" Del asked.

"Small one," she said.

He got Sonny a treat from the pantry but didn't immediately give it to him. "Watch this," he said. "He's a true police dog. Okay, Sonny, don't let me down." He held up the treat. His other hand made a gun. "Bang," he said. Sonny, who'd been on his back legs, promptly fell over, legs in the air.

"That's terrible," Celia said, though she was smiling and laughing. "But smart as hell."

Sonny popped up, took the treat, and hurried out of the room. It would comfort him for the moment.

"Does he do other tricks?" Celia asked.

"We could bore you for hours." Del opened a cabinet and pulled out two tumblers. "I hope a glass is okay. It's the way my parents drank their wine."

"When in Rome," she said.

"Turin." He pulled a bottle of Italian Chianti from another cabinet. "Why a Shih Tzu?"

Del glanced at her as he poured two glasses half full. "I bought him for my ex, but she didn't want him and he didn't want her."

"Well, I think he made the right choice then."

Del held up his glass to hers. *"Salute."*

"Salute," she said. "How long have you been divorced?"

"More than four years."

"How long were you married?"

"Six. I got married late in life. It was a mistake," Del said.

"Getting married?"

"Getting married to the wrong woman. We had too many fundamental differences we both tried to overlook. In the end we couldn't." He led Celia into the back room, his sanctuary. He was about to flip the light switch, but she caught his hand.

"It's beautiful," she said. "Can we leave the lights off?"

"Did I tell you?" he said, admiring a view that never got old. "Best room in the house."

They sat on the leather couch, sipped their wine, and looked out over the sparkling but still-sleeping city.

"You think Evans is telling the truth?" Celia said.

"About Trejo? After what Tracy told me, yeah, I think he is. But I did before somebody put a bullet in his head. Frankly, I don't see Evans as the type of guy to read the newspaper or watch the news, so it's unlikely he would have known about Trejo being arrested for the hit and run. This also explains why Trejo didn't stop that night when he hit that kid."

"And it explains how Trejo's car ended up in that woman's backyard," Celia said.

The name Evans had provided was Eric Tseng. Tseng rented a home in Rainier Beach. "It could," Del said. "But it doesn't explain who took the videotape. Tseng didn't do that."

"*If* someone took it," Celia said.

Del sipped his wine, thinking about that. "Heck of a coincidence, if someone didn't."

"Let's assume Evans is telling the truth," Celia said. "There's a bigger issue here, Del."

"I know. Where's Trejo getting the drugs?" Del said. "Funk said it's a very pure form of heroin."

Celia lowered her glass. "And depending on how much he delivered and how much has been delivered to others . . . more people will die, Del."

"Narcotics is working with patrol to get the word out." Del sighed.

Celia set her wine on the coffee table and shifted toward him. "You okay?"

"Yeah, I was just thinking of Jeanine Welch," he said. "It brought back the memory of that morning when my sister called, when she'd found Allie."

"I'm sorry."

"I just can't imagine anything being worse, Celia. I know I said this before, but I'm sorry about your son. I'm sorry I was so insensitive to you that morning."

She leaned forward and kissed him, then folded into his side; he wrapped his arm around her shoulders. "I don't try to figure out why it happened anymore, Del, and I don't try to change what I know I can't. I just accept that there had to be a reason for it, that maybe I can save another one or two kids with the work I'm doing now."

Del said, "I read that Seattle is likely to pass that law, the one that would create places where addicts can go to get high under a doctor's care."

"It's getting closer," she said. "But there's still opposition."

"I hope it passes," Del said.

She leaned back to look up at him. "Are you going soft on me, Delmo Castigliano?"

He laughed. "Let's just say I've come to realize the error of my ways. You were right. I can't make a difference this way, arresting people."

She shook her head. "I was too hard on you that night too, Del."

"No," he said. "I'm a big enough man to admit when I'm wrong, and I was wrong. Nothing I've done has removed the sting of Allie's death, not in the slightest. I feel like I'm swimming in mud and my arms and legs keep getting heavier, and I'm making less and less progress."

"That's not true, Del. If you're right about this, you could be responsible for taking down a major drug supplier and getting a dangerous drug off the street."

"And another four will step forward to take his place and 'round and 'round we go, like Sonny."

She smiled. "There are no easy answers, Del."

"I know, but I'm starting to agree that this is not a police problem—not one that we can fix. And it's going to get a hell of a lot worse before it gets better."

Sonny, finished with his treat, trotted into the room and came to an abrupt stop, staring up at Celia as if she'd wronged him.

"Let me guess," Celia said. "I'm in his spot, aren't I?"

Del laughed. "Yes, you are." Celia shifted a bit and Sonny jumped onto the couch, snuggling between the two of them. Del rubbed Sonny's head. "You hardly touched your wine."

Celia stood and took Del's hand. "Come on," she said. "Let's go to bed."

Her abruptness surprised him; Del had hoped to ease into this moment. "Celia, not to be presumptuous, but it's been a long time since I've been with a woman . . ."

She smiled. "I'm not surprised."

Del chuckled. "Ouch."

"You're a good man, Del; you're moral and ethical and kind. So I'm not surprised. Don't worry. I won't hurt you." She winked.

Del stood, surprised that he didn't feel nervous, not in the slightest. He felt comfortable with Celia, and this felt right.

They walked to the staircase where Del had put Celia's bag. Del picked it up. At the same moment Sonny came running around the corner and bolted up the stairs. He turned at the top landing and looked down at them. Del smiled, stifling a laugh.

"Let me guess, he also sleeps on the bed, doesn't he?" Celia said.

"He does," Del said. He made a ball with his two hands. "But he's small and doesn't take up much room."

CHAPTER 37

Tracy slept for a few hours at a hotel in Bremerton, awoke, and called Dan. She'd called him the night before, but well ahead of everything that had happened. After assuring Dan that she was fine, she called Billy Williams, her detective sergeant, to also give him a heads-up. Williams had spoken to Del earlier that morning, and he relayed to Tracy what they knew about Nick Evans and Eric Tseng.

"I got a detective out here at the Bremerton Police Department who wants to be kept involved," Tracy said.

"You need me to have a talk with his sergeant?" Williams asked.

"He is the sergeant."

"I can give him a call, let him know of our involvement and the potential tie between Trejo and the recent heroin deaths."

"I can handle it for now. We're meeting with Battles this morning. If things change and he gets territorial, I may need you to make that call."

"You think she could have killed Trejo?" Williams asked.

"Ordinarily I'd say this is a drug deal gone bad, and someone is eliminating the pieces, but that doesn't explain the missing video," Tracy said. "How are we doing on that warrant to get a copy of the security footage from inside the Defense Service Offices?"

"Ron's working on it," he said, meaning Ron Mayweather.

"I'd like to get it today, while I'm out here."

"Understood. We're going to need an affidavit to support the warrant."

"I'll type one up and send it over," she said.

"Did Battles see the video?" Williams asked.

"She said she did, and she says there's nothing on it, but I'm dotting i's and crossing t's at this point."

"Okay. Just watch your back," Williams said. "Kins isn't there to watch it for you. He called, by the way."

"I spoke to him also."

"He's driving us all crazy, so I guess that means he's getting better."

―――

Tracy typed up an affidavit on her laptop to support the search warrant and e-mailed it to Ron Mayweather after speaking with him on the phone. Then she drove back to the Bremerton Police Station. She would have preferred to talk to Battles someplace else, someplace more private, but that wasn't going to happen. She compromised and met with Owens. After some discussion, he agreed to let Tracy talk to Battles alone in one of their conference rooms, since they'd already established a rapport.

Tracy opened the door and stepped inside the room. Battles sat at a round table with her feet propped on an adjacent plastic chair, though she didn't look comfortable or relaxed. She wore her blueberries, as if it were just another workday. Battles was not under arrest. Nor was she being detained, not yet anyway, but being a lawyer, she had to know she hadn't been called in to the police station just to say hello.

Battles gave Tracy a sly grin. "'Intriguing. Arousing one's curiosity or interest. Fascinating.'"

Tracy gave her an inquisitive look, uncertain what Battles meant.

Battles took her legs off the chair and sat up. "The dictionary at Zeitgeist Coffee—I told you it was prophetic."

"Ah." Tracy readjusted the chair and sat. "You have a photographic memory?"

"No. Just very good. It's why I'm so good at chess. I can remember my opponents' moves and draw upon that the next time we play. It's judgment that has always been my Achilles' heel. How am I doing so far? People think I stole a video to get my client off of a murder charge. Now they think I shot him."

"Did you?" Tracy asked. *What the hell?* Battles had opened the door.

"No. But would that be enough to convince you?"

"You want coffee?" Tracy asked.

"I'm having enough trouble sleeping," Battles said.

"You don't seem like the type who'd have trouble sleeping."

"I usually don't." Battles sat forward. "So what are you doing here? And what am I doing here?"

"Trejo's my case," Tracy said, not wanting to offer anything more.

"I saw the press conference. It was convincing, but we both know King County wasn't going after Trejo."

"No?"

"Not without the tape," Battles said. "Same problem the prosecution here would have had. Trejo would argue that without the tape he could not effectively cross-examine witnesses. That being the case, why would Seattle's DA want to interject himself into that mess?"

Battles was sharp, perhaps too sharp to give away anything. Tracy felt, at the moment, like she was in a chess match, and she wasn't the better player. "Has the Navy made any decision about going forward?" Tracy asked.

"Against me?"

"Yes."

"There's an ethics investigation under way. Whether there will be a court-martial, I don't know. The best I might do is a plea to an honorable discharge in lieu of a court-martial and I get to keep my dignity and my pay. Most people in my shoes might be happy with that."

"Not you?"

"No."

"Why not?" Tracy asked.

"Because someone set me up to take this fall, Detective, and I don't like being set up. And I really hate losing."

Battles sounded sincere, but then Tracy had interviewed others who'd sounded sincere about their innocence and hadn't been. "Some people would argue that's the reason you took the tape."

"They already have," Battles said.

Tracy knew she meant Cho. "So where were you last night?"

She smiled softly. "Do I have an alibi?"

"Do you?"

"I was at home. I went to work, sat there twiddling my thumbs, then realized that I was likely going to be court-martialed and assigned an attorney to defend me. Well, I'm not exactly great at listening to others—it was a real problem in grammar school—so I decided I'd better start defending myself. I left at four o'clock, took the ferry back to Seattle, went to a workout class, and went back home and did some research."

"How late were you up?"

"Midnight."

"Anyone who can verify that?"

"I wish." She shook her head. "I live alone. But my computer won't lie."

"Did you make any phone calls?"

Battles smiled. "Okay. You play detective and I'll play suspect."

"Actually, I'm *intrigued*," Tracy said.

Battles smiled softly. "Do you play chess, Detective?"

Is that what this was? Tracy wondered. "Like golf. Poorly. But I still think I should be better every time I go out."

"I used to be a junior champion. Now I go into the Seattle parks looking for games. I'm good. I rarely lose. I think it makes me a better lawyer because it forces me to think several moves ahead of my opponent."

"Who are you playing against now?"

"I don't know. But I'm convinced Trejo knew, and that's why he's dead."

"Tell me your analysis."

"You already know it. You were in court. You saw Trejo's reaction—or lack of reaction when he heard the tape went missing. You think, like I do, that he expected the video to go missing. He expected to get off."

"So the tape wasn't just randomly misplaced."

"What are the odds of a critical piece of evidence being misplaced, Detective?"

"You were the last person to have the evidence box. All indications are the security tape was in it when you returned it."

"True, but the real question isn't who took the tape. It's why. And I'm pretty sure why has something to do with what Trejo was doing over in Seattle that evening."

"He didn't tell you?"

"He never even admitted being there, not even after I showed him the convenience store tape." Battles shrugged. "And before anyone accuses me of violating an attorney-client privilege, it expired when Trejo died. He said it wasn't him. He said it was someone who looked like him. I couldn't understand it then, why he wouldn't take the plea. But now I do."

"The video was never coming into evidence," Tracy said.

"And Trejo knew it," Battles agreed.

"You said you saw the tape from inside the DSO building."

"It shows Cho leaving for the night, and it shows me putting back the evidence box and then leaving. Nobody else but the janitor came in or out before six o'clock the next morning."

"Is there an alternate entrance into the building?"

"Not after hours. Not easily anyway."

"Let me ask you," Tracy said. "Trejo worked as a logistics specialist?"

"That's right."

"How would I find out where he'd been deployed?"

Battles's gaze narrowed. "His service record would show every destination where he was deployed. Why?"

"How hard would it be for him to smuggle a package onto and off of a ship?"

Battles gave the question some thought. Finally she said, "Not that hard." Tracy could see the wheels spinning inside her head.

"How would he do it?"

Battles considered her for another long moment, then sat back. "Hypothetically, say a ship stops in Thailand. A box is put in the ship storeroom. Trejo, as the logistics specialist, logs everything in. But instead of eight boxes of bananas, he only logs in seven. The ship comes back and goes into the yard for repairs. People and cargo come off the ship, including seven boxes of bananas, which complies with the ship's manifest. The eighth box never got recorded. The Navy had a problem not that long ago with guys stealing cargo from the storeroom and selling it on the street. They caught them by pulling all the manifests and comparing them to what was being logged in. Someone like Trejo, however, could manipulate the manifests so that something coming on board never did, and something going off never did."

"So it's possible."

"It's possible." Battles gave Tracy a small, inquisitive smile. "Drugs?"

Tracy didn't answer.

"Intriguing," Battles said.

CHAPTER 38

After her conversation with Battles, Tracy debriefed Owens and left the building, but not to head back to Seattle, not right away. Battles had not known the name of the janitorial service, but she had been able to describe the uniforms and the trucks she'd seen in the DSO parking lot. She said both were embossed with the logo of a cartoonish man in a white suit and cap, his lower legs spinning like the brush of a vacuum cleaner, and his uniform impressed with the initials IJS. After a ten-minute search on her laptop, Tracy located Industrial Janitorial Services on West G Street, close to the naval base. She made a few phone calls, spoke with the owner, and made an appointment to meet the janitor working in the DSO building the night before the Article 32 hearing.

Tracy pulled into a parking space in front of a one-story brick building with a parking lot containing several white trucks with IJS on the door panels. The temperature remained cool but for the moment it was dry. A seagull strutted along the pavement, cawing in complaint when Tracy approached the building's front door. She entered a dated lobby of wood paneling, black-and-white photographs, and lamps and furniture straight out of the 1950s. The building even held an old, musty smell.

She had an appointment with Gary Buchman, president of IJS. Tracy announced herself to the receptionist, and Buchman entered and greeted her. He fit with the décor, his salt-and-pepper hair combed into a modified pompadour. Tracy estimated Buchman to be mid- to late sixties. His white polo shirt protruded slightly at the waistline and bore the initials IJS on the left breast. When he shook Tracy's hand, she noticed his fingers were adorned with several rings. A chain medical bracelet wrapped his wrist, the kind Tracy had seen worn by diabetics.

Buchman did not look or sound nervous greeting a detective, though she noted that his hand had a tremor. Buchman offered her coffee, which she declined, and led her down a long, narrow hallway cluttered with file cabinets and stacks of papers and files. Buchman's office was at the rear of the building, and it too had the same dark wood paneling and dated furnishings. On one wall hung a black-and-white portrait of a man with a crew cut, black-framed glasses, and a passing resemblance to Buchman. A window with blinds afforded a slatted view of a gas station and car wash across the street.

"Thanks for seeing me on short notice." Tracy sat in an avocado-colored cloth chair across from Buchman's large desk, which was adorned with three computer screens.

"Not a problem." Buchman lowered himself into a leather chair.

"Is that your father?" Tracy asked, pointing to the portrait.

"It is," Buchman said.

"You've been in business a long time," she said.

"Since 1956," he said. "My grandfather started the company and my dad expanded it with the Navy contract." Buchman switched gears. "I called the janitor who worked that shift you were inquiring about. He should be in any minute."

"I appreciate it," Tracy said. "I hope I didn't get him out of bed."

"I'm sure it's fine."

"How long have you had the naval contract?"

"Almost forty-five years. It's a big contract for us, as I'm sure you can imagine. We've never had a problem before."

"You're a civilian contractor?"

Buchman nodded. "The naval base is the largest employer in the state. I'm not sure if you knew that."

"I didn't," she said.

Buchman seemed to perk up. "The base employs more than 10,000 contractors and about the same number of Department of Defense civilian employees."

"Impressive."

"Like I said, we've never had a problem. We're the longest tenured employer."

"And I'm not trying to create any problems for you," Tracy assured him. "As I said on the phone, I was meeting with detectives from Bremerton and thought I'd stop by before taking the ferry back to Seattle. I'm just running things down."

"Is this about the missing videotape?"

"It is," she said, though she hadn't mentioned the tape specifically in their brief conversation on the phone to set up the meeting. "This isn't the first you've heard of it?"

"No," Buchman said. "I got a call from NCIS when this whole thing happened. They sent out an investigator to take my statement and my janitors' statements."

Tracy made a mental note to get copies of those statements. "Who would that be?"

"The janitor that night was Al Tulowitsky. Al's been with me almost fifteen years," he said, as if jumping to the man's defense. "The last ten he's worked on the base. We've never had a complaint. In fact that's one of the reasons I put him there. All of our employees have to be vetted by the Navy. Al's salt of the earth."

A knock on the door drew their attention to a tall, thin man who stood, looking tentative.

"And right on time," Buchman said, standing from behind his desk.

Perhaps midforties, Tulowitsky had a shock of prematurely white hair. He motioned vaguely behind him. "Debra said to just come in?"

Buchman moved to the door. "Al, this is Detective Crosswhite with the Seattle Police Department." Tracy shook his hand. Tulowitsky wore several sterling silver bracelets and had the dark-red complexion of someone who lived in Arizona or maybe frequented tanning salons.

"Detective Crosswhite has some questions about the missing videocassette from the DSO."

"NCIS took my statement." Tulowitsky had a tattoo on his right forearm, a red heart with a scroll and the words "You Are Loved."

"I haven't seen those statements yet," Tracy said. "I appreciate you coming in." She motioned to the red heart tattoo and took a guess. "Did you serve?"

"I did," Tulowitsky said.

"Navy?"

Tulowitsky gave a thin smile. "They were my ride," he said. "I'm a Marine."

"But no longer active, I presume."

"You never retire from being a Marine," he said.

"I've heard that before. So you said NCIS took your statement?"

"They called the next day, said that a tape was missing and wanted to interview the janitor who'd worked the DSO building that night," Buchman said.

"I never saw a cassette tape," Tulowitsky said. "And I don't touch anything on the desks, ever."

"I understand," Tracy said. "I'm just trying to get a better understanding of your process cleaning that building."

Buchman suggested they all sit. Tulowitsky took the chair next to Tracy, pulling it away and angling it before sitting. He smelled of fresh cigarette smoke and had the telltale signs of a chain-smoker—lips deeply wrinkled, his teeth yellowed, along with the fingernails of his right hand. He'd likely puffed down a cigarette in the car or parking lot just before coming in.

"You want me to tell it to you?"

"Please," Tracy said.

"Okay. First I empty the trash cans. Then I clean the bathrooms, vacuum, and straighten up. But I don't touch anything on the desks," Tulowitsky again offered.

Tracy needed to slow him down and press him for details. She took out a notepad. "So you go into the offices? You clean inside the offices?"

"Yes, ma'am," Tulowitsky said, though they were likely about the same age. He had a habit of shutting his eyes and tilting back his head, as if defiant, but it was likely a tic of some sort. "But we don't touch anything on the desks. A scrap of paper to you could be an important name or phone number to the person working there."

Buchman gave him an approving nod, and she got the sense that Tulowitsky had properly recited a company mantra.

"Do you remember cleaning Lieutenant Battles's office that evening?"

"I do, but only because I was asked about it. I clean all the offices on the first floor."

"You don't remember seeing a box on her desk?"

"No. No box."

"And there was nothing on the floor?"

"Not that I saw. Like I said, NCIS called the day after. What I told them is likely most accurate. I would have remembered a videotape. The most I would have done—if one had been on the floor—would have been to maybe pick it up and put it on her chair so I could vacuum, but that didn't happen. I never saw one."

"Can you run me through your routine in that building?"

Tulowitsky shrugged. "The DSO? Okay."

He glanced again at Buchman and it made Tracy wish Buchman wasn't present, but she knew if she asked Buchman to leave it would make everyone even more uncomfortable.

"That's building 433," Tulowitsky said. "It's the first building we clean. It's the first building inside the Charleston Gate."

"Is it just you or do other janitors also clean that building?"

"That building there's two of us, me and Darren, but I clean the first floor."

"Does Darren clean the upper floors?"

"That's right. Fewer offices up there."

"NCIS took his statement also," Buchman said. "I tried to reach him this morning but wasn't able to get him."

"I understand you enter the last four digits of your Social Security number to gain entry into the building," Tracy said.

"The door is locked; you can't access the building without your Social Security number," Tulowitsky confirmed. "And your number, the last four digits anyway, have to be approved."

Buchman sat up. "It's computerized," he said. "There's a security office where the numbers are stored. As I said, we've never had a problem."

"Nobody's ever stolen someone's number?" Tracy asked.

"Not one of our employees," Buchman said, but then added, "Not that I know of anyway."

Tracy asked Tulowitsky the last four digits of his Social Security number, then said, "Okay, you were going to run me through your routine inside the building."

Tulowitsky wrinkled his brow as if to indicate that he already had. "Like I said, first thing I do is empty all the trash cans in the offices."

"Everything has to be shredded," Buchman interjected. "Some of the Navy personnel do it themselves. And the garbage is taken to a designated facility on base and destroyed."

Tracy looked again to Tulowitsky. "So you empty the trash. What's next?"

"I take the trash out to the truck and get the cleaning supplies and the vacuum. I clean the restrooms on the first floor, and just sort of tidy the offices. I vacuum and work my way out of the building." He shrugged.

"How long does that take?"

"Everything altogether?" He glanced up at the ceiling. "The whole thing is about forty-five minutes to an hour—sometimes a little longer if we have to spot clean the carpets, but the offices are never really bad so it's fairly straightforward."

"So when did you arrive?"

"I usually arrive right around eleven o'clock, and I'm usually done in that building by about midnight."

"And do you recall seeing anyone else in the building that night?" Tracy looked at her notes. "March 18."

Tulowitsky shook his head. "I told NCIS the same thing. If someone had been in there, I would have remembered seeing them."

"And when you leave the building to take out the garbage, do you lock the doors?"

"The doors lock automatically. All I have to do is exit. Doors close behind you. Simple as that," Tulowitsky said.

Maybe, Tracy thought, except nothing in this case, it seemed, was simple.

CHAPTER 39

Del and Faz had inadvertently opened a can of worms, and a good many of those worms were sitting around the conference room table just outside Chief of Police Sandy Clarridge's office midmorning. The two detectives sat with their sergeant, Billy Williams, and their captain, Johnny Nolasco. Kevin Dunleavy, the King County prosecuting attorney, sat with Rick Cerrabone. Also present were Anthony Rizzo, sergeant of the SPD Major Crimes Task Force, and Scott Disney, detective with the Narcotics Proactive Squad. Disney had long hair and a wispy beard, which meant he'd been working undercover for some time.

At the moment, Del had the floor, explaining their arrest of Nick Evans, and Evans's subsequent statement that his supplier had fingered Laszlo Trejo. "Was this firsthand knowledge?" Rizzo asked. Clean-cut, Rizzo looked like an accountant and sounded skeptical.

"No," Del said. "He was relating what he was told by his supplier, Eric Tseng." Evans had provided Tseng's name in exchange for a plea of guilty with a reduced sentence in the county jail. Further research revealed that Tseng was twenty-nine years old, had no criminal record, and had not served in the military. He was flying well under the radar.

Narcotics had no knowledge of him. "Could it have been bullshit?" Rizzo asked.

"Anything's possible," Del said, "but I don't think so."

"Why not?" Rizzo challenged.

Williams leaned forward, taking up Del's defense. "For one, they found Trejo's body in a deserted park in Bremerton last night." That tidbit got everyone's attention. "Bremerton Police are currently calling it a suicide, but we had a homicide detective out there and she said it looks to her like somebody executed Trejo with a bullet in the head."

"And I doubt Nick Evans was regularly reading the morning newspaper over a cup of coffee," Del said. "So unless someone told him about Trejo being arrested, it's doubtful he would have known either that name or anything about Trejo's arrest unless someone filled him in. Second, one of the things we've been trying to determine since this whole thing started was why Trejo simply didn't stop his car when he hit D'Andre Miller—why he fled the scene. This explains it. Third, somebody helped Trejo find a vacant lot in which to ditch his car and further helped him get back to Bremerton. Fourth, somebody stole the security tape, which showed Trejo at the convenience store the night the kid got hit. It couldn't be used against him at the Article 32 hearing."

Williams jumped in. "And we don't think it was a coincidence— that someone simply misplaced it, not with everything else that has happened."

Rizzo frowned. It looked like a pout. "Trejo could have been dealing drugs for years and might very well have known about the vacant lot on his own. Second, he might not have stopped because he knew he was looking at a hit and run while under the influence. We have any indications he uses?"

"I can check his autopsy," Faz said, making a note on a legal pad.

Rizzo continued, "Third, his wife could have helped him get home and is covering for him or possibly for a friend. Maybe this guy Tseng."

Rizzo looked to Williams and Nolasco. "I thought I heard that the Navy defense counsel was under investigation for taking the video?"

Del didn't back down. "If Trejo was supplying heroin on a regular basis, it raises the logical question. Why didn't you guys know about him . . . or Tseng." Rizzo visibly stiffened. "Not that I'm casting any stones."

"They talked to Trejo's wife last night after finding his body," Williams said, relaying what Tracy had told him. "She admitted Trejo had been out the night of the hit and run, but swears she didn't know where he went or what he was doing. She says he told her he had errands to run for work and would be home late. When he came home, he told her the car was in the shop for an oil change and he'd get it back later the next day. Nothing to indicate she's lying, and frankly, she wouldn't have any reason to, given that her husband is dead."

Clarridge spoke to Rizzo. "So you have nothing going with respect to a heroin ring in Rainier?"

"We have a lot going, just not with Tseng," Rizzo said. "We were made aware of a problem by the medical examiner's office after those two overdose deaths in the north end. We had bike officers reach out to known users and asked them to spread the word. What we believe, given the timing of the deaths and the geographic proximity of the two overdoses to a dozen others, is that the victims bought from either the same person or from persons supplying from the same source. But there are a number of gangs and drug cartels in the Pacific Northwest running meth and heroin."

"China white?" Del said.

"We don't know it was China white," Rizzo interjected.

"It wasn't black tar," Del said.

Clarridge jumped in. "But is it accurate that Tseng was not on your radar?"

"If Trejo was providing Tseng heroin, he and whoever he was work-ing for were keeping it quiet, and with good reason," Rizzo said. "If the

Mexican drug cartels find out someone is dealing in their territory, there will be hell to pay."

"So let's take Tseng and see what he knows about Trejo," Del said.

"We take him, we're going to need to find the product," Rizzo said. "Without any product, and without Trejo, why would Tseng talk, especially if he was working behind the Mexican drug cartels' backs?"

"Maybe that's the pull to get him to talk."

"You take Tseng, and he's part of a much larger operation, you risk losing the bigger fish."

"There's a bad product out there," Del said. "People are dying."

"That product has likely been distributed by now," Rizzo said. "Best thing we can do is get the word out far and wide."

"So we do nothing?" Del said, looking to Clarridge.

"That's not going to be acceptable," Clarridge said, rubbing his chin. "Not to the mayor and not to African American community leaders. There's a perception the Navy had a hand in Trejo walking, and now there are all kinds of theories circulating that the Navy also had him killed."

"So it sounds like our best bet is this guy Tseng in Rainier Beach," Dunleavy said, who, up until this point, had remained quiet. Tall, with a ruddy Irish complexion and deep voice, Dunleavy asked, "How long are we looking at, realistically, if we were to try to get something in place?"

"You mean people on the inside?" Rizzo looked and sounded dumbfounded. "First, we don't know how long this has been going on, but they certainly weren't making much, if any, noise. That's a problem. If they know we picked up Evans and that Trejo is dead, you can forget about it; they will have likely shut everything down and are on the move."

"So then there's no harm taking Tseng now," Del said.

"How long?" Dunleavy asked again.

Rizzo blew out a breath. "Months. I'd say three to six, minimum."

Del shook his head.

"That's too long," Clarridge said. He took a moment, considering their options. "All right, let's pick up Tseng, start applying pressure, and see if he'll give us Trejo as his contact, maybe more. If he IDs Trejo, at least maybe we solve the public perception problem."

"And possibly save a few more lives," Del said.

"Then let's make it happen," Clarridge said.

Late in the afternoon, an MA escorted Tracy into the office of Rebecca Stanley, Leah Battles's officer in charge. Stanley's office was located on the first floor of the DSO building, just down the hall from Battles's office. It seemed too small and too austere for an officer in charge, almost as if Stanley were using a spare office for their meeting. But on the wall behind her hung a series of diplomas with Stanley's name embossed in black script—degrees from college, law school, and the JAG Corps. They hung next to a square window not much bigger than the picture frames.

Ron Mayweather had busted his hump to get the warrant signed by a King County judge and have it properly served on Kitsap's commanding officer, Peter Lopresti. The warrant had apparently then been transferred to the security officer, also located in the DSO building. He advised Mayweather that he'd made a copy of the security video for the night in question and provided it to Stanley, which Leah Battles had also confirmed. After a phone call, Tracy had a meeting.

Stanley begged off shaking Tracy's hand. "I'm feeling a cold coming on," she said. She had an officious demeanor emphasized by piercing brown eyes. She folded her dark hair, cut short, behind her ears, revealing gold stud earrings. The haircut framed narrow features, but Stanley was not small. In her boots she stood perhaps five foot six or five foot seven, and though it was difficult to tell from her baggy uniform, she didn't appear petite. She sat behind a gunmetal-gray desk. Tracy took one of the two chairs across from her.

"I understand Laszlo Trejo shot himself last night at Old Mill Park," Stanley said, subtlety apparently not part of her repertoire.

"Where did you hear that?" Tracy asked.

Stanley sat erect, hands folded on her desk pad. She maintained a serious, no-nonsense demeanor. "Word travels fast on a military base, Detective."

"Yes, Laszlo Trejo was shot."

Stanley's eyebrows, well groomed, inched together. "You seem to doubt it was self-inflicted."

"I don't know that it was or wasn't," Tracy said. "That's Bremerton's jurisdiction, and the results of an autopsy will take time."

"And what's your jurisdiction?" Stanley pulled open a drawer, unwrapped a cough drop, and put it in her mouth.

"D'Andre Miller," Tracy said. She didn't like Stanley's attitude. Didn't like the way she treated Tracy like a subordinate. Tracy had never been in the military, but she knew the officers, in particular, could be rank conscious.

"Does SPD plan to pursue D'Andre Miller's death?"

"I'm just a worker bee. That decision is well above my pay grade. I'm sure you can appreciate that," Tracy said.

Stanley's lip curled slightly as she worked the cough drop, but she didn't verbally respond. She picked up the search warrant from her desk pad, the only visible piece of paper in the room, and considered it as if seeing it for the first time. Somewhere down the hall an unanswered telephone rang. Voices called out. After a minute, roughly, Stanley set the warrant down.

"You're interested in the security video taken inside this building the night before Petty Officer Trejo's Article 32 hearing."

"I understand from your security officer that you asked to have the tape copied and he provided it."

"I secured a copy the day after the hearing," Stanley said. "I thought it prudent."

"Why was that?" Tracy asked.

Stanley gave a small shrug. "Leah Battles works for me and the allegations being made are serious. It has been suggested that she had something to do with the cassette tape being missing. I wanted to confirm who was in the building after her departure."

"What did you find?"

She shook her head. "Just the janitors."

"No one else entered or exited?"

"No." Stanley pulled open a desk drawer and removed what looked to be a multipage document. "Your warrant also asked for the list of persons who entered the building that evening and the last four digits of their Social Security numbers." She handed the document across the desk. Tracy took it and considered the names.

Stanley said, "Between approximately eleven p.m. and six a.m. the following morning, no one entered the building . . . other than the janitors."

Tracy would review the document in more detail later. She set it on her lap. "Do you know how the video system works?"

Stanley smiled. "I'm not very computer literate, Detective. I was a poli-sci major in college. What I can tell you is what the security officer told me when he provided the tape."

"Please," Tracy said.

"It's an IP system. The video footage for the day and night feeds into a computer in the security office, and sits on the network until the tape rolls over and it gets recorded over."

"How long is it on the system before it's recorded over?"

"I don't know."

"You asked for a disc?"

"I didn't have a choice. From what the security officer told me, the cameras are of high quality, which means the footage takes up a lot of storage space. To upload more than six hours of high-quality camera footage would require multiple gigabytes, which I'm told, in unscientific terms, is a lot—enough to crash my computer. So they burned me a disc. I asked them to burn you one as well."

She reached again into the drawer and handed Tracy a five-by-eight manila envelope. "You've watched it?" Tracy asked.

Stanley nodded. "Several times. I also showed it to Lieutenant Battles. You see anything I might have missed, I'd welcome knowing. Leah is a good person and an excellent lawyer. I'd hate to lose her."

With that, Stanley stood, their meeting over.

—

On the ferry crossing back to Seattle, Tracy quickly slid into a booth near the big plate-glass windows, opened her laptop, inserted the DVD disc, and waited for the computer to load the video. Rain spotted the glass as the ferry crossed into the wind, and she smelled theater popcorn and hot dogs from the cafeteria. It reminded her that she hadn't eaten since the prior evening, but she put off food for the moment.

An image popped onto the screen—a camera angle looking down on the interior of what she recognized from her earlier visit to be the DSO office lobby. She noted a date and time stamp in the lower right-hand corner and scribbled it on a legal pad.

March 18 2016 10:00 p.m.

She hit "Play." The seconds on the time stamp ticked forward. She kept the pen and notepad close at hand.

Her cell phone vibrated and rattled on the table. Habit caused her to answer it, though she let the tape continue to play. She expected the caller to be Dan, but the 360 area code indicated the caller was from Bremerton.

"I'm assuming you're long gone?" John Owens said.

"I am," Tracy said, not elaborating. "What can I do for you?"

"We didn't find the slug that killed Trejo," he said. "However, the medical examiner indicates it was likely .40 caliber."

"The caliber of Trejo's weapon, which we know had been discharged."

"Correct. I thought you should also know that Battles owns a Glock .40 and we've secured it."

"And?"

"It hasn't been fired anytime recently. We also spoke to Trejo's wife. She confirmed Trejo was right-handed."

"So it's unlikely Trejo shot himself."

"Seems that way, but here's the problem I was having with that theory—Trejo brought the gun out there with him for a reason, right?"

"Seems logical."

"So we can assume he wasn't exactly comfortable with the situation, whatever it was, and likely would have been on guard. Assuming that to have been the case, I'm wondering, how would someone get ahold of his gun?"

It made sense, but Tracy heard something in the tone of Owens's voice, a lilt indicating he had something else, another piece of information. "You have something more you can share?" she asked.

For a moment Tracy thought they'd been disconnected. Then Owens spoke. "I got a video I want you to take a look at. I found it today online. I'll send the link to your e-mail."

"What is it?"

"Just look at it. I don't want to color your perception. After you do, call me back." Owens disconnected.

Tracy stopped the video playing on her computer and went into her e-mail account. She saw Owens's e-mail, opened it, and clicked on the link. As she watched, she leaned forward, feeling a rush of heat much like when she'd been having hot flashes.

"I'll be damned," she said.

A little more than an hour later, Tracy dropped her briefcase on the floor beside her cubicle closet. Del and Faz, seated at their desks, both took notice. "You got to see this," she said.

"Got a lot to tell you," Del said, pushing away from his desk and approaching.

"Got a lot to show you," Tracy said. She sat at her desk without taking off her jacket, entered her password, and pulled up her e-mail.

Del and Faz stood behind her. "What is it?" Faz asked.

"Just watch."

They hovered over her as she pulled up the link in Owens's e-mail and skipped the advertisement. As the video played, she rolled back her chair to give Del and Faz a better view of her screen monitor. In the video, a man and a woman stood arm's-length apart. They each wore black T-shirts, the man in shorts, the woman in sweatpants. The man held a faux yellow-colored gun at the woman's chest, while narrating in a thick British accent. In a split second, he no longer held the gun; the woman had disarmed him, and aimed the gun at his head.

"What is this?" Del said.

"YouTube," Tracy said. "The Bremerton detective sent it to me. The woman in the video is Leah Battles."

"The defense attorney?" Faz asked, sounding incredulous.

"Same one."

They watched as the instructor went back through the disarming, this time step-by-step. Battles held the gun at his chest. Moving slow and deliberately, the instructor pivoted sideways, out of the line of fire, while simultaneously gripping the wrist holding the gun with his left hand and violently snapping the barrel in the opposite direction with his free hand.

"If her finger was on the trigger," the instructor said, *"it would be broken."*

He moved to the next technique. This time Battles held the gun at his abdomen. As with the prior example, the instructor moved too quickly for Tracy to fully assess his actions, but somehow he'd again disarmed Battles and aimed the gun at her.

"Damn," Faz said.

The instructor went back through the four-step technique that resulted in his yanking the gun free.

As the third technique started, Tracy said, "This is the one I wanted you to see."

The instructor pointed the barrel of the gun at Leah Battles's forehead. *"The key,"* he said, *"is once you make the decision to move, you cannot hesitate."*

Battles ducked while raising her arms. She gripped the weapon and shoved the barrel toward the ceiling as her right knee simulated a blow to the groin. Stepping away, she bent the barrel into her assailant and snapped his wrists down, yanking free the gun.

"What is this stuff?" Del asked again.

Tracy sat back, still staring at the video. "Krav Maga," she said.

"Krav what?" Faz said.

"It's the way Leah Battles could have taken Laszlo Trejo's gun and shot him."

CHAPTER 40

After a very long night working to put together a coordinated effort between the Seattle Narcotics Unit, SWAT, and the Violent Crimes Section, Del and Faz accompanied a SWAT team to the home of Eric Tseng at just before four in the morning.

Tseng's rental in Rainier Beach was not far from the intersection in which Trejo ran down D'Andre Miller, as well as the easement where they'd located Trejo's Subaru. The address likely explained who came to Trejo's rescue the night of the hit and run. If Tseng was a seasoned drug dealer, he might also have had the forethought to wipe down the interior of the car, including the air bag, to eliminate prints. It didn't, however, explain how the convenience store videotape had gone missing.

Earlier surveillance revealed the home to be a rambler—a rectangular structure with pea-green wood siding. Instead of just the one story, which was traditional for ramblers, the house had two stories, with the two-car garage located below the front walk and the three stairs leading up to the front door. The door and ground-floor windows were protected by black security grates. Most problematic, however, were the two dogs roaming a cyclone-fenced front yard. They looked to be a mixed breed and they weren't small. They also barked when any-one walked near the fence. Sneaking up to the house would not be an option, even armed with a "no-knock" warrant from the King County court, which allowed SWAT to raid the home without announcing themselves.

As agreed, the tactical team used two armored vehicles and multiple officers to cordon off the street and the easement behind the home. Once the officers were in place, two animal control officers went through the gate, secured the dogs, and moved them out of the yard. At the same time, to distract anyone inside the house from the dogs' barking, a SWAT team negotiator called the cell number Tseng had provided to Evans. She shook her head.

"No answer."

The SWAT team leader, a burly man named Glenn Ekey, asked her to call the number again. She did, with the same result.

Not wanting to wait and potentially give Tseng time to arm himself or dispose of evidence, Ekey gave the order to proceed.

At just after 4:00 a.m., Del watched SWAT members, dressed in full tactical gear, move toward the front door carrying a battering ram. The metal security door opened with a loud clatter and the wood door gave way with what sounded like a pop. The SWAT officers entered quickly and with practiced precision. Del heard their voices broadcast over the radio as they searched room to room, clearing them. Lights in the adjacent houses and across the street snapped on. Dogs barked. A few of the neighbors stepped out onto their porches in pajamas, shorts, and T-shirts.

Del and Faz waited.

Within minutes of entering, two of the SWAT officers stepped back out the front door to speak to Ekey. Ekey listened, then turned and gestured for Faz and Del to approach.

"Do you know what this guy looks like?" Ekey asked.

"Just from DMV photos," Del said, not getting a good feeling about what the SWAT team had found inside the house and what he was about to see.

Ekey led Del and Faz inside. The upper floor was sparsely furnished. Descending stairs, Del heard music and smelled a pungent odor. The music and smell became more prominent when they followed Ekey into a daylight basement with a 72-inch television, recliner chairs, and a fully stocked bar. Someone shut off the music. Eliminating the pungent smell would not be so simple. Eric Tseng sat slumped in one of the recliners, head flopped to the side, blood splattered on the leather and pooled on the floor. Del estimated the kill was at least a couple days old, very probably the same night as Laszlo Trejo.

CHAPTER 41

Tracy arrived at the cottage in Redmond in dire need of sleep. After managing just a few fitful hours in the Bremerton hotel room, she'd worked through the day and the night, waiting to hear from Del and Faz about the raid on Eric Tseng's home.

Del finally called at 5:00 a.m. The news was not good. He told her that they'd located a concrete room adjacent to the man cave where they'd found Tseng's body. The room had been secured by a steel door. Inside they'd found a glistening metal table and a floor with a drain. Everything else had been cleaned out, and the room held the smell of lemon and bleach. Del said the room was built for someone to clean up quickly, and they likely had. They found no remnants of heroin, no scales or plastic bags. Detectives from CID would go over the house anyway, including pulling the trap on the drain to take samples.

A canvass of the residents in the neighborhood had also failed to reveal any of the telltale signs of a drug operation. The neighbors did not recall random cars or people showing up at all hours of the day and night. In fact, they described Tseng as friendly but private, and said he kept mostly to himself. One neighbor recalled several different women at the home, but she couldn't identify any of them and didn't think much of it since Tseng was single. Tseng told his neighbors he ran a software consulting business out of his house, but that fieldwork often required him to leave at odd hours of the day and night to troubleshoot client problems.

Tracy kicked off her boots and set them outside the front door, entering in her socks so as not to wake Dan, if he were still sleeping. However, the sound of the lock disengaging, and the door rattling open—it stuck in the jamb in the winter months—awoke Rex and Sherlock, and the two dogs bolted from the bedroom, barking. Dan followed several steps behind them. Dressed in shorts, socks, and a sweatshirt, he looked to be on his way out the door for a run. "I'll bet you're going to be glad when your night shift is over," he said.

She made her way to the dining room table where she discarded her briefcase, purse, and her jacket. "I don't even know what shift I'm working anymore." She shook her head and immediately regretted doing so. Her temples pulsed—a sleep-deprivation-induced headache.

Dan bent to kiss her.

She pulled back. "Better not. My breath must smell like moldy cheese, given what my mouth tastes like."

"I'd ask if you wanted to go for a run, but I think I know the answer."

"The only thing I'm running to is the bed." She walked into the kitchen and filled a glass with water. Then she rummaged in the cabinets for aspirin.

"Why so late?" He looked at his watch. "Or should I say early?"

"We raided the home of the guy Trejo was supposedly supplying. I wanted to wait and find out what happened."

"And?"

She drank in large gulps. "We found *him*," she said, lowering the glass. "Nothing else. No drugs, no drug paraphernalia."

"Doesn't sound good," Dan said.

She exited the kitchen and walked into the bedroom. "Shot in the temple, like Trejo. Del said it was probably about the same time too."

"Somebody cleaning up," Dan said.

"Looks that way. They're processing the house, but no one is optimistic." She shimmied her jeans over her hips and sat on the bed to pull them off. "This one just gets more and more confusing."

Tracy pulled back the covers and climbed into bed. Sherlock, seizing his chance, leapt onto the duvet cover and plopped down in the center of the mattress. Dan sat on the edge, Rex at his feet, looking up at him as if to say, *I thought we were going on a run!*

Dan stroked Rex's head. "We'll go in a minute," he said. He looked to Tracy. "You want to walk through it?"

She didn't, but she also knew Dan was not offering just to be kind. He had enough on his plate at the moment. With a criminal defense background, he was a good sounding board, and she needed one, with Kins out of commission. Dan also knew she would stew on her thoughts, preventing her from sleeping. Talking to Dan was the equivalent of writing it on a sheet of paper to get the thoughts out of her head.

"Sure." She sat up and adjusted the pillows at her back, considering where to start. "Laszlo Trejo runs a red light and hits a kid in Seattle. Why was he over there?"

"He had heroin in his car and was making a delivery."

"Right," she said. She rubbed her face and shook off the cobwebs. "Who helped him ditch the car and get back to Bremerton?"

"The most obvious choice would be the guy he was delivering the heroin to, but you're not going to be able to verify that with both men dead."

"Agreed. Highly doubtful we can verify it; highly probable Tseng helped him." She grimaced, her head now pounding. "I don't know where to go with this. Ordinarily, I'd say this is a drug deal gone bad, but we have the issue of the missing convenience store videotape, and I no longer believe it was just a bad coincidence."

Tracy put her head back against the pillows. She could feel the fatigue settling into her joints and her eyelids becoming heavy.

"Who had access to that videotape?" Dan said.

"Anyone who had access to the evidence room in the DSO building."

"Which is who?"

Tracy took a deep breath. "Battles, the defense attorney; the prosecutor; his assistant; the court reporter; the janitors. The problem is, I got a copy of the security tape for the building before I left Bremerton and no one came in or out of the building the night and morning that the tape disappeared, except the janitor."

"You viewed it?"

"Not yet."

"Then—"

"I was told what was on the video by Leah Battles and by her officer in charge. She pulled it the day the convenience store tape went missing."

"Could it have been the janitor?"

Tracy thought of Al Tulowitsky and his boss, Gary Buchman. "It's possible, but it seems unlikely."

"What about Battles?" Dan said.

Tracy told him about the link to the video Owens had sent her, the one showing Battles disarming a person holding a gun.

"I know you don't want to believe it was her, Tracy, but everything seems to point to her. She lives in Seattle. She had the opportunity, certainly, to take the security tape. She has no seeming alibi for Trejo's death and now, apparently, she had the ability to get his gun. How much do you really know about her?"

"Not a lot," Tracy said. "Maybe not enough."

"Maybe that's where you should start."

"Okay," she said. "But I'm not doing anything until I get some sleep."

"The less you have the more you crave it," Dan said.

She smiled.

"You said you have a copy of the security tape for inside the building that night? Tracy?"

"Huh?"

"The security tape. Do you want me to watch it?"

"It's on a disc in my briefcase."

He stood watching her sleep. "I'll take that as a yes."

Dan braced the front door to prevent it from shuddering and stepped inside, the dogs following. He'd taken the dogs on his fifty-minute run into the trails behind the house, roughly five miles, then spent ten minutes walking and stretching to cool down. He didn't want the dogs to run into the house like two drunkards and wake Tracy. He'd closed the bedroom door before leaving, but in their small confines that was only so effective, and he knew she was exhausted. Detective work was a lot like legal work. You could leave the office, but you couldn't escape the case. Dan thought about his cases and his clients when he went to bed and when he awoke. He thought of them in the shower, when he went for a run, and when he shopped in the grocery store. He knew Tracy did the same thing, looking for that piece of evidence she'd not seen or had overlooked. When they were home at night they had a rule—"no work," unless the other needed a consult to get it off his or her mind.

He filled the dog bowls at the tap in the kitchen and set them on the floor. As Rex and Sherlock slurped, he filled a glass at the sink and grabbed vitamins from the cabinet, including glucosamine. He wasn't getting any younger, and his knees reminded him of that fact each time he ran. Running on the dirt trails was a marked improvement over the concrete sidewalk along Alki Beach, but it didn't eliminate all his aches and pains.

He brought the glass and vitamins into the main room and retrieved Tracy's briefcase. Sitting at the table, he powered up her laptop, inserted the disc, and waited for it to boot up. He downed his vitamins with gulps of water and wiped sweat trickling along the sides of his face. He'd had experience with videotapes during his legal career, though usually he'd been on the other side, trying to keep a tape out of evidence. In civil cases, defense attorneys would hire private investigators to follow their injured clients, hoping to videotape the clients during a moment when they weren't as incapacitated as they claimed. The rules of admissibility were rigid. The biggest hurdle for an attorney seeking to have a tape admitted into evidence was establishing a proper foundation—proving that the tape was a reliable depiction of what had actually occurred. That meant putting someone on the witness stand who could testify that the tape had not been edited or tampered with. And that's where Dan usually focused his initial attack.

The video loaded. Dan looked down on the interior of an office space with a reception area and desk counter off to the right. He hit "Play" and sat back, watching like a spectator, occasionally hitting "Fast Forward" to skip the moments when nothing appeared to be happening. He wiped another drip of perspiration from his temple and watched a tall Asian man descend stairs and approach an office at the back of the video. He knocked on the door and pushed it open. Dan noted the time to be 10:31 p.m. and deduced from Tracy's recounting of the Article 32 hearing that this was Brian Cho, the prosecutor. Dan again hit "Fast Forward." Cho exited the office, shutting the door at 10:37 p.m. Again he paused, this time to slip on his camouflage hat. As he approached the camera, he shook his head, grinning as if bemused by something.

Shortly thereafter, a woman exited the same office carrying a box. She walked away from the camera. This he assumed to be Leah Battles, the defense lawyer. Dan noted the time to be 10:49 p.m. He hit "Fast Forward," then slowed the tape when Battles returned. The counter indicated the time to be 10:54 p.m. He sped up the disc, then again hit "Play" when Battles departed her office. She'd changed from the camouflage attire into athletic clothes. Approaching the camera, she snapped on a bike helmet as she departed. He scribbled on his notepad that she wore a backpack and raised the question: *Could Battles have hidden videocassette in her backpack when she left for the night?*

He sat back, sipping his water and glancing over at the dogs. They lay flopped on their sides in a stream of sunlight through the windows. He returned his attention to the video when the janitor entered the building. Dan scribbled the time: 11:03 p.m. The janitor began empty- ing trash bins. Dan hit "Fast Forward," and the janitor moved quickly about the reception area and the offices. When he exited the front door, Dan hit "Pause" and noted the time to be 11:17 p.m.

On the notepad he wrote, *Second-floor janitor?* He hit "Play."

The first-floor janitor returned at 11:26 p.m. carrying a bucket of what looked like cleaning supplies, and a vacuum, which he left in the lobby. He carried the cleaning supplies to the back of the camera's coverage, presumably to the bathrooms.

Dan again hit "Fast Forward" and then "Play" when the janitor reappeared, set the supplies on the reception desk and vacuumed. When he'd finished vacuuming, the janitor exited the building carrying the vacuum and cleaning supplies. The time stamp indicated it was 12:13 p.m. No one else entered or exited the building until the following morning. Cho returned at 7:15 a.m. and disappeared down the hall to the stairs. Others arrived. Leah Battles entered the office at 7:42 a.m.

Dan hit "Stop" and scribbled on the notepad.

Janitor have motive?

Court reporter?

Leah Battles?

Cho? Arrived early the following morning. Was court reporter in office yet? Why would Cho take the tape?

He set down the pen, sipped his water, and gave the tape some additional thought. After a moment he hit "Rewind," and played the disc contents backward. He'd learned the technique from an experienced trial lawyer in his firm in Boston. The man said he played tapes and discs backward to prevent his eyes, and his subconscious, from anticipating what he was about to see, instead of seeing what actually occurred. He said it also allowed him to focus not on the people in the tape, but rather on the environment.

After a few minutes, something caught Dan's eye, or so he thought. Uncertain, he played the tape forward, then played it backward a second time, then a third and a fourth time. He was considering the door across the hall from Leah Battles's office, trying to determine if it had changed positions. That is, the door seemed to have partially closed—only about a foot—though no one had touched it, at least no one on the videotape. Dan rewound the tape and played it forward yet again. The janitor left the building at 11:17 p.m. with the rolling garbage can. Dan watched the office door. Just before the janitor's return at 11:26 p.m., the door was slightly more closed than it had been when the janitor had exited. Dan played the tape back again to be certain, confirmed what he'd seen, then let the tape run. The janitor took the cleaning supplies into the bathroom. Dan noted that the door again seemed to move, this time slightly more open, and again without anyone being present, at least not on the tape.

He took out his legal pad and made three entries—the position of the door at 11:17 when the janitor left the building, the position of the door at 11:26 when the janitor reentered the building, and the position of the door when the janitor left the building for the night.

Either the Navy had a ghost, or someone had edited the tape.

CHAPTER 42

Tracy awoke, startled at the man standing over her bed, and screamed. Sherlock too sat up and barked.

Dan winced, feeling guilty. He stood at the edge of the mattress holding her laptop and looking down at her with a goofy grin, apologizing for having wakened her but not looking sincere.

After a few moments to catch her breath and regain her bearings, Tracy said, "Well, that would just about scare the crap out of Stephen King."

As Dan continued to apologize, Tracy looked across the room to the clock on the dresser. Noon. She had three hours until her shift started again. She could use three days. She felt groggy and sleep deprived.

"I have something to show you," Dan said.

"You better. I set the alarm for one o'clock. You owe me an hour of sleep."

Dan sat on the edge of the bed and played the tape on her laptop, going through the sections he'd noted on his pad, and pointing out what he'd noticed about the door to the office across the hall from Leah Battles.

"Somebody edited the contents of the disc," she said, recounting what she'd seen, but also asking Dan for confirmation.

"Sure seems like it."

She got out of bed and began to put on clothes. "This changes things. Really changes things. How could they do it?"

"I don't know exactly."

Tracy thought of Mike Melton. "I know someone who will."

—

At just after 3:00 p.m., the start of her shift, Tracy walked into the Washington State Patrol Crime Lab on Airport Way carrying the envelope with the computer disc. Detectives called Mike Melton "Grizzly Adams," but Tracy called him "Oz," as in *The Wizard of Oz*, only Melton wasn't a sham hiding behind a curtain. He was the real deal.

Melton's office smelled like vinegar from the wilting, unfinished salad in the bowl on his desk. He looked up as Tracy entered his office, considering her over reading glasses resting on the tip of his nose. He set down a document he'd been reviewing and sat back. "You look like you've seen better days."

"Thanks," Tracy said, sounding hurt. "I really needed that."

Melton leaned forward. "I didn't mean anything by it; you just look tired."

Tracy chuckled. "You have a wife and six daughters, and you still haven't figured out when a woman is playing you?"

Melton laughed, rich and full. "And I doubt I ever will." He had the sleeves of his plaid shirt rolled up meaty forearms, like Paul Bunyan about to swing an ax and fell a tree.

Tracy pointed to the salad. "You going soft on me or is another one of your daughters getting married and you need to fit into your tux?"

"I fit for the first three, but I'm not sure I'm going to be able to squeeze into it again, no matter how many salads I eat." He picked up the bowl. "This is my wife telling me, 'You better fit into that monkey suit, given what it cost us.'"

"Have you seen Del?" Tracy asked.

"He and Faz came in a few days ago. He looks good. Maybe we'll rub off on Fazzio."

"I doubt it."

Melton pointed to the manila envelope in her hand. "Is that it?"

She'd called him from home, told him what Dan thought he'd detected, and asked him to take a look. She handed him the envelope, along with the yellow legal paper with Dan's scribbles designating the times he'd noticed the changes in the office door's position.

Melton pulled the disc from the envelope and inserted it into his computer. He looked down his nose through his reading glasses at the computer screen. Tracy walked behind him and peered over his shoulder as he typed in a command to pull up the video and started through it.

He watched for a few seconds and said, "Superficially, it looks legit." He pointed. "Date and time stamp in the lower-right portion of the screen."

"That's the office door," Tracy said, pointing over his shoulder to the office across the hall from Leah Battles's office.

Melton spoke while continuing to view the screen. "And you need me to tell you if you're crazy, the naval base is haunted, or the tape's been edited."

"Correct."

"Is this a copy?"

"The tape? Yes," she said, recalling her conversation with Rebecca Stanley.

"Hmm."

"What?"

"Be better if we had the original."

"I'm working on it. Tell me why."

"Whoa." Melton had come to the first door movement. He hit "Stop," rewound the tape, then hit "Play." "There it is. Definitely moved." He sat back, continuing to watch.

"Why would you need the original?" Tracy asked.

Melton looked down at Dan's log of times on his desk as his fingers clicked more keys. "It's nearly impossible to monkey with an original tape." He looked up at her over his shoulder. "So I'm told. I'm not a computer guy. I was born too early, but I know it's difficult from what I've been told. If somebody wanted to monkey with the video it's easier, as I understand it, if they make a copy. They can then use certain software programs to remove the date and time stamp, edit the video, and replace the date and time stamp so it looks continuous. There it is again," he said. "Definitely a ghost." He again hit "Stop," rewound the tape, and replayed it. This time he pointed with his finger. "Did you see this?"

"The door movement?"

"Not the door. Take a look at the crack between the door and the jamb. Watch the shadow."

Tracy leaned closer—her chin over Melton's shoulder. She could smell his cologne. The crack between the door and the jamb darkened. "Somebody's behind the door."

"Sure looks like there could be. Something's creating the shadow. Look. Now it's gone again."

"Why couldn't somebody edit the original?"

"Again, as I understand it, these security videos are watermarked by the manufacturer with a code to prevent someone from tampering with them. It could be like 000111000111. If this was edited, we'll know because the watermark will have been broken."

Tracy straightened. "How long will it take?"

Melton hit "Stop" and ejected the disc from the computer. Tracy picked up the paper with Dan's log and walked back to the other side of his desk.

"I have a guy in the lab who does a lot of this," Melton said. "It will be right up his alley."

"Does he need the log?" Tracy asked.

"Shouldn't." Melton considered his watch. "Not sure if he's still here, but if he is, it shouldn't be too long to determine whether the tape's been edited, depending on what he has going on. Let me get him working on it. I'll call later and let you know."

—

Back in her car, Tracy lowered the volume on the radio as she made her way across town to Police Headquarters. She contemplated a scenario in which the tape had been edited to eliminate someone coming in and out of the building. She could think of two immediate problems.

First, whom could she tell?

She couldn't go to Stanley. Stanley had provided Tracy with the tape, and could, somehow, be involved in editing its contents. Tracy also couldn't call up the security officer who produced the tape because, again, he could have been the person who did the editing, maybe on his own, maybe at someone's request. She also couldn't go to Leah Battles or Brian Cho because either—on their own or on someone's order—could have been the person who went into the building, stole the tape, and hid in the office until the janitor left. Both knew where to find the tape as well as the evidentiary significance of it. Working in the building, they both also likely knew the court reporter's schedule and would have known that he had already gone home that evening. They also knew the janitor's schedule. It didn't, however, explain how they could have edited the security feed, unless they were working for or with others—which meant maybe there was something more to the rumors that the Navy was involved in a cover-up. About the only thing the tape did was eliminate the janitor.

But if Tracy was right about any of the suspects, the tape didn't explain how the person got into the DSO building without entering the last four digits of his or her Social Security number. Before leaving home to meet with Melton she'd tried to match the people on the tape with the Social Security numbers entered for that evening. She confirmed that neither Cho, Stanley, nor Battles had entered their Social Security numbers to get back into the building after they'd departed. At least the log provided to her by Stanley did not note any of those three numbers. Could the log also have been tampered with? A thought came to her and she pulled to the side of the road. She retrieved her briefcase and pulled out the log of numbers. On the tape, it had taken Al Tulowitsky nine minutes after leaving the building to dump the garbage and return, which seemed like a longer time than necessary. She checked the log and noted his arrival at 11:03 p.m. Scrolling down further, however, she did not see the same four digits. Tulowitsky had not reentered his code when he'd returned from dumping the garbage at 11:26 p.m.

She sat back, wondering if the janitor could have taken the cassette with him when he cleaned Battles's office and put it in his truck, or had given it to someone when he went outside. It would have been simple enough for him to do so, but again, it didn't provide an explanation for why he didn't reenter his Social Security number. It also didn't explain why someone was clearly hiding from him.

So why had it taken Tulowitsky so long to dump the garbage? Tracy wondered if there was some other way to gain access to the building, despite Battles telling her that there was not.

Tracy had another problem. She looked at the date on her cell phone and wondered if the original video even still existed, or if it had been copied over. According to Rebecca Stanley, the Navy had a retention policy, but Stanley either didn't know that policy or deliberately didn't tell Tracy. Then again, the retention policy might not matter;

someone could have already recorded over the tape, inadvertently, or deliberately.

Tracy found Detective John Owens's 360 area code in her recent calls, and pressed the number. Owens answered on the second ring. Tracy explained what she'd learned from the tape and what she was contemplating. Then she asked, "You said you had experience dealing with the Navy?"

"It comes with the territory out here," Owens said.

A gust of wind rattled her car. The rain continued to fall, and dark-gray tendrils reached down from a cloud layer suffocating the city. "I need to get into the security office, today. Can you make it happen?"

"I can try," Owens said.

"I don't want anyone to know we're coming."

"I understand."

"I also want to talk to the janitor again, Al Tulowitsky, but not at work, not in front of his boss."

"You think he's involved?"

"Maybe unintentionally. I have a theory. See if you can find a contact for him. I'm going to catch the next ferry, if it isn't full."

"This time of evening, with the commuters, it's likely full. Just walk on," Owens said. "I'll pick you up at the dock."

—

Leah Battles had been sitting at her desk going stir-crazy since her banishment. She'd endured a telephone interview with the ethics investigators from Washington, DC, which made her want to puke, and was now waiting for them to make a decision on bringing an ethics charge, which would no doubt be a precursor to a court-martial. It hung over her, constantly on her mind. She couldn't even go out of her office and engage the staff to distract her thoughts and kill time. She remained radioactive, and, as such, others gave her a wide berth when they saw her coming. They weren't unfriendly. They smiled or nodded. A few even said hello on occasion, but no one ever stopped to ask how things were going. At times it made coming into the office almost intolerable. If the brass was going to court-martial her, Battles wished they'd just get on with it. At least a hearing would give her something on which to focus her energy, which was better than sitting at her desk slowly dying of boredom.

It seemed everything had been put on hold since Trejo's death, including her fate.

Nearing four in the afternoon, she lifted her head to the sound of a light tap on her door. It startled her only because it was the first visitor she'd had in a week. She expected Darcy, who was the only person who engaged in anything beyond superficialities.

"Come in."

Rebecca Stanley pushed open the door and stepped into the office. Battles quickly turned off Pandora, which she was streaming over her computer to keep her company, and stood.

And just like that, Battles found those nerves of anticipation.

Be careful what you wish for, she heard her mother say.

Stanley did not visit often, and never just to chitchat. Battles also knew that bad news was always best delivered in person.

"It's depressing in here," Stanley said. The only light came from the Tiffany desk lamp. Stanley flipped on the overhead fluorescent tubes. "You need an office with a window, though given the weather this past month, I'm not sure it would offer much."

Battles wondered if the mention of a different office was a good sign. "Seattle natives use weather to keep people from moving here," she said.

"So I've heard." Stanley walked to one of the two chairs and sat. "We all could use some vitamin D."

There was an awkward pause. Finally, Battles broke the silence. "I'm assuming this isn't a social visit." She even mustered a smile.

"I'm afraid not. Part of my job is delivering bad news."

"I figured as much."

"But this time there's an element of good news and bad news," Stanley said. "Which do you want first?"

"Let's just shoot the works. Give me both."

Stanley smiled softly and gently pursed her lips. "Okay." She paused another beat, as if trying to decide where to start. It made Battles wonder if the news wasn't actually bad news and really bad news.

"First, I've been advised that after considerable debate, the ethics investigation is not going to recommend proceeding to a court-martial."

Battles breathed a sigh of relief, but it was brief. She knew what "considerable debate" meant. "So they don't believe they have sufficient evidence to convict me."

"They can't definitively say what happened to the videotape," Stanley confirmed, "and they can't draw a conclusion without something more substantial to base it on. The tape could have simply been misplaced, discarded inadvertently, or taken by someone for nefarious purposes. Under the circumstances, there's insufficient evidence to bring a charge as serious as dereliction of duty."

"So their decision has nothing to do with guilt or innocence."

Stanley shook her head. "The decision will specifically state there was insufficient evidence to proceed to a resolution."

Battles sat back. "Insufficient evidence," she said, mulling over the words. She briefly contemplated telling Stanley she wanted a hearing, growing confident she could defeat the charge, but she recognized that a decision made in haste, when she was emotionally upset, would not be wise.

"I know it's not exactly what you were hoping for," Stanley said.

"No, it's not," Battles said.

"But with Trejo's death, there's just no way for anyone to be certain about what happened to the tape. And the surveillance tape for this building is inconclusive."

"I could have hidden the tape in my backpack," Battles said.

"Everything is circumstantial," Stanley said.

Battles looked at an abstract painting of the Seattle train depot, a view from outside her apartment window. It was one of her best paintings, but she doubted she'd ever appreciate it. She'd painted it during her recent hiatus. "So is that the good news or the bad news?"

"I guess that depends on how you consider it."

"I'm hoping it's the bad news."

Stanley sat back. "You're being transferred," she said. "That's not necessarily bad news, except for me. I need you here, Lee. You're my best defense attorney."

The news came as a surprise, even in a profession where transfers were frequent. Battles was not just a good attorney, she'd twice been named the Defense Counsel of the Year. This was clearly not a decision that had anything to do with performance or merit, which meant they were getting rid of her, sending her away, basically implying to everyone that she was guilty but they couldn't prove it.

"Command doesn't believe you can fulfill your duties as a JAG officer here, in light of what has transpired. They think it best that you be transferred to another base."

"Where am I going?"

"DSO North."

"Washington, DC?" They couldn't have picked a spot farther from Seattle if they'd tried, or closer to the ethics panel. They were, in essence, pulling her back, close to home, where they could keep an eye on her by no doubt sticking her at some meaningless desk job.

"Yes."

"Will I still be trying cases?"

"Not initially."

"Will I at least be in a DSO office?"

"No. Not initially, but I understand you will be reevaluated, in time."

"So . . . No," she said, seeing the handwriting on the wall. She'd be deskbound until her commission expired. Then she'd be sent on her way. Maybe it was for the best. She could get out of the Navy and get a real job, earn some real money defending cases for clients with a lot to lose. Maybe she'd hang her own shingle.

"I'm sorry to see you go, Lee. I hope you know that I did what I could to keep you here. But Washington, DC, is a terrific city."

"When do I ship out?"

"Your last day here is the end of the month. You'll have two weeks to report to DSO North."

Battles nodded, taking it all in. It wasn't like she had a choice. She'd pretty much forfeited freedom of choice about where she lived and worked when she'd been commissioned.

"Take some time to clear your head. Travel a bit before you get settled."

She'd have to find a new place to live and a new Krav Maga studio. She suspected she would need the energy release after a week of meaningless filing. "Maybe."

"You were never going to make the Navy a career," Stanley said. Before Battles could protest, Stanley continued, "You're too good an attorney, and for the good attorneys, this job is always a means to an end. You've gained a lot of experience, trial experience civil attorneys your age rarely get. Any number of the top law firms in any city would love to hire you."

"I guess," Battles said, thinking perhaps that it had all been worth it, despite the consequences. "What about Trejo?"

"What about him?"

"What have they determined? I saw the police detective here yesterday."

"I don't know. She did tell me that she doubts Trejo killed himself."

"She thinks someone killed him? Did she say why?"

"No. She asked for a copy of the security tape for the building. I told her I'd already viewed it and didn't see anything concerning."

"But she asked for the tape anyway?"

"She had a warrant."

Battles sat back, wondering what Tracy Crosswhite was doing, and why.

Stanley stood. "Come on. Let me buy you a drink. We can go to The Bulkhead."

Battles was still deep in thought. If Crosswhite wanted the video-tape, it meant SPD was continuing to pursue the matter. Why? Trejo was dead, which was seemingly their only involvement. The security tape was a Navy matter. She thought again of her conversation with Crosswhite at the Bremerton Police Department, about how Trejo could have brought something on and off a ship without anyone knowing. Then she thought again of the tape.

"Lee?"

"What's that?"

"Let me buy you a drink."

Battles had gone out with Stanley before, but usually at lunch to discuss her cases. They'd never gone out after work. "I appreciate the offer," she said.

"This will be what you make of it, Lee. DC could be a great move for you. It's a military town and there are a lot of opportunities, especially for someone young and talented."

"Thanks," Battles said, though she noted that Stanley had stopped short of offering a letter of recommendation.

Stanley noticed Battles's bike. "We can put your bike in the back of my car and I'll drop you off at the ferry after we're done. Have you looked outside lately?"

"No," Battles said.

"The weather is brutal. It's raining hard and the wind is gusting. You don't want to be riding a bike in this weather, not on that road. It's a good way to get yourself killed."

The ferry ride across Elliott Bay rivaled a roller coaster at an amusement park. With the wind increasing in intensity, the waves also grew, making the ferry pitch and roll. Occasionally the whitecaps would crash over the bow with enough force to trigger car alarms. Tracy wasn't in the car hold; the ferry had been full, as John Owens had predicted. She'd walked on, but now wondered if that had been such a good idea. If the storm got worse, and maybe even if it didn't, the Department of Transportation could shut down the ferry system, and she'd be stuck in Bremerton for the night without a car.

She sat in one of the booths, watching the whitecaps out the window. Unfortunately, the bad weather didn't stop the tourists from being tourists. Some stood on the deck, dressed in raincoats, seeing how far they could lean into the wind, as if walking up a hill.

When the ferry docked in Bremerton, Tracy departed on unsteady legs and with a queasy stomach. She raised a hand against the wind and rain to search the parking lot for John Owens. A car flashed its headlights twice and she moved toward it, seeing Owens in the shadows between swipes of the car's windshield wipers. She pulled open the passenger's-side door and quickly slid into the seat.

"I'll bet that was an E ticket ride," Owens said, dating himself; E tickets had not been in use at Disneyland for several decades.

The inside of the car felt like walking into a sauna, fully dressed. Owens had the defroster blasting air at the front windshield, and Tracy could see where he'd wiped uneven streaks on the inside of the glass in an attempt to clear it. He reached out again with the sleeve of his jacket and swiped several more streaks. "The defroster is the shits in this car," he said.

Tracy removed her raincoat, deposited it on the floorboard in the backseat, and helped him wipe the windshield. "You have any luck locating the janitor?"

"Yeah, I got an address." Owens pulled back the sleeve of his jacket to consider his watch. "Not sure if he's home, but he's close enough to the base that we can drive over and knock on his door before we go meet my friend."

Owens had arranged to get on base with a captain he knew well. He said the captain would get them through the Charleston Gate and escort them to wherever they needed to go. Frustrated at his inability to clear the windshield, Owens cracked his driver's-side window, which allowed in spittles of rain, and pulled from his parking spot.

Tracy's cell rang. She recognized the number on her screen and quickly answered. "Mike?"

"Nice weather, huh? I hope you're not out in this."

"Unfortunately I just took the ferry to Bremerton."

"Bet that was fun."

"I won't be eating anytime soon. You got something on the security tape?"

She noticed Owens glance over at her.

"Watermark is broken," he said. "Several times. Someone definitely edited it in the places you found."

That raised another series of questions, but they weren't questions Mike Melton could answer in a lab. "Okay," she said. "Good to know, Mike. I'm hoping to get a copy of the original while I'm over here. If I do, I'll send it over to you."

"Stay dry," Melton said, and disconnected.

"What about the security tape?" Owens asked.

"I had the crime lab analyze the tape given to the OIC, Rebecca Stanley. They say it was edited," she said. "The watermark is broken."

Owens squinted as if having trouble seeing. With the window cracked and the defroster on high, he'd opened a half-moon-shaped gap in the condensation. "How can somebody edit the tape? Doesn't it have a date and time stamp on it?"

"Apparently you can edit a copy. There's software available."

Owens shook his head. "I guess there would be, wouldn't there? Can he tell where it was edited?"

"It was edited after Tulowitsky left the building and then again when he returned."

"To hide someone's presence inside?"

"That would be the most logical reason for someone to do it."

"Battles?"

"We won't know for certain until we get the original, if it still exists."

"What do you mean, 'if'?"

"My understanding is the security office keeps the tapes for a designated period of time. Then they roll over the contents."

"How long before the rollover?"

"Stanley didn't know."

"You want me to make a call?"

"I'm worried that could sound alarms. I'd rather go in person, serve the warrant, and get the tape without giving anyone a reason to destroy it. Otherwise, this could all be a wild-goose chase."

"We got the weather for it," Owens said. "You want to go to the base first?"

Tracy checked her watch. Tulowitsky would be leaving for work soon. "No. Let's talk to Tulowitsky first. If my theory is wrong, the tape might not matter."

—

Al Tulowitsky lived in a modest, one-story home not far from the naval base and his employer, IJS. The front of the house did not face the street. Rather, the home was situated perpendicular to the road. A dirt-and-gravel easement extended for perhaps a hundred yards and served as the driveway for three homes. Owens pulled down the easement and parked beneath the limbs of a gnarled pine. Forsaking her raincoat, Tracy followed an uneven stone walkway strewn with spent pine needles to a front door protected by a tiny overhang that offered little relief from the wind and rain. A gutter to the right of the door overflowed, the water splattering the ground and kicking back up at Tracy's shoes and ankles.

Owens, who wore slacks and black dress shoes, stepped lightly around the puddles and joined Tracy at the door. Water dripped from the overhang onto his Gore-Tex jacket. Tracy used a door knocker to rap three solid beats. The door pulled open as if Al Tulowitsky had been standing on the other side, expecting them. The surprised expression on his face refuted that assessment.

"Mr. Tulowitsky," Tracy said. "We met the other day at IJS's office."

"I remember," Tulowitsky said, clearly confused by her presence. He glanced at Owens. Tracy introduced him.

"I have a few more questions I'm hoping you can answer for me."

"What kind of questions?" Tulowitsky wore his work uniform—blue pants and a white short-sleeve button-down with the company logo of the energetic man on the breast pocket.

"I just need to nail down a few things for a timeline." Water continued to drip from the small overhang, and the pine tree shed water like a shower burst with each gust of wind. "We won't take up much of your time," she said.

"I have to get to work pretty soon."

"Just a few minutes," she said.

Perhaps conceding more to the weather than Tracy's request, Tulowitsky opened the door and stepped back to allow them entry. They stepped onto a couple of rows of cracked tiles leading to a front room. The shades had been drawn over both windows, giving everything a yellowish tint, and the air held the thick smell of cigarette smoke. After the hellish ride on the ferry, Tracy's nausea didn't need much to be reactivated. She quickly felt queasy. Sufficient time in here, and she'd breathe enough secondhand smoke for an entire city. Tulowitsky picked up a remote from a cluttered coffee table and turned off the television. He seemed uncertain about what to do or to say next.

"Can I get you something to drink?" he asked, then made a face as if he regretted the offer. "I don't really have much."

"We're fine," Tracy said. She gestured to the living room. "Maybe we could just sit for a minute."

Tulowitsky sat in a brown leather recliner. The faded color of the chair's arms, and the pile of newspapers on the floor beside it, indicated the recliner was his preferred seat. An ashtray on a side table overflowed with butts, and the smell of cigarettes intensified. Tracy took shallow breaths to fight off her nausea.

They sat across the coffee table from her on a worn cloth couch. Hot air poured out of the floor vents with enough force to shake the leaves on a fake palm in the corner of the room. "You said you had a question?" Tulowitsky asked.

Tracy read from a blank page in her notepad to give Tulowitsky the impression these were follow-up questions to their prior conversation. "I've had a chance to go over the security tape for that evening we talked about. It looks like you arrived at the building at just after 11:00, 11:03 to be precise, and began emptying garbage cans, as you said."

"That's what I do first," Tulowitsky affirmed. He had his hands on the arms of the chair, like a man about to be strapped down for an electrocution.

"Right." She returned to her notepad. "You left the building again at 11:17." She glanced up at Tulowitsky. "That was to take out the garbage, correct?"

"That's right."

"I was wondering, did you take the garbage anywhere to be shredded or incinerated when you left?"

"No," Tulowitsky said. "No, we just drop off the bags before we leave the base."

"So you just take it out to your truck, grab cleaning supplies and a vacuum, and continue on with your duties."

"Pretty much," Tulowitsky said.

"You don't do anything else at that point, right?"

"Like what?" He gave her an inquisitive stare.

"I mean when you go outside, you don't fill out paperwork or call in to the office?"

"Oh, uh, no," he said. "Nothing like that."

"Did you have a cigarette when you went out, Mr. Tulowitsky?"

That question got his attention. Tulowitsky glanced between her and Owens. "What's that?"

She pointed to the pack of cigarettes on the side table. "When you stepped out to empty the garbage, did you have a cigarette? Is that part of your routine?"

"No," he said. "There are designated areas for smoking on the base. So . . . no."

She got a sense he was not being honest. "Is there a designated area near that building?" She was playing a hunch. She doubted Tulowitsky could go long between cigarettes.

"No." He shifted as if someone had started to apply electrical current to the chair.

"Mr. Tulowitsky, I'm not passing judgment, and I'm not here to create trouble for you, but you left the building and you didn't return for nine minutes. That's a long time to just dump the garbage and grab cleaning supplies."

"I might have been looking for something," he said quickly.

"Such as?"

"Oh, I don't know. It's been a long time now."

"I understand. But you didn't recall doing anything other than loading the garbage bag and grabbing supplies. That's also what you told NCIS."

"But that doesn't mean I didn't."

"You would have told NCIS if you had, wouldn't you?"

He paused again. "I don't know."

Tulowitsky hadn't. She had his statement. "Did you see anyone when you went out?"

"Meaning what?"

"Anyone standing by your truck or near the building?"

He shook his head. "I don't think so, no."

She took a different tack. "You shut the door to the building when you go out, right?"

"It shuts automatically," he said.

Tracy set down her notepad and picked up the log of Social Security numbers entered on the pad that night. "This is a list of people who entered and left the office that evening. It should show you initially logging in at 11:03, and then logging in again when you returned at 11:26, correct?"

"I guess so," he said.

"How come it doesn't for that day?" Tracy said.

Tulowitsky didn't immediately answer. When he did, he said, "What's that?" He was stalling.

"How come the log for that night shows you arriving at 11:03 but doesn't show you returning nine minutes after leaving to dump the garbage, at 11:26?"

"You said it did."

"No. The security tape documents your return at 11:26, but the security door does not."

Tulowitsky pressed his lips so tight they nearly disappeared altogether. "I . . . I don't know."

"Mr. Tulowitsky, did you leave to have a cigarette and prop the door open so you wouldn't have to log back in nine minutes later?"

Tulowitsky folded his hands in his lap, fidgeting with his thumbs. His lips began to move as if he were craving that cigarette right now. After another beat, he said, "I could get fired."

Tracy felt a twinge of excitement and had to calm herself. "For having a cigarette?"

"In a non-designated location? Yeah," he said.

"And you had one that night?"

Another nod.

"Some place out of view?"

"I go around the side of the building," he said. "Just one cigarette."

"When you go around the side of the building, can you see the door to get back in?"

"No."

"And did you prop it open so you could get back inside without using your code and thereby registering how long you'd been out?"

"Yes."

Tracy glanced at Owens before reengaging Tulowitsky. "Is that something you do every night?"

"You mean have a smoke?"

"And leave the door propped open?"

Again he paused. "Pretty much every night; there might be a night when I don't."

"How do you prop the door open?"

"There's a wood block, a wedge. I just pop it between the door and the jamb. Look, there's nobody else there that late, not usually anyway, so it's really not a big deal."

Only this night there had been, and whoever it had been, Tracy was betting they also knew Tulowitsky's routine.

They knew it well.

CHAPTER 43

During her three years at Bremerton, Leah Battles had ridden her bike to and from the ferry in some pretty nasty storms, and this storm certainly rivaled, if not surpassed, the worst of them. The wind gusted in sustained bursts, enough to cause Rebecca Stanley's Chevy TrailBlazer to shudder. Battles hated to consider what that wind would do to a rider on a bike.

Her bike was currently in the back of Stanley's car.

"Thanks again for the ride," she said. "This storm is nasty."

"Not a problem," Stanley said. The wheels of the car plowed through another puddle, sending up a wall of water outside Battles's window.

The darkened sky had brought an early dusk that was quickly fading to night. Rain had overwhelmed the gutters, and ponds of water extended well out onto the surface streets. The car's tires sprayed rooster tails each time it ripped through the puddles.

Battles looked down at the driver's-side floorboard. "How's the ankle?"

Stanley had stepped in a calf-deep puddle just outside her door in the parking lot. "Wet and cold," she said. "Do you mind if we stop at my apartment so it doesn't feel like I'm sitting the rest of the night with my foot in a bucket of ice?"

Battles smiled. "Sure."

She touched her side and felt the comforting presence of her Glock just beneath her blueberries.

"How do you feel about The Bulkhead?" Stanley asked.

Bremerton being a Navy town, there was no shortage of bars using Navy terminology. The Bulkhead was in favor because it offered frequent discounts for military personnel, like two-buck beers on Thursday nights and eight-dollar "Bell" hamburgers, which came with french fries and the drink of your choice.

"Sounds good," Battles said.

"It's close to my apartment," Stanley said. "I can quickly change and we can grab that drink and maybe a bite to eat and still get you back to the ferry at a reasonable hour. You think they'll continue running in this weather?"

"It wouldn't be the first time they cancelled them," Battles said. "I have the app and the number for the ferry system on speed dial. I can call for an update if the weather doesn't clear. I heard on the radio this was supposed to blow through later this evening."

"Hopefully we don't lose power."

"Hopefully," Battles said.

Stanley lived east of the base, across the Manette Bridge, which spanned the Port Washington Narrows. They drove the road that hugged the coastline to an apartment complex designated The Crow's Nest, likely because there wasn't anything else around the two multistory apartment buildings situated directly across the Narrows from Naval Base Kitsap.

"Do you sometimes go home and feel as though you never left?" Battles asked, admiring the view.

"I've always been partial to water," Stanley said. "I have a killer view off my deck. Come up and see."

Battles pushed out of the car. She felt the wind gusting at her back and gripped the bill of her hat to avoid having to chase it across the lawn. She followed Stanley through a glass door into a small entry with mailboxes and an elevator. Stanley retrieved her mail and they took the elevator to the top floor. Stanley's apartment was three doors to the right of the elevator. She unlocked the dead bolt and doorknob and stepped inside, turning on lights. Battles followed her inside and shut the door.

Battles considered an apartment to be an extension of the person. Hers was somewhat cluttered, with an ever-present easel holding her latest painting, and a chessboard on the kitchen table with a game in progress. She played against herself, making a move in the morning before she left for work and a countermove for the opponent when she returned home. Her longest game to date was three weeks.

Stanley tossed her keys on the Formica counter separating the kitchen from the living room. "Make yourself at home. I'll just be a minute." She disappeared down a hallway.

Battles walked farther into the front room, which was neat, but sparsely furnished. A sliding glass door led to a narrow balcony that barely fit a small metal table and two matching chairs, but which did have a killer view looking across the water to the lights of the shipyard.

She stepped to the mantel. Framed photographs displayed Stanley with a dark-haired man and a small girl, perhaps two or three. Stanley kept no such photographs in her office, and she'd never mentioned being married, or being a mother, or from the looks of the apartment, being divorced. Things were starting to add up.

Battles heard Stanley returning and reached for the Glock, pulling it from her holster and holding it at her side.

"Told you it was a hell of a view," Stanley said.

Battles turned and raised the Glock. "Actually, you said it was a killer view."

Tracy now knew how someone had entered the DSO building without having to punch in a Social Security code and without having been seen. Whoever that person was, they'd simply waited for Al Tulowitsky to take his regular, prolonged cigarette break, and prop the door open with the wooden wedge. It confirmed that the convenience store videotape had not been misplaced. It had been an intentional act, stolen by someone who knew Tulowitsky's routine. That meant, in all probability, that the person was someone who worked within the building. Battles and Cho were Tracy's first choices. Stanley also could not be dismissed.

All three knew where the evidence room was located, as well as the significance of the videotape. It provided a direct link to what Laszlo Trejo had been doing in Seattle the night he'd run down D'Andre Miller, which meant he'd likely been delivering heroin smuggled on and off his last naval ship.

"You think Tulowitsky could have been in on it?" Owens asked. They were back in his car on their way to meet his contact at the naval base.

Tracy had considered that same question, whether Tulowitsky could have left the door open on purpose.

"No," she said. "Whoever snuck in went to great lengths to remain hidden from Tulowitsky. They wouldn't have bothered if he'd somehow been involved. I'm betting that same person also killed Trejo to prevent him from testifying, if it came to that, which makes involving Tulowitsky too big a risk."

Owens and Tracy presented credentials to the MAs manning the Charleston Gate, then waited until the friend Owens had called to gain admission met them and escorted them to the security office on the first floor of the DSO building.

David Bakhtiari's office was loaded with computers, video screens, and blinking lights. Bakhtiari wore the same blue-and-gray uniform as everyone else on base, but that was where the similarities ended. He was as big as Del, and bordering on 300 pounds. He wasn't fat, far from it.

He looked like an NFL offensive lineman. After introductions, Owens's friend remained outside the office.

"You want the disc for the night of March 18," Bakhtiari said. It wasn't a question. "I copied that tape once, for OIC Stanley."

"I understand," Tracy said. "We'd like to see the original."

Bakhtiari's eyes narrowed with interest. He was clearly wondering why, and likely processing the possible answers. "You have a subpoena, I assume." He said it in a tone that sounded like a challenge, but more likely was intended to cover his ass in case anyone ever asked.

Tracy handed him the subpoena. Bakhtiari read through it in some detail. After a minute or two he nodded and said, "Okay. I'll burn you a copy. Where should I send it?"

"We'd like to see the tape now," Owens said. He reached into his coat pocket and handed Bakhtiari a business card. "After we see it, you can forward a copy to this address, but we'd like to see it now."

Bakhtiari let out a held breath and quickly checked his watch. Tracy wondered if he was covering for someone.

"You need to be somewhere?" Owens asked, letting a hint of sarcasm creep into his tone.

"My daughter's birthday is today." Bakhtiari shrugged. "We're supposed to be having a party in the backyard, but with this weather . . . My wife is a bit stressed-out. She asked that I get home as soon as possible."

Tracy fought the urge to smile; nothing could take down a man, even a very large man, faster than his wife's irritation. He'd stand up to other men, even go to blows to save his ego, but when the wife asked for something, he shuddered at the thought of not delivering.

"I have the time stamp with the time we're interested in," Tracy said. She reached into her pocket for the piece of paper on which Dan had scribbled the times that the door to the office appeared to have moved. "We just want to see a particular section of the tape. After we do, you can mail Detective Owens a copy and we'll be out of your hair in time for you to get home and celebrate your daughter's birthday."

Bakhtiari seemed to exhale in relief. "I appreciate that. What sections?"

Tracy handed him the slip of paper. He studied it, then said in a brighter tone, "Okay. This makes it easy."

They followed Bakhtiari to a computer terminal, standing behind him as he sat and pecked in commands. Within minutes he'd pulled up a familiar lobby. Bakhtiari pointed to the first series of numbers on the scrap of paper he'd set on the desk and confirmed it as the first location.

Tracy said, "But take it back thirty seconds earlier."

"Yes, ma'am." Bakhtiari gave her a slight nod and continued to type. He compared the time on the tape with the time on the sheet of paper, then pushed back his chair, about to hit the arrow to play the tape.

"Can you stand on the other side of the computer?" Owens said.

Bakhtiari looked between the two of them, uncertain of the request.

"In case this becomes evidence, you might have to testify regarding the chain of custody," Owens said. "I think it best if you also don't become a witness to what's on the tape."

"No problem." Bakhtiari rose from his seat. "Just press that button to go forward and that one to go back." He stepped around to the other side of the screen.

Owens sat, surveyed the keyboard for a second, and hit the arrow to start the video. When he did, Tracy hit the stopwatch on her phone.

"What are you doing?" Owens asked.

She kept her voice low. "I want to be sure this tape wasn't tampered with either."

On the screen, Al Tulowitsky exited the second office with two plastic waste bins, one for trash and the other for recycling. He emptied them and returned both bins to the office. He then rolled the garbage can to the front door, exiting.

Several minutes passed. Tracy was tempted to hit "Fast Forward."

"It would take him a minute or two to empty the garbage," Owens said, eyes locked on the screen.

Another fifteen seconds and someone stepped into the lobby. Owens and Tracy leaned close to the monitor. She felt a rush of adrenaline. It wasn't Tulowitsky. It was someone dressed in the same baggy, blue-and-gray uniform, the hat squarely on the head, which was turned to the left, away from the camera.

"Holy shit," Owens said under his breath. "There really is somebody. I—can't tell who it is. Can you?"

"They know the camera is there," Tracy said softly. "Whoever it is, they're avoiding it, avoiding showing their face."

Owens leaned closer. "Then they work in the building."

"Or just know where the security camera is," she said.

"Can you tell if it's male or female?"

"Not in those uniforms," Tracy said. "Everyone looks the same." The angle of the camera also made depth perception difficult.

The person walked down the hall between the two offices to the staircase leading up to the evidence room.

"Play it back," Tracy said.

Owens did, but even viewing it a second time, Tracy could get very little from the tape.

They let the tape run. Tracy checked the stopwatch on her phone. Four minutes and twenty-four seconds had passed. Then five minutes. Six. At six minutes and forty-two seconds, the uniform returned from down the hall, but again the person kept his or her head lowered so the bill of the cap prevented Tracy from seeing the face in any detail.

"I think it's a woman," she said.

"How can you tell?"

"The facial features are soft. The chin."

Rather than proceed to the front door, the uniform turned quickly into the second office and partially closed the door.

"That explains the first door movement," Tracy said.

"Anything?" Owens asked.

"Not yet," Tracy said.

"Could it be Cho?"

"I don't think so. Cho was more erect in his walk and his features were stronger. It could be Battles or Stanley. They're about the same height and build."

At eleven minutes and four seconds, Al Tulowitsky came through the front door carrying the cleaning supplies and the vacuum cleaner.

"Somebody cut about two minutes," Tracy said. "The tape I have, Tulowitsky is gone for nine minutes."

"He's heading for the bathrooms," Owens said.

Seconds after Tulowitsky exited the reception area, the office door opened and the uniform stepped out.

"There's the second door movement," Tracy said.

The uniform moved quickly toward the front entrance, head still down, face still partially obscured by the bill of the cap. Tracy's heart quickened for just a beat before the image was out the door. "Go back."

Owens hit the keys and went back. "How far?"

"That's good there. Can we slow it down frame by frame?" Tracy asked Bakhtiari.

Bakhtiari came around the desk and Owens pushed back his chair to provide him space. Bakhtiari hit a couple of keys, and again departed. Owens pushed the "Forward" button and Tracy leaned closer to the monitor. The uniform came out of the office and walked toward the door one frame at a time. Tracy had her finger on the keyboard as the uniform approached the entrance. She hit the "Stop" key, freezing the frame.

"I know who it is," she said.

Tracy and Owens exited Bakhtiari's office, hurrying down the hall to Leah Battles's office on the same floor. Battles wasn't there.

Tracy moved quickly to the woman at the reception desk. "I'm looking for Leah Battles," she said, holding out her shield and ID.

"Can I ask what this is about?" the woman said.

"Make it happen, Petty Officer," Owens's friend ordered.

"She left," the woman said. "She left with the OIC."

"Rebecca Stanley?" Tracy asked.

The woman nodded. "Yes."

"Do you know where they went?"

"No, ma'am, I don't."

"Where's her office?" Owens asked.

"The OIC? She's down the hall, first floor."

Tracy followed Owens and his friend down the hall. Stanley was not in her office. They started back to reception.

"Detective Crosswhite?" Brian Cho stood above them on the stairs, his brow furrowed. "What are you doing here?"

"I'm looking for Leah Battles or Rebecca Stanley. Have you seen either of them?"

Cho nodded. "Earlier today, but they left together about half an hour ago."

"Do you know where they went?"

"I do," another woman said. She came out from behind a desk in the hall. "They were going to The Bulkhead, for a drink to celebrate."

"To celebrate?" Cho sounded skeptical. "More likely to drown their sorrows."

"Why do you say that?" Tracy asked.

"Because the ethics committee came back with its decision today. They're recommending a court-martial against Lieutenant Battles."

CHAPTER 44

Leah Battles stared at the gun in Rebecca Stanley's hand, though it had not come as a surprise. The gun in Battles's hand, however, had clearly surprised Stanley. Now they were at what some referred to as a Mexican standoff.

Anticipate your opponent's moves and be prepared to counter. One of the first rules of competitive chess.

Battles had started to put things together after Stanley indicated that the detective, Tracy Crosswhite, was still involved and seeking the original security tape, despite having the copy from Stanley. Based on Crosswhite's questions the night the two of them went for coffee, the detective was either pursuing a theory, or had evidence that Trejo had been dealing drugs the night he ran over the kid in Seattle. The logical conclusion, if Crosswhite was seeking the original tape, was that she had reason to believe the copy had been edited. If it had, Stanley, who supplied the tape, was the most likely suspect. Stanley also had access to the building and to the court reporter's office. She also knew, from her discussions with Battles, the significance of the convenience store video and the likely outcome if that tape went missing. Finally, the invitation to get a drink was out of character.

"You stole the tape that night," Battles said. She circled to her left as Stanley circled to her right and came farther into the room.

"I had no choice. Like you said, the tape was damning. Trejo would have been convicted."

"And you edited the DSO security tape so that you wouldn't be on it. That's why Crosswhite wanted the original. You're on the tape?" She stepped again to her left.

"I always said you were a good attorney, Leah." Battles stepped right.

"You should see me play chess." Battles continued circling. "So you took the tape to get Trejo off, and then you killed him because you couldn't trust that he'd keep quiet about the heroin."

Outside the apartment, thunder clapped. Stanley flinched, but Battles resisted the urge to pull the trigger.

"Easy, Captain," Battles said. Despite outward appearances, Stanley was clearly on edge.

The thunder became a distant rumble but the rain intensified, pecking on the roof and the deck furniture—not rain but pellet-size hail pinging off the table and chairs.

"So why are we here?" Battles asked, trying to keep Stanley talking, looking for any opening to strike and take her gun. She had to get closer. "Trejo's dead. You have the tape. The ethics investigation isn't going to be pursued. Why bring me here?"

"Yeah, well—I lied."

"They intend to pursue it? I figured they would. I didn't expect anything less of those coneheads."

"They've recommended a court-martial. I told you, chain of command wants someone's ass."

"Too bad they're not going to get it."

"It isn't personal, Lee. But we both know the first thing your defense attorney will request is the security tape for the building."

"And they'd find you on that tape?" Battles said.

"I doubt they could positively identify me. I knew where the camera was located. But . . ."

"You couldn't take that chance. So if I'm dead, there's no reason for the hearing. No hearing, no reason for anyone to seek the tape."

"Simple, really," Stanley said.

"So what's in this for you? The drugs?"

Stanley didn't answer.

"Your back," Battles said, nearly smiling at the simplicity of it. "You started using after you hurt your back."

"Heroin was easier to get in Afghanistan than pain medications, and some days it's the only way I can cope," Stanley said. "So, you're an unfortunate problem."

Battles stepped again to her left. "This isn't going to be as simple as making Trejo look like he committed suicide."

Stanley smiled. "Maybe not, but that's not going to be what happens."

"No?"

"No."

"What is going to happen?"

"This time, I'm pretty sure a police detective is going to kill you."

—

Tracy followed Owens out the door. She covered her head with her jacket against the hail. The balls were large enough to sting when they hit skin. The windshield was covered with accumulating ice and, inside the car, the glass had again fogged over. Owens turned on the engine and the defroster kicked into high, but it had little impact on the glass.

The wiper blades scraped away the balls of ice as Tracy and Owens furiously swiped at the windshield to open a viewing hole.

Owens couldn't wait. He backed out and drove toward the Charleston Gate. "How do you know it was Stanley?"

"The earrings," Tracy said. "Stanley wore the same gold stud earrings when we met in her office."

"I'm betting a lot of women on base wear those earrings," he said. "And I'm betting regulations are fairly stringent."

"Battles doesn't," Tracy said. "And she and Stanley are the two women with the means and opportunity to get that tape. And, they're going to court-martial Battles. What do you think would be the first thing Battles's defense attorney would demand for her defense?"

"The security video," Owens said.

"And Stanley knows she's on it."

"So how do we find them?" Owens asked.

"She's not going to kill her in a bar," Tracy said.

"The secretary said The Bulkhead is near Stanley's apartment across the Manette Bridge. I'd say that's our first stop."

"We're going to need backup."

"I've called in the car make and license number. Uniforms will meet us at the apartment." He handed a slip of paper to Tracy identifying Stanley's car type and license plate number. "We check the cars parked outside the bar. If her car isn't there, we haul ass to her apartment, unless someone calls in that they've spotted the car elsewhere."

Owens drove across the Manette Bridge and took the first exit onto Wheaton Way, pulling quickly into The Bulkhead parking lot. Given the weather, there were just five cars in the parking lot, none Stanley's. Owens exited the lot and continued toward Stanley's apartment complex. Minutes later, he pulled into The Crow's Nest. Patrol cars had not yet arrived.

"That's her car." Tracy pointed to a Chevy TrailBlazer parked in one of the spaces.

"Let's move," Owens said. "Patrol has to be close behind."

Owens parked and they both pushed out of the car. Tracy looked in the back of the Chevy TrailBlazer and saw Leah Battles's bike. "She's here."

They made their way toward the glass door entrance and the lobby. "What floor?" Tracy asked.

"Third," Owens said, viewing a directory and proceeding inside. He ignored the elevator, climbing the stairs two at a time. Tracy was winded just trying to keep up.

On the third floor, Owens exited the stairwell door with his head on a swivel, searching the apartment numbers embossed on brass plates on each door. Stanley's apartment was to the left. Owens moved quickly down the hall and stopped outside the apartment. Tracy heard voices inside, looked at Owens, and nodded.

Quietly he said, "I'll kick it in. You go in first and to the right. I got your back."

Tracy held her Glock muzzle up. "Ready."

Owens kicked at the door, which was made of cheap materials. It exploded in. Tracy slid into the apartment. To the right was a kitchen. Empty. She slid two steps farther and saw Stanley and Battles holding guns on each other.

"Drop it! Drop the gun! Drop the gun!"

Stanley let the gun slip from her hand onto the carpet, but Battles hesitated.

"Drop it," Owens said.

Battles too let the gun drop.

Tracy exhaled, rising from her crouch. About to speak, she felt the barrel of John Owens's Glock 22 press against her temple.

CHAPTER 45

One moment, and it was all over. One moment, and Tracy had arrived in time to keep Rebecca Stanley from pulling the trigger, from killing Leah Battles. She hadn't been there the night Sarah had been abducted and she hadn't been able to save her. Failure had a terrible way of lingering in the recesses of your mind, waiting for another opportunity to smack you with horrible pangs of guilt. But that wasn't going to happen this time. They'd arrived in time. She'd arrived in time. Leah Battles was alive and Rebecca Stanley had dropped her gun.

And just like that, everything evaporated.

She'd been played the way a street magician played a tourist.

See this red ball? Follow the red ball. That's all you have to do. Follow the red ball and tell me which cup the ball is under. The one in the middle? Are you sure? Of course you're sure. You have good eyes and you watched it the whole time.

Only the game isn't about what you can see. It's about what you fail to see, and you failed to see the magician squish that red ball into his palm. It never even went under a cup. You couldn't win. The game had been rigged, but your ego wouldn't allow you to admit it, and now you're standing in an apartment looking for the red ball that never was there. Meanwhile, the magician is holding a gun to your temple.

"You're going to lower your arm and let the gun slip from your hand and fall onto the carpet, Detective."

Still confused, her brain still processing what had just transpired, Tracy couldn't move.

"I said, drop the gun."

Tracy lowered her arm and released her finger, letting the gun slip from her grip. It hit the carpeted floor with a dull thud. Owens took a step back, but kept the gun trained on Tracy. Stanley moved forward and picked up Tracy's weapon.

Battles looked at Tracy. There was fear in her eyes but not in her voice. "I guess you know who took the tape of Trejo." She almost smiled when she said it.

Tracy said, "I guess you know the ethics committee is going to court-martial you."

"Who told you?"

"Brian Cho."

"I never liked him," Battles said.

"And the first thing the defense attorney will request is the security tape, which we can't have because the detective here noticed your earrings," Owens said, his voice becoming angry. Stanley reached up with her free hand and touched the gold nubs as if just remembering them.

"Trejo was working for you," Tracy said to Owens. She felt like one of her students—all those years ago—the ones who'd failed her chemistry exams because they hadn't studied, and afterward still felt compelled to know the right answers to the questions, though it wasn't going to change their grade or, in this instance, her circumstances.

"I'm a Navy man," Owens said. "It was right there on my office wall. If you'd done your research you'd have known I was also a logistics specialist."

"So you knew where the ships were docking overseas."

"And I knew what could be obtained when the ship docked, how to obtain it, and how to get it on and off the ship. And from my years working narcotics I know a bit about where to sell it."

Battles looked at Stanley. "You became addicted after the explosion in Afghanistan."

It explained Stanley's role, why she'd taken the tape.

"My back will give me a lifetime of torment. The pain will never go away. The doctors said I had to learn to live with it. They wouldn't prescribe me any more pills. Do you have any idea what it's like to live in pain every hour of every day?" She noticed Battles considering the pictures on the mantel.

"My ex," Stanley said. "He left when I started using heroin." She seemed to be fighting back tears. "He said he wouldn't raise a daughter with me. He said that I could either let them go or he would let the Navy know about my problem." She appeared bleary-eyed. "Do you have any idea what that was like? What choice I had to make? Of course you don't. You're not even married."

"How did you get past the drug tests and the mandatory medical exams?" Battles asked.

"Finding urine isn't difficult, especially for money, and I inject in places that aren't readily obvious."

"So here's how this is going to go," Owens said. "We went to the security office after Detective Crosswhite here learned that the tape you provided had been edited. I'll testify that the actual tape showed Leah Battles entering and leaving the DSO that night. Since the original will be destroyed, there won't be anything to refute what I say. The ethics decision is fortuitous. After the ethics committee issued their decision to go forward with her court-martial, Lieutenant Battles knew you possessed a copy of the security tape and asked to meet with you outside the office for a drink," he said to Stanley. "When you agreed, she forced you at gunpoint to come to your apartment to get that tape, which she believed to be in your briefcase."

He addressed Battles. "Detective Crosswhite and I, upon reviewing the original tape, learned that the two of you left together in Captain Stanley's car. Using deductive reasoning I won't bore you with, we found you here. You had Captain Stanley's gun, which won't be difficult for anyone to believe once they review the Krav Maga video I sent to Detective Crosswhite earlier this week. Detective Crosswhite entered the apartment first and you managed to shoot her, but I managed to shoot you."

Tracy looked at Stanley and her mind went white, completely and totally blank. It was as if someone had wiped it clean, removed all the clutter, then started it again, allowing her to see things as she might not have, in a manner she hadn't even considered until that very moment. She'd read somewhere of a phenomenon referred to as "the eureka effect"—when a person suddenly understands a previously incomprehensible problem or concept.

"He's going to kill you," Tracy said to Stanley.

Battles and Stanley shifted their gaze, uncertain to whom Tracy was speaking. Tracy looked directly at Stanley. "He's going to kill you."

Stanley looked perplexed but tried to laugh off the comment.

"He has to. You had the copy of the tape and provided it to me— that copy has been edited. But the original still exists. And you're on it."

"The original will be destroyed," Owens said, his voice calm.

"Think about it," Tracy said. "How is he going to explain that tape in my office that came from you? How's he going to explain who edited it?"

"I'll say it was Battles," Owens said.

"But I never asked for the tape," Battles said, seeing Tracy's logic.

"You'd be questioned, at the very least," Tracy said to Stanley. "He can't take that chance any more than he could take the chance that Trejo might have talked. Or that his dealer in Seattle might have talked. So now he's going to get you to shoot me. Then he's going to kill you."

"Shut up," Owens said. Tracy turned to him. She knew he couldn't shoot her, not with his own gun, which was a different caliber than Stanley's weapon, a .38. He needed Stanley to use her gun for everything to work.

"Think about it," Tracy said to Stanley. "That gun, your gun, has your fingerprints all over it. He's going to say you shot me and he shot the two of you."

Stanley glanced at Owens, perhaps beginning to comprehend her situation.

"She's trying to confuse you," he said.

"You pull that trigger and he's going to shoot you. It's common logic. It's the only way he walks out of this."

"We're going to walk out of this together," Owens said.

"He's lying," Tracy said. "Did he let Trejo walk out of it?"

"We'll get out of it and after things die down we'll both walk away, just like we discussed."

"He's lying," Tracy repeated. "He never meant anything he said. He sees you as nothing but a junkie and he's been playing you, just like he played me. He's a con man and he's conning you."

"Shut up," Owens said with greater force. Then to Stanley he said, "Shoot her."

Stanley pointed the gun at Tracy.

"You pull that trigger and you're dead," Tracy said again. "Just think it through."

"Shoot her, Goddamn it!"

She spoke over him. "He can't tie all the pieces together with you still alive."

"Shoot her!"

"He has to blame someone for the edited security tape. How's he going to do that with you still alive?"

"She's lying. I'll say it was Battles. Shoot her."

"But the tape came from you," Tracy said. "You requested it. And they're not going to destroy the original. I told them to hold it as police evidence. You're on that tape. He knows it."

Owens redirected his aim at Stanley. "Shoot her, dammit. Or I'll shoot you."

"That's the evidence he needs, irrefutable. You're on that tape, a junkie. You were working with Battles and Trejo to get the heroin because you're a junkie. That's the story he's going to tell. It's the only story that makes sense."

Stanley's hand quivered. Her eyes became two black spheres of doubt. She was figuring out that Tracy was telling the truth.

Tracy flinched on purpose, as if going for her gun. Owens redirected his aim at her but didn't pull the trigger. "You see, he can't shoot me. It's the wrong caliber gun. He needs you to do it."

"Shoot her," Owens urged.

Tracy spoke louder, her voice rising over Owens's voice and the increasing noise from the storm outside. "Don't do it. It's the only way you might walk out of here alive."

"Idiot," Owens said and he shifted the gun to Stanley. She too readjusted her aim. The guns exploded in the small apartment, three reverberating blasts, two from Owens's gun and one from Stanley's. The shots propelled Stanley backward as if she were a puppet tied to a jerked string. She crashed hard into the wall, slumping to the floor.

Owens had turned his upper body sideways, reducing the size of the target. Stanley's bullet exploded in the Sheetrock behind him, leaving a large pucker wound.

Tracy didn't deduce this as it all happened. She hadn't deduced any of it in real time. She'd dropped at the first movement, as she'd been trained, knowing escape was impossible, knowing that her gun remained on the floor and was her only hope. She hit the ground, grabbed her gun, and rolled onto her side, taking aim at Owens.

About to pull the trigger, Tracy froze. Leah Battles struck in a series of lightning-fast movements. Battles had Owens's gun and arms raised over his head and delivered a debilitating knee to his groin, dropping him as she wrenched free his weapon and stepped back, out of Owens's reach. She spoke over her shoulder to Tracy, though her focus, and her aim, remained on Owens. "Do you play chess, Detective?"

"Like I said, not very often and not very well."

"Too bad. I got a hunch that, with some practice, you'd be a badass chess player too."

CHAPTER 46

Aneighbor who'd heard the shots called the Bremerton Police Department and police descended on The Crow's Nest. They first encountered Tracy, who'd stepped outside of the building holding up her badge. She spoke calmly, deliberately explaining what had happened, and told them that the weapons had been secured. Inside the apartment, the police found Detective John Owens seated on the carpet, hands cuffed behind his back. After another half hour of explanation, Owens was removed from the apartment, and Tracy and Battles were allowed to leave the apartment and go outside while forensics did its work. They were each told not to go far.

The sky remained a frothing mix of clouds, but, for the moment at least, the rain had stopped. The parking lot had filled with Bremerton and Kitsap County police vehicles and enough officers to take down the army of a small country. Fire trucks, ambulances, and the Kitsap County coroner's van had also arrived. There was no rush. Rebecca Stanley had died from the two gunshot wounds to her chest. Along the street, behind a police line, several news vehicles and apartment residents stood waiting and watching.

Battles talked on her cell phone. Tracy had requested that she call the security officer, David Bakhtiari. Tracy wanted to be certain nobody destroyed the DSO security tape for March 18.

Battles disconnected and stepped toward Tracy. "He'd already tagged the tape before he left for the day. It wasn't going to get destroyed anytime soon. I also spoke to our CO. He's sending out NCIS."

"When they get here, tell them to take a number."

Tracy and Battles stood silent, watching the officers. In time they both would have to give statements.

"What will you do?" Tracy asked Battles.

"What do you mean?"

"I mean in the future, when this is resolved; what are you going to do?"

Battles shook her head. "I don't know, Detective. That all seems a long way off right now. And things are going to be pretty screwed up around the base for a while. I imagine they'll undertake a full-blown investigation of Trejo, whether he had assistance and for how long. It could take some time. I doubt they'll get anything out of Owens except a request for a lawyer."

Tracy nodded. Battles was likely right. After a beat, she asked, "How much longer are you enlisted?"

"How long is my commission? Four years on active duty followed by four years inactive status. I'll be done with my active duty in less than a year."

"Then what?"

Battles shrugged. "I don't know. At the moment I'm just trying to process what went on here and how the hell I got in the middle of it."

"You defended Trejo," she said. "You rode your bike down to the jail and asked to see him."

"Be careful what you wish for," Battles said.

"What's that?"

"Nothing. Just some good motherly advice."

"You think you'll stay here?"

"Bremerton?" She shook her head. "No."

"Seattle?" Tracy said.

Battles shrugged again. "I don't know. I guess it depends on the job opportunities, and the men."

"My husband's a lawyer."

Tracy liked Battles. She was a strong personality, but so was Tracy. Maybe the two of them would be too much for Dan to handle, but it sounded as if Battles had plenty of experience and could hit the ground running.

Battles raised an eyebrow. "I assume you're happily married, so . . . what type of law?"

"Mostly plaintiffs' personal injury, but also some criminal defense work."

"Is he any good?"

"He's had to turn down cases because he doesn't have the time to work them. He's thinking about slowing down and taking on help."

"Slowing down? What are you, forty?"

Tracy smiled. "He's done pretty well."

"He must have." Battles seemed to ponder the idea for a moment. "I like the sound of that," she said.

"Plaintiffs' work?"

"Retiring at forty."

Tracy smiled. "Slowing down, not retiring; I don't want him around the house that much."

"Lieutenant?" A detective approached Battles. "We'd like to take a statement."

Battles nodded and stepped toward him. She stopped and looked back at Tracy. "Tell your husband I'm interested. But also tell him I don't come cheap."

CHAPTER 47

The following morning, Tracy knocked on the door in Rainier Beach. She was under orders from Clarridge to speak to the family in person, though she hadn't needed an order to do so. This was a conversation she wanted to have. She took a deep breath and the door pulled open. Shaniqua Miller's mother gave Tracy an inquisitive glare.

"Good morning," Tracy said. "Is Shaniqua home?"

The mother grimaced. Tracy thought she might close the door. "Hang on a moment, please."

Tracy heard voices inside the house. She also smelled coffee and perhaps something baking in the oven.

Moments later, Shaniqua Miller appeared in the doorway and gave Tracy the same inquisitive glare as her mother. Behind her, down the hall, her two young boys stood watching, dressed in their pajamas.

"Good morning," Tracy said.

"It's awful early for a house call, Detective."

"I apologize, but it got too late last night to bring you the news, and I didn't want to tell you over the phone or have you find out from the news media."

Shaniqua Miller's brow furrowed. She turned back to the interior. "Mom, can you take the boys into the kitchen, please?" After the mother had ushered the boys from the hallway, Shaniqua said to Tracy, "What kind of news?"

"We know what happened to your son and we know why. And the people responsible are going to be tried. I know you've heard this before, but I'm confident this time they'll go to jail."

Shaniqua Miller pressed her lips tight but did not cry. Her mother, who had reappeared at the door, reached for and gripped her daughter's hand. "Are you sure?" Shaniqua said, her voice rough with emotion.

"Yes," she said. "We're sure."

The two women turned and hugged, crying without reservation. The two little boys, ignoring their grandmother's instructions, came down the hall and buried their faces in their mother's clothes. Tracy didn't try to interrupt them. She didn't try to say anything. She just let them cry.

After several minutes, Shaniqua recovered her composure and wiped at her tears, taking deep breaths. "Thank you," she said.

Tracy nodded. "I can tell you more later, when it's a little better time. I just wanted you to know that we never forgot about your son." She handed Shaniqua a business card. "Call me when you get a chance and we'll set up a time to talk." She started down the steps to the concrete path.

"Detective?"

Tracy stopped and turned at the foot of the steps.

"I'm sorry," she said. "But he was my boy and . . ."

"You don't need to apologize, Mrs. Miller. I know exactly what you mean. And I would have been just as frustrated and disillusioned. But I'm not going to let this one go. I'll stay involved until the people responsible are behind bars. Some of them are dead, but the person most responsible will have a first hearing very soon and he'll be arraigned on multiple charges."

Shaniqua stepped down to Tracy and motioned back to the front door. "Please," she said. "My mother just made coffee and I'm baking scones. We have homemade jam."

Tracy nodded. "I'd like that," she said.

EPILOGUE

Leah Battles reinserted her identification back beneath her riding clothes and coasted to the bottom of the hill, to the DSO building. It had been two weeks since the events at Rebecca Stanley's apartment, and things were still weird, but slowly getting back to normal. She'd met with Dan O'Leary about a job, and he'd called her two days later and offered her a position as an associate in his law firm. She told him she'd think about it and get back to him, but she'd already made up her mind to stay in Seattle after her commission expired. She'd even put in a request to senior trial counsel to finish her commission at Kitsap, and there was at least a decent chance her request would be granted.

She locked her bike in one of the racks out front and unsnapped her helmet as she went inside.

"What's up, ma'am?" Darcy asked from behind the reception desk, smiling.

Battles returned the smile. "Sun and sky, Darcy. I'll let you know when they're not."

She went into her office and closed the door, proceeding to the closet behind her desk where she set her helmet and exchanged her clothes for her blueberries. After lacing and tying her boots, she turned on her computer and opened her file drawer, fingering through her dozen active files. She looked up at a knock on her door.

Brian Cho opened it and stepped in. "Am I interrupting anything?"

Battles shook her head. Cho shut the door behind him. He looked at the newest painting on her wall, a view of downtown Seattle and the Puget Sound from Battles's apartment window. "This is new," he said.

"I painted it when I had all that free time," Battles said.

Cho turned to her. "Yeah, about that."

"Don't worry about it," she said. "I would have accused you too, if the situation had been reversed."

Cho smiled. "Thanks," he said. "I think."

"And I will beat you," she said. "It's just a matter of time."

"Well, I guess that's why they actually run the races," Cho said, smiling. He opened the door but didn't immediately exit. "But if anyone is going to beat me? I'd be okay if it was you," he said.

—

Del parked the Impala in the street and shut off the engine. He made no move to get out of the car. It wasn't because of the weather. March had finally passed, and he was glad to see it go. He loved the four seasons in Seattle. He didn't even mind the rain, usually—but he'd had enough of it. April, at least, looked like it was going to be a whole lot drier and a whole lot better month all the way around. The persistent veil of darkness that seemed to descend in the winter had lifted, if only temporarily, and the days were getting longer and seemingly filled with more sunshine. He needed some brightness. His sister needed some brightness.

"She's a little high-strung," he said to Celia McDaniel, seated in the passenger seat of his Impala.

He felt nervous. Del never felt nervous, not even at work, not when he'd been out on patrol, and not in all his years as a detective. He loved every aspect of his job—not that he liked seeing dead bodies; everyone could do without that. He just never got nervous, figured what was, was, and what was to be, would be.

Celia smiled. "Stop worrying about it, Del. She has a right to be high-strung."

In the interim two weeks, with Del back on the more hospitable day shift, he and Celia had seen each other almost every night. Celia had monitored the legal case against Nicholas Evans and was putting together the complaint against Detective John Owens. It would include a number of charges, including the murders of Rebecca Stanley, Eric Tseng, and Laszlo Trejo, and drug trafficking that had led to the deaths of more than ten Seattle residents. For now, that number did not look like it would increase. They'd spread the word about a potentially dangerous heroin, which seemed like an oxymoron, but they'd had no deaths in the past two weeks. Funk had called and said the lab's analyses confirmed that the heroin found on Allie's dresser and in Jack Welch's garage apartment had been cut with fentanyl.

Despite Celia's reassurances, Del had half a mind to put the car in drive and go get a nice dinner at a restaurant where he wasn't nervous about who might say what to whom. "You're sure you don't mind?"

"Do I mind meeting your family? Why would I mind?"

"The boys can get . . . a little curious. You know?"

"About the fact that I'm black?"

His nerves became more pronounced. "Well, there could be that," he conceded.

"Did you happen to mention that I was black?"

"I did," he said. "Not that it really matters. I just thought it might make it a little easier on everyone."

Celia laughed. "You're like a seventeen-year-old girl on a prom date. Color is a fact of life, Del. The people who say they don't see color, or race, are the people who do. We see good-looking people and funny people, obnoxious people. Why shouldn't we see something so obvious as color?"

"I'm not sure anyone is going to see black or white with what you're wearing tonight." Celia wore a maroon skirt with pleats that reached to just above her knee, and a matching jacket and white shirt.

"Too much?" she said.

"Too beautiful," he said.

She leaned across the car and kissed him. "Relax. As for your nephews and what they might say, I grew up with three brothers, and I raised my own boy. I don't think they'll intimidate me too much."

"Right," Del said, exhaling but not relaxed.

Celia started to push open the passenger door. Del reached across the seat and touched her shoulder. "You know there's going to be a natural bond."

"Is your sister black?"

"You know what I mean," Del said. "I just don't want you to feel obligated."

Celia smiled. "The only way to get through this, Del, is with a strong family, a strong faith, and strong friends." Her eyebrows arched. "I can't help with the first two, but I can help with the third. It's not an obligation; it's what I know my son would want me to do."

Del leaned across the car and kissed her. "Now, did I mention my nephews?"

Celia slapped at his hands.

They walked hand in hand to the front door. Del reached for the doorknob, but the door pulled open before he had the chance to knock. Stevie stood in the entry shoving half his shirt into his khaki pants. He had his shoes on, but untied. No doubt he'd run upstairs from their room in the basement when he heard Del's car. He gave Del a brief glance but his real interest was Celia.

"Hey, Stevie," Del said.

"Hey, Uncle Del." Stevie said it as if Del were an afterthought.

"You look good," Del said.

"Mom made us get dressed up," he said, still staring at Celia.

Mark hurried around the corner into the living room. His shirt was not tucked in and he had his shoes in his hand. He scowled at Stevie, then he too stared at Celia as he approached the front door.

"Hey, Mark."

"Hey, Uncle Del."

"Stevie, Mark, this is Celia."

Celia stuck out her hand and the boys reciprocated.

"Nice to meet you," they said.

"It's nice to meet you both," Celia said. "I've heard a lot of good things about you. I've heard you are exceptional baseball players. Del promised to take me to a game soon."

The boys beamed. "We play on Saturday," Stevie said.

"Uncle Del's the coach," Mark said.

"I heard," Celia said. "Maybe he'll invite me."

The Little League had been short on coaches. Del had agreed, so long as he didn't have to wear the pants.

Stevie looked to Del. "How come you haven't invited her, Uncle Del?"

"Yeah, where are your manners?" Mark said.

"Yeah, where are your manners?" Stevie said.

"You're like a stereo," Del said. "Where are *my* manners? You two goofballs have left us standing out here in the cold. All right, step back and let us in."

The inside of the house was spotless, the coffee table cleared, the couches free of food crumbs and newspapers. Soft jazz played from the speakers. "You guys cleaned up in here," Del said. "It looks good."

"Mom made us."

"Yeah, Mom made us."

"It smells terrific," Celia said.

"Mom's cooking manicotti," Stevie said.

"We never get manicotti unless we have guests," Mark said.

Maggie walked out from the kitchen. She wore blue jeans, a light-pink blouse, and flats. When she saw Celia, she smiled. "Hey," she said to Del, pecking him on the cheek. "I was just checking on dinner."

"It smells terrific," Celia said.

"I hope you like Italian food," Maggie said.

"Who doesn't like Italian food?" Celia said. "You're going to have to teach me how to make it."

Maggie smiled and gestured to the couches. "Come in. Sit down."

Del and Celia sat on the longer of the two couches.

"Stevie, bring out the hors d'oeuvres," Maggie said.

"The what?"

"The hors d'oeuvres," Maggie said.

"The plate with the olives and the prosciutto?"

Maggie rolled her eyes. "Yes. Mark, bring the wine and the glasses."

"Do we get wine?"

"No," Maggie said.

"It'll stunt your growth," Celia said.

The boys froze. "It will?"

"I knew a man who was six three. His son drank wine at dinner and never got taller than this." She held her hand about three feet off the floor.

The boys' eyes got as big as saucers. They looked to Del for some type of confirmation or refutation but he just shrugged as if to say, *Don't ask me.*

The two boys turned and ran into the kitchen.

"I hope Del warned you about the two of them," Maggie said.

"They remind me of two of my brothers. Eleven months apart. One never did anything without the other."

Stevie carried in a plate loaded with Italian meats, olives, crackers, an eggplant spread, and various cheeses. He set it on the coffee table. Mark followed with a bottle of Chianti and three glasses.

"I hope you didn't go to too much trouble," Celia said. "This looks terrific."

"Uncle Del got it," Stevie said.

Del gave him the evil eye. This was supposed to be Maggie's dinner party.

"Yeah, he, like, lives at Salumi," Mark said.

"It's his favorite restaurant," Stevie said.

"At least he used to when he was fat," Mark said.

"Thanks a lot," Del said. He'd lost nearly twenty pounds.

The two boys laughed.

"He must really like you if he's losing all that weight," Stevie pressed.

Del cleared his throat. Celia held a hand over her mouth. "This is an Italian spread," Del said, and he poured the three glasses of wine.

"Are you Italian?" Stevie asked Celia.

"Can I be an honorary Italian?"

Stevie shrugged. "I guess so."

"She's African American," Mark said, popping an olive in his mouth and grabbing a piece of cheese.

"Is that so?" Celia said.

"We learned it in school." Mark shrugged as if it was no big deal. He rolled a piece of prosciutto around two olives, eating it. "But you can be Italian."

"All right, you two," Maggie said. "You're like a swarm of locusts. Leave some food for the guests and go finish setting the table."

The two boys got up from their knees, grabbed a handful of olives and slices of meat, and went into the kitchen.

"Sorry about that," Maggie said. "They can get a little personal."

Celia smiled. "My son was a lot like them at that age."

Maggie lost her smile. "Del mentioned you lost a son. I'm very sorry."

"Thank you. I'm very sorry about Allie."

Maggie nodded. Her eyes watered but she fought back the tears.

"It's okay," Celia said. "You're going to cry."

Maggie wiped the corner of her eyes with a napkin. "Does it ever get better?"

Celia set down her wine and put out a hand, taking Maggie's. "You know I'd be lying if I said it did, right?"

Maggie nodded. "I know."

"In time, though, you learn how to live with the pain. You learn how to live with all the memories, and you learn not to fear them. You learn to embrace them, to welcome them."

Maggie started to cry. Celia got up and sat beside her. "It isn't going to be better, Maggie. It's going to be different, and different is okay. You just have to learn how to embrace it. Like anything, it takes time. What you have to realize is that crying is God's way of helping us wash away the pain. So don't you ever apologize for crying; it's a reminder to us all that we're human, and that we love our family with our entire being. And that's a beautiful thing."

Maggie smiled and wiped her tears. She inhaled a breath. "Your accent, where's it from?"

"Georgia," she said. "And it can get thick as syrup at times." She smiled at Del, who sat on the couch with a tear in his eye. "Other times, people hardly even notice."

"I notice," Del said, raising his glass.

"It's beautiful," Maggie said.

"Yes, she is," Del said, and he heard the snickers of two little boys who'd snuck back into the room behind him.

Tracy held Dan's hand as they walked the dogs along the trails behind their house, which was actually a backward way of looking at it. Once off leash, the dogs walked the two of them. The rains of March had passed. April offered spring and, now that she was off the night shift, more sleep and more time with Dan.

She was busy, gathering the evidence that Celia McDaniel would use to charge Detective John Owens, and she imagined she would remain busy for some time.

Somewhere in the fading light, Rex and Sherlock thrashed through the underbrush, taking in all the different smells and sounds of the second-growth forest. Birds chirped and trilled, and overhead the trees knocked and creaked in the breeze.

Ordinarily, after a day working downtown, this was Tracy's nirvana. This evening, though, she felt queasy and light-headed. Maybe it was the accumulated lack of sleep. She'd always had trouble switching back to working days after a month pulling night shift.

She stopped and took a deep breath of the fresh air, but she had a metallic taste in her mouth and had all day.

"You okay?" Dan asked.

"Queasy," she said. "And I feel like I'm having hot flashes." She fanned her jacket, then unzipped it. The cool air felt refreshing.

"You want to turn around?" Dan asked.

"If we do, we'll pay the price with the two of them running around the house all night. I'm all right. The cool air actually helps me feel a little better."

They started walking again. "Maybe you got a bug. The flu is going around."

She shrugged. "It could be menopause. My mom went through it early."

Dan stopped walking. "You know it's okay, right? I mean whether we have children or not. I'm okay with it just being the two of us, so long as I have you."

Tracy smiled. "It will never be just the two of us, not with Rex and Sherlock, and Roger."

"You know what I mean."

"I do."

"And you're okay with it?"

"There's not really a choice, is there?" She squeezed his hand as they walked. "In time, I'm sure it will be fine. I'm disappointed that I couldn't conceive, but things happen for a reason." She thought of Leah Battles. *Be careful what you wish for.*

Tracy couldn't mask her disappointment that she could not conceive a child, but she had a good life now. She had Dan and a place to call home, a career that gave her a purpose, and a feeling that she was doing something for the greater good.

Dan kissed her and they continued toward home.

"Did you talk with Leah Battles?" Tracy asked.

"I did."

"And?"

"She seems competent. It will take her a while to get up to speed on criminal and civil procedure outside of the military, but she's had an awful lot of experience on her feet. I liked her."

"Are you going to hire her?"

"I already made her an offer."

"What did she say?"

Dan smiled. "She said she'd think about it and get back to me in a week."

Tracy laughed. "I told you she was a pistol."

"She has several months before her commission expires," Dan said. "She's not in any rush. But I'm fairly certain she'll accept. I can't see her working for one of the large law firms."

They finished their walk and returned home. For dinner, Dan had made his famous enchiladas. They came out of the oven bubbling cheese and red sauce, and bursting with flavor. After just a few bites, however, Tracy set down her fork.

"Still not feeling well?"

"I think I'm going to lie down. I'm sorry. I'd rather eat these when I can enjoy them." She stood and picked up her plate and fork.

"I'll clean up," Dan said. "Just leave everything."

"Thanks," she said. "Sorry."

"Don't worry about it."

She paused, feeling again like she could throw up.

Dan started to get up. "Let me help you."

She waved him off. "No. It's fine." Then she laughed. "It's only a few feet to the bed."

She went into their bedroom, changed into a T-shirt, and climbed under the covers. Sherlock and Rex had already found spots on Dan's side of the bed, curled into balls and trying to look as small and inconspicuous as possible so they wouldn't get booted. They were not allowed on the bed when Tracy and Dan went to sleep, but occasionally they'd sneak on early in the morning. Tracy didn't bother to move them. She enjoyed their company.

—

She awoke after dark. The clock on the nightstand indicated it was just after 2:00 a.m. Dan snored lightly beside her, and the dogs grunted from their beds on the floor. She hadn't heard Dan come into the room, and she hadn't heard or felt Rex or Sherlock get off the bed, which meant she'd really been out of it. Now, however, she feared she might be up the rest of the night.

She got out of bed and shuffled out of the room and into the bathroom, which was lit by a night-light. She felt better than she had earlier, still a bit light-headed, but not nearly as nauseated. She shut the door three-quarters, and sat, but didn't immediately go to the bathroom. She looked at the cabinet beneath the sink and wondered. Then it dawned on her that she might have one more.

She stood, flipped the light switch, and rummaged in the cabinet until she'd found the box. Inside, one pregnancy stick remained. She removed it, but didn't immediately open it. In her heart, she knew the odds were stacked against her. They'd had no success on the Clomid, and Dr. Kramer had said the chances she could get pregnant on her own were less than good.

She was tired of getting her hopes up only to be disappointed. She shook that thought. Her father would have called it a defeatist attitude. If she expressed doubt before a shooting competition, he'd tell her not to compete. "If you go in thinking you're going to lose, you've already lost. If you go in thinking you're going to win, you'll be disappointed if you lose. So just go in to the competition with the attitude that you're going to compete, which is all you can control anyway."

This wasn't quite like that, but she really did have no expectations.

She thought of Dan, of that night when she'd been content to just go to sleep. The night he'd held her and told her that she was all he wanted in this world. They'd made love, not to make a baby, just to be close.

She unwrapped the pregnancy stick, peed on it, and set the stick on the top of the tank while she went to the sink to wash her hands. She dried them on a hand towel, glancing in the mirror behind her at the stick. She wasn't going to have any expectations. She wasn't going in thinking the results would be positive or negative.

She walked back to the toilet, but no matter what she told herself, she couldn't quiet her heart, which was pounding.

That could be the flu.

She reached and picked up the stick, staring at it.

Two parallel lines.

She closed her eyes. Tears spilled over, running down her cheeks. She fought against the urge to both laugh and to cry, to shout out. There was a long way to go, she knew. Pregnancy sticks were unreliable and could produce false positives. She needed to make a doctor's appointment. Then there were the chances of a miscarriage, much higher for her because of her age.

She needed . . . She needed . . .

She needed to stop. She needed to just stop and enjoy this moment.

She smiled and looked out the bathroom door, to their bedroom, to where Dan slept, though not for long.

ACKNOWLEDGMENTS

The subject of this book is troubling, especially for parents. I never fully understand the subject I am writing about until I have written the first draft of the novel. Often my novels start with an idea, spurred by a newspaper or magazine article. In this case, however, the idea came from real life.

In the year prior to writing *Close to Home*, I read of multiple students at a local high school dying of heroin overdoses. The loss of a person so young is always tragic. The loss of that person, often after years of the torment heroin wreaks on the entire family, is shocking. As I researched this topic, I was surprised and dismayed at the long-term and long-range ramifications of the legalization of marijuana. I had no idea that the loss of marijuana income had led to the Mexican, South American, and Chinese drug cartels plowing under their marijuana fields to plant poppies and to flood the United States market with cheap and affordable heroin. This came at an unfortunate time in the United States, when so many people had become addicted to prescription opioids.

While I don't profess to know all about this mess, the substantial amount of information that I read in books and in newspaper and magazine articles, as well as conversations I've had with many intricately involved in treating those addictions, was sobering and frightening. I'd always believed heroin addicts were people living in rodent-infested apartments. The words that had the greatest impact on me during my research were those describing so many addicted as "good kids from good families."

Despite my best efforts, I'm sure I still made mistakes, and for those I take full responsibility. During the course of my writing career, I have become much like Blanche DuBois in *A Streetcar Named Desire*. I depend on the kindness of strangers, many of whom have become friends.

My special thanks to Detective Ron Sanders, Seattle Police Department, Traffic Collision Investigation Unit. Ron walked me through working for the TCI, then helped me in particular with a hit-and-run scenario and the steps that might be taken to uncover the driver of the vehicle. The new technology is amazing, and it just keeps getting better.

Two years ago I was teaching a class on novel writing on Whidbey Island and one of my students was Alexandra Nicca. "Nicca," as we soon called her, had a unique and humorous way of looking at life in general and at particular incidents. I asked her what she did for a living and she advised that she was a lieutenant in the United States Navy, a Judge Advocate General. In short, that's a military lawyer. Stationed at Naval Base Kitsap, Nicca arranged for me to tour the legal building, to sit in the courtroom, and to ask her hours of banal questions that likely threatened to put her to sleep. At the time I just thought she had a really cool job and wanted to learn more about it. At that point I had no novel in mind. As I started to put this novel together, I knew that others would also see her job as interesting and want to learn more about it. As I told Nicca, I have great respect for anyone who puts on the uniform to defend and serve this country, and that includes her. I am appreciative of her time and expertise.

As with all the novels in the Tracy Crosswhite series, I simply could not write them without the help of Jennifer Southworth, Seattle Police Department, Violent Crimes Section, and Scott Tompkins, King County Sheriff's Office, Major Crimes Unit. As I was writing this novel, Jennifer was working the night shift. I met her and Scott for dinner at Shawn O'Donnell's American Grill and Irish Pub on the first floor of the famed Smith Tower. Not only did they educate me, I found another setting for several scenes in my novel, as well as an overall mood. It was cold and rainy that night, and I could only imagine what that must be like for the detectives called out to investigate a murder.

My thanks also to Kathy Taylor, forensic anthropologist, King County Medical Examiner's Office. Kathy is busier—as they say— than a one-armed paperhanger, yet she always manages to find time to answer my questions. In addition, I asked Kathy to read a scene from my novel for its accuracy. She did and she informed me that the scene indicating that the King County medical examiner had four heroin overdoses in a week was sadly unrealistic. The medical examiner often has four overdoses in a day, and the heroin epidemic is far worse than I had portrayed. As we writers well know, writing is rewriting, and I went back and made the changes.

Thanks also to Eric Yurkanin of Max Technologies in Seattle. My knowledge of computers and computer systems extends about as far as my reach to my keyboard. I asked Eric many questions about security cameras, how they work, how they record, how long those tapes are kept, whether they could be copied. I appreciate his patient explanations. Over the years, I have learned that computers, like guns, have a rabid community that is just waiting for me to make a mistake so they can correct it. Some of these people are very kind and e-mail me. I appreciate their input and I keep every e-mail for future books. Others rip me all over the Internet. I don't keep those. So let me just say, if I made a mistake, it was inadvertent and not because of a lack of effort. I'm open to an e-mail so that, hopefully, I don't make the same mistake again.

Thanks also to Dr. Scott Kramer, obstetrician-gynecologist. Scott helped me with the details of Tracy and Dan's attempts to get pregnant, as well as all of the potential options and ramifications of each option. Scott is also my brother-in-law, and let me tell you, that man has cooked up some wicked Christmas dinners over the years. So you might say that I'm twice blessed to have him as part of the family.

Thanks to Ms. Meg Ruley, Rebecca Scherer, and the team at the Jane Rotrosen Agency. They've been guiding me for my entire career, and at times I'm sure it felt like a parent guiding a teenager. I've had my ups and downs, but they've stuck by me through it all and kept me moving forward with relentless enthusiasm and optimism. I just can't say thanks enough.

Thanks to Thomas & Mercer. This is novel five in the Tracy Crosswhite series and my sixth novel with the team, but it never feels old. They're always looking for new ways to promote my work and to get my novels into the hands of as many readers as possible. As an author, that's all I've ever asked for, a chance to be read.

Thanks to Sarah Shaw, author relations, who always makes me feel special. The post office has threatened to close my PO box if I don't get down there and pick up all the packages she sends. These are terrific surprises, and my family and I greatly enjoy them.

Thanks to Sean Baker, head of production, and to Laura Barrett, production manager. I've said this before, but I love the covers and the titles of each of my novels, and I have them to thank. Thanks to Justin O'Kelly, the head of PR, and to Dennelle Catlett, Amazon Publishing PR, for all the work promoting me and my novels. Thanks to publisher Mikyla Bruder, associate publisher Galen Maynard, and Jeff Belle, vice president of Amazon Publishing.

Special thanks to Thomas & Mercer's editorial director, Gracie Doyle. My novels usually start with a lunch with Gracie at which I say that I have a couple different ideas. Then I begin to lay out those plots. Gracie analyzes them and helps me find the plot with the most emotional bang. From there, I'm off to the races. When I'm done, Gracie is the first to read the novel and help me bring the idea to life. So, once again, thanks, Gracie, for your direction on the story, thanks for your editorial suggestions, and thanks for your friendship. I'm truly glad to have you leading my team.

Special thanks to Charlotte Herscher, developmental editor. This is our sixth book together and she has made me infinitely better. At times I can hear Charlotte in my head asking for more character development and I try my best to heed that call because her advice is spot-on. Thanks to Sara Addicott, production editor, and Scott Calamar, copyeditor. When you recognize a weakness it is a wonderful thing—because then you can ask for help. Grammar and punctuation were never my strengths, and it's nice to know I have the best looking out for me.

Thanks to Tami Taylor, who runs my website, and creates my newsletters and some of my foreign-language book covers. I ask Tami for help and she gets things done quickly and efficiently. Thanks to Pam Binder and the Pacific Northwest Writers Association for their support of my work. Thanks to Seattle 7 Writers, a nonprofit collective of Pacific Northwest authors who foster and support the written word.

Thanks to you, the readers, for finding my novels, and for your incredible support of my work. Thanks for posting your reviews and for e-mailing me to let me know you've enjoyed them—always a writer's highlight.

Special thanks to Bob Grassilli, Serra High School Class of 1966, and David Bakhtiari, Serra High School Class of 2009, for making generous donations to the Serra High School "Fund a Dream" program. One of the cool things I get to do is auction off the name of a character in my novels to raise money for worthy charities. Serra High School is my alma mater, and the "Fund a Dream" program raises money to provide scholarships to kids in need. Serra has produced notable alumni like NFL Super Bowl MVPs Lynn Swann and Tom Brady, MLB's Barry Bonds and Jim Fregosi, scholars such as *New York Times*–bestselling author John Lescroart, and the preeminent portrait photographer in the world, Michael Collopy. Bob Grassilli is the former mayor of San Carlos and David Bakhtiari plays left tackle for the Green Bay Packers. Thanks to both of you for your generosity.

I've had a great year professionally, but a little less great personally. My wife, Cristina, and I are learning how to let go of our children and send them off to college. When you're blessed with two of the best kids a parent could ask for, that's a tough thing. So thanks to my son, Joe, and to my daughter, Catherine—you've given this guy more fun than he has had a right to experience. I'll never forget traveling in London with Joe, who I am convinced was born with radar. That kid can find a restaurant or a pub with just one look at a map. Astonishing. And Catherine continues to make us all laugh. She's promised to take care of her daddy when he becomes old and senile. What more could a guy want?

The person who holds all this together is Cristina. How blessed am I that I get to publicly thank her each time I complete a novel? She's stood by me through the ups and downs, and her support has never wavered. So this past Christmas, 2016, I gave her the gift she'd waited for ever so patiently during our twenty-two years of marriage. She knows what it is, and it is as beautiful as she. Forever and a Day, with you.

ABOUT THE AUTHOR

Robert Dugoni is the #1 Kindle bestselling and #1 *Wall Street Journal* bestselling author of The Tracy Crosswhite Series, including *My Sister's Grave, Her Final Breath, In the Clearing,* and *The Trapped Girl.* He is also the author of the Edgar Award–nominated *The 7th Canon*; the *New York Times* bestselling David Sloane Series, which includes *The Jury Master, Wrongful Death, Bodily Harm, Murder One,* and *The Conviction*; the stand-alone novel *Damage Control*; and the nonfiction exposé *The Cyanide Canary,* a *Washington Post* Best Book of the Year selection. Dugoni is also a two-time nominee for both the International Thriller Award and the Harper Lee Award for Legal Fiction, and he is the recipient of the Nancy Pearl Award for fiction. Visit his website at www.robertdugoni.com and follow him on Twitter @robertdugoni and on Facebook at www.facebook.com/AuthorRobertDugoni.